REALM G

THE
BLOOD BANK

REALM F

THE WASTES

REALM E

REALM H

REA

United States

Realm G

The Blood Bar

AGE OF VAMPIRES

FORSAKEN RELIC

CAROLINE PECKHAM
SUSANNE VALENTI

2

New York

Belvedere Castle

Interior Formatting & Design by Wild Elegance Formatting
Map Design by Fred Kroner
Artwork by Stella Colorado

ISBN: 978-1-916926-18-9

Forsaken Relic/Caroline Peckham & Susanne Valenti – 2nd ed.

This book is dedicated to Count Dracula. He can't possibly have known his legend would end up here as modern day growly hot vampires who want to keep you in their castle, but here we are bitey D. Here we are.

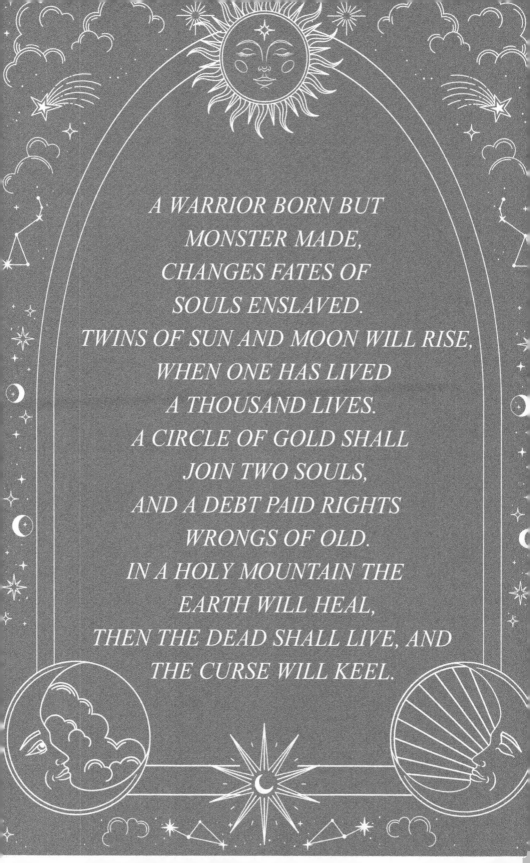

*A WARRIOR BORN BUT
MONSTER MADE,
CHANGES FATES OF
SOULS ENSLAVED.
TWINS OF SUN AND MOON WILL RISE,
WHEN ONE HAS LIVED
A THOUSAND LIVES.
A CIRCLE OF GOLD SHALL
JOIN TWO SOULS,
AND A DEBT PAID RIGHTS
WRONGS OF OLD.
IN A HOLY MOUNTAIN THE
EARTH WILL HEAL,
THEN THE DEAD SHALL LIVE, AND
THE CURSE WILL KEEL.*

CALLIE

CHAPTER ONE

Silence echoed endlessly over the water. I stared at the gentle swell of the waves as the moonlight highlighted them beyond the back of the speed boat and tried to hold the shattering pieces of my heart together.

I chewed on my bottom lip, wondering if it had already happened. Had Montana changed beyond all recognition? Her features smoothed and perfected? Her canines filled with venom and sharpened just the right amount to pierce human flesh and give her the one thing she would crave above all else?

Perhaps she'd already awoken and had realised what had happened to her. What I'd let happen to her. Would she hate me? Would she wish I'd let her die a mortal death? Or would she forgive me for my weakness? Maybe she'd even *like* being a monster…

I'm so sorry, Monty. I should have saved you. This should never have happened.

I reached out and touched the freezing water with my trembling fingertips, trying to distract myself with the bite of cold, but nothing could dull the fear I felt for my sister. It had all happened so fast in the end. She'd been there with me, warm and alive until somehow she'd been falling and then-

I closed my eyes and tried not to re-live that moment, tried not to hear the horrifying crack as she'd struck the ground, tried not to break over how close I had come to losing her, tried to convince myself I hadn't lost her at all.

Julius had taken us out to sea, chasing the horizon until New York City was reduced to a cluster of glimmering lights in the distance and our blades had stopped burning with the proximity of so many vampires. Then he'd cut the engine.

The silence stretched between us and I knew that the brothers had no idea what to do now. We'd brokered some kind of fragile peace with Erik Belvedere, united over our hatred of the gods. But what did that mean for us now?

He was still our enemy. Even if he had wanted to halt the fight in the end. It didn't change anything. And yet it changed *everything*.

I wished the phone would ring, this endless torment of waiting for news burning me up from the inside out. But I had no idea what I'd say to my sister when she did call. I'm sorry? But was I even sorry?

You're selfish. You couldn't bear to lose her, so you cursed her instead.

But hadn't she been considering the idea of turning anyway? She'd been the one to insist the prophecy wanted her to be a vampire. And though I'd never have agreed to her doing it under any other circumstance, with her body broken beyond all chance of recovery, what other choice could there have been?

Magnar still hadn't said anything to me about what I'd done. He hadn't spoken a word about the choice I'd made, and I hadn't dared broach the subject because I knew exactly how he felt about it. He wouldn't have made the same choice. But I could feel the unsaid words hanging between us like this heavy weight which just kept growing, making the air simmer with tension and my frayed nerves shiver within every piece of my flesh.

I should turn to him, open my mouth and say...well what could I really say? He'd killed his own father rather than see him walk the Earth as a vampire.

I didn't need to ask him if he agreed with what I'd just done. I knew he didn't. Given the opportunity, I couldn't even be sure he wouldn't end Montana's immortal existence if he saw her again. My actions went against everything I'd sworn to do when I took my vow.

Or did they?

If this ended in us breaking the curse then Montana would be human again. The vampires would all be destroyed and reborn in mortal bodies. So perhaps my actions *were* following the path I'd chosen. If creating one vampire led to the end of their reign, then it had to be worth it. But I was trying to convince myself of the truth of that with everything I was. I only wished that gamble hadn't had to be made with my sister's soul.

I twisted my mother's ring on my finger and wondered if the gods had figured out that I had it. They'd certainly felt its power when I'd forced them away from us, but would they have recognised what was being used against them? Magnar thought they'd want to take the ring from me if they knew I had it, but I wondered how they'd ever be able to retrieve something they couldn't even see.

There were so many questions twisting through my mind and nowhere near enough answers.

The boat shifted as someone moved towards me and I closed my eyes, withdrawing my fingers from the water as whoever it was took a seat beside me. I wasn't sure I wanted to hear what the slayers had to say to me but I guessed the least I could do would be to hear them out.

"I'm sorry," I said before he could speak. "Not for choosing what I did; I can't bring myself to regret that. But for the position it puts you in. Both of you. I know you think that that fate is worse than death but I... I just couldn't say goodbye."

"Normally I'd have to agree with you," Julius said and I turned to him in surprise, having expected it to be Magnar beside me if I was being entirely honest with myself. Or perhaps hope was more accurate than expectation. "But your sister had plenty to say on the subject of her becoming one of them. She thought it might have needed to happen, even before she had no choice in it. And I think she would have asked the parasite to turn her in the end if she believed it meant the curse could be broken." He spoke the words with a roughness that betrayed his own dislike of them, but I could tell that he was trying to see this situation from all angles, trying not to hate everything about it on principle alone.

I looked up at him and my heart swelled with hope as I clung to his words like they were a life raft upon a tide which had been hell-bent on ripping me away with it.

"You think she would have chosen this? She would have wanted to turn instead of dying?" The idea would have been unthinkable just weeks ago when we'd been two girls from Realm G but after everything we'd been through, I really wanted to believe he was right. That she would have chosen a life as a vampire over a death as a mortal. Not for her own sake. But for the idea that she might have been able to change the fates of everyone tangled up in the curse the gods had given to the Belvederes so many years ago.

"I think she wanted to solve the prophecy," Julius replied slowly. "And that she was willing to sacrifice a great deal to try and do so."

"So maybe I did the right thing?" I breathed hopefully.

Julius glanced at his brother before answering, though I didn't dare follow his gaze, and a dark look crossed his eyes. "I think if the curse ends up broken then any kind of payment will turn out to be worth it."

"But?" I asked, sensing how carefully he was picking his words and that there was a lot he wasn't saying.

Julius shifted in his seat and looked at Magnar once again. I forced myself to follow his gaze, chewing on the inside of my cheek as I waited for the words I'd been trying to avoid hearing. Because I already knew how they felt about it. Their own father had begged for death rather than live with the vampire curse. And Magnar hadn't hesitated in giving it to him.

With some difficulty, I forced my eyes to meet with the golden gaze of the man who I had laid my heart out for, who I had sworn an oath with, and who I owed my life to countless times over. The silence stretched as we looked at one another, my emotions too raw and bruised to hide, while his were a roiling tempest of the unknown. But my heart still upped its pace beneath this weight of his penetrating gaze, my breath still catching in my throat as he stripped me apart piece by piece with nothing but his endless stare.

"But nothing," Magnar said, surprising me. He leaned against the wheel and continued looking down at me in that way which stripped me bare. If I wasn't utterly delusional, then I could have sworn that wasn't anger or hatred simmering in his sandstorm eyes. "If Montana had to do this to break the curse then it isn't for us to cast judgment on her. The parasites have developed ways to sustain themselves without killing so she should be able to survive this transformation with her soul as close to intact as is possible. Now we can only hope that her guesses about the prophecy were right and that she won't have to remain a monster for long."

I stared at him with my lips parting in shock. I'd expected him to hate me for the choice I'd made. I'd thought that this would have created a divide between us so great that even with the gods forced aside, we would still struggle to be together. But that wasn't the truth I found in his expression.

I pushed myself to my feet and approached him, the boat rocking beneath me as I moved and making my steps slower as I adjusted to the unfamiliar motion.

Magnar watched me come for him, his gaze drinking me in, his posture rigid, but it felt more like restraint than rejection.

I reached up to touch his face, my fingertips scraping across the stubble that graced his strong jaw line. The blood and filth of battle still coated his skin, though now it had begun to dry and flake away, revealing the man beneath the mask of the monster.

"Thank you," I breathed, knowing what it must be costing him to alter his views on this. To go against everything he had been raised to believe in and fight for. But I knew what the cost of such consideration had to be. If he was able to believe Montana could be saved, then that would open up all kinds of doubts about what had happened to his father. Or what the vampires were, deep down inside. They'd all been human once after all.

Magnar's fingers brushed down the length of my arm until he reached my hand and took it in his. He ran his thumb over the ring which still shielded us from the gods and it throbbed beneath the power of his touch.

15

He said nothing more and I could almost feel the pressure of his world, his beliefs and even the foundation of all he was cracking beneath him, but he did not break. Didn't even buckle. Because he was made of something far more powerful than simply the gifts of the gods and that was why I had been his from the moment he'd shoved me up against that wall.

"So what now?" Julius asked as he leaned back in his seat and put his feet up on the chair in front of him. He was looking brighter already, the colour returning to his skin as his gifts helped him to replenish the blood he'd lost to Erik in their fight, and I was relieved to have one less thing to worry about.

I squeezed Magnar's fingers and looked around us at the water which stretched on and on, the waves rocking the speedboat beneath our feet. A cool wind blew, raising goosebumps along my skin and I could feel an ache in my stomach which spoke of a desire for food.

I still wore the white dress Idun had given me, though it was now so stained with Fabian's blood that it had turned mostly red. My feet were bare and my body cried out with fatigue.

The others weren't much better off. Their clothes were torn and bloodied and countless wounds marred their flesh, slowly healing with the aid of their gifts but surely still causing them plenty of pain.

We hadn't grabbed our packs when we'd left the island and the speedboat was open to the elements, leaving us exposed and vulnerable on the open water. We couldn't stay out here long, but I had no idea where we were supposed to go. I only knew that I didn't want to travel far from Montana. She could be awake already and I needed to see her as soon as possible to apologise and to make sure that whatever had happened to her now, she was still herself. That she loved me as her sister, that she was still in some way human.

"Have you checked the cell phone?" I asked, shaking off my mounting fears.

Julius pulled it from his pocket and glanced at the screen with a small shrug. "Nothing. It could be hours before she calls. Or days. Who knows how long it takes a new paras- I mean, *vampire* to think of anything other than blood?"

I tried to ignore the fact that he'd nearly just referred to Montana as a parasite but the sting of his words drove deep into my chest.

"Then we need to find shelter," Magnar said, pulling me against him so I could feel the warmth of his skin and hear the steady rhythm of his heartbeat beneath my ear. "Is there anywhere that we can go which will be safe from the vampires without taking us too far away?"

Julius pursed his lips as he considered it. "We could head north of the city. Maybe find somewhere along the coast to hole up so that we can use this boat to escape again if necessary. I don't think many vampires live outside of the city limits, so it should be safe enough."

"Let's go then. We need to find fresh supplies and get some rest. Who knows what trials we're going to have to face next?" Magnar replied, casting a dark look towards the sky which I knew was aimed at the gods.

I flexed my fingers. The shield provided by the ring would continue to conceal us from their wrath and I had no intention of removing it any time soon.

Julius nodded and got to his feet, heading for the wheel. I let Magnar guide me down onto the leather chairs at the back of the craft and he pulled me into his lap as Julius started the boat up.

I curled myself against him, the ache in my chest lessening slightly as he wrapped his strong arms around me and the heat of his body banished a little of the cold from my limbs.

"This moment will pass," Magnar murmured into my hair, his fingers tracing back and forth across my thigh in a soothing motion. "Every moment does. And when pain strikes its deepest, each second which slips by beyond it will lessen that ache. The world will keep turning and the sun will shine brighter, some days more than others. You will be ready to bask in it when it does."

The boat wheeled about in the inky water as Julius turned it north and loosed the throttle. I settled myself against Magnar's chest, allowing his presence to ease the knot of anxiety within me and relaxing just a little.

Icy droplets sprayed around us as the powerful vessel carved a path through the sea and we bounced over the waves as our speed increased, the motion lulling me towards a sleep my aching body begged for.

I closed my eyes, letting my thoughts drift to memories of my sister and I as children. I'd always been the reckless one, getting myself into all kinds of messes through boredom or sheer stupidity. But she'd been right by my side; getting me out of trouble and fixing the problems I'd created. She'd always been able to solve every issue and I'd relied on her to help me in every way imaginable.

If anyone stood a chance of solving this riddle and ending the vampires' curse, it was her. It had to be. Because I refused to believe it had all been for nothing. I refused to accept that this was our fate: to stand on opposite sides of a war we'd never chosen to take part in.

No. We'd never been divided in anything in our entire lives. So the gods had drawn battle lines and set us apart? I didn't care. I didn't dance to their tune anymore. Perhaps vampires and slayers had been created to destroy each other, but that would never define us. Because we had something so much purer than hate. We had love.

MONTANA

CHAPTER TWO

A thousand smells found me in the chasm of darkness I'd fallen into. The fresh scent of grass, the sweetness of fir trees, the crispness of the air. Sounds were near and far away at once. I could pick each of them out, honing in on one until it was all I could hear. The twitter of birdsong, the rumble of a distant engine, the wind shifting branches and rustling leaves.

My tongue was swollen, heavy. At the base of my throat, a fresh rawness started to grow. It expanded from a nagging ache to a persistent, screaming, demanding *burn*.

My eyes flew open and a starlit sky stared down at me, and the bulbous moon hung above, surveying and impossibly bright. The more I focused, the more the sky lightened and a million pinpricks filled the heavens, more stars than I'd ever seen before. It was an expanse of endless beauty, of more colour than I had ever realised lay above. Deepest blues, swirls of purple, shimmers of green.

This was surely death. And it wasn't as cold or as brutal as I'd imagined it to be, nor as empty. But it wasn't exactly inviting either. The pain in my throat was growing to an unbearable ache, so this had to be something other than death. Was I still teetering on the edge of life, about to fall into a dark oblivion? But if I was, why didn't my body hurt from the fall from the statue, why couldn't I feel my shattered bones and punctured skin?

I scraped my tongue against the roof of my mouth and sucked in a breath as I brushed something sharp. My canines were pointed and longer than usual, the touch of them like the kiss of a knife-point.

No...wait. This isn't right.

The pain in my throat sharpened to a blinding agony and I sat upright with a gasp, suddenly drowning in the need to end this torture. Because that was what it was, a torment that ripped at my insides and required something of me. Something I couldn't deny. No force in this world or the next could deny it. This insatiable want.

I grasped at my neck, taking in the garden that sprawled out before me which ended in a group of trees. There was dew on the grass and the way the morning light shimmered through it made it look like diamonds were glinting upon every blade. And I could perceive each of those blades too clearly, like they were right in front of my eyes.

On the horizon sat the glittering skyscrapers of New York City, and my mind spun as I realised where I was. Yet it wasn't possible. Not unless-

"Erik!" I cried in panic, my voice somehow softer, more musical.

It was all clicking together, reality slamming into me like a ton of bricks and leaving me breathless. Only there was no need for breath, no movement stirring within my lungs, no request for me to draw oxygen into my body. All was still, my body in a kind of stasis apart from that ripping, roaring burn in my throat.

The sound of a door opening punctured my ear drums like a gunshot. I winced as I tried to adjust to the swarm of sound around me, even the gentle wind like a bellowing wail. I clapped my hands to my ears, trying to block it out, but even the sound of my skin against my own was too much.

Erik appeared before me, falling to his knees in the grass. He was dressed in sweatpants and a white t-shirt, a stark contrast to the last time I'd seen him. Bloodied and bruised.

"Focus," he commanded, that word drawing all of my attention.

"You can dial down each noise, make it fade, Montana."

I nodded, trying to do as he said and finding it all too simple to do so, each noise slipping back to a normal level at nothing but my will.

I slowly lowered my hands from my ears, taking him in without the need to blink even once. His dark hair was pushed back more carelessly than usual, and there was no hint of exhaustion in his glass-cut features, but there was a touch of something in his storm-grey eyes. Concern and perhaps even a glint of fear.

He was alive. His fight with Magnar was over. And we were somehow here together despite what I knew had happened. How I'd leapt from the top of that towering statue in a bid to save this very man before me from the curse that had been laid upon his soul. But instead of salvation, I found myself damned along with him, Andvari's words nothing but a trick I'd dived so foolishly into.

I was in too much of a daze to move toward Erik, too confounded by this impossible situation. That I was actually, truly sitting here, alive. No...not alive. Not really. I was one of them. Of the creatures I had feared my entire life, and only my stubbornness was still denying it.

Erik held a silver bottle in his hand and the sweet scent that sailed from it filled me with a longing that took over everything in me. I was nothing but an animal in that moment, ruled by instinct alone.

"Here, don't look, just drink," he ordered.

My throat flamed and a groan escaped me, filled with so much desperation it was nearly impossible to resist. But I knew in the pit of my soul what was in that bottle and I couldn't – I wouldn't-

Erik cupped my cheek and I stilled in surprise. He didn't feel cold. He felt...not warm exactly, but something in between. Something that didn't send a chill through me but instead made my skin tingle with desire. I took his wrist, turning his hand over and admiring the strangely different feel of our fingers intertwining. His cypress scent was everywhere, invading my senses and making me somehow forget the bottle in his hand. I eyed his face, able to see through the darkness of the night as easily as if it were day. I reached for him, brushing my thumb along the strong line of his cheekbone, along the slanted lines that made up his painfully handsome face.

"Drink, rebel," he insisted, handing me the bottle.

A lump swelled in my throat and I bit down on my lip to try and hold back the urge to do as he bid, instantly drawing blood with my teeth.

Oh shit. I have fangs. And if I accept what that means, I'll scream.

The pain was nothing but a minor throb and in seconds, it departed as the welt on my lip healed over.

I shook my head, panic rising in me at the impossibility of what was happening and Erik lunged at me, knocking me to the ground and taking hold of the back of my neck.

"What are you doing?" I cried, leaning away from him.

He held me firmer, his hand fisting in my hair and drawing me closer as he lifted the bottle to my lips.

My mind stopped working as the stronger scent hit my nostrils. I was reduced to one primal need. A hungry wolf given a helpless lamb. Erik pressed the bottle to my mouth but I battled my way out of the darkness trying to consume me, refusing it with everything I had. I was not a monster. I would not drink the blood of the people kept caged to feed Erik's kind.

I shoved him hard in the chest, and he was thrown off of me with such force that he slammed onto the ground on his back, only keeping the bottle upright by sheer luck.

I stared at him in disbelief, my gaze shifting to my outstretched hands in awe.

I'm strong. Like him. Like his kin.

He released a low chuckle as he sat up in the dirt and my senses realigned.

"Drink or you'll go mad," he insisted.

"Then I'll go mad. I can't drink the blood of my own people," I snapped as emotion dug a deep pit in my chest. I reached for my heart and released a sob as it didn't beat, didn't even flutter with life.

I was dead. And yet not remotely in the way I'd imagined.

Panic crept through my bones and threatened to overwhelm me.

I was one of the creatures I'd despised all my life, the ones that had taken my mom away to the blood bank. Who had killed her and killed Dad too.

Erik rose to his feet with the bottle in his grip. "Montana, you have to drink."

I shook my head violently, springing upright. I should have been dizzy from how fast I'd moved, but my body was made for it, my mind too sharp to be affected by something so trivial. My eyes were trained on Erik as he advanced again and I held out a hand to keep him back.

Fuck, he was beautiful. He seemed to glow under my heightened vision. The shadow of his cheekbones, the deep glittering iron of his gaze. He was like a comet tearing through the sky toward the Earth, growing brighter as he approached.

That salivating scent reached me again and I held my throat, willing the forceful need away.

"Please don't make me do this," I begged, trembling as I eyed the bottle. The want was growing too fierce, my determination already cracking. How I ached to drink every drop of that blood. I knew it would be ecstasy, that it would sate this blazing need inside me.

Erik frowned deeply, his gaze tinged with concern. "I don't want to make you do anything, but you must drink or you'll go insane with hunger. It is only a matter of time before you cave, and frankly, it's a miracle you haven't drunk the whole stock in the house already."

"There's more?" I breathed, my thoughts abandoning me again.

I cursed myself for the desperation in my tone, hating this new desire that lived in me. It didn't feel like it was a part of me more that it was my ruler now. A vicious demon perching on the throne of my desires, and this was what it wanted most of all.

"As much as you need." Erik nodded. "It's Realm A. No humans were harmed in the making of this blood," he teased, and I gaped at him, unable to believe he was joking about right now.

He gave me an apologetic look. "Alright, maybe that was in poor taste, but you need to drink or it's only going to get worse, rebel."

Tears seared my eyes as I stared at the bottle in his hand. He was waiting for me to take it. Waiting for me to break. But how could I?

To do so would be to abandon my humanity. It was unthinkable. It was damn cannibalism.

Except it wasn't. Because I wasn't human anymore. I was one of *them.* The creatures who'd been my sworn enemies my whole life. But that didn't mean I had to be like them, I didn't have to give in. I could refuse, I could hold out.

I backed up and my bare feet pressed into the soft grass. I glanced down to find I'd been dressed in a black tank top and matching sweatpants. I should have been freezing standing out here in the winter air, but the breeze was the same temperature as me. Although, I wasn't quite sure what temperature that was. I wasn't cold, but I wasn't warm either. I was suspended in an equilibrium that was unaffected by nature, and something about that scared me even further.

I glanced toward the trees at the base of the garden, energy burning through me and urging me toward them.

I'll run. I'll hide. He can't make me do this.

"Rebel," Erik warned, sensing the decision I was about to make.

I ran, darting through the grass so fast that I was sure I would fall. But my legs were sturdy, incredibly strong and able to carry me as far as I wanted to go. I slipped between the trunks and expected darkness to swallow me, but my eyes adjusted and the world brightened so I could see the winding path that led deeper into the woodland.

A rush of air sounded before a weight slammed into me. I toppled, but no pain found me as I hit the ground and Erik pinned me in place, his thighs clamping my legs together. He rolled me over beneath him and tilted his head, surveying me with a kind of hunger which lit a fire in me.

The rune on my left palm scorched with the need to be closer to him. My lips parted as I reached up, skating my fingers across his skin in admiration. My eyes picked out every fleck of silver in his eyes, the way his mouth moved and his throat bobbed. "You're so-"

"Blood. Drink. Now," he barked.

"*Bossy*," I finished my sentence, and the strength of my feral tone took me by surprise, like a wild animal had tempered my voice with a snarl.

Erik laughed, seeming so at ease with this entirely world-altering situation. He held the bottle out once more with a roguish grin. "Fine, I propose a deal. You drink this and I'll give you a phone to call your sister."

"Callie?" I gasped. "She's okay, right?" Shit, this thirst was stealing away my thoughts. I had to know she was safe. That the slayers were too. But then...what if they despised me? What if they couldn't bear to face what had happened to me? What if my sister could never look me in the eye again without wanting to plunge her blade into my heart?

"Yes, she left with the other slayers. I gave them the speedboat."

I lurched upward, unable to gain any control over how fast I moved as I wrapped my arms around Erik. "Thank you." Relief spilled through me at knowing they still lived, but shit, what did Callie think of me now?

Erik pulled me into the tightest hug I'd ever had and I fell still in his hold, drinking in the moment with all my heart, knowing I had almost lost the chance at ever being this close to him again.

"So?" he asked, pressing me back.

I tentatively took the bottle, shutting my eyes as a wave of disgust mixed with the thirst that clawed at my insides. "I can't," I rasped.

"Montana, look at me."

I did, my fingers gripping the bottle so tight, it must have been on the verge of cracking.

Erik gripped my jaw in his hand, and the touch sent a wave of goosebumps skittering across my skin. I leaned into his palm, practically nuzzling him as all these new sensations set my flesh ablaze. I could feel so much at once, his fingers like roughened satin grazing against me.

"You need this," he spoke evenly. "You will hurt people if you don't drink. You cannot see your sister again until you have a handle on your urges. And the best way to keep your mind as your own is to stay well fed."

Acceptance washed over me, the truth undeniable as he laid it out for me like that. I'd seen the rotters in the ruins. That was the fate of hungry vampires. They became mindless, starved creatures that were little more than husks of their former selves. I couldn't risk becoming that. I had to find a way to handle this so I could reunite with Callie, or at least have the chance to. Because in all honesty, I didn't know if she could ever accept me into her life like this.

I touched the bottle to my lips then drew it away again with every ounce of strength I had left. I was torn, knowing I had to do this and equally repulsed by that truth.

I groaned with longing as a ravenous creature hollowed out my stomach. My hand shook as I tried to keep the blood away, but my traitorous arm moved closer and tilted the bottle to my lips. I had to. I just had to.

The moment the first drop touched my tongue, I fell into a frenzy, my mind sparking with a blur of frantic light. I tipped the bottle up, drinking deeply, intoxicated as the sweet, metallic liquid rolled down my throat, quenching that unbearable burn at last. I couldn't stop until it was all gone and my body reacted with an explosion of ecstasy which seeped into my veins, awaking a predator in me that demanded more. So much more.

Erik gripped my arm, giving me an intense look as if he was waiting for something. Slowly, the pain died away entirely and bliss took its place, a sea of perfect tranquillity that was nothing but nirvana. I bathed in the moment of satisfaction like I was standing in the aftermath of an earthquake, relief settling into my bones and releasing me from the demands of the thirst.

I placed the bottle down and guilt took the place of my satiation, my brow furrowing in judgement at myself. Erik slid a hand into my hair, leaning in to place a kiss on my forehead. I lifted my head so his lips met mine instead and he released a feral noise against my mouth.

Love swelled in my heart and the mark of partnership on my palm sung with joy. Everything felt heightened, my lips tingled from his kiss and I couldn't get enough as I gripped his neck, devouring the feel of his skin against mine.

"Please," I moaned and I didn't know where my begging came from or what I really wanted. I just needed him closer. In the aftermath of the blood, a primal part of myself had awoken and she was an animal with one need in mind.

"Please what?" Erik growled, his fingers skating up my sides and sending a fire burning along my flesh.

I tilted my head back, pulling him toward my neck with a desperate groan, wanting to feel more of his skin against mine.

"Rebel," he rumbled against my throat. "We should really talk-"

I clawed his shirt apart, silencing him as I slashed the material to shreds with barely any effort. He cocked an eyebrow at me, lifting his head long enough to take in my yearning expression.

I spotted a bandage peeking out from under his shirt and frowned deeply.

"You're hurt," I gasped.

"Your sister drove a slayer blade into me. But she can hardly be blamed. Andvari took control of me. I lost myself for a while. If anything, she saved me."

My mouth parted as I ran my thumb close to the bandage. "Does it hurt?"

"Nothing will ever hurt like the fear of losing you," he said darkly.

His pupils dilated and his mirth fell away into a look that was utterly animal. He dipped his head again, branding my skin with fierce kisses that set my soul alight. I couldn't think straight. I couldn't gain control of myself as my body starved for something else entirely.

I pushed my hand beneath the torn material of his shirt to feel the hard plane of his muscles. His throat rose and fell as he watched me explore his body and liquid heat blazed between my thighs. I needed him to the point of insanity, my skin igniting from each of his touches, and I despised every shred of clothes parting me from him.

"I've got one ounce of self-control right now. You'd better tell me to use it," he warned, and I caught him by the neck, yanking him down to kiss me.

His tongue met mine and I nearly died all over again with how good it felt to be this close to him. My skin was electrified, connecting to his with currents of energy that shuddered through my body and made me moan.

I clawed at his back and he arched above me, snatching the front of my tank top and ripping it off in one clean swipe. I was bare beneath it, my breasts exposed to him and I grasped them, squeezing the soft flesh and delighting in how damn good that felt. Everything was heightened, each touch eliciting an earth-shuddering explosion in my body, but it wasn't enough.

Erik's eyes trailed over me, a sinful want in them that had me undone. My clit throbbed from his hungry looks alone and I bucked beneath him, tugging on my nipples and sighing his name.

"You are the answer to all my desires," he said with grit, his head tilting down and his eyes becoming more shadowed as the moon haloed him from behind.

His hands pressed into the soft earth either side of me as he dropped his mouth to my ear, grazing his fangs across the shell of it. A thousand volts of electricity coursed down my spine in response, and I cursed as my clit pulsed again, sure I could come at these simple touches alone.

His palm slid between us, and I inhaled deeply, my lungs swelling even though they didn't need air. I could taste the trees on the night air, but most of all I could taste *him* and it sent me spiralling into madness.

He brushed his nose against mine, toying with the edge of my waistband as he sucked on his lower lip. I could see the question he was going to ask building in his gaze. But whatever hesitation I'd felt towards this in the past had thoroughly abandoned me. I loved Erik. Wholly, deeply, profoundly. Nothing could change that. Nothing could unwrite it. We were made for each other. And even though my dad would have hated me for this, I was far beyond following the path he might have chosen for me. I was Erik's kin now. His blood flowed in my veins. His venom had changed me in more ways than one. But it was the leap I'd taken from the statue that had really shifted who I was. In that moment, I'd proven my love beyond any reasoning. No one would deny me of it.

I pressed two fingers to Erik's lips with a slow smile spreading across my face. "I'm yours tonight."

"What about tomorrow?" he asked beneath my fingers, his tone unravelling me.

I brushed my knuckles across his jaw with a grin. "If you behave."

He snorted a laugh, pushing my hand aside and slamming it into the mud, pinning me there. He didn't need to be gentle with my newly made body and I didn't want him to be.

He captured my lower lip between his teeth and I gasped as he bit down, a flare of excitement rearing in my chest.

"No deal," he growled, pushing his hand beneath my waistband and finding my slick core.

My back arched as he drove three thick fingers inside me, and I cried out as he stretched me for him and pleasure tore through my flesh. Erik raked his mouth across my throat and I lost myself to his hands, his tongue, even his teeth. Of all the things I'd wanted from Erik, his fangs had been the last on that list. But as his canines grazed my skin, I came apart from the sensations pouring through me.

Erik released a low noise against my lips as his thumb slid over my clit and rolled across my skin in the perfect way. I cried out again, pleasure darting through me so violently that I didn't know what to do with it. His fingers pumped and a growl built in his throat as he watched me delight in the feeling of his body taking control of mine. His skin was rough yet smooth, cool yet warm, and every nerve ending in my body was primed for his, like my skin was made to connect with him this way.

"You're made for me," Erik said darkly. "See how your body bows to mine, rebel?"

I couldn't answer, my moans turning frantic as he ground the heel of his palm down over my clit and pushed another finger inside me. My pussy clamped tight around his hand and my back arched as I bucked against the ground, coming apart at the seams and screaming as ecstasy exploded through my body. I couldn't think straight as every muscle in my body tensed then relaxed and my head spun from the needy desire in my flesh. I had to have more. It was a taste of perfection, but not the full dose of it, and there was only one way he could provide that to me.

Erik slid his fingers out of me, watching me with a wicked kind of lust in his gaze. He lifted his glistening fingers to my left breast, wetting my nipple with my own arousal and circling his thumb over it, making me whimper for him. I could see the thick outline of his hard cock pressing against the inside of his pants, and I reached for it, squeezing and caressing him, making him growl with want.

I knew he was as desperate as I was for this to go further, his gaze tracking over me with a sinful hunger that went far beyond the thirst that racked his soul. This want was just between us, a thing that grew more demanding with every passing minute. There were no more doubts in my mind about him. I wanted him to possess me as no man had ever possessed me before.

"I'll have you now and always, Montana," Erik declared. "I will not be denied of you again. You are mine as I am yours, understand?"

"Yes," I said fiercely, moaning again as he toyed with my breasts, my nipples raw from his sweet torture. "Now claim what's yours and show me what you have been holding back on with me. Because I can take every ounce of strength you have to give now, and I want all of you. Every piece of this monster you hide so poorly."

As if my words had summoned the beast from within him, he reared over me, pressing the bulk of his weight down on me, forcing me deeper into the earth, no longer being gentle with me as he had when I was mortal. He shoved his knees between mine, reaching down and shredding my sweatpants along with my panties, baring me fully to him.

I hooked my thumbs beneath his waistband, tearing his pants away too and a low laugh left him at the show of my own strength.

"This will take some getting used to," he said, then he lifted his hips, reaching between us to fist his cock and drive the slick tip of it against my entrance.

I whimpered, needing this and not knowing what it would be like to feel him inside me, only sure I wanted it more than anything. He showed me no mercy as he rammed his hips forward and filled me entirely, making me cry out in delight at the wholly new sensation. I scraped my fingers through his hair as I drew him down onto me, our skin velvet on velvet, sparks of pure energy igniting along my limbs. He started fucking me with a brutality that had me crying out with every thrust of his hips, my legs locking around his waist as he took me with the full force of his strength, no pain finding me despite this being my first time. I didn't want for more, he gave me exactly what I needed as his cock pulsed inside me, the huge length of him pounding into a sensitive spot that had me shattering for him again.

I could hardly withstand the powerful feelings he caused in me, clawing and scratching, marking his body with my desire as another climax rocked the foundations of my soul.

His hands scored through the earth beside my head, gouging great craters in the mud. We were filthy, desperate, and nothing but carnal creatures as we claimed each other. But I didn't care about anything but his weight on me and the way our souls seemed to inch closer, demanding to be joined as one.

I tore at his neck with muddy fingernails, wrapping my thighs around his waist to try and get nearer. I never grew tired and neither did he, and a pressure was mounting at the base of my spine, promising me more pleasure as we fell into a hungry rhythm.

"Come all over my cock again, sweet girl," he growled in my ear, and I fell apart for him all too easily, giving him what he wanted, what I wanted. He roared as he came with me, fucking me furiously and stilling for only a moment before he continued on, chasing another release just as I was.

I rolled us in the mud, the filth caked against my skin as I straddled him instead, rolling my hips and fucking him as he drove his hips up to match my pace.

He leaned up, capturing one of my nipples between his lips and raking his fangs over it, making me gasp and shudder. His fingers bit into my ass, taking control of my movements and I let him guide me towards another tide of oblivion. The wind on my skin was like a caress of its own, and I pawed at myself, my fingers sliding through the mud on my flesh and feeling so fucking good. Erik's mouth on me was the centre of it all, his lips, his fangs, he was everywhere all at once, and somehow, as my clit ground against his body, I was coming again, falling into bliss and letting him catch me in his arms.

He shifted our position once more, moving with speed until we were standing and he was driving me against a tree, the huge bough groaning from the force he used to pin me there. Leaves fluttered down around us as he fucked me raw, the sensation of my back scraping the rough bark feeling incredible against my immortal skin.

Erik's hand fisted in my hair and he made me look at him as he fucked me slower, our eyes locked.

"This is only the beginning of us," he swore. "I will chase life with you to the ends of time."

He pulled me into a fierce kiss, his tongue meeting mine with a wild kind of passion. No matter how long this went on, I didn't pant or lose my breath, my body so strong I knew I could handle anything.

His hips slowed and I ground my teeth with urgency as he brought me toward a climax that took my entire body hostage. My toes curled as my ankles locked around his waist, and my mind exploded with stars. I was his to shape, moulded like clay and sculpted by his will.

He pressed his forehead against mine, groaning my name as he reached his own end again, falling still inside me. A thrill danced under my skin at seeing him shatter for me, and I held him tighter as my muscles clenched and finally unfolded.

"Fuck," he breathed with a boyish smile.

My arms fell either side of me as I laughed, the tension floating out of my body and up, up, up into the sky. Erik joined me in my laughter and I felt like the earth had flipped on its axis.

How was it possible we were here naked in the forest when I should have been dead just hours ago?

Because I'm a vampire.

The word resounded in my head like a broken record, and I fully accepted the weight of the curse that now had hold of me. There was no coming back from this without finding an answer to the prophecy. If my turning had been a part of it, then perhaps we were on the right path, but the rest we still had to figure out.

Erik lowered me to the ground, and I stared at his powerful body as he gazed down at me. "Just so we're clear, that was not my intention this evening."

"What was your intention?" I asked with a wide smile I couldn't get rid of.

"Well an hour ago, I was scared out of my fucking mind that I'd lost you forever. So making sure you survived the curse was my priority. And then..."

"And then?" I prompted.

"My turning was so fucked up, I wanted to make it better for you.

Easier. You like being outside, so I thought if I laid you in the grass..."
he trailed off and my heart lifted at his words.

"Thank you," I whispered, then swallowed hard, worried the
bloodlust might creep up on me again. "How often do I have to drink?"
I asked, my nose wrinkling.

"Every few days," he said. "But once a day is best, it keeps you
sharp."

I frowned, hating the idea and he rubbed a muddy thumb across my
cheek.

"Let's go inside. We can talk. You'll feel better once we talk."

"I do feel better and not because we *talked*."

He grinned, stepping back and I looked to my clothes which were
in ribbons on the ground. Erik's gaze lingered on me, his cock still
hard and his eyes telling me he was far from done with me. But it was
probably time I dealt with reality.

I expected to blush from his penetrating stare, but my blood wasn't
warm and instead a strange coolness ran through my blood.

He stalked closer once more, and he pressed a hand to my waist,
brushing his thumb up and down my skin. "Let's find you some clothes.
I am far too easily distracted by you like this."

I laughed and the sound was a musical thing that had no business
coming from my throat. Erik kept close as we headed back through
the garden and up to the house, naked as the freaking dawn. I eyed the
brightly lit porch with a flicker of concern as I searched for guards.

"Everyone's off duty tonight," Erik said, evidently reading my
thoughts. "Except the guards outside the gates. But if they could see
you from here, I'd have wrapped you in a plastic tarp by now."

I released a soft laugh.

Mud clung to my skin and a few leaves tumbled from my hair as I
followed Erik into the house. Quiet reached my ears but I listened harder
and found all kinds of sounds filling the building that I'd never noticed
before. The buzzing of the refrigerator in the kitchen, the ticking of a
clock, and suddenly, the hum of something I knew as well as my own
pulse.

"Nightmare!" I started running, moving in a burst of speed as I tore upstairs into my old bedroom and found it waiting for me on the wooden table at the heart of the room.

I hurried forward, reaching for it before a flutter of fear passed through me. What if I couldn't touch it anymore? It was designed to hurt vampires. *Me.*

My heart ached but I knew I had to try. It was too tempting not to pick up my old friend. I gently brushed my fingers over the hilt and it purred in response. With a breath of relief, I took it in my grasp and a swell of victory filled me.

Moon Child has been made, it whispered and a shiver darted down my spine. So it was true. This had been the line of the prophecy. And the fact sent a ripple of relief through me.

At least jumping from that damn statue hadn't been for nothing.

Erik appeared in a pair of sweatpants, and he gave me a faint look of surprise as he spotted Nightmare in my hand. "I wondered if you might still be able to wield it." His eyes brightened further. "Perhaps the sun won't weaken you either." He moved toward me at speed, cupping my cheek and pressing a feather-light kiss to my lips, nothing like the fervent kisses we'd shared in the woods.

"You're filthy," he said with a grin, plucking a twig from my hair. "Go shower. I'll join you shortly, I just have something I need to do first."

"What?" I frowned and he gave me an awkward smile.

"Fabian's still in the trunk of my car. Your sister ripped his head off and I'm delaying letting him heal."

"He can heal from a severed head?" I asked, a savage grin pulling at my lips over what Callie had done to the asshole.

"Yes, but I might wait until tomorrow...I should bring him inside at least."

I nodded and he headed away, leaving me with my skin still humming from the contact of his and far too many dirty memories replaying in my mind.

I made a path for the shower, taking Nightmare with me and placing it beside the basin in the ensuite. I ran the water hot, then swung it to cold, feeling the gush of it over my hand. I could sense the change, but not in any way that affected my blood. I left it somewhere in the middle, moving into the stream and washing the mud from my body, wondering vaguely if Erik had already washed me after the battle. There certainly must have been a lot of blood on me after I'd hit the ground...

I shuddered, horrified at the thought of my sister finding me like that. Of all of them finding me like that. I wondered where she was now. If Erik had let her go, I hoped that meant things were mending between him and the slayers. Or they were tolerating him at least, which was certainly something worth holding onto.

I knew I was putting off the inevitable as I lingered in the rushing water. I needed to call Callie to tell her I was alright, but I was terrified of what her reaction would be.

Time slipped away and the more my thoughts overwhelmed me, the more I couldn't feel the pass of the seconds. It could have been minutes or hours before I exited the shower and wrapped myself in a towel, confused by the strange way time felt now. Or perhaps it was me that felt strange. Everything was so different. I was still me at my core, I knew that. And I held onto that truth with all I had. But at the same time, I couldn't forget the way my throat had burned for blood or how good it had tasted on my lips.

I took a measured breath as I prepared to face the full weight of my situation. I was a bloodsucker. One of the creatures I'd grown up despising. But so long as I had Erik, I was somehow sure I'd be alright. That we'd figure out the prophecy together. We'd already taken a step in the right direction. And surprisingly...I didn't feel all bad. In fact, I felt kind of invincible. The blood was my biggest issue. Even the prospect of having to face another bottle sent a wave of nausea through me. I tried to convince myself that I despised it, but as I thought about human blood, a desperate longing grew in me, and I was never going to be rid of that need until the curse was broken.

Taking Nightmare in my hand, I stepped into the bedroom, finding the lights low. My eyes adjusted to the darkness and the clock on the wall told me it was well past midnight.

How long had I been in that damn shower?

I spotted a still form leaning against the headboard of the bed and my heart softened as I found Erik asleep. He was still half-naked and muddy all over, but it was the sweetest sight I'd ever seen. Everything he'd been through must have taken its toll on him. The fight with Magnar was enough, let alone what we'd done together in the woodland.

His face was totally relaxed and his awkward position told me he'd practically fallen asleep the second he'd sat down. I wondered how long it had been since he'd slept before now.

I crawled onto the sheets beside him, gently lowering him down the bed into a more comfortable position, surprised at how easily I could move his huge body. He murmured something incoherent, but I was pretty sure my name was among his words as he slid an arm around me and pulled me to his chest.

I soaked in the closeness of him like a wolf with her mate, coiled up against him and basking in the afterglow of claiming him at last.

Sleep didn't come for me. My mind was swirling with a thousand thoughts, and no tiredness found me in my new state. But I didn't move, because being that near to him, safe, alive and nowhere near the slayers' fury, filled me with so much happiness it was hard to believe my body could contain it.

ERIK

CHAPTER THREE

1000 YEARS AGO

We had to abandon the village and run north. North to the snow, the wind, the rain. Moving in the daytime was a severe disadvantage to us. We needed more hours of darkness to ensure the slayers wouldn't catch up. The cover of clouds and shorter days.

I despised running from the slayers, but I was badly injured and the others had confirmed there was a whole host of them on our tail. Perhaps we could have taken them in a fight if we'd planned our attack better, pushed ourselves to our limits. It was pointless to chew over it, but I had nothing else to occupy my thoughts as we journeyed on.

Fabian had suggested we recuperate a while and ask Andvari to assist us again, but I'd pushed for another option. The battle of Atbringer was still fresh in my memory. I'd killed too many with the god's power, spilled too much blood. Even if we could manage it that way, it didn't sit right with me.

My decision wasn't out of kindness to the slayers. The fact that they'd hunted us across an entire ocean set a rage burning in me that

Instead, I came up with a simple plan that would ensure Magnar and Julius Elioson would never be a threat to us again. Once we reached the snowy lands, we'd break apart, head separate ways and remain deeply hidden for a hundred years. By then, Magnar and his companions would be long dead. The Blessed Crusaders would be no more. And all without spilling a single drop of blood.

My siblings had finally agreed. I sensed they were eager to stop killing for a while too. Our time in the village had proven peaceful. Trust had been built between us and the humans. Blood had been given willingly in exchange for our help. That was the sort of life we wished to build for ourselves again one day. And I held onto that dream with all my heart.

We're not monsters. We can be better. There is a way to live like this that doesn't result in more death.

We'd taken shelter for the day in a dark cave after we'd found our way into a mountain range. The ache in my side had finally dulled and it was slowly knitting over. The damage done by the slayer's blade would leave an eternal scar, but I didn't care. The mark would only serve to remind me of the man who had made it. Magnar Elioson was determined to make himself my enemy. But we would outsmart him and the others in a way that they could never fight against. We had time on our hands. And a hundred years was nothing if it meant we would be rid of them.

Rain formed puddles beyond the cave, the world turning to a deep shade of blue outside our haven.

Clarice stalked back and forth in her dress; it was shredded in places and she'd soon need something new to wear if she wasn't going to be walking around naked for the next few weeks. I doubted she'd care about that. I, on the other hand, would rather my sister wasn't baring it all for the rest of our trip. She might not have been a sibling by blood, but since we'd been turned, our bond had grown more familial, and I knew Fabian and Miles felt the same way about her. We were protective of each other, nothing more.

"We should seek out a village soon," I said.

Fabian moved for the first time in a while, stepping away from the cave wall.

"Blood," he rasped, nodding firmly.

"And clothes." My own shirt was in tatters after my fight with Magnar. "But we must do so without leaving a trace. Without killing anyone."

Fabian nodded, moving to the edge of the cave. "I'll find a bird. In fact, I might find a few so we can keep an eye on the slayers too."

"Good idea." Miles jogged to follow him and the two of them stepped into the pouring rain, disappearing off through the trees.

Thunder rumbled overhead and energy spiked in my veins, storms always awakening something primal in me.

Clarice drifted toward me, perching on the rock at my side. "They'll never stop hunting us."

"That's why we're going to hide."

"And what of their children? And their children's children?" A flicker of fear flamed in her dazzling blue eyes and I rested a hand on her arm.

"They will not hold the same anger in their hearts as these slayers. As generations pass, they will not feel so wronged by us."

"How do you know that? Idun could instil the same hatred in them. We could be facing an eternity of being hunted. And one by one, we will fall. Eventually we have to. The odds won't always be in our favour."

"Clarice," I sighed. "This is our only option for now. What else can we do?"

"Talk to them?" she suggested quietly. "It's the gods who drive this fight. What if we went against them?"

I shook my head, knowing it was pointless. "The slayers do not see it that way."

"But maybe we can make them," she begged, her tone laced with desperation. "I don't want to live in caves, watching my back at every turn. I want to have a *real* life, Erik. We had one at the village of Bel Vedere and they stole it from us." Her voice broke and I sensed she was on the verge of tears.

I pulled her closer, rubbing her back in soothing circles. "We will have it again."

"When?" she growled.

"I cannot know, but I promise we will. I'll make sure of it."

"You always did know the right thing to say to make a girl feel better." She sighed, sitting upright.

"I'm not sure about that," I grunted. "But you know I'll do everything in my power to look after those I love."

"I know," she whispered, reaching up to place a kiss on my temple. "It's why Kyla loved you so fiercely."

A chasm of regret opened up inside me at the mention of my dead lover's name. She'd died by my teeth on the night I'd been turned, lost to the bloodlust. A woman I'd promised to look after had been killed by my own hands. How could I declare myself some valiant protector when I could not keep those I cared for safe in the past?

I glanced away from Clarice, and she took in a breath. "I'm sorry, I didn't mean to upset you."

"No, you're right to mention her. We rarely talk about them anymore. I think of my sister often. When I see my reflection, I recognise her in some parts of my face."

"I see her too," Clarice whispered, running her thumb over the line of my cheekbone. "You'll find her again one day in the afterlife. We'll find all of them."

I nodded vaguely, unsure if that was true. Our souls were tainted now. Even if we could somehow break the curse and become human again, perhaps we'd already done too much wrong to afford us a place with our families in the afterlife.

A sniffing sounded beyond the cave and I lifted my head, spotting a wolf and its three cubs eyeing the shelter intently. The mother was perfectly still, her eyes pinned on me as water dripped from her grey muzzle.

I tilted my head, seeing something of myself in her as she padded into the cave and her three little cubs followed.

Clarice's lips parted in surprise as the animal shook off the rain and curled up on the dry floor to nurse her cubs.

"Why isn't she afraid? Or aggressive?" Clarice breathed into the cool air.

"Maybe she knows we're not her enemy. Maybe she knows we are just like her," I murmured, a strange feeling stirring in my chest.

A wolf protected its own at all costs. No one lay judgment on it for that. Wasn't that the same as what we were trying to do? If that was the case, maybe the gods really would forgive us one day.

We travelled further north, using Fabian's Familiars to scout out small tribes. It was easy to fall into a routine, sneaking into their villages at night, taking unsuspecting people and knocking them unconscious before feeding from them. We never drank too much, never killed, and left as little trace as we could. When they woke, we hoped they'd put the painful bites down to snakes. It was the best we could hope for. And at least no one had to die in the process.

When we finally reached a snowy land where mountains huddled on the horizon, I knew it was time for us to part. We'd each head deeper into the northern territories, spreading out, east and west until we all found somewhere we could live undetected.

We'd taken clothes from the towns, wrapped ourselves up in furs so we resembled the natives as much as possible. We couldn't do much about our pale skin, but that was why we'd all agreed to continue with our plan of taking people surreptitiously for as long as possible.

Now, we stood in a ring with snowflakes dancing between us. One drifted down to land on my hand and didn't melt. I couldn't feel its icy touch, my own skin was impervious to it.

"We reunite in a hundred years," I said as Miles rested a hand on my shoulder. The others did the same so we were linked in a circle. "Return here when the times comes."

Fabian took a knife from his hip, striding away from the group towards a black boulder that jutted from the ground at an angle. He swept the snow from the side of it and etched a cross into the stone.

Clarice embraced me and a sadness weighed down my heart at the thought of parting with them all.

"We're family. Forever," Miles vowed. "Never forget that."

"We won't," Clarice promised and tears slid down her cheeks as she pulled Miles into a tight hug.

"We should unite under one name," Fabian said, strolling back to join us. "As true siblings."

"We could name ourselves after the people of Bel Vedere?" Clarice suggested, raising a brow.

I liked the idea. The village had been full of people who'd loved us. Even if their belief in us had been wrong, that didn't change who we really were. But maybe it was something to hold onto. Something to remind us that we could be better than the thirst. Stronger than it.

"Belvedere it is," Fabian announced, gazing around at us with a sad smile. "I'll miss you all."

"See you in a hundred years," I said in a low voice, an ache growing in my heart. "And when we reunite, we will be free of Magnar and his bastard friends at long last."

CALLIE

CHAPTER FOUR

The dank boathouse we'd found to take cover in smelled of rot and mildew which wasn't exactly what I had pictured when hoping to find shelter.

The meagre fire Magnar continued to care for was resisting every effort to get going, which meant my hopes of warming up and feeling a little more human again were dwindling by the minute. Everything was damp and refused to burn with any true heat. I longed for a real fire which might just banish the wet from my bedraggled dress, but I was beginning to lose hope that it would ever set light properly. Even my slayer gifts couldn't keep out this level of cold.

Rather than stare at Magnar while he worked, I paced up and down the wooden jetty beside the water in some vain effort to coax a little warmth into my limbs and stop my mind from racing.

Julius had gone in search of supplies but I didn't hold out much hope. Aside from the wooden structure we'd claimed for our shelter, the landscape around us had looked close to deserted from the water.

Very little had been left standing here after the Final War and this battered boathouse had been the only viable option for miles.

He'd left the cell phone with us and had shown me how to call Erik's number, but the bloodsucker hadn't picked up when I'd attempted it.

I'd called so many times that I'd lost count. It just rang and rang endlessly, leaving me in this eternal torment. How could I be sure the transformation had even worked? She should be a vampire by now. Her body should have healed. So why hadn't she called me? Was she angry with me? Or had something gone wrong? I didn't know. I didn't know anything at all and the not knowing was tearing me apart.

I released a scream of frustration and slammed my foot into the jetty beneath me, my strengthened muscles splintering the wood and breaking a hole right through it.

I regretted the outburst instantly as pain lanced through my ankle as I wrenched my foot back out of the hole and the jagged wood tore through my skin.

I swore, turning my anger onto myself as blood flowed over my bare foot in payment for my stupidity.

Magnar got to his feet, abandoning the pathetic fire as he approached me, his brow furrowing as he drew closer.

I wanted to punch something. I wanted to punch Erik fucking Belvedere in his stupid lying face. He'd *promised* to call me. I'd let him take her from me because he'd made me believe it was the only way, and now I had no idea what he'd done with her. He'd taken my sister from me for the second time and I had no way of knowing if I'd ever be able to get her back. She was one of his creatures now. And if he'd lied about letting me speak to her once she was turned, then he could just as easily have been lying about everything else too.

"Take a breath," Magnar murmured, and I turned to glare at him.

"*You* take a fucking breath," I snapped.

My anger was the only thing I had left in this moment and if I let it go too, then I wasn't sure what would remain of me.

He tilted his head and raised an eyebrow at my tone as if it amused him rather than riling him like I'd been aiming for. "You're bleeding."

"No shit." I stomped away from him, but he caught my arm before I could get more than two paces.

I spun back towards him, fully intending to hit him or start screaming or do anything at all other than fall into his arms sobbing.

Magnar released a heavy breath as he pulled me close to his chest and my tears fell against his skin as something within me began to shatter despite all my best efforts to hold it together. I didn't know what to do. I felt so helpless and hopeless and utterly alone without my sister. I didn't even know if she was still *her* anymore and it was eating me up.

I couldn't bear not knowing. She might need me. Or she might never need me again. But how could I even begin to try and deal with any of it when I just didn't know?

"When we were hunting the Belvederes a thousand years ago, we often had to split up. My mother didn't always know where I was and after what became of my father, the fear of something happening to us would sometimes grow too hard for her to bear," he said gently. I had no idea why he was telling me this but I managed to rein in some of my tears as I listened to the deep rumbling of his voice. "She was born of your clan and she shared your gifts. So when she wanted to know that I was alright, she would come and find me. In my dreams."

I sucked in a deep breath as I realised what he was suggesting. If Montana was sleeping now then maybe I could find her in her dreams. I didn't know how likely that was, but her body had been so badly damaged that it could at least be possible. Fabian had slept a lot when he was recovering from the wounds Magnar had given him after the wedding. So maybe she'd be resting now as her immortal form repaired her broken body.

"Okay," I breathed, wondering how the hell I was supposed to sleep with everything charging through my brain like a stampede. "But I don't know if I can sleep now. I feel so wired up, like there's a fire burning beneath my skin and I've got too much energy to spare."

"My mother didn't have to sleep to use her gifts. She would simply close her eyes and hunt for whoever she needed," he replied softly, his fingers tangling in my knotted hair before tugging slightly, angling my face up to his so he could look at me.

But I couldn't handle the intensity of his stare or face the truths which lingered there in his eyes.

My mind spun with the possibility of his words though and I pushed out of his arms, dropping to the floor so I could lean against the wall

51

and close my eyes.

"Can I at least look at your wounds while you try?" Magnar asked in exasperation.

I peeked up at him from beneath my lashes as he crouched down in front of me. "Sorry for biting your head off," I muttered.

"Don't worry about it." He pulled my ankle into his lap and tutted as he eyed the splinters lodged in my skin.

I bit my tongue against the pain as he started to remove them, and I turned my attention back to finding Montana.

My eyes fell shut and I opened myself to my gifts, trying to remember how it had felt the last time I'd hunted for someone's sleeping form.

I pictured Montana clearly in my mind, focusing on the feeling of her, the familiar shape of her soul taking form within my imagination until I could almost reach out and touch it.

After several long seconds, I felt something tickling on the edge of my consciousness and focused on it, throwing myself towards it and sucking in a sharp breath as I began to fall. My gut lurched as I tumbled into the place between dreams where a thousand stars marked all the sleeping souls I could ever wish to find and satisfaction pulled at me.

The feel of Magnar's hands on my ankle slipped away from me as I danced closer to the stars and I fell into the power of my gift.

I stared around, searching for anyone who felt familiar to me. At first, there didn't seem to be anyone I knew but as I concentrated, I noticed one of the points of light shone a little brighter than the others.

I drifted towards it, reaching out as I tried to work out who it was. Erik's presence washed over me and I recoiled, drawing back as fear ran down my spine. I still didn't trust him despite what he'd seemed to do to help us. He'd taken Montana from me and he hadn't kept his word about contacting me since.

I searched the space around him, hoping to find my sister's presence but there was no one else sleeping nearby.

I hesitated.

I'd visited Fabian's dreams twice but my bond to him made him feel somehow safer to be around. Erik was something...else. Everything Magnar had told me about him was more than enough warning for me to be cautious, but Montana seemed to have seen something entirely different in him.

There was only really one way for me to find out about him for myself though.

So I took a deep breath and pushed my consciousness into his.

I summoned Fury into my hand as the dream materialised around me, feeling safer with the blade in my grasp even if nothing in this place was real. I blinked against the bright light that greeted me and looked up in confusion as I took in where Erik's dream had taken me.

A periwinkle blue sky opened up endlessly above my head and the sun beat down, warming my skin like it was the middle of summer.

The heat was uncomfortable in the winter clothes I'd given myself so I switched my outfit to a thin blue shirt and a pair of denim shorts, the clothes fizzling into existence on my skin.

A warm breeze rustled the long grass and it tickled my knees as I looked out at the sweeping landscape. I was standing on a hill which rolled away from me before ending in a glittering blue lake, nothing but nature all around.

Halfway down the hill, I could just make out the shape of someone lying in the long grass.

I glanced about once more, unsure if sneaking up on a monster was the best idea. But I'd already come this far and I wasn't about to turn back. Besides, I reminded myself that I could take control of this dream at any time. He wasn't the one at an advantage here and I needed to remember that.

I stalked closer and found Erik laying in the grass beside my sister. She was holding his hand and twirling a daisy between her fingers above them. His head was turned towards her and he smiled as he watched her toying with the small flower.

They were both dressed for the hot weather and his skin wasn't pale and translucent, it was warm and lightly coloured by the sun.

The false Montana noticed me and a wide smile lit her face. "Shall we swim, Callie?" she asked excitedly, sitting up and pointing at the lake.

She pulled off her shirt, revealing a black bra which was weirdly shiny. She removed her shorts too and was wearing matching bottoms beneath them. I guessed they were intended for use in the water but there was a small issue with that.

"You can't swim, Monty," I reminded her.

She stared at me for several long seconds, blinking more times than was natural. "Shall we swim, Callie?" she asked again, the dream version of her unable to do more than play out its role in this place.

I sighed and shook my head. "You go. I'll join you later."

"Okay," she smiled brightly and jogged away from us towards the lake where I noticed Clarice, Fabian, Miles and another male vampire I didn't recognise swimming already. Except when I looked more closely, I realised they weren't vampires; they were human too.

"Come on, Callie," Erik said teasingly as he pushed himself upright. "Don't you want to join in?"

I got the weirdest sense that we were friends in this dreamed up scenario and the ridiculousness of the idea sent a shudder racing down my spine.

I observed him for a moment, trying to gauge whether or not he'd realised what I was. He was acting like he hadn't, but I knew by now that everyone I visited worked it out pretty quickly.

"Maybe I just don't like the sunshine," I replied with a shrug, willing a rain cloud into existence.

As its dark shadow fell over us, goosebumps covered my skin and I fought the urge to shiver.

"Come now, I think we both know that's a lie," Erik replied with a smirk.

The cloud dissolved and the sun beat down on us again. He raised an eyebrow at me tauntingly and I surveyed him with suspicion. This wasn't the monster Magnar had described and yet I knew every foul tale of this creature to be the truth. So was Erik Belvedere a man or a monster? Or was he simply both depending on what mood took him?

I heard someone approaching us and looked up as Fabian jogged our way. He was beaming at me, his arms outstretched as if he expected me to step into his embrace. I could tell this dream version of him was supposed to be with me. False memories fluttered over me of the four of us spending time together like some weird happy family and I balked instinctively.

I scowled at the dream Fabian and swiped my hand angrily, causing him to disappear entirely.

"As if that would ever happen," I said irritably.

"This is my dream," Erik countered. "So if I like the idea of you making my brother happy then that's what you do here. Is that so bad?"

Fabian reappeared and I gritted my teeth in frustration as Erik wrangled the dream from my grasp.

"He's a murdering psychopath and the last time I saw him I ripped his head off. So why the hell would you ever think I'd be happy with him?" I glared at the false Fabian and his head fell off a fraction of a second before I stabbed Fury through his heart and he dissolved into dust which blew away on the breeze.

I could feel Erik trying to regain control of the dream, but I hadn't come here to play games with him. I stole the sun from the sky and filled it with stars instead. I imagined Montana out of existence then filled the lake with the biters who had attacked us in the Hudson.

As Erik's family started screaming, I forced him back into his vampire form and made him watch them bleed.

His will batted against my own as he tried to reclaim his dream and banish the nightmare but I had it under my control and I wasn't letting go.

"What happened to my sister?" I demanded.

Erik bared his teeth, revealing those sharp fangs, and I could feel the fear he was trying to contain.

"Release my family and I'll tell you," he growled.

I glanced at the lake which was slowly filling with blood as the biters fed from his siblings. They were dragged beneath the surface one by one and the water fell still.

Erik stared at the bloody lake, his hand clenching into a fist.

"What's the matter?" I asked coldly. "Don't you like having your *family taken from you?"*

"Alright, I get it," he muttered as he turned back to face me.

"I really don't think you do," I hissed.

The hill disappeared and we were standing outside the Blood Bank with Wolfe glaring at me, his eyes full of murder. He leapt towards me but my father pushed me aside, taking the wound which had been meant for me. I let Erik feel my pain and see every drawn out moment that led to my father's death, made him suffer through every second of it just as I had.

I didn't allow him to speak as the view shifted again to our tiny apartment. He gazed around at our squalid living conditions, his face written with shock as he took in the two little girls whispering together on the threadbare couch, their cheeks a little too hollow, their waists a little too narrow.

The door burst open, causing us to scream in fright and the vampires flooded in, dragging our mom away while I hid beneath the table with Montana, our tiny fingers curled around each other's as our father begged and sobbed.

My pain was gilded in fury and I couldn't help but relish the way each truth lashed at the creature standing beside me, forced to bear witness to his own crimes.

"This is nothing compared to what the rest of our kind suffered. Tale after tale of agonising reality lays at your feet, Prince Erik, if only you cared to look for them," I sneered.

I let it all fade away and gave the dream to him once more. Erik dropped his eyes and I could feel shame pouring from him in waves, the truth of him filling this false landscape and offering itself up to me. He'd never intended for the Realms to be like that. He'd thought he could trust Wolfe to do as he'd been instructed.

But I wasn't sure if his regret meant much to me. I could understand why Montana had felt she could forgive him as I tasted his remorse on the air, but I wasn't convinced that I could. She always had been the more forgiving of us, the more understanding. But his kind had taken everything from me and he was one of their rulers, so surely that made what had happened to us his responsibility? And claiming ignorance

56

just didn't seem like a good enough excuse to me.

"So. Tell me what's happened to my sister," I snarled. I'd come here for a reason and I didn't want to waste any more time wondering.

"She's fine," he said, abandoning the games he'd been trying to play with me and aiming to appease me instead. "Better than fine; she's incredible." He began to conjure an image of her in her vampire form but I shook my head, willing it away again.

"Don't," I breathed. "I don't want to see her like that...not yet. I just, can't."

Erik nodded sadly and I could tell he was disappointed but he didn't press the issue.

"She really is okay," he said softly, reaching out like he might touch me, but I recoiled.

"So why hasn't she... I mean, you promised she'd call me. Does she blame me? Does she wish I hadn't let you do it, or-"

"No," he said quickly. "She's glad I managed to save her in time. I hope that it means something for the prophecy too. I think she's just afraid."

"Afraid of me?" I asked in confusion.

Erik eyed me like he thought I was being dense on purpose. "Well you don't exactly like our kind, do you?"

The way he said 'our kind' sent a shudder through me. It was like he was claiming her as his own. Like she was his instead of mine now. But becoming a vampire wouldn't change anything about what made the two of us, us. At least not if I had anything to do with it.

"Well she isn't your kind," I replied angrily. "She would never do any of the things you've done."

"We were all human once," Erik reminded me, and I wondered if he knew I'd been thinking that exact thing earlier or if it was just a weird coincidence.

"Perhaps. But the things you've done with your immortality have turned you into monsters. I know what you did to the slayers. What you did to Magnar's father."

"You realise you've only heard one side of that story?" he asked irritably. "Why don't you let me show you mine if you want to cast judgment?"

I frowned at him, half wanting to refuse but the scene around us was changing already and curiosity got the better of me.

Everything fell dark and I could feel the years piling upon each other as Erik tried to refuse the hunger. He fell into madness, Andvari's taunting voice calling out to him in the depths of his despair. He was so lonely, so empty and so, so hungry.

A shaft of light fell on him and an arm pulled him from the darkness. Fabian carried him, running, fleeing, racing to get somewhere and when they arrived, there it was. Blood. The deepest most desperate desire of Erik's tainted soul, all that the darkness had left him with. The answer to all of his prayers. As Erik fell towards the battle I felt Andvari's glee and his power flooding into him. He used Erik just as he had in the battle with Magnar; stealing his will and urging him to kill over and over again until all that was left was blood.

When the god finally let him be, no one remained but the four devils, coated in the blood of their enemies. Just one slayer was still alive, glaring at the Belvederes with hate in his eyes. I could see Magnar and Julius in him. I knew who he was.

It wasn't hate that drove Erik to turn him. It was pity. Regret. And Andvari whispering in his ear. He wanted him to have a chance to see his family again. He hadn't meant for him to harm any of them.

Once he was a vampire, Magnar's father raced away from them and the memory faded.

I swallowed a thick lump in my throat as I struggled to deal with what I'd just seen. If it was true - and I was convinced he couldn't lie to me here - then it did change things. At least I thought it did. And perhaps Magnar and Julius would agree too.

"You still murdered the rest of the clans a hundred years later," I breathed. "If you felt so bad about it then why fight them that day?"

In place of answering, images flooded past me so quickly that I couldn't count them. Magnar and Julius chasing the Belvederes across the sea, hunting them to the ends of the Earth. Every time Erik and his family tried to hide from them, the slayers would show up again, hell-bent on killing them. Years passed and even after Magnar and Julius *disappeared, the slayers kept coming.*

"We had no life at all while the slayers still lived. It was war. I'm not proud of it but it seemed like the only way at the time. Us or them."

"And now?" I asked.

The 'us' was down to three as far as I knew and the 'them' numbered in the thousands.

"Now... I think the gods were to blame all along. They cursed my family and made us what we are. They created the slayers and set them against us. They used our hatred as a distraction so that we forgot who was really to blame for our misery."

"Well you were all stupid. I knew Idun was the problem from the first moment I heard that bitch's name," I growled.

Erik gave me a dark smile and I was struck with this weird sense of camaraderie toward him. "Then maybe it's time we figured out what to do about it."

I hesitated. The idea of taking on the gods was sorely tempting but I had more pressing issues than deities at the moment.

"The only thing I want to do right now is see my sister," I replied.

Erik's gaze darkened. "I don't think that's a good idea for a while. She might have trouble resisting the call of your blood. If she were to hurt you, bite you, then I don't know if she'd ever forgive herself."

"She'd never hurt me," I replied instantly.

Erik's jaw ticked, and irritation filled me as I could tell he didn't agree.

"Just because she's like you now, don't start thinking you know her better than me," I snapped before he could say anything to contradict me. "So just get her to call me. Because if you don't, I'll come for her myself and if you want to stop me, you'll have to kill me. And you can find out how much she loves you after that."

I didn't give him the chance to respond as I stepped away from his dream and moved back to my own body. I didn't push myself into wakefulness though. I needed to rest and my best chance of sleep would be to stay close to it now. I just hoped to be woken by the cell phone ringing soon. Or Erik Belvedere was going to find out that I always kept my promises.

MONTANA

CHAPTER FIVE

I laid in Erik's arms longer than I should have, knowing I was putting off the inevitable, but the idea of talking to Callie was terrifying. What if she despised me now? What if she couldn't stand to be around me anymore? She'd only just started to see the vampires differently, would she be able to look at me as I used to be? Or would she only see a monster?

I crawled out of bed, flexing my limbs which were so strong it was hard to adjust to. Every movement I made felt powerful, like the sweep of a blade. I was a weapon given life. And I was afraid of what I might be capable of.

Moving to the bedside table, I hunted through the drawers, determined to find Valentina's phone.

When I didn't, I gazed at Erik a moment, drinking in the sight of his peaceful face. My eyes raked down to the packed muscles of his abs and energy pounced into my veins.

I shook my head at myself, forcing my legs in the opposite direction and heading to the closet. I found some jeans and a shirt to wear, pulling them on before quietly slipping out of the room. And I really was quiet. Entirely silent. Like a cat padding around the house.

I walked downstairs into the open plan kitchen-lounge where moonlight spilled in through the window and all was achingly quiet. My gaze landed on a large shape on the couch covered with a blanket, the back of my neck prickling as I stared at it. Was someone sleeping here?

I crept toward them and steeled myself as I tugged the blanket back to see who it was. My heart lodged in my throat at the vile sight before me. Fabian's body lay in a heap next to his severed head.

My mouth parted in horror as his eyes gazed up at me, glassy, blank and seeming so void of life I didn't know how it was possible that he could come back from this. But Erik had said he could heal. And I couldn't bear to look at him like that, no matter what I thought of him. My senses told me what to do and I nudged his head toward his neck with a grimace.

As the jagged skin met, it immediately began to fuse together.

I watched in horror and awe as his head knitted back onto his body then his limbs jerked to life. He flew upright in a rush of motion, rounding on me with a vicious snarl. My lip curled back on instinct and a feral growl escaped my throat.

I gasped, covering my mouth at the reaction I'd had and Fabian stilled, blinking at me in surprise as he took in his new surroundings.

"Holy fucking shit," Fabian gasped as he took me in. He was filthy, caked in dried blood and filth, his bare chest gleaming, but there he stood, alive as any immortal, undead creature could be.

"Hi," I said weakly, dropping my hand.

I had no idea of how the hell I was supposed to explain the fact that I was his kind now, but I guessed the truth was staring him straight in the face.

"You're..." He moved forward, reaching out to me with bloody fingers and I recoiled.

"How?" he demanded falling still. "And where's your sister?" He threw a hopeful glance over my shoulder, his eyes dancing with light. "We killed the slayers, right? That's why you're here." His excitement was evident and it burned a furious hole in my chest.

I reached out and struck him across the face. The blow was so hard, he flew away from me and smashed into the wall, sending a huge crack splintering across it. I swore at what I'd done, gazing at the palm which had landed the hit, feeling no ounce of pain from the collision with his face.

Fabian scrambled upright, turning to me with a glare. "What the fuck?"

"You listen to me," I snarled, pointing at him as I forced the shock aside and focused on the bigger issue. "My sister is not yours and the slayers are damn well alive. No thanks to you. They're far away from here with Callie. And you'll never find her. I'll make sure of it."

Fabian's eyes simmered with heat as he approached me, his muscles tensing as if he intended to hurt me, his upper lip peeling back to reveal his fangs. I backed up, suddenly not trusting my strength against him. He was a Belvedere. He was certainly stronger than me, and I wasn't trained to fight.

He moved within two inches of me and then fell to his knees, grabbing hold of my legs. "Please tell me where she is. I'd never hurt her. I love her," he pleaded, and my lips fell open in alarm as he clutched at me with desperation.

"Stop it." I tried to shake him off, but he held on tight.

"She's my life," he begged and I sighed as I stared down at his pitiful form, the work of the gods clearly affecting him powerfully.

"Get up," I urged more gently.

He rose shakily to his feet then clutched my arm. "Look at you," he cooed, changing tact. "So beautiful. Did Erik make you? I can offer this to Callie too. Eternal life. Then the two of you will be together for all of time. Princesses. Adored and worshipped by-"

"She'd never want that." I tried to pull my arm free but he didn't release me.

"I can't believe she ripped my head off...she's so damn *passionate*." He shifted closer, his eyes raking over my face. "You look like her in ways..."

"You're creeping me out." I jerked back and he finally let go.

"Sorry," he muttered, rubbing the skin above his heart. "I just miss her. All I wanted was to bring her here. My love for her is all consuming and I need her by my side. Why did Erik let them go?"

"Because he knows it's the gods who set up that fight. They're our true enemy."

Fabian grumbled something under his breath, not seeming entirely content with that explanation.

I glanced around the room, looking for what I'd come here for and spotted the cell phone on the coffee table. A jolt of energy raced through me as I snatched it up.

My hand trembled just a little as I stood, gazing at the screen. When I tapped it, a whole list of missed calls were revealed from Julius.

My heart sang with hope. If they'd been trying to call, surely that meant they still cared? They hadn't written me off as a parasite.

I found my way to his number, my thumb hovering over the call button.

"Do it," Fabian urged, bouncing on his heels beside me.

I threw him a frown. "Go away, asshole. I need to do this alone."

He gazed at me like a wounded dog expecting me to hit him again.

"Go," I insisted and he padded off through the room with his head hung low, stepping out of a door into the hallway. I was sure he'd hear me anyway, but there wasn't much I could do about that. The last thing I wanted was for Callie to hear his voice and have to wrestle with the mark that bound her to him.

I sank into an armchair, drawing in some air, though it was useless to me. Then I pressed dial.

I lifted the phone to my ear, chewing anxiously on my lower lip.

One ring, two-

"Monty?" Callie answered, her tone raw.

"It's me," I confirmed, squeezing my eyes shut as fear raged inside me.

Don't hate me.

"I'm so sorry," she blurted. "Are you mad at me? I didn't want to do it, but I couldn't lose you and-"

"I'm fine," I promised, a tear of relief rolling from my eye, but it was icily cold instead of the heat I was used to. "Are you okay?"

"Am *I* okay? Fucking hell, Monty, are *you* okay? Are you...did

Erik..." She seemed unable to get her questions in line and my heart went out to her. She must have been driven insane with worry, and guilt consumed me that I hadn't trusted that she'd want to hear from me. I should have called sooner. I shouldn't have waited.

"I'm alright, I promise. It's strange, but it's not all bad. And Erik is looking after me."

"Did you drink blood?" she asked in a deathly quiet whisper.

There was no judgement in her tone, just fear. As if she was grieving over the mere idea of me having to consume it.

I didn't answer for several seconds, hating having to admit it. But I couldn't keep anything from her, and she would figure it out regardless. "Yes," I rasped. "I couldn't help myself, Callie. I didn't want to but it was the only way to stop the pain and if I refused, it would only get worse. Plus it was from Realm A, the place the humans live happily. So I guess that's the best option I have."

A whimper escaped her and another tear rolled down my cheek.

"I wish I didn't have to," I added.

"I know," she choked out, then a heavy paused passed between us. "Why did you jump?" she asked, her tone laced with hurt, like my action had been a betrayal of her. Leaving her behind in this savage world, but I'd never have chosen that path if I could have seen any other.

"Andvari," I said in answer, and she released a breath of anger.

"I hate them. Him and Idun, they're monsters. Worse than anything that walks on Earth." I knew she meant the vampires and my heart cracked at her tone. At least she was making some progress with seeing them in a better light. But they weren't just *them* anymore, they were *me*.

"We'll work out the prophecy," I breathed. "We'll finish this."

"But how? What are we going to do?"

"I don't know. Maybe the answer lies at the holy mountain?" I suggested.

"Yeah maybe..." She cleared her throat. "You sound different, Monty. Like you but not you."

"I am still me," I swore, feeling sure of that right down to my bones. "And you know I'd never, *ever* hurt you. I don't care what this curse makes me feel, it doesn't mean I'd act on it, Callie, I swear."

"I know," she said on a breath. "I trust you. And I want to see you."

"She can't." I turned sharply at the sound of Erik's hard voice, finding him watching me from the doorway. "It's too risky. You could succumb to the bloodlust and hurt her."

Callie fell silent on the other end of the line and more tears found me. "I would never hurt my sister," I growled.

Erik shook his head firmly. "Until you've had time to adjust, it's best you don't-"

"No," I snapped. "We've been apart long enough. And we're so close to figuring out the prophecy. I have to see her."

"I'll come, Monty. Wherever you are, I'll be there," Callie said at last and relief ebbed through me.

Erik's jaw ticked as he observed me. "Not her. One of the other slayers first. As a test. There's a cottage on the estate, I can pick them up and bring them there. But only Julius can come to the house. Not your sister."

I released a hollow laugh. "Fine, but once you have your proof that I'd never hurt any of them, I *will* see Callie."

Erik moved toward me, taking the phone from my hand and talking down the line. "Hello, Dream Walker. Are you haunting me in my waking hours now too?" he asked, his tone cool.

My brows arched in surprise. Callie had gone to him in his dreams? Did that mean they were forming some semblance of a friendship? I didn't think that was likely from Callie's side, but I wondered if she was trying for my sake.

My heightened hearing picked up her answer on the other end of the line. "I'm pretty sure it's you who's haunting me, Belvedere. So where is this cottage? Where can we meet you?"

"Only Julius can see Montana," Erik pressed. "Neither you or Magnar should stray too close to my home just yet. There is still the issue of Fabian-"

"Yes," Fabian cut in as he stepped into the room. "If that slayer comes within a mile of me, I'll finish him for real this time and take my wife back."

I glowered at his causal vow to kidnap my sister, and Erik turned his back on him. "I'll text you where to meet me," he murmured before cutting the line.

An ache filled me at not having a chance to say goodbye, but I suspected he'd done it to avoid the chance of Fabian getting his hands on the phone.

"So you're awake," Erik turned to his brother, passing the cell phone back to me.

"Your new vampire helped me heal. How long have I been on that couch?" Fabian asked irritably, his hands curling into fists.

"After the slayers dumped you in my boat and I stuffed you in the trunk of my car?" Erik goaded him and tension crackled in the air between them.

"Yes," Fabian gritted out.

"It's been several hours," Erik said, folding his arms.

"Who the fuck do you think you are? We were on the verge of defeating the slayers. Why did you let them go?" Fabian demanded, taking a step towards his brother.

I rose to my feet and moved to Erik's side, protectiveness washing through me. He wasn't alone if Fabian decided to start something. I was able to defend him now.

"Because we found some common ground for once," Erik explained. "The gods took over our bodies during that fight. They are to blame for everything. They were the ones who pitted us against each other in the first place. It's time we faced that fact and put our differences aside."

"The slayers hunted us to the ends of the Earth!" Fabian bellowed, and Erik released a weary sigh.

"That was then, this is now. We have to adapt," Erik insisted. "And if you don't drop the issue, I'm going to ask my wife to help me detach your head again because I can't deal with your bullshit right now."

Fabian fell quiet, his eyes whipping to me. "Why did you turn her?" he asked, changing the subject, his head cocking as if assessing my new form, sizing me up.

"Andvari tried to kill her, I'll tell you everything later," Erik clipped. "All you need to know right now is that she's one of us."

My skin tingled at his words. I was one of them. No longer a food source or a weak being to be put under the thumb. And although the idea still made me uncomfortable, it felt good to be on equal ground for once.

Fabian stalked past us toward the stairwell. "I'm gonna have a shower."

"Great," Erik muttered as he passed.

"And jerk off while thinking about your wife's twin sister," Fabian taunted him and my mouth parted in disgust.

"Can we cut his hands off?" I asked Erik as Fabian disappeared into the stairway.

"Much as I'd enjoy that, I'm sure Fabian would find other ways to pleasure himself. That's just the level of stubbornness he'd stoop to in defiance of anyone telling him what to do."

I breathed a laugh, praying Fabian had been joking about what he'd said and forcing my mind sharply away from the idea in case he hadn't.

Erik took my hand, his grey eyes brightening, and energy raced across my skin from the contact.

"You should wash too," I said, eyeing his mud-caked body.

"Mhm," he hummed, pulling me after him toward the staircase. "So you don't like your royal husband dirty?"

I laughed as he tugged me along. "It's pretty embarrassing, your royal assness."

"I didn't realise what high standards you had for me."

"Oh I do, and I expect you to come up to the mark, Prince Erik."

He cornered me on the stairs and his smile fell away to an intense look. "It's so good to have you back, rebel."

He brushed his thumb across my cheek and my heart squeezed with my love for him, all the barriers between us seeming to crash away to the dirt. I'd chosen to turn from him, to run and never stop running, but fate had had other ideas. Now I was with him again and there were no gilded cages in sight, I couldn't find a single reason not to indulge the wants of my heart. Because despite the circumstances, and all the terrible things that came with this reality, I felt freer than I had in a long time. My destiny had been laid in my own hands and as scared as I was about what this new body meant for me, I was hopeful of what it might lead to as well.

I took Erik's hand from my face, placing a kiss on his muddy skin. "I'm glad you turned me," I breathed. "And I don't ever want to be apart again."

"Promise," he commanded and for once I didn't mind giving into his commands, because this vow was one I gave freely from my lips.

"I promise."

MAGNAR

CHAPTER SIX

I sat by the fire, listening in on Callie's conversation with her sister even though she'd taken the call outside. I'd seen the relief in her eyes when the cell phone had woken her with its incessant jangling and despite my concerns, I hadn't made any move to stop her from taking the call.

I hadn't followed her when she'd wandered away from me while they spoke. The excitement in her tone, the relief, the love… It brought up ideas I'd never wanted to have.

If it turned out that Montana was still able to love her sister, and that becoming a vampire didn't automatically make her a monster, then what of my father's fate?

He had begged for death so that he wouldn't succumb to the bloodlust and hurt any of us. But what if I hadn't taken up his blade that day? What if I'd offered him my wrist instead?

Perhaps he could have stopped himself from drinking too much. Perhaps his love for us would have been enough for him to contain the murderous impulses of their kind. Perhaps he could have still been alive, even now.

I frowned into the flames, my heart growing heavy as I forced myself to consider that possibility.

What if…

"I'm guessing that's Montana on the phone?" Julius asked as he slipped through the door and moved to join me by the pathetic fire.

"It is."

"It seems to be going well enough," he said.

One look at him was all I needed to let me know that his scavenging trip hadn't gone to plan. He held nothing in his hands and exhaustion weighed on him heavily.

"If Montana turns out to be…Montana," I began hesitantly. "Then surely that means that our father was still-"

"Don't do that," he said sharply, shifting closer to me. "You can't think of it like that."

"How can I not?" I asked, refusing to meet his gaze.

If we were willing to accept that Callie's sister might be fundamentally the same despite her transformation, then surely it followed that all vampires maintained their humanity when they were created. And only their own choices turned them into monsters. And if it came down to a choice, then I knew our father would have chosen to remain true to himself.

Julius's hand fell on my arm as he forced me to meet his gaze. "Father begged you to end him. He never could have accepted that life and you know it. It would have been far crueller to make him exist as one of them. You did him a great kindness and I know how much it cost you to do it. What a sacrifice you made. The burden it put on your soul."

"I don't know how you can still look on me with love after watching me end his life," I muttered, voicing the thoughts which always found me in the darkness. How could my brother and mother have ever loved me the same way after watching me do that? Despite our father begging it of me. They saw me drive a blade through his heart.

I couldn't even look at myself the same way I had before that fateful day. Let alone expecting them to.

"You didn't end his life," Julius growled. "You ended his torment. I love you more because of it. Not less. You are a much greater man than I could ever hope to be. I'm not sure I could have done it. But I have

72

never once doubted the sacrifice you made that day. And I have *never* judge you poorly for it."

He pulled me into his arms and I gripped him fiercely, pressing my forehead against his.

"And what if he could have survived the curse?" I asked. "If Montana can-"

"You know in your heart he never would have wanted that life. If you hadn't ended it for him, he would have done it himself. They have ways for humans to donate blood to the vampires now but a thousand years ago he could only have fed himself by biting. And even if we'd been willing to offer our blood to him, do you think he could have lived with that? Feeding off of his children? His wife? Any of his people?"

"Never," I muttered.

He was right. Our father had given his life in the fight to destroy the vampires. He never could have known happiness as one of them. It was unthinkable. Impossible.

"Don't doubt yourself, brother. I certainly never have," Julius said firmly.

"I've never doubted you either," I replied, pulling out of my brother's arms and smiling at our overt display of affection.

He clapped me on the shoulder hard enough to leave a bruise.

"No more of this moping shit," he said bracingly. "We've got real problems to deal with."

"That's true enough," I agreed.

"Like the fact that you have laid claim to the only remaining mortal woman we know. Do you realise how pathetic that makes me feel?"

"Are there no other issues that concern you at this moment?" I asked in amusement.

"None so pressing," he sighed in exasperation as he leaned back on his elbows. "You know I haven't bedded a woman in a thousand years. A *thousand* years!"

I laughed, punching him in the bicep playfully. "You're an ass. You were asleep for all of those years. I'm sure if you hadn't been, the women of the world would have been semi-satisfied by you while they pined for the better looking brother."

"Keep telling yourself that, Magnar. When I was put into that slumber, the women of our clan wept with the knowledge that they'd never again know the level of pleasure I was able to provide them."

"And their husbands cheered with the relief of knowing they'd never again have to chase you from their tents."

Julius laughed, and I smiled as I thought about our people. I hadn't allowed myself to think about them much since I'd woken but I missed them horribly whenever I did. It was hard to wrap my mind around the fact that they'd all been lost to time so long ago. Elissa, Aelfric, even their children would have grown old and had lives of their own. And I missed my mother most of all. I guessed I'd never know how their lives had panned out. Or how they'd ended.

"I don't know if I would have agreed to come if I'd known the future held no women," Julius joked.

"No women for *you*," I teased in response.

"Well I suppose that seeing you this happy is worth the sacrifice," he said with a sigh. "I don't think I've ever seen you look at a woman the way you look at her."

"That's because I haven't," I replied. "Callie is everything I'd given up on having. From the first moment I saw her racing towards a group of vampires unarmed in the name of helping her family, I knew she was it. I just didn't believe I could truly have her at the time."

"Well happiness suits you, brother. It's been too long since I saw what it looked like on you."

The door eased open and Callie slipped back in. Her cheeks were damp with tears but a hopeful smile lit her face.

"She's alright?" I guessed, getting to my feet.

"Yes," she breathed, moving towards me and slipping into my arms. "Better than alright. She sounds good, *really* good and I…" she trailed off as her arms tightened around me and I got the sense that she was afraid to voice what she'd been about to say.

"Go on," I urged, trailing my fingers through her golden hair as the feeling of her body in my arms made my soul hum contentedly.

"I told her I want to see her."

I glanced at Julius as doubts crept through me and he shrugged unhelpfully.

"Are you sure that that's the safest thing to do right now?" I asked.

"Why wouldn't it be?" she demanded, leaning back to frown up at me.

Her eyes blazed with a challenge, and it was plain that she'd already made her mind up despite anything I might have to say on the subject. My jaw ticked with irritation. She was so damn wilful sometimes, and though I loved that about her, it also drove me to despair.

"Probably because you'll smell entirely tempting to her right about now," Julius supplied casually.

Callie glared at him, pushing her way out of my arms as tension grew in her posture. I didn't want to release her but she didn't really give me any option.

"Montana would *never* hurt me," she snapped.

"Well, *human* Montana wouldn't have," Julius agreed.

"You sound just like Erik," she muttered, and tension licked down my spine at the mention of that creature's name.

"Why were you talking to him?" I asked irritably.

We may have called time on our conflict, but I found it hard to imagine any real way for us to work together on solving the prophecy. At least not face to face. My hatred for him still burned as strongly as ever and leaving him and his evil brother alive had been one of the hardest things I'd ever done in my life.

"Well if you must know, I went to his dream last night."

Silence followed her statement and my hands curled into fists as I tried not to let my anger get the better of me.

Julius sucked in a sharp breath and I glared at him as he got to his feet.

"That's my cue to leave," he said hastily. "Because this conversation is about to turn violent and this one is the dick-punching type." He passed me and moved outside as fast as he could without actually running.

"Before you start," Callie said. "Will you at least hear me out?"

I narrowed my eyes at her, wondering what she expected me to say.

"Fine," I bit out, folding my arms as I waited to hear her story.

Callie sighed dramatically as if she thought that *I* was the one who was behaving unreasonably, and she dropped down to take a seat beside the small fire.

She raised an eyebrow, waiting until I lowered myself down beside her, and she gave me an assessing look before she spoke.

"When I fell asleep last night, I went in search of my sister like we'd planned, but she wasn't sleeping-"

"And Erik Belvedere was?" I growled, realising why she would have been tempted into approaching him. She'd been distraught with worry and he would have held the answers she so desperately needed.

"He was," Callie confirmed. "And once he'd told me that Montana was okay, he asked to show me something else; something that I think you should know about."

"I have no interest in anything that parasite had to tell you," I replied.

"He didn't tell me; he showed me."

I sighed heavily, sensing she wasn't going to let this drop until she told me what she'd discovered. "Showed you what?"

"How he came to turn your father into a vampire," she breathed.

I stared at her, wondering how on Earth she could have come to discuss such a thing with him. Why would he show her that? But I was curious despite myself. I'd always regretted the fact that I hadn't been present for that battle. Always wondered if my presence there could have made any difference at all. Callie seemed to sense the fact that I wanted to hear more and she reached out for my hand before continuing.

"Before the battle, Erik had locked himself away from the world, trapped himself inside a cave and refused the call of blood for two hundred years. He was trying to deny his nature. Trying to pay a debt in suffering so that the gods might release him and his family from their curse-"

"And you believed that?" I scoffed.

It was true that Erik hadn't been sighted for hundreds of years prior to that battle, but I highly doubted he'd been doing anything so noble as that.

"It's true," Callie said firmly. "I saw it. I felt what he felt, he showed me true memories and I don't believe he could have lied to me there even if he wanted to."

I frowned at her. My mother had always said the same of her gifts. No man could lie to a Dream Walker. They had a window into your soul and while they visited you, you could only show them the truth.

"Well he obviously decided to abandon his sacrifice," I growled.

"He didn't. Fabian came and got him when the battle began. The rest of the Belvederes needed his help and when he arrived at the battlefield he was starving, insatiable. And Andvari seized control of him."

"You mean to say the god had a hand in it?" I growled angrily, wondering why that even surprised me. It seemed the deities lived to heighten our suffering. Every foul thing in my life always led back to them one way or another.

Callie nodded, her brows drawing together as she tightened her grip on my hand. "By the time Erik regained his senses, only your father was left alive. He was mortally wounded and he was murmuring about his love for his wife and his sons. Andvari whispered a line from the prophecy in Erik's ear, making him believe that turning your father might be the answer to solving their curse."

"How could he possibly believe such a thing?" I demanded but a crater was opening up in my chest.

My hatred for Erik Belvedere ran in my veins, it had moulded me into the man I was. If he had never planned to send my father back as a monster in the hopes of destroying the last of my people, if he'd never intended to murder hundreds of my kin, if he hadn't even had control of his own flesh at the time…

I shook my head, unable to chisel away at my hatred for him despite the questions which were now burning through my mind.

"You know how convincing the gods can be when they want something," Callie said softly. "Your father was the first human Erik ever turned. He never planned to do it. I don't know if that changes anything or if it changes *everything*."

I stared into her deep blue eyes as I tried to make sense of what she was saying. It was so much to take in. I had no idea how to process her words.

It altered the most monumental moment of my life. It meant so many things could be viewed differently. But it also didn't change others. I just didn't know where to begin with unravelling it.

"Thank you," I breathed finally. "For telling me. It can't have been easy for you to see all of that."

Callie shifted onto her knees and moved before me, trailing her fingers along the side of my face.

"I'm so sorry that that happened to your father. But when he thought his life was over, all he was thinking of was you and your family."

I held her gaze and she leaned forward to press a soft kiss to my lips. I pushed my fingers through her hair as I pulled her closer, wanting the reassurance of her touch. I didn't know what to think about what she'd said but I did know how I felt about her.

She melted against me, moving into my lap as she trailed her fingertips down my chest and my blood rose beneath the pressure of her body, the all-consuming need I felt for this woman so present once again.

"Is that true?" Julius asked as he stepped back into our shelter.

He obviously hadn't gone very far in his mission to escape our row and had clearly been listening in to our conversation.

Callie pulled away from me to look at him and I reluctantly let her go. "Yes."

Julius nodded thoughtfully and I could see the same confusion warring in his eyes as I felt jostling within me.

"So what now?" he asked.

"Now we have to go and see my sister," Callie said firmly.

I shook my head. "I really don't think we can risk-"

"It's not a risk," she interrupted stubbornly. "But if you're that worried about it then feel free to stay here while I go."

I released a growl of frustration as I realised this wasn't a negotiation. "And how exactly do you expect us to get to her in a city full of vampires?"

"Easy," she replied with a grin. "Erik's going to pick us up."

MONTANA

CHAPTER SEVEN

I sat on the bed in silk pyjamas, watching as Erik pulled on clothes after his shower, still feeling wide awake despite still being in the depths of night. I couldn't get enough of him. I didn't know if it was our time apart which drove this passionate, insatiable desire for him, or if it was always going to be like this.

Reuniting with him had healed my shattered heart, and despite all the reasons I'd had not to claim him in the past, I found them paling in the face of all the good that we were building between us now.

Erik walked toward me with a grin, tugging down the hem of his long-sleeved t-shirt to conceal his defined muscles.

"Want something, rebel?" he mocked, and I bit down on my lip as I smiled. "Did I not satisfy you well enough?"

"Not even close," I taunted, though even the thought of how much pleasure we'd found between us had my skin tingling.

"You seemed sated enough when you were moaning my name. Maybe you need a reminder." He smirked and a hungry shiver darted down my spine. "Perhaps I will keep you here in my room until I have wiped all memory of other men from your body."

"Well that might not take all that long," I admitted, tucking a lock of dark hair behind my ear. "In fact, it wouldn't take any time at all."

Erik frowned at me then released an arrogant laugh. "All the better then. And if you fuck me that well without practise, I look forward to seeing you learn from me."

"Oh wondrous sex guru, teach me your ways," I scoffed and he reached out to grip my throat, smiling darkly at me.

"Gladly."

My mirth fell away, the taint of sin in his eyes filling me with a twisted kind of desire. I had the feeling I hadn't seen the most depraved side of him yet, and I was far too curious for my own good. Luckily for me, I wasn't a cat, or I would have been dead a long ass time ago.

He dropped his hand from my neck and my gaze dropped to Nightmare beside me, my thoughts shifting to Callie and the slayers. They'd be on their way here now, but we had hours to kill before they arrived. There was only one thing I wanted to do with that time, but an even more pressing issued filled me.

"Could we talk?" I looked up at Erik and his brow furrowed.

"Of course."

"Could you fill me in on this whole vampire thing? I feel like my soul has been planted in a loaded gun and I have no idea how to adjust to it."

He took my hand, pulling me up with ease and twirling me under his arm. My feet moved with grace as if they knew what to do before I did. I'd never been so assured in my movements before. My body reacted before my mind did.

"Well, your dance moves have improved," he jibed, and I rested my hand on his shoulder as I raised a brow.

"I was always a wonderful dancer."

He laughed. "That is painfully untrue."

"Do you miss my clumsy human ways?" I asked.

"No, because now I get to do this." He twirled me again then moved fast and shoved me back against the wall, my spine colliding with it, though no pain found me.

I glared at him. "You're happy you can push me around without hurting me? How very gentlemanly of you."

He caught my waist, tugging me close again. "I never said I was a gentleman and you knew that well enough before you fell in love with me." He grinned in amusement, eyeing my mouth, but I darted out of his arms, spinning back to face him with a triumphant smile.

"You're only turning me on more by running away. Remember what fleeing from me resulted in earlier," he said with a lustful glint in his eyes.

"You're getting greedy," I teased, retreating as he hounded after me. "I think you've had quite enough of me, Erik Belvedere." My toes curled against the floorboards as I stopped moving, knowing I was just as desperate for more of him too, but I loved this game of cat and mouse.

He halted, folding his arms with a sideways smile. "Alright, dear wife, perhaps you have a point. We should focus on something more constructive."

"Good, because I need some pointers on how to be a monster."

He winced minutely at that word. "Montana, you will never be a monster. Not like me. You are too pure. But you're right, you need to learn how to handle that body of yours," he said. "In some other ways," he added with a devilish expression.

"Then tell me how." I waited for him to go on and he moved forward, taking my hands. The runes on our palms met and electricity pounded between us, setting the hairs rising on the back of my neck. "Your nails are one of your best weapons. They're razor sharp against your enemies." He slid his hand up to my biceps. "And you might still look fragile, but you're strong. You're my sireling. Meaning you're an Elite - more powerful than any vampire sired by another Elite or less."

I nodded, eyeing my pristine skin with awe, trying to absorb the fact that I was really stronger than so many of the vampires I'd been pushed around by in my life.

"Wait, does this mean I have to call you master now?" I asked dryly.

"Only in the bedroom."

"Not unless you call me your highness." I jutted up my chin, enjoying the way his eyes roamed over me.

"That doesn't sound so bad." He slid a hand to my face, sliding his thumb into my mouth and brushing it over my canines. "These are your best weapon of all."

I pulled back from him, revulsion darting though me. "I can't bite someone," I said in horror. "I won't."

"If it came down to a fight with an enemy, you would have to," he said, his eyebrows pinching together.

I glanced at Nightmare where I'd left it on the bed. "I have my blade, that will always protect me."

He pressed his lips together. "The thirst is your biggest enemy anyway. You cannot resist drinking. If you do, you will succumb to it and sink your teeth into the nearest human neck you can find."

I knew he meant the slayers and my gut knotted at the thought. "I'll drink the bottled blood," I said firmly. "I'll do anything to stop that from happening."

"Good," he said, his tone softening. "Have you had any more thoughts on the prophecy? You seem to be pretty good at figuring it out."

"Nightmare helps sometimes," I said thoughtfully. "The blade seems to know the answers. Or at least...it guides me toward them occasionally."

Erik nodded as his gaze fell on the slayer blade. "Then ask it," he urged and I didn't miss the longing in his voice. He wanted this curse broken as much as I did, probably far more considering how long he had been trapped in his immortal form.

I headed to the bed, dropping onto the mattress and folding my legs beneath me as I took Nightmare into my palm.

Moon Child, it purred happily as I caressed it.

"What more can you tell me about the prophecy? What is the debt paid?" I asked.

A debt paid rights wrongs of old.

"But what is the debt?" I pleaded.

In a holy mountain the Earth will heal. Then the dead shall live and the curse will keel.

I sighed heavily, looking to Erik as he stood at the edge of the bed with a desperate hope sparkling in his gaze.

"It's just reciting the prophecy to me."

"Make a guess. Maybe it can answer if you're right," he prompted, looking like I held all the answers he'd ever needed. And I wished I did.

"I don't know." I gazed down at Nightmare with a frown.

Erik crept onto the bed, kneeling before me. "My parents spoke of a ring. Andvari was hunting for it. I believe the one Callie possesses is the one he was looking for. They stole his treasure and hid it in a mountain. But when my siblings and I sought it out, we couldn't enter."

My frown deepened as I tried to find the answer hiding within his words. "So the debt could just be returning the ring to Andvari at the holy mountain?"

Erik's eyes glazed with thought. "It seems too simple."

"What else could it mean?" I begged of him, but he didn't have a response.

I turned my attention to Nightmare, pressing my will into it and attempting to search out the secrets it held.

"What's the debt?" I whispered again.

The debt is that which will be lost.

"The ring?" I asked. "The ring was lost."

The debt is that which will be lost, it repeated and I gave up, placing the blade on the bed beside me.

"I hate riddles," I muttered. "My dad always loved them. He'd be great at this."

Erik rested his hand on my knee with sorrow in his gaze. "I'm sorry he's not here to help. It kills me the way he was taken from you. Callie showed me how it happened when she came to me in my dreams."

I blinked hard, fighting away tears. "He suffered so much," I said on a deep breath.

I'd forgiven Erik for trusting Wolfe with my father's life, but the sting of his loss still cut me deeply. The curse hadn't taken that pain from me, and I was glad. Grief was the only way he was still present with me. That and the precious memories of him.

"You have dealt with too much death in your life. And I hate that I can't make it right." Erik's eyes dropped and guilt consumed his expression. "Callie also showed me your home in the Realm. She replayed the moment your mother was taken," he said tentatively. "The

Blood Banks were only ever supposed to be for law-breakers. But blood supplies waned over time...the laws changed and I was just happy to keep my people fed with a constant supply. There was always the greater fear that if the empire grew hungry, the humans wouldn't be safe. It is a fragile balance and one Valentina and her Biters are a threat to."

I ground my teeth at the mention of her, but my thoughts returned to my mother. She had been taken to feed the vampires. How long had she lasted in the blood bank? I'd seen visions of its interior when my mind had connected to Callie's at the choosing ceremony. The humans were kept in pods, alive...almost as though they were sleeping. Mom had been in so much pain with the disease that had claimed her. I knew she'd have died one way or the other, but our final days with her had been taken from us. Was it better she'd slept peacefully in one of those tanks?

I shook my head, horrified that the thought had even crossed my mind. She should have died at home in her bed, surrounded by her family. More tears slid from my eyes and Erik pulled me against him, murmuring his apologies. Nothing could bring her back. Nothing could change the past, no matter how much I wanted it to sometimes.

The scent of cypress and rain caressed my senses, and I sighed as I pulled myself together, leaning away from Erik and absorbing the sight of his pained expression. I didn't want to dwell in pity and the sadness of my old life. It was time to face the new dawn.

I ran my thumb across his jaw, a question sliding into my mind. "What is it you actually do in the empire? I never see you working."

He released a rumbling laugh. "I've been rather distracted of late." He squeezed my waist and a slow smile crept over my face, wiping away the ache in my chest.

"So?" I pressed.

"I have jurisdiction over several areas of the empire. My main focus is on clearing the ruins in the south. Miles runs the farmlands that my people clear for him to grow food for the humans. The rest of my efforts are focused on expanding the city, building wind and solar farms in the desert. My sirelings can only work at night there, but the projects have ensured that our entire empire runs off of renewable energy."

"What's that?" I asked, fascinated by his knowledge of the planet.

I'd been kept in the dark in the Realm. There was so much I didn't understand. My dad's stories had provided limited knowledge of the life humans had once led. Most of his stories of *before* had focused on his favourite memories.

Erik continued, "Before the war, the land was pillaged by humans for other means of creating electricity and fuel. There were so many humans in the world, the need for it was great and the cost to the planet was nearly catastrophic. When I gained power over the lands after the Final War, I pledged to improve this world. My life has held too much destruction in it, I wanted to build an empire that could withstand the test of time. One that could live in harmony with nature."

"That seems awfully noble of you," I teased, tugging on his sleeve.

His lips twisted at the corner. "I try."

"Oh do you? How modest you are," I said playfully, slipping my hands under his arms in an attempt to tickle him.

"That won't work on me. But *you,* however-" He flipped me back onto the bed, tickling my sides and I cried out, laughter tearing from my throat.

He pressed his weight onto me and I fell still as his hands stopped their torment. He brushed his nose against mine, his eyes boring into my own, that wild connection flaring between us and casting our souls in starlight. I felt like he was staring right into the depths of my being, and my heart almost beat with how much it wanted to get closer to him.

No words passed between us as he took my wrists, pinning them to the bed and grinding his hips against mine in a demand. He started tearing my clothes off as well as his, and I wondered vaguely if we were going to destroy the entire contents of our closets.

When we were skin on skin, his hard cock rutted between my legs and I lifted my hips, our bodies aligning perfectly as he slid inside me in a slow, torturous movement.

His mouth came down on mine, his kisses filled with an intensity that spoke of his love for me. We moved in a slow, rhythmic dance as he possessed me in a new way. One that made me feel like we were a single being, as if he was knitting my soul to his with an unbreakable thread. And I knew without a doubt, that this was the kind of love that could never die.

I lay at Erik's side, still thoroughly awake even though I should have been exhausted after how much sex we'd had. His skin called to me over and over again and I wondered at what point I was going to burn out of energy, if ever.

A sweet scent floated from his skin from the shower he must have had hours ago now. Dawn had spilled into the room, but clouds were veiling the sunlight and raindrops tinkled against the balcony. It seemed I was in the most blissful dream of my life.

I ran my fingers across Erik's chest in slow circles, thinking about the slayers as I eyed the bandage on his shoulder. They'd be on their way here now and Erik was going to fetch them as soon as they got close to the city. A riot of nervousness coursed through me, but I was certain I wouldn't hurt Julius when I saw him. There was no way I'd bite one of my friends. No matter what Erik thought. And as soon as he realised I could handle myself, he'd let me see my sister.

Fabian was watching television downstairs and I was pretty sure it was a romantic film from the emotional music that reached us. Every now and then, he would release a lament at the characters' actions, demanding they find a way to be together. I blew out a breath of amusement as Erik's hands brushed over my spine, making me arch into him like a cat.

"We have to break that bind between your brother and my sister," I whispered, turning his right palm over to trace the lines of the silver cross there. My own mark throbbed hungrily and I pressed it gently against Erik's, making him groan. Our souls seemed to connect at that very point our palms met, like we were an extension of each other. It sent a rush of energy through me that made me want him all over again, but we couldn't lie here all morning. I had to get dressed, prepare for the slayers arriving.

"I think only the gods can break it," Erik said thoughtfully, his eyes growing darker.

"Callie's bound to Magnar too. He's her mentor, but they love each other and their bind stops them from being together," I revealed. "It's so cruel. The gods have no hearts."

"Hm, the last I heard he was betrothed to Valentina," he said thoughtfully and I wrinkled my nose, certain Magnar had no such intentions toward her now.

Fabian shouted at the TV downstairs, "If you love her then tell her, you asshole! She's going to marry Kyle! Fucking *Kyle*!"

"Fabian's acting like a psycho," I said with a frown. "He can't be here when the slayers come."

"He won't be, I promise."

"How are you going to make him leave?" I asked curiously.

"I'll ask him nicely, then order him if he says no. And if he still refuses, I'll call Miles and Clarice to take him home." At the mention of his brother and sister, his brow creased with lines. "I haven't spoken to them yet. They're going to start wondering where we are soon. But they'll listen to me about the gods, I think, it's Fabian I'm concerned about."

"Why?"

"Because he has no interest in breaking the curse. He enjoys being immortal. And while that mark drives him toward your sister, he's only going to have one task in mind."

"We can't let him near her," I said urgently.

"We won't." He leaned up to kiss me and I slid my hands across his shoulders. He winced as I accidentally touched the wound Callie had given him.

"Sorry." I bit into my lip.

He caught my waist with a dark grin, pulling me up to straddle him, holding my wrists in one hand.

"It'll heal," he growled. "But I do have something else you can tend to-"

"Erik." Fabian strode into the bedroom, shirtless but freshly-washed with his brown hair loose about his shoulders.

Erik sat upright with a snarl, pushing me down onto the bed and shielding me with his body. I clutched the covers with a growl, dragging them up to my collar bone as Fabian walked toward us.

"Ever heard of knocking, asshole?" Erik snarled. I shot him a look. Erik had never been one for knocking either.

Fabian was disregarding our nudity, clearly not giving a shit about it. But I sure as hell did. I'd been bared to the world when his brother had walked in.

"Callie is on her way," Fabian said with a whine in his tone. "And I know you're going to tell me to go before she arrives but hear me out. I'll just talk to her. She can come here and we'll go to my room. Just the two of us, no other slayers, no trouble."

"You're not seeing her," I snapped before Erik could answer.

"Exactly," Erik agreed. "And this is my house. You don't own a single room in it."

"Callie tried to kill you the last time she saw you," I pressed. "And you hurt her when you tried to kill Magnar."

Fabian frowned deeply, taking something from his pocket. "Alright..." He gave in with a heavy sigh as if he'd known we were going to refuse. "But give her this, please." He held out a folded piece of paper and I reached for it, unable to fight the pity his sad expression sparked in me.

I started unfolding it, but he shook his head.

"It's for her. Don't read it." Fabian's eyebrows pinched together and I gave him a terse smile.

"Okay." I placed it down on the nightstand and he seemed to relax.

"I'll go then." Fabian backed up to the door slowly as if he expected us to tell him he could stay and see Callie after all.

"You can take the Ferrari," Erik said. "The keys are in my desk in the office."

"Thanks." Fabian lingered by the doorway like a dog who wanted to be taken for a walk.

"Bye Fabian," I said, unable to fight a snort of amusement as he drifted out of the door with a look of defeat.

Erik turned to me, shaking his head. "At least he's behaving better now he actually gives a shit about one of the women he's pursuing."

90

"You guys seem like you have some issues," I said tentatively as he stretched his arms above his head and moved toward the closet. I eyed the flexing muscles on his back and the firm planes of his ass, losing my train of thought.

"We have our differences, but I still care about him. He's my brother."

I got off the bed and followed him to the closet. He picked out a blue dress and handed it to me with a slanted smile. "For you."

"Choosing my clothes, Erik? Old habits die hard, huh?" I wafted the dress away, reaching for a long black one and taking some underwear from a drawer.

"Ever the rebel, *princess*," he murmured, tugging on some jeans and a shirt.

When we were dressed, I moved to the mirror on the wall. It hit me that I hadn't seen myself since I'd been turned. I hadn't dared to look in the bathroom mirror last night, but now, I couldn't shy away. I had to know if I was still me on the outside, just like I felt I was on the inside.

I swallowed hard as I approached the oval glass and took in my reflection.

My lips parted in shock. I looked just like the vision Andvari had shown me back in the ruins. Ethereal, captivating. I was me and yet not me at all. And I didn't know if I liked it. As I approached the pane, I ran a hand over my smooth cheek. My skin was pearlescent, near-glowing. I was radiant and yet I shouldn't have been anything of the sort after a night rolling beneath the sheets. Even my hair was barely affected. It hung in loose curls, silky soft and seeming even longer than it had been before. The black dress I'd chosen hugged my figure which was thankfully the same. Although perhaps I was slightly fuller in places. As if the venom had washed away any sign of the starvation I'd faced in the Realm.

I slid a hand across my stomach in awe. I was remade. But I didn't like the idea that my human life was lost completely. I was still the same girl beneath this veil of beauty and I didn't want this change to take that from me.

Erik appeared behind me, brushing the hair from my neck and

placing a kiss beneath my ear.

"Do you find me more attractive now. Like this?" I asked, a knot of concern tying in my chest. What if this was an improvement on the human Montana that Erik knew? What if he had seen my human flaws and found them lacking?

His mouth skated to my ear. "I have no idea what you mean," he purred, sending a shiver down my spine.

I reached back to cup his neck and pulled him around to look at the mirror. "You know exactly what I mean."

Erik gazed up and down my reflection, then shrugged. "You've always looked like this to me." He turned to me and though I expected to find mirth in his gaze, I only found a shining honesty.

"Oh," I breathed, my heart squeezing at his words. "Really?"

He took my hand, pressing it to his shirt where his quiet heart lay beneath it. "If you could see what I saw the first day I met you, the first time I kissed you, and the moment you woke beneath the stars, you would see the woman that holds my heart. And she is the same woman in every single one of those moments, and all of them in between."

My throat constricted and a smile crossed my features. Before I could respond to his beautiful words, the phone rang and anticipation spilled through me.

Erik released me, heading across the room and answering the call. "Hello?...right, see you soon." He hung up and turned to me with an anxious frown. "Ready?"

I nodded firmly and he moved toward me in a flash of movement, pressing a lingering kiss to my lips. When he stepped back, he pushed a hand into his hair, revealing his concern. "There's blood in the refrigerator. Drink some. You'll want to be as well-fed as possible before you see Julius. I'll bring him here within the hour."

He stepped out of the room and my shoulders dropped as the weight of what he'd asked seeped over me. I didn't feel hungry but at the thought of blood, a small fire lit at the base of my throat, urging me to drink. And I sensed that now that my mind had moved to that desire, it wouldn't be purged of it until I'd answered its call.

The front door sounded as Erik left and I moved toward the door, hating the thought of what I was about to do. But if it would ensure I didn't hurt Julius, I had to do it. I liked to think that even if I was a starving husk, I wouldn't lay a hand on my friend. But it was better to be safe than sorry.

MAGNAR

CHAPTER EIGHT

1000 YEARS AGO

Days turned into weeks which bled into months and years.

We hunted the monsters who now called themselves the Belvederes across the great continent they'd discovered, often slaying their foul creations but never coming close to them. They ran from us whenever we drew near and their damn rune-stones made it almost impossible for us to track them down again.

I was beginning to lose hope. It was pointless. What was it all for? I'd given my whole life to this cause and I'd achieved nothing. It had been eight years since they'd murdered my father and justice still hadn't been served.

I felt cheated. Cheated by fate, the gods, life. I'd sacrificed everything to this search and what did I have to show for it?

A betrothal to a woman I could never love. A vendetta which I was beginning to fear would never be set right. An aching desire for revenge which tainted every good moment that was presented to me so that I couldn't fully enjoy it.

For all that I had offered the gods, they'd given me very little in return. Idun never answered my calls anymore, but I was sure I could feel her presence, her amusement when I was feeling my lowest. As I did at this moment.

"Why watch me if you won't speak with me?" I demanded of the deity. "Is my misery so interesting to you?"

The wind shifted in the trees and I looked up at the rustling branches with a scowl. It was the height of summer; there was no natural reason for such a cold wind to blow. She wanted me to know she was here. She wanted me to know she still refused to speak with me. *Cruel whore.*

"I hate you," I murmured. "I hope you know it. You are stealing my life from me with this crusade, and you offer me no assistance. I would end them all, each and every one of them if only I could find them. But you won't help me, will you? Even though I am sure you know where they are."

A rat scampered out of the hedges and paused before me, tilting its head as it inspected me. I frowned at the rodent as it rubbed its paws across its face before shifting closer to me.

I stayed still, wondering if this creature had been sent by the goddess. It certainly seemed too tame to be natural and yet I knew it was no Familiar.

The rat hopped onto my boot and proceeded to take a shit before scampering away from me again.

I couldn't help but laugh as I shook my head.

"Bitch," I muttered.

She could force a rat to take a shit on me, but she couldn't guide me to my enemies.

I got to my feet, shaking my boot to remove the animal droppings from it before heading into the trees. I was late to return and no doubt my betrothed would be scouring the camp for me already. I'd promised to dine with her tonight out of sheer frustration from the amount of times she'd asked me, but I was sincerely regretting it now.

It took me longer than expected to make it back to camp and by the time I arrived, the sun was setting and the blue sky was streaked with pink and orange. I must have wandered further than I'd realised and I sighed as I passed the sentries, knowing I was about to get a mouthful from Valentina.

I was sure she'd already been informed of my arrival by one of her many loyal followers within the clans. I wasn't entirely sure how she'd managed it but Valentina had gathered a sizeable group of admirers from each and every clan. They called her my queen even though they knew we weren't wed yet and I was fairly sure their loyalty to her now rivalled their loyalty to me.

I supposed it should have annoyed me more than it did, but somehow, I couldn't bring myself to care enough to do anything about it. If it kept her busy, then all the better. And if she was so interested in being called queen, then why not? Though sometimes I could see the pain it caused my mother to hear her referred to as such. But the days of my father's rule were long behind us now and as much as I'd prefer not to hold his title and have him back among us, it was a futile hope. Life went on.

I'd been Earl for eight years already, my father had only ruled for eighteen. It wouldn't be long before I passed him in that too. Especially as the Belvederes continued to evade us and I wasn't likely to receive a warrior's death any time soon.

I wondered if Valentina was building up her following so that she could force my hand in finally honouring my commitment to her. But if that was her plan, she was a fool. The clans weren't just loyal to me because they loved me - and I didn't much care if they did or not - they were loyal because their vow demanded it. Turning from me would have been the same as abandoning their vow and doing so equalled death from the goddess.

"Magnar!" Julius called as he spotted me, and I summoned a smile as I made my way towards him through the mess of tents.

"Brother," I replied, clasping his forearm in greeting. "Allow me to hazard a guess - am I in trouble?"

"The strangest thing is that I don't think you are," Julius teased. "But I have been tasked with hurrying you along all the same."

"Oh? And how long ago did you promise to find me?"

"Well, I had to eat first," he replied with a shrug. "I couldn't very well wander into the woods on an empty stomach. What if I'd come over all faint? Half the women in camp would be heartbroken if something ever became of me in the wilderness."

"So now she's angry with both of us no doubt," I replied and I couldn't help but feel a bit pleased that Valentina's anger would be split between my brother and I. "I'm a little surprised she didn't send a storm cloud after me again."

"Well you did stay out in that rain for nearly three days last time," he reminded me. "So it wasn't an entirely successful attempt to rein you in."

I chuckled in response as we drew closer to the fire pit. I'd been fucking miserable out in that storm for days, watching the sun shining brightly over our camp from afar while I refused to return. But there was no way in hell I'd let her whip me like a dog and chase me home with a storm. I'd only come back when she'd finally given in and withdrawn the cursed clouds and even then I'd waited several hours. I'd been soaking wet, freezing cold and as angry as the beasts of Ragnarok, but I'd beaten her at her petty game so it had been worth my suffering.

"And where is my bride to be?" I asked, scanning the clansmen around the fire and not finding her among them.

"She said you were dining in private. Which I imagine is why she's been in and out of your tent all afternoon 'getting ready.'"

I sighed and clapped him on the back before heading away from the fire to find my tent.

It wasn't long before I arrived outside it, and I reached for the flap just as I heard my name.

"Magnar!" Elissa called and I paused to glance at her as she emerged from her tent which was pitched beside mine.

"Do you mean *me* this time?" I asked, cocking an eyebrow.

She and Aelfric had named their first born after me which had seemed like a touching idea at first but had quickly become confusing when I constantly heard her calling my name.

"Yes," she replied with a smirk as she adjusted their second born, Ferne, over the swell of her stomach. She was yet to tell me that they were expecting their third child, but it was fairly apparent. "And I still don't regret naming him that so you'll have to put up with it."

I grinned at her, unable to pretend to be angry with her over it. "So as you do mean me this time, what is it you want?"

"Apples," she replied. "But Aelfric is taking too long about fetching them and I fear he's accidentally ended up drinking ale instead. He took little Magnar with him but I don't want to carry Ferne all that way..."

I smiled at the little girl and snatched her before Elissa could even finish asking. She was as light as a feather in my arms as I swung her into the air, and she giggled excitedly.

"Mag-mag!" she cried, reaching towards me until I let her grab my hair.

"You're the best." Elissa hurried away and I waited until she was out of sight before lifting Ferne up to look me in the eye.

"You wanna go high?" I asked her in a low whisper.

She was nearing her first birth moon and didn't have many words yet, but she nodded excitedly.

I double checked that Elissa was gone then tossed her up into the air. She squealed with excitement as she flew towards the sky and fell into raucous giggles as I caught her again. The sound made my heart lighten and I laughed too before throwing her into the air again.

"You know, we could have some of our own if you'd just marry me," Valentina said loudly as I caught Ferne for the fourth time.

I held the little girl close to my chest and she instantly started tugging on my hair again.

"That is probably the first thing you've ever said to me that might tempt me into action," I replied teasingly as I turned towards Valentina.

She was wearing a grey dress which was cut low to reveal her breasts and she'd left her hair loose for once. The effect was quite striking; she seemed somehow softer, more feminine. Her eyes drifted to the child in my arms and I was fairly certain discomfort flickered across her gaze. I'd never once seen her playing with any of the village children and the fact that she was suggesting that she'd like to be a mother quite frankly surprised me.

"Well we could have a go at making one tonight?" she suggested.

"You know you wouldn't get pregnant unless we were wed first," I reminded her, though no doubt that was why she was offering it. It was another of the goddess's rules which bound our people; slayers were unable to conceive children outside of wedlock.

"We could do that tonight too."

I laughed as if it had been a joke and turned my attention back to the little girl in my arms. I pressed a kiss to her head and she giggled appreciatively.

"Mag-mag," Ferne cooed, yanking on my hair again and I laughed properly.

"Go high?" I whispered and she nodded enthusiastically, releasing her grip on my hair so that I could toss her towards the sky again.

"If my wife catches you doing that she'll castrate you!" Aelfric called as he approached us.

"Doing what?" I asked innocently as I tucked Ferne against my chest once more.

"Nothing. So long as you don't tell her we stopped for an ale on our way back."

"We? I don't see your son anywhere," I pointed out.

"Oh for the love of the gods!" Aelfric looked down at his legs then started hunting the spaces between the tents for little Magnar.

The sound of laughter reached us as the two year old peeked out from his hiding place behind my tent and Aelfric made a show of pretending to be mad at him.

After listening to his father for half a minute, little Magnar sidestepped him and ran towards me.

"Hi Mag-mag," he said with an impish smile. "Go high?"

"On your head be it," Aelfric said as I gave him an imploring look, then he took Ferne from me so I could throw their son into the air instead.

Valentina watched us playing but made no attempt to join in, and I wondered again why she'd suggested for us to have a child. If I truly thought she meant it, I might have been tempted to set a date for our wedding after all. It wasn't as though I was any closer to fulfilling my promise to Idun anyway and I was yet to meet a woman who held my interest for more than a few weeks. Perhaps that kind of love just wasn't in my future. But the love of a child was something I could still have if I went through with the wedding.

"Magnar Elioson!" Elisa yelled angrily as she spotted me tossing her son high above my head.

I laughed as I placed little Magnar on his feet then hurried into my tent, pushing Valentina ahead of me so that I didn't have to face Elissa's wrath.

"You really want a child, don't you?" Valentina asked thoughtfully as I stepped around her and unstrapped the sheathes which secured my swords to my back.

"One day," I replied vaguely, not wanting to think on it too much.

I'd dedicated my life to removing the Revenants from the Earth in the hopes that I could make those kinds of decisions once they were gone, but maybe she actually had a point. The longer I put my life on hold, the more I prolonged my own suffering. Perhaps I should have been thinking about my own future rather than letting it pass me by in my quest for revenge. I was mortal after all. I wasn't going to live forever.

I placed my swords down and turned my back to my betrothed, wondering why she'd been in and out of my tent all afternoon because I couldn't spot anything different about it...although everything did look very clean.

Valentina moved to sit at the small table which I used for meals when I didn't feel like interacting with the other clansmen, which wasn't particularly often. Two plates of food sat waiting on it and I grinned as I took a seat opposite her.

"Cold food, good idea," I said with a smirk as I ripped a hunk of bread apart.

"Well at least I knew that when you were late it wouldn't have gone bad," she replied lightly.

"And I am always late."

"Well you are when you're meeting *me*," she agreed though her voice didn't hold any irritation at the fact.

"So how was your day?" I asked as I filled my stomach.

"Good. I cleaned up in here a bit." She pointed around the tent and I nodded, though I couldn't have said specifically what she'd done.

"Thanks," I said a little late as I realised that was what she was waiting for.

She slid a full jug of ale towards me and I offered her a smile as I emptied it in one long drink. She didn't usually encourage my drinking but if she'd decided to allow it without protest for once then I wasn't going to complain.

"Have you ever thought about what you'd like to call them?" she asked as she refilled my jug, leaning forward as she did so and offering me a view down her dress.

"What?" I asked with a frown as my head swum for a moment.

I had no idea where she'd gotten that ale, but it was strong as shit. I emptied the second jug and she laughed like I'd said something amusing.

"Our children. What will you call them?" she pressed.

"I haven't thought on it," I replied.

"Imagine if they inherited both of our gifts," she said softly.

I felt a heavy pressure building in the air for a moment as she drew electricity from the atmosphere then released it again, her eyes flaring in time with her power.

Though it was possible, it wasn't likely. Children almost always inherited the gifts of whichever parent was stronger. Though I couldn't be sure who that would be between Valentina and I; our gifts were too different to easily compare their strength. There were only a few cases of children inheriting both lines of gifts anyway.

"They would be a force to be reckoned with, with parents such as us whatever way their gifts fell," I said before wondering why I was entertaining this fantasy. I normally shot down any conversation about us as a couple, but somehow that one had slipped past me by accident.

"They would," she agreed with a warm smile as she refilled my jug again. "Imagine inheriting the strength of the most powerful man on Earth and being able to harness the wildness of the storms like I do. They'd be unstoppable. Legendary," she breathed, that last word captivating me.

I found myself smiling at the idea. Valentina held my eye and dipped her finger into my drink before raising it to her mouth. I watched as she sucked the ale from her finger and my attention caught on the curve of her lips, the intention behind her action clear. Lightning flashed in her eyes as thunder rumbled overhead. A storm was coming and I wondered if I might like to be caught in it for once.

I drained my jug again and my head swam from the strong drink. Valentina leaned over the table, her dress seeming even lower cut than it had before as she gave me a view of her breasts again.

I blinked in confusion, forcing my gaze away as the unwanted thoughts kept swimming across my mind.

"I could bear you sons and daughters who the gods themselves would sing songs about. No one has blood so pure as ours or gifts so potent," she breathed, and the dream was a little intoxicating.

Valentina refilled my jug for a fourth time but she placed her hand around it before I could lift it to my mouth. She slid from her seat and moved towards me, perching on the table as she raised the jug to my lips. I kept my eyes on her as I drank it and the warmth from the alcohol fizzled into my blood. I shouldn't have been feeling as drunk as I was and I began to wonder where the hell she'd gotten this ale. But she distracted me by sliding from the table onto my lap.

She pressed herself against me and I couldn't help but feel a little aroused as she held my eye. She reached out to refill the jug again, but I snared her hand in mine and knocked it from her grip instead. She stilled in my arms, watching me as I looked at her in a way I'd never allowed myself to do before. She was beautiful and loyal and the picture she was painting of the life we might have was tempting me in a way it had never done previously.

"What do you want, Magnar?" she breathed seductively. "Just tell me and I'll give it to you."

"Love," I replied, a faint frown pulling at my features as I wondered why I'd just told her that.

"I love you," she replied instantly and I found I liked the way it sounded. She smiled, reaching up to trace her fingers along my face. "I love you and I want to show you how much. I want to be your lover, the mother of your children, and your *queen.*"

My heart leapt and I shifted my grip to her waist, feeling the warmth of her body beneath my palms.

"I want that too," I said although I wasn't sure if the words were mine or not. But I didn't have time to think on it before my desire for her took over and I pulled her towards me.

Her lips were full and demanding against mine. I kissed her like I never had before and my body ached with lust as I realised I wanted to do so much more than that to her.

Valentina shifted on my lap, straddling me as her fingernails bit into my shoulders and she devoured my kisses.

She gripped my shirt and tore it off of me, and I groaned as her hands moved over my flesh. I wanted more of her. All of her. I pushed her dress up and smiled when I realised she wasn't wearing anything beneath it.

She started pulling at my belt and I couldn't help but wonder why I hadn't done this before. She was mine. She'd always been mine. As soon as I took her to my bed, I knew there would be no going back on it. I'd marry her and she'd have my children and-

I yanked my head back and frowned at her in confusion.

She looked at me uncertainly and I could see a flicker of concern in her eyes.

"What's wrong?" she breathed as she shifted her hands beneath my waistband, but I caught her wrists in my grasp, halting her as I tried to work out what was happening.

My head felt thick with desire for her. It was like I'd seen her a thousand times before but I'd never really looked at her until now and it turned out she was everything I'd ever wanted. Except that couldn't be right. She'd offered her body to me plenty of times before and I'd never felt tempted enough to act on it.

She leaned closer, trying to kiss me again and I wanted it. I wanted it like I wouldn't be able to breathe again until I lost myself in the feeling of her skin against mine and I bound our souls together in marriage like I'd always intended to do.

I stood up suddenly, knocking her off of me.

"What was in that ale?" I growled as she stared up at me in fright.

I half wanted to grab her again and spend the night losing myself in her body, but I shook my head harshly, trying to clear the cloud from my mind.

"I...nothing," she gasped, shaking her head fearfully.

"Tell me if you want to keep your head on your shoulders," I growled. "An attack against your Earl is punishable by death."

"It wasn't an attack!" she said desperately. "Idun gave it to me for you. She said it would help you find happiness, that's all, I swear it."

I cursed at her as another wave of desire racked my body and I turned and strode out of the tent before I could do something that I would regret.

I headed away as quickly as I could without running and set my sights on the fire pit in the distance.

I still ached with a longing to satisfy the need for Valentina in my flesh, but that was easily solved. Any brown haired woman would do. And if Valentina had even an ounce of sense at all, she wouldn't come near me again any time soon.

CALLIE

CHAPTER NINE

W e waited on the quiet road for Erik to arrive. My hands kept
trembling as I thought of reuniting with my sister and I had
to keep reminding myself that there was nothing to be afraid
of. She was my Monty. No change could ever alter that. It didn't matter
what she looked like now or what her body was capable of. Inside, she
was still my Monty.

I glanced down at the ruined dress for the hundredth time, wishing
we'd managed to find some new clothes. I was still filthy with Fabian's
blood and accepting the bloodsucker's hospitality while we were clearly
in such desperate need of it felt like a form of defeat.

I heard the van approaching in the distance long before it turned
onto the dusty street. We were on the farthest outskirts of the city and I
was as sure as I could be that no vampires were nearby.

"This feels all kinds of wrong," Julius murmured as the black van
drew closer to us and I spotted Erik behind the wheel.

He pulled over and my gaze swept across the empty passenger seat
hopefully, but she wasn't there.

"Are you coming?" he called as the three of us hesitated.

I squared my shoulders and marched towards him, trying to look dignified despite my ragged appearance. His window was down and he watched our approach with as much mistrust as I was sure we were showing him.

"Where's-" I began.

"We agreed that she won't see you yet," Erik reminded me firmly. "She'll meet Julius back at the house and test out her resistance like we said. If she can control herself, then we'll figure out the rest after that."

I sighed as I nodded in acceptance. If Montana was even half the person she always had been then I didn't think for one second that she would hurt me, but it seemed I was alone in that belief.

A few feet separated us from the truck and I could feel Magnar and Julius standing right behind me as I eyed the seats beside Erik warily.

"You're going to have to ride in the back," he said before any of us made a move closer. "No offence, but you don't look like us and I can't risk anyone seeing mortals in the city at the moment."

"That's not offensive," Julius replied. "It would be offensive if you thought we *did* look like you."

Erik pursed his lips but didn't bite back. "As Fabian's wife, you can have more freedom," he said to me instead. "After you're cleaned up that is."

"Don't call me that," I snarled. "And don't presume to tell us how much freedom we have."

"You're a princess of the New Empire," he reminded me. "I'm sure there are a lot worse things that you could be."

"You're right," I replied scathingly. "I could be pregnant with a demon too."

Magnar and Julius chuckled and I walked away from Erik before he could reply, climbing into the back of the van. The space inside was cold and empty but at least it was dry. I took a seat, leaning against one of the walls and Magnar dropped down beside me. He pulled Venom from his back and rested the point on the floor between his legs as he kept hold of the hilt.

Julius took a seat opposite us and laid Menace over his lap before pulling the door shut and covering us in darkness.

"I must be fucking insane," Erik muttered from the cab before starting up the engine. "This is like letting the Trojan horse in."

The truck started moving and I felt Magnar tense beside me. It wasn't like I had a whole lot of experience with these kinds of vehicles either but it was easy to forget that everything like this was completely alien to him. I placed a hand on his thigh and he relaxed slightly as I leaned against him. I didn't say anything about it though, knowing Erik could hear us.

We stayed silent throughout our journey but I could feel Fury growing hotter and hotter at my hip as we were surrounded by the vampires once more.

I grew tense, wondering if we'd just done something insanely stupid. We were trusting a Belvedere with our lives; he could just as easily deliver us to our execution as he could to my sister. But Montana trusted him. And I trusted her, so I had to stick to this plan no matter how uncomfortable it made me.

After a while, Fury began to cool a little and the sounds of the city were left behind. Erik drove quickly, taking hairpin turns left and right which almost sent me flying more than once. I was pretty sure it was intentional so I refused to make any sound in protest.

We finally rolled to a stop and we got to our feet as we heard Erik exiting the cab.

"There's no handle on the inside," Julius muttered and a prickle of uncertainty ran through me again.

Magnar stepped forward and kicked the doors so hard that they flew open and the one his boot had hit was left with a huge dent in it.

Erik's mouth fell open in surprise as we stepped out. "I was about to open that for you," he said incredulously.

"If you like your doors in one piece, then I'd suggest not locking us in again," Julius replied with a taunting grin.

Erik shook his head and pointed towards a stone cottage which stood a little way back from the driveway. In the distance up on the grassy hill, was the wooden structure of the main house on Erik's fancy ass estate.

"After you," he said stiffly.

"Afraid to turn your back on us, parasite?" Magnar asked with a dark laugh as he placed an arm around my shoulders and started guiding me towards the cottage. He kept Venom in his other hand and I was pretty sure he didn't want to present his back to Erik either but he didn't look around as he set a quick pace towards the stone building.

We stepped into the cottage and I stared about at the open space in wonder. Everything was so clean; there was a long white couch which curved before a huge window that gave a view over the rolling hills. To the right, the space opened up into a sleek kitchen with cream cabinets and a heavy oak dining table divided the two areas.

"I stocked the fridge. There are clean clothes and hot water that way," Erik said, pointing to a wide corridor which led out of the living area before turning his eyes to Julius. "We can get going as soon as you're changed."

"Already trying to get me out of my pants, huh?" Julius joked as he strolled away from us to wash up, removing his belt as he walked. "You know I'm really not that kind of girl."

"Could have fooled me," Erik muttered, and Julius's brows rose in surprise at the comeback, his lips quirking like he was about to laugh before he caught himself and scowled instead.

My stomach growled as I eyed the refrigerator, but I felt uncomfortable approaching it with Erik standing there watching us.

"You shouldn't leave the cottage while I'm gone. It'd be better for all of us if you're not seen," he said.

"Fine," I agreed. We didn't have anywhere else to go anyway. "Anything else we should know?"

Erik hesitated for a moment before answering. "Fabian's still keen to see you; he knows you're here but he promised to stay away for now. I don't know how long he'll be able to resist the urge to come looking for you though."

"Just remind him why I ripped his head off then," I replied darkly. "And that I'll happily do it again if he ever so much as looks at the man I love with a squinty eye, let alone tries to hurt him again."

Erik's eyes slid from me to Magnar whose arm was firmly around my shoulders. He was about three times my size and still held Venom in his grasp. I was sure that my promise to protect him seemed foolish on face value, but I didn't care. If Fabian came for me again I'd plunge Fury through his heart without a second thought. My mother's ring protected me from my bond to him so there would be nothing to stop me now.

Tension coiled around us as Magnar and Erik stared at each other. I wondered if they'd ever really seen each other like this, standing so close while neither of them made a move to attack the other.

They couldn't have looked more different; Erik was dressed in a crisp shirt and jeans, his hair styled and skin so clean it practically shone. Magnar stood shirtless, sword in hand and the filth of their battle still coating his skin. He looked wild, like some untameable beast, his humanity undeniable in contrast to the polished lifelessness of the vampire.

I cleared my throat as the silence thickened and moved between them, breaking their death stares.

"We should eat," I said, forcing Magnar to look at me.

He nodded but didn't move, so I caught his hand and towed him after me to the kitchen.

"Montana told me you couldn't be together because of the novice bond. Is the ring blocking that too?" Erik asked.

It was a pretty odd subject to use for small talk but I grabbed onto it in an effort to end this awful silence.

"It did but I broke my bond to Magnar so that I could stop the two of you from destroying each other. So that's gone now, ring or not." I opened the refrigerator and my mouth fell open as I spotted all of the food inside. It was more than we would have been given in a month in the Realm.

"Callie is a full slayer now," Magnar added darkly. "More than capable of destroying your kind."

I grabbed an apple and passed it to him, hoping to shut him up with food. None of us needed reminding of what we were; the air was alive with it already. Magnar eyed the fruit but didn't take a bite.

"I assure you, if I wanted you dead I wouldn't go to this much effort just to poison you," Erik said, noticing his hesitation. "That would seem to be more your style."

Magnar smirked and took a huge bite from the apple. "I'd hazard a guess that the one Idun gave us for your wedding didn't taste so sweet."

"How about we just don't mention the many ways we've all tried to kill each other?" I suggested.

"I think you made a mistake with these clothes," Julius said loudly as he re-entered the room. His hair was wet and his skin was clean. He was wearing a pair of jeans but the shirt he'd pulled on with it was stretched to breaking point across his huge chest and rode up several inches to reveal his stomach. "I think you got us your puny size by accident." He grinned at Erik tauntingly and the vampire rolled his eyes in response.

He shot out of the room in a rush of motion and returned just as quickly with another shirt in hand.

"You're wearing a woman's shirt," he said, tossing the new one to Julius. "But feel free to keep it on if you like it."

I couldn't help but laugh as Julius ripped the old shirt off of him and switched it out for the one Erik had retrieved.

"Well women didn't wear such garments in our day," Julius replied with a shrug. "Neither did men for that matter. Everything is a lot more confusing now."

Erik almost looked like he was going to smile, and my heart squeezed with hope. We were all standing in the same place and no one had tried to kill each other yet. Perhaps we would be able to find a way to work on solving the prophecy together after all.

"Shall we go then?" Erik asked impatiently and the moment dissolved as if it had never existed.

"One second." Julius crossed the space between us and started rummaging in the refrigerator. He filled his arms with a loaf of bread, a block of cheese and a mound of fruit before taking a carton of milk too. He kicked open several cupboards and smiled triumphantly as he found a bag which he filled with his meal. He tossed several packets of chips on top for good measure until the bag looked like it might burst, then started eating as he headed for the exit. I could tell Erik was more than a little disgusted by his lack of manners, but he said nothing.

"What are we waiting for?" Julius asked around a mouthful of food and Erik moved to open the door for him.

"I want to give her plenty of time to make sure she can control herself," Erik said, looking back at me one last time, his eyes filled with concern. "If it all goes well, we'll come back in a few hours."

I sighed, wishing he wasn't forcing us to go through this nonsense, but if that was what it took, then I'd simply have to bite my tongue. A few hours I could cope with. I just wanted to see my sister again.

"Fine. Two hours," I reiterated, glancing at a large clock on the far wall. That would be midday.

Erik nodded and Julius stepped past him before he shut the door, leaving us alone.

My gut churned with worry but I forced it aside. Whatever differences there were to my sister now, I knew deep down she'd still be the same. Nothing else mattered.

I grabbed a hunk of bread and some butter and quickly started filling my stomach. Magnar followed my lead, placing his swords down on the table and we silently devoured as much of the food as we wanted until the ache in my belly was fully satisfied.

I glanced around at the opulent living space uncomfortably. It was at least five times the size of our entire apartment back in the Realm and it didn't even seem like anyone lived here.

"We should get cleaned up," I suggested as Magnar finished eating too.

"I'd sooner find a river than use whatever infernal devices reside in this house," he replied.

"Well I didn't see a river anywhere and we can't go wandering about outside," I replied, raising an eyebrow at him.

"Then I can just-"

"Come on." I snatched his hand and tugged him after me through the house. He resisted a little but I kept pulling so he had no choice but to follow me.

The corridor opened up and several doors led off of it. I opened the closest one and found a huge bedroom decorated in grey tones. On the other side of the room, another door stood open and I spotted a bathroom beyond it.

I dragged Magnar after me as he frowned at the lavish surroundings and didn't release him until we were in the bathroom. White tiles lined the walls and a huge shower stood at the back of the room, promising to free me from the lingering filth which coated my flesh. I approached it and spun the dial to start the water running.

Magnar scowled at it suspiciously and I reached out to let the flow run over my fingers. It was deliciously warm and I grinned at the prospect of washing the dirt and blood from my skin at last.

"I don't like it," Magnar grumbled behind me, and I turned to look at him with a frown.

"I know you're not a fan of modern technology, but you're going to have to suck it up."

He folded his arms and I could tell he was going to refuse.

"Fine," I said before he could. "I guess I'll just have to shower alone if you won't join me."

His gaze brightened as he caught on to what I was implying but he didn't move. I held his eye as I hooked my fingers around the straps of my ruined dress and slowly slid it from my shoulders.

His gaze slipped to the material as I pushed it lower and I bit my lip as I noted his desire. The moment hung between us as I held the dress in place and heat raced through my body.

We had two hours after all and we were all alone in this huge house.

I released my hold on the dress and it fell to my feet, leaving me naked before him. Magnar's face lit with a wicked smile and knots formed in my stomach as I backed up, forcing him to follow me.

He stalked closer as the water cascaded over my body and he released a groan filled with lust.

"You don't play fair," he muttered as he paused just outside the shower.

I tilted my head back so that the water raced across my skin, his eyes tracking the movement.

"Come and get me if you want me," I teased, smiling at him as I watched his resolve shatter, my hands running over my body, teasing my nipples and brushing between my thighs.

My teeth sank into my bottom lip as I looked at the beast of a man who I had claimed for my own and remembered all the ways he had destroyed me the last time I'd been naked in his presence.

"You're going to regret taunting me," Magnar promised darkly and my heart leapt with excitement.

"I doubt it," I breathed.

He unbuckled his belt and I held my breath in anticipation as he started to undress, my eyes roaming over his body and heat building between my thighs.

With a force of effort, I turned my back on him as I rubbed shampoo through my hair and scrubbed the blood from my skin, needing to remove all evidence of that place and the battle so I could be entirely myself again.

My heart pounded as I heard him kicking his boots off, the sound of clothes hitting the floor quickly following and I could sense him moving closer. Anticipation clawed at me and I chewed on my lip to stop myself from turning back to him, waiting for the promised feeling of his flesh against mine.

Magnar's hands landed on my waist and I sighed in pleasure as he moved beneath the shower too, letting the water cascade over him. I arched my back as he pressed himself against me and the hard plane of his muscles pushed into my spine, the thick ridge of his cock driving against my ass and making me release a low moan.

He slid his hands lower and I sucked in a breath as he moved his knee between my legs, nudging them apart, taking control as always, making my body bend to his demands.

Magnar dipped his mouth to my neck as his hands roamed over my breasts, tugging at my nipples and making me moan again.

"The sight of you like this is enough to bring a man to his knees, drakaina hjarta," he growled, his words rough against the shell of my ear. "I want to worship and devour you in equal measure."

"Then what are you waiting for?" I panted, rocking my hips so that my ass ground against his cock.

He chuckled darkly at the provocation, one hand sliding from my breast and over my stomach before trailing between my thighs. He didn't linger at my clit, instead rolling his fingers straight over it before sinking two of them inside me. The heel of his hand pressed down on my clit as he began to pump his fingers in and out of me, murmuring praises in my ear about how wet I was, how tight, how hard he was going to fuck me just as soon as I came for him.

I whimpered at the torture, and I reached over my shoulder, holding him in place as I gripped his hair in my fist.

His cock drove against my ass with more force and I rocked my hips, loving the feel of every solid inch, wanting it inside me with a desperation which had my head swimming.

I released a moan of longing as he continued to toy with me, building a pressure in my body which ached to be set free. I was always at his mercy in this, his creature, bound to his bidding and it was the one place where I was willing to relinquish all control to his desires.

My breathing started to escalate as my skin tingled beneath his touch. I was a slave to the motion of his hands, every inch of my flesh longing for a moment of his attention.

His mouth moved along my neck, his teeth grazing my skin in the most delicious way.

I turned my head towards him, catching his mouth so I could feel the heat of his lips as his tongue danced against mine. My heart pounded life through my veins, waking every desperate part of my soul and binding it to his. The hand toying with my nipple released it and travelled up my body, caressing my skin before wrapping around my throat as he drew me closer to the edge.

"Come for me," he demanded, driving his fingers in and tightening his grip on my throat.

I moaned as my body buzzed with energy, locking my muscles as I fought his command, wanting this to go on and on, but as he growled that word again, his fingers pushing deeper and hand grinding against my clit for a final time, I gave in, shattering for him and calling his name.

Magnar groaned his approval, shifting his hand from my throat to grasp my chin and drag my mouth around to meet with his.

I turned sharply, my tongue sinking into his mouth as I dislodged his hold on me and I wound my arms around his neck, wanting to see this monster of mine when he lost control in my arms. I lost myself in the heat which burned in his eyes, dragging him closer so that I could kiss him deeper, my nails digging into his flesh and devouring the taste of him on my tongue.

He took hold of me, making to push me backwards but I slapped his hands aside, taking control for once and pushing onto my tiptoes so I could deepen our kiss further. Magnar released a deep laugh which resounded all the way through my body, right down to my bones and I smiled against the wicked curve of his lips.

The water cascaded over us endlessly as I dragged my hands down his chest, feeling the rigid curves of his muscles beneath my palms. I wanted every piece of him to be mine. Every wound, each tattoo, the scars which stood out across his perfect body, all of it.

I skimmed my fingernail along a tattoo which crossed his collarbone, biting my lip as I felt him shudder beneath my touch. I moved my mouth to it next, running my lips along the ink on his skin as his hands travelled down my spine while he explored me in turn.

I shifted my attention to his arm, raising his hand in mine as I kissed four scars which marked his bicep like the marks of some beast's claws.

I held his gaze as the warm water ran through my lashes and my mouth claimed a star which was tattooed on his forearm.

Magnar groaned, twisting his arm in my grip and catching the back of my neck so he could drag me into a world-altering kiss.

I pressed my body against his, the water making our skin slide against each other in a way which made my heart race, and I took his cock in my grasp, delighting in the size of it, still surprised by the way he filled my hand, my fingers unable to close around his girth.

His other arm tangled around me, increasing the pressure of my flesh against his and I knew he was about to give in to his desire and take me, the rapid pace of our breaths merging and his cock jerking in my fist.

Magnar gripped my leg and tugged, angling his hips toward mine and I almost gave in, but I wanted to take him to his knees for once instead of forever bowing to his commands.

I bit his lip hard enough to make him jerk back and his eyes lit with a fire which I so wanted to burn up in as he looked down at me in surprise.

I used my gifted muscles to shove him back against the tiles before he could have me, letting my eyes roam over every breath-taking inch of his body as he leaned back against the wall and surveyed me in turn.

"Not yet," I breathed with a smile, and he groaned in protest but gave in, remaining in place before me.

I inched back, enjoying having this power over him and taking my time as I decided what I would do with it.

I wasn't done exploring his body and I was going to make him wait while I did it. And if that drove him crazy with desire, so be it. I'd gladly let him release that energy on me in time.

I caught his chin in my hand, pushing it up so I could kiss the bruised skin on his neck where Erik had bitten him. He sucked in a breath at the mixture of pain and pleasure, and I trailed my hand down his chest as I moved my mouth to his side next.

I kissed the ribs that Fabian had broken, awe filling me at the perfection I found where the wound should have been. Idun had healed his injuries as if they'd never existed at all. I could almost forgive her cruel ways in light of that one miracle which had saved this man who I loved so terrifyingly.

Magnar's hand moved to grip my hair as I shifted my attention ever lower, seeking out every mark on his skin.

I trailed kisses over each of them, branding them as my own.

His muscles tensed beneath my attention and I smiled as I turned the table on him, playing with him as he so enjoyed to do to me. The more I could feel his desire rising, the closer I came to breaking. My body yearned for him in a way that made me feel like I would never be able to get enough.

"Callie," he breathed and I knew he was begging me to give in to him and keep going in the same breath.

"Magnar," I murmured in response but I didn't give in. He would have to break first.

As my lips made it to a sweeping scar which curved over his hip, he cursed, his fist rolling down the length of his cock like he was desperate for the relief.

My knees pressed to the tiles and I looked up at him as I peeled his fingers away from his cock then slowly leaned in and wrapped my lips around it in their place.

Magnar released a low growl, his hands driving into my hair, urging me on as I took him into my mouth. He was so big that his cock was grazing the back of my throat long before I managed to take all of him and I wound my fist around the base of his shaft as I started moving.

"Fuck," Magnar panted, his hips jerking as I took the length of him again, his cock driving to the back of my throat and making me moan at the tight fit. I pulled back, rolling my tongue over the head of his cock and tasting his arousal.

I met his simmering gaze as I took him in again and again, and he watched me with a wild desire in his gaze which made my heart pound furiously.

I moaned around his shaft, caressing his balls in my hand, and he threw his head back with a deep groan that was followed by the heat of his cum filling my mouth.

Magnar caught my chin and dragged me back up into his arms with a growl of longing as I swallowed the taste of him down and he kissed me roughly, praising my name while the water crashed over us, never once growing cold.

I relaxed into his arms, trailing my fingers along his jaw and looking up at him as he backed me up against the wall.

"You," he growled, pinning me there with his grip on my jaw. "Are fucking everything, Callie Ford."

I blinked at him through the torrent of water, sucking on my bottom lip and wondering at the fact that he wasn't slowing down. His cock was still rigid, his eyes wild with want and I got the distinct impression that he wasn't close to done with me yet.

"Then stop holding back," I taunted.

Magnar's eyes flashed at the challenge, and I gasped in surprise as he yanked me to him, his mouth colliding with mine in a brutal kiss which promised so much more. He was done waiting and the look in his eyes set my blood alight.

He hoisted me into his grip and I wrapped my legs around his waist as he bit down on my lip just as I'd done to him and slammed me back against the wall, joining our bodies as he silenced me with his mouth.

I cursed into his kiss as his cock drove into me and stole the breath from my lungs, my pussy throbbing as he pinned me at his mercy and began to fuck me like the heathen he was.

I groaned against his lips as he took my body hostage and I was lost to the intensity of this feeling, his cock pounding into me relentlessly, my heels driving into his spine and my nails ripping into his back. Somehow, impossibly, this man, this beast, was *mine*.

My nails tore into his flesh as he held me there and the feeling of his body taking mine hostage set a fire blazing in my veins. He was all I wanted. All I needed. And I knew I'd never, ever get enough of him.

There was an urgency to our kisses which yearned to be satisfied. It was a greedy, desperate ache which drove us together with the force of the wildest storm. He wasn't careful with me and I didn't want him to be. I just wanted more and more of everything he was offering. I was hungry for this, starving for it, for him. Each moment in his arms driving me towards the sweetest of conclusions.

His breathing grew harsher against my lips as he fucked me with a rabid fury, and I felt myself falling apart in his arms. He was the only thing keeping me in one piece. I was sure if he wasn't holding me there, I'd break apart and dissolve into the endless spiral of pleasure that was waiting to devour me whole.

Magnar's hands gripped my ass and he tilted my hips so his cock could drive in deeper, his pelvis grinding against mine and finding my clit while I cried out as he drove me to the edge of ecstasy and beyond.

I called his name as I came for him, my pussy tightening around his cock and forcing him to come with me. He cursed as he fucked me through it, making the pleasure echo on through every single piece of my flesh until even my soul was buzzing in the aftermath of him.

Magnar's kisses grew less demanding and more worshipping and he finally lowered me to the floor where I forced my trembling legs to hold me up.

"I'm yours for however long you want me, Callie," he breathed as he pushed my wet hair over my shoulder so he could look me right in the eyes. "Fuck the gods and their rules. Fuck Valentina and Fabian and every other thing that might want to get between us. I want to be yours and I want you to be mine. You're all I've ever wanted for myself and the moment I saw you I knew that you were precisely who I'd been waiting for, for a thousand years."

I gazed up at him, running my fingertips along his jaw as I studied his achingly perfect face and the intense desire which simmered in his eyes.

"You're mine," I agreed because no matter how furious he made me, no matter how often we clashed and how ferociously we fought, there was something which always drew me back. This tie between us wasn't the kind that could be undone. These words didn't make it so because it already was. He belonged to me and I belonged to him. That was simply the way it was.

"And I'll be yours," I breathed. "Because I already am."

MONTANA

CHAPTER TEN

An engine growled as it pulled up the drive and I rose from my seat in the lounge, having continued with Fabian's movie to occupy my mind. I'd never seen anything like it, though Dad had told us about such things. A story told by people pretending to be other people. Strange. Though weirdly entertaining. And Fabian had been right. Kyle fucking sucked.

An empty bottle of blood stood on the coffee table and I eyed it with a niggle of guilt. Snatching it up, I carried it to the trash can and dropped it inside, wringing my hands together.

What if I can't control myself?

You will. You can do this. Just remember how much you care about Julius. You'd never hurt him.

The front door opened and my heart clenched. I didn't know where to stand, suddenly panicked as heavy footfalls approached.

"Nice house. Being an asshole clearly pays well," Julius's voice reached me.

"Definitely better than being a giant fuckwit does," Erik replied smoothly.

I moved to the couch, gripping the back of it, half tempted to duck down and hide behind it. But I had to keep it together. I had to do this.

They approached the door and I smelled it. Blood. Thrumming through Julius's veins. His rampant heartbeat called to me, telling me he was as uncertain as I was.

I won't hurt you, I swear it.

The door opened and Erik entered first, seeming concerned but Julius shouldered past him, his eyes landing on me. His mouth opened and I wrapped my arms around myself, feeling horribly scrutinised. Did he see a monster standing here? A vile creature he longed to kill? Did Menace scream my death in his ear?

"Hey, damsel," he breathed as if I was a frightened animal he wanted to lure closer.

His blood smelled even sweeter than the bottled stuff and I felt a tingle in my canines that frightened me. Taking a breath, I took a step towards him and Erik looked ready to jump between us, his gaze swinging from me to the slayer.

"Hey," I said, sighing when the urge to kill Julius didn't come. I could sense the curse pushing at my will, but it wasn't remotely strong enough to make me act on my thirst. In fact, after my recent drink, it was surprisingly easy to stand before him without the scent of his blood overwhelming my senses.

"You're looking...um," Julius struggled for the word.

"It's okay," I sighed. "I know you must hate this." I dipped my head. "If it's too hard-"

"It's not," Julius said firmly, and Erik took a step forward as if he was still afraid I might lunge at my friend. "I'm just glad you're okay. You know, not dead. Or not, *not* dead. If you know what I mean." He ran a hand down the back of his neck and I nodded, breaking a smile.

"I know what you mean."

He frowned and a moment of tension passed between us.

"Fuck it," Julius muttered, then strode toward me, dragging me into his arms.

Erik was at our side in a flash and I shook my head to warn him off, his fierce look telling me he was half a second from ripping Julius away from me. I wrapped my arms around Julius's broad shoulders and the scent of his blood rolled over me in a delicious wave. My fangs ached, my tongue scraped the roof of my mouth. The curse pushed at me, telling me to feed. But as I concentrated, I started to will the sensation away until it reduced to a quiet throb in my throat. Totally manageable.

A noise of relief left me and I clutched onto Julius, delighting in the pounding of his heart against my silent chest.

I could actually manage this. I'd really done it.

"How's Callie?" I asked as he released me.

"Well I've left her alone with Magnar, so I imagine she's *really* good right now." He winked and I grimaced.

"Ew."

He laughed, gazing over me with a look of awe. "I didn't think it'd be like this. I mean, you're still *you*. You don't even have that monstrous air the others have." He glanced at Erik with a pointed look.

"Better than the caveman look you and your brother excel at. Has Magnar heard of clippers yet or is he still mentally bound to the Middle Ages?" Erik taunted.

Julius released a laugh and my brows shot up, hope darting through me at the way they were talking. Even if they were hell-bent on throwing insults at each other, it was still progress.

"I'd consider mentioning modern hair styles to him but I think I'd end up with a broken jaw for it," Julius replied.

"I've been trying with my own brother for years, but Fabian insists on walking around looking like a wild goat."

Julius snorted. "Scissors aren't that hard to find."

My mind spun at their casual interaction. I couldn't believe the difference in them. They'd been trying to rip each other limb from limb just yesterday.

"So can I go see Callie now?" I asked Erik hopefully. "I'm fine. See?" I gestured at Julius to prove it.

"No," Erik growled. "We'll wait a couple of hours. Give yourself time to adjust."

"I've adjusted. Come on, look at me."

He did and his eyes trailed right down to my toes, making me feel like he was seeing right beneath my clothes to my bare skin. "I don't know how you're doing it, rebel. Even I'm tempted to eat this motherfucker."

Julius cocked a brow. "I knew you'd come back for more." He gestured to the wounds on his neck, and I frowned. "You can't get enough of my sweet nectar."

"That's disgusting." I wrinkled my nose and Erik scowled.

"I'm quite content never to taste your *nectar* again," Erik muttered.

Julius shrugged, dropping down onto the couch and planting Menace and his bag on the floor. He picked up the TV remote from the arm of his seat. "What are we watching then?"

I clucked my tongue in annoyance. "Can't we just go? I want to see my sister."

"Have you seen Bone Breaker?" Erik suggested, sitting in an armchair and turning his attention to the TV.

"No, but it sounds like a fucking blood fest. I'm in," Julius said keenly.

"Er, hello?" I folded my arms as they put on the movie.

"Shh, it's starting." Julius patted the seat beside him and I huffed my frustration, glaring between them.

I glanced at the door and remembered I could move pretty fast now.

"If you run, I'll catch you, tie you down and make you enjoy the movie from my lap," Erik said causally.

I scowled at him, but he didn't look my way, his muscles flexing just enough to tell me he was ready to launch himself at me if I made a move. So instead of giving Julius a show of me being rounded up like a rogue sheep, I gave in and sat down next to the slayer on the couch. He opened the bag between his knees and took out a pile of food, peeling open a block of cheese and taking a huge bite out of it.

I looked to Erik pleadingly but he just offered me a firm look and turned his attention back to the screen.

I sat back in my chair as Julius gulped down a whole pint of milk and a smile took over my face at how well this had gone. His blood was present, sure, and his pounding heartbeat drew my attention now and again, but I could control any urges I had towards him.

And at least if I was going to be stuck here a while longer, I was in

126

the company of two of my favourite people in the world.

As the movie drew to a close– which had contained practically nothing but blood, gore and guts – a knock came at the front door.

Erik stood in a flash, charging across the room.

"Stay here," he commanded before exiting and slamming the door.

Julius raised his brows at me, swallowing a mouthful of food. "He's jumpy."

He reached for Menace beside him, and I strained my hearing toward the front door.

"Fabian just came to my house with a very strange story, Erik. He said Montana is a vampire and you've teamed up with the slayers. What the hell is going on?" Clarice's voice carried to me and I rose from my seat, feeling on edge.

Julius got up too, lifting Menace into his hands, his eyes darkening to a formidable glare.

"Don't," I hissed, but he didn't lower his weapon.

I heard Erik explaining about the gods and what had happened at the statue. When he was finished, Clarice sucked in a breath.

"What's that smell?" she demanded.

"Wait-" Erik snarled, but the door flew open and Clarice appeared beyond it dressed in a low-cut pink dress that hugged her figure and amplified all of her curves.

Her bright blue eyes fell on Julius and she bared her fangs. "*Slayer*," she snarled, but Erik caught her arm before she could advance.

"We're working *with* them now," Erik said to her. "Accept it."

Julius rolled his shoulders, lowering his sword slightly as he drank in the sight of her. He lifted a bag of chips from the couch and held them out to her. "Snack?"

"What the fuck?" Clarice snarled, looking ready to rip him apart.

"Oh sorry," Julius said with a mocking grin, dropping the chips and holding out his wrist instead. "Snack?"

Clarice released a feral snarl and Erik pulled her back a step.

"How can you trust him?" Clarice bit at her brother.

"I told you, we have a common enemy now: the gods. And we're uniting against them," Erik insisted.

Clarice's eyes whipped to me and her expression softened. "Oh Montana, you look beautiful."

"Er- thanks," I said awkwardly, taking Julius's arm and squeezing as I tried to make him drop Menace.

"*Ow*," he murmured, attempting to shake me off, but I didn't let go.

"But Erik, what about the prophecy?" Clarice looked to him in fear. "If Montana's a vampire now, she can't bear any children."

I ground my teeth at her words. "I wouldn't have done that anyway."

"And neither would I," Erik added. "Besides, I told you the prophecy doesn't mean that. You have to trust me, Clarice. I know what I'm doing."

Clarice scowled as she shifted her attention back to Julius. "Are you sure? Because this looks insane to me. Shouldn't we just kill him while he's outnumbered?" Her eyes glittered dangerously and a flicker of concern ran through me.

"Bring it on, Golden Whore," Julius said with a wicked smile.

"Let's all take a breath." Erik planted himself between Clarice and Julius. "We must try to set aside our differences."

Clarice looked to Julius with a grimace. "The last time I saw him, he tried to cut my head off."

"Foreplay." Julius shrugged and I bit down on my lip to hold my laughter back. How could he be so damn calm right now?

Clarice very nearly broke a smile at his joke, then schooled her expression and scowled again.

"You don't know what real foreplay is, slayer boy," she said coolly.

"I'm sure you're desperate to show me your version, sweetheart, but I don't go for blood-sucking parasites who like their men weak and abiding. Not really my thing, Clarice. So you can stop eye-fucking me because we need to go."

"I am not-" Clarice started, but Erik held up a hand to stop her.

"Enough," he snarled. "You can stay here. We're leaving."

Clarice caught Erik's arm. "Fabian's in the car. He insisted on coming. He said Callie's here too and he's not allowed in the house."

Erik pressed his fingers into his eyes. "She's down at the cottage. Don't let him follow us."

Clarice nodded, giving in although she still seemed uncomfortable with the situation.

Julius sheathed his blade and I released his arm as we moved across the room toward Erik. Clarice still barred our way to the door and her lip peeled back as Julius got close.

"You've got something in your teeth," Julius muttered, and Clarice threw a hand to her mouth in horror. "Oh never mind, I think it was just bullshit."

Clarice glowered, lunging forward, but Erik shoved her back before she could reach the slayer.

"Ignore him," I said to her and she threw me a glance, her eyes suddenly blazing with emotion.

She stepped around Erik and moved toward me, pulling me into a hug. "I'm so glad you're a part of our family."

I gave her a tight sort of smile as she released me. "We're going to break the curse. We'll figure it out."

"Do you really think so?" she asked, looking desperate for that to be true. Honestly, I wondered why she of all the Belvederes longed for humanity so much; it seemed like she had everything she wanted in this life and more. I'd never seen the torment in her that I had in Erik.

"Yes," I promised, squeezing her hand.

"Come on then," Erik encouraged, and I moved to his side, poking Julius to get him moving. The sooner he was away from Clarice, the better.

She watched us walk from the room with a mixture of discomfort and disbelief. I hoped she'd come around to this idea soon, because if we were going to take on the gods, we needed all the help we could get.

CALLIE

CHAPTER ELEVEN

I laid on the impossibly soft bed and looked up at the ceiling as Magnar brushed his fingertips over my skin. His movements were getting more intentional again and I turned to smile at him as he eyed my exposed body like I was something he wanted to eat.

"You're insatiable," I murmured as he placed a kiss on my shoulder.

"You're irresistible," he countered, his mouth against my skin.

"Well that may be, but we're also out of time." I smirked at him as I rolled away and sat up on the edge of the bed. "And though you might have been a good distraction, I've got somewhere to be."

"A good distraction, am I?" he asked as he followed me over the bed and I had to stand before he could snare me in his arms.

"Fairly good," I agreed as I moved across the room and opened the drawers filled with clothes.

"*Fairly* good?" He raised an eyebrow at me and got to his feet, stalking after me as I hurried to pull on some underwear. His eyes fell on the garment which pushed my breasts up and I realised it wasn't doing anything to tame his desire.

"Above average," I said, biting my lip as I tossed a pair of boxers at him.

He caught them and pulled them on but didn't slow his pursuit. Adrenaline bubbled in my gut as I backed away, smiling at the game.

"I think it was a bit more than above average," he said. "And I think you're going to say it."

"Okay," I breathed as I hopped up onto the bed and looked down at him. "It was a bit more than above average."

Magnar laughed as he lunged for me and I squealed, leaping from the bed and sprinting for the door. He chased me and I ran as fast as I could, feeling him closing in on me with each passing second.

I made it to the front room and he tackled me, knocking me to the ground and trapping me in his arms. I laughed as he flipped me over beneath him and he pinned my wrists above my head as his weight pressed me into the floor.

"So, tell me how it was again?" he asked, dipping his head to my neck and marking a path along the length of it with his tongue.

My traitorous body ached with desire for him, a rush of energy storming through my flesh and pooling in my core. I pulled in a heady breath.

"Good," I whispered.

His mouth trailed lower and his weight pressed me into the soft carpet.

"Just good?" he urged, his free hand running the length of my body and causing my spine to arch against my will.

"Really good," I conceded as he moved his mouth to mine and I melted against him. "Really fucking good," I sighed.

An engine sounded outside and we stilled. It cut off and the sound of three doors opening and closing quickly followed.

I laughed as Magnar dragged me to my feet before tossing me over his shoulder. He strode back to the bedroom with me captured like that and I put a half-assed effort into making an escape.

Magnar turned his head and sank his teeth into my ass, making me shriek in protest before he tossed me down onto the bed where I bounced as I looked up at him.

"The things I plan to do to you," he murmured, making my blood heat but I shrugged as if I was utterly unaffected by the sight of his powerful body looming over me.

"Promises, promises," I replied, rolling away from him and moving to the closet once more.

I snatched the first thing I found and pulled on some faded blue jeans and an emerald green crop top as I heard the front door opening.

I turned to Magnar and jerked to a halt as I found him in a pair of jeans and a black t-shirt. I blinked. Twice. He rolled his eyes as I continued to gawp at him in the modern clothes. I wanted to make some smart-ass remark but I simply stood there staring because the outfit made him look so...

"Callie?" someone called from the front of the house and I stilled at the sound of my name. No, not just someone, that was Montana. Her voice was the same but somehow entirely different as well.

Suddenly my feet were fixed to the ground. I couldn't move. I couldn't go out there and see what stood in place of my sister. I didn't know if I could face the changes brought on by her transformation. All of the fears which had been festering since the moment I'd let Erik Belvedere take her from me rose their heads and taunted me with my own stubbornness in coming here.

Magnar moved closer and took my hand in his, his expression grave but resolute. "Come on," he murmured. "You can't leave her waiting forever."

I nodded, stealing some strength from him as I inched towards the door. I padded silently along the carpeted corridor on my bare feet, closing in on this new reality with fear gripping my heart.

Please still be you. Please be the same. Please just be my Monty.

I stepped into the front room and released Magnar's hand. I was vaguely aware of Erik and Julius watching me but I didn't spare them any attention. Montana stood looking out of the window at the view, her back to me and her dark hair coiling down her spine.

"Hi," I breathed, so gently I wasn't sure the word actually left my lips.

She stilled and not in a human way; she ceased moving entirely. She was a statue filled with life and my heart leapt in fear at that one difference. If that much terrified me then how was I going to cope with the rest?

She turned towards me slowly and my lips parted as I took in the changes in her.

Her skin almost seemed to shimmer with a translucent sheen which was so pale it made her appear like moonlight given flesh. Her eyes were brighter, wider and yet somehow the exact same shade they'd always been. Her lips were fuller, redder. She was beyond beautiful, but it was in that unnatural way which only those creatures possessed.

And yet... she was still the same. Still my sister. My other half.

"Hi," she replied.

My face fell into a wide smile and I launched myself at her as tears sprung from my eyes. A surprised laugh left her lips just before she caught me. Her body felt unnaturally solid and too cold as I wrapped my arms around her, but it was still her. I knew it deep in my soul. I could feel it as we were reunited. We belonged together. My heart ached for her when she wasn't with me and I only felt whole again when we were holding each other like this. And that hadn't changed. It was exactly the same. We still fit together. Two pieces of the same puzzle. We completed each other.

"I love you, Monty," I breathed, wishing I'd said it more often because when she'd died it was all I could think. That I hadn't told her enough, even though she already knew. She should hear it more.

"I love you, Callie," she whispered back.

I was well aware that everyone else in this room could hear us easily, but it felt like we were alone for a moment. United against the world. I didn't care if we weren't supposed to love each other now. No power on heaven or Earth could stop me from feeling like this.

I stepped back reluctantly and looked at her more closely. She wasn't that different really. It was like I'd always looked at her in a dim light before but now she stood in full focus.

"I just realised something," I said excitedly. "I'm the oldest now!"

"No way," she replied with a frown. "Eighteen minutes, Callie - it makes all the difference."

I grinned at the phrase she'd thrown at me all throughout our childhood.

"You stopped aging two days ago, little sister," I countered with a grin. "So now I'm in charge."

"No! Tell her she's being insane, Erik." Montana turned to look at him expectantly and I followed her gaze, finding him staring at us with the strangest look on his face. Like he didn't quite know what to make of our exchange.

"Well, technically..." he began and Montana glared daggers at him.

"Ha!" I said triumphantly.

Montana pursed her lips and Erik shrugged at her apologetically.

"This is nice and cosy and all," Julius said as he moved to take a seat on the couch. "But before we start swapping friendship bracelets and coming up with an awesome name for our new gang - my vote goes to 'Julimacalana and the vampire scum' - how about we figure out what the fuck we're going to do now."

"He's right," I agreed. "The sooner we figure out the rest of the prophecy and end this curse, the better."

"Okay," Montana said enthusiastically. "Well I think at this point all we really need to figure out is how to get to the mountain and what debt needs to be paid."

"We've had an idea about that," Erik added, giving me a pointed look. "When Andvari first cursed us, it was because our families had stolen his treasure. They gave all of it back. Every piece but one which they couldn't find. A ring."

I glanced down at the ring on my hand and spun it on my finger. The longer I wore it, the better I was getting at wielding its power. I was already shielding the whole of this cottage from the gods without even giving it much thought.

"I told you they'd be searching for it," Magnar said heavily and I pursed my lips.

"Well they can't find it, can they? It's hidden from them." I shrugged defensively.

I didn't want to stop using the ring. I didn't want to give the gods the opportunity to find me again and learn what they thought about me using its power. And I certainly didn't want to feel my bond to Fabian again.

"Which would explain why they'd need it to be returned by someone who walks the Earth. The holy mountain is a place between the living and the afterlife; if we return it to them there then maybe the debt will be paid," Erik said.

"Or we just end up giving them the only thing we can use against them for no reason at all," I countered.

"Callie's right," Magnar said, moving towards me. "We shouldn't return it to them unless we are sure it's what the prophecy refers to. Without it, we will all be placed at their mercy once more and I don't want to risk that unless we're certain."

Montana sighed and dropped down onto the white couch. "So how can we be certain?" she asked.

No one had an answer to that and we all fell into silence.

Erik's phone rang and he answered it quickly. "Yes. She's fine." His eyes flicked to me and I bristled as I realised he was talking about me. "No. No, I don't think that's a good idea right now. I..." There was a long pause and I strained to hear whoever was on the other end of the line, but he was too far away even for my gifts.

Montana caught my eye and mouthed 'Fabian'.

My scowl deepened.

"Look, we only just got here but I'm sure she'll give it to her in a moment... No... I said *no*. Hold on." Erik glanced at us apologetically and headed outside.

"Do I even want to know?" I asked.

"He's a little obsessed," Montana said with half a smile. She pulled a folded piece of paper from her pocket and handed it to me. "I promised I'd give you that."

I glanced at Magnar before flipping it open and found him frowning at the letter with his arms folded, but he offered no comment on it.

"I'm hungry," Julius announced loudly. "Come brother, you look famished. Have you been working up an appetite in my absence?" He slapped a hand on Magnar's arm and guided him across the room to the kitchen.

I glanced down at the long letter in Fabian's elaborate cursive. At a push, I could read my own name written on the top line but the rest was indecipherable.

"I can't read that," I said, holding it out for Montana.

She hesitated as she took it. "He asked me not to read it," she explained. "He said it was just for you."

"Well if you don't then I'll have no idea what it says, so do you think he'd rather I don't read it at all or have you do it for me? Because I honestly don't care much either way."

Montana gave me a long look and I narrowed my eyes at her, knowing I'd said something that she didn't like.

"What?" I asked.

"I just feel a bit bad for him that's all. He didn't ask for that mark any more than you did."

"Not true," I countered. "He wanted me for a wife but I didn't want him for a husband. And surely he would have wanted to love his wife, right? He even told me as much himself; he's *glad* Idun did this to us. So if it's making him miserable then that's on him. It's the least he deserves."

Montana nodded and looked down at the paper for several seconds before shaking her head.

"I can't read that either," she admitted as she failed to interpret Fabian's handwriting. "We'll have to ask Erik."

"Okay then." I stood up, taking the letter with me as I headed for the door but Erik opened it before I could get there.

"Sorry about that, he's being...never mind. Did I miss anything?" he asked as he noticed me lurking in front of him.

"Can you read this?" I asked, shoving it under his nose.

He took it from me, scanning the paper briefly before pushing it back at me. "Fuck no. That's not meant for me anyway. Why don't you just read it yourself?"

I scowled at him, waiting for the penny to drop, but it didn't, so I spelled it out for him. "Because I can't read, which you can take the credit for if you like as you didn't think providing us with schools was important. So you owe me, wouldn't you say?"

"For fuck's sake." He held his hand out for the letter and I gave it to him. *"For my dearest wife, Callie."* He cleared his throat awkwardly

137

and I glanced over my shoulder to see Magnar frowning at us from the kitchen.

"Would you rather I just throw it away?" I asked him before Erik could continue.

I didn't really care what Fabian had to say to me and it certainly didn't interest me enough to let it bother Magnar.

"Let's hear it, brother," Julius answered before he could, his face set with amusement. "That parasite has walked the Earth for over a thousand years, he must know many things we could never hope to learn. Maybe it'll teach us a thing or two about how to win a woman's heart."

"Go on then," Magnar agreed, his expression softening in response to his brother's joke. "Let's hear it."

"He meant this for you alone," Erik said in a low voice and I could tell he was reluctant to read it aloud to everyone.

"Even if I could read it myself, do you really think I wouldn't tell them what it says anyway?" I countered.

"Alright," he sighed, rubbing a hand over his face like he was regretting this already. *"For my dearest wife, Callie, I hope you know how deeply sorry I am for any hurt that I have caused you. I understand why you felt you had to rip my head off but the fact that I am still alive can only be a testament to your true feelings for me."* Erik raised his eyes from the letter and I waved a hand for him to continue whilst trying not to let Fabian's assumption annoy me. I hadn't left him alive because of my true feelings; it had been because of my *false* feelings.

"I only want the chance to explain to you why I did what I did and to try and make it right. I can't bear to think of you in pain. It kills me. It tears me apart and burns the pieces. It eats me alive and spits me back out... There are a lot of these, can I skip over them?" Erik asked.

"Sure," I agreed as Montana drifted closer to me, clearly having changed her mind about this being a breach of privacy and enjoying the show.

"I would take any punishment you would dish out to me. You can beat me, whip me, chain me and have your way with me in any way you desire so that I might right what is broken between us – for the love of

the gods," Erik muttered before continuing. *"I have written you a poem so that you can understand the depths of my feelings for you.* Do I have to read the damn poem?" Erik asked, clearly not wanting to.

"Yes!" Julius and Montana said at the same time, and I had to bite my lip to stop myself from laughing. If I ignored the fact that Fabian was one of the most dangerous creatures in existence and his obsession with me could be deadly for the people I cared about, then I might actually be able to find this a little funny.

"I take no responsibility for this," Erik added before reading it out.

"Your eyes are so bright.
I think about them every night.
Your golden hair shines, just like sunlight.
I'm always worrying if you're alright.

Your skin is as soft as a chick's feather.
I will love you forever and ever.
You look amazing whatever the weather.
I won't stop loving you, not now, never.

Your mouth is the subject of my desire.
Each moment my love for you grows higher.
You make my loins burn with a raging fire.
If I said I could leave you, I'd be a liar.

Truly, my Callie, you have no flaws.
You smell like sunflowers and apple sauce.
So this is my promise: I'll always be yours.
I'll win you from Magnar's big meaty paws."

Julius started laughing first and Magnar cracked a second later. I tried to fight against it for Erik's sake but honestly, it was fucking hilarious.

"I look amazing whatever the weather?" I raised an eyebrow and I could see Erik fighting against the impulse to join in as Montana started laughing too. I actually kinda admired his loyalty to his brother as he managed to school his expression.

"I'm sure it sounded romantic in his head," Erik muttered, trying to salvage whatever remained of his brother's reputation. "He hasn't had a lot of practice with being in love."

"Let's hear the rest of it," Magnar demanded, his eyes dancing with amusement. "I need to know how hard I'm going to have to fight to keep you, Callie."

"It's not really meant to be funny," Erik said tersely but no one was listening and he shook his head as he returned his attention to the letter. "*I love you more than I could ever put into words, please end my torment. I need you. I crave you. I want to take you in my arms and feel your full lips against mine once more. I want to feel them on my neck, my chest, my...* You know what? If you want to find out what the rest of this says, then I suggest you just fuck him because it's really fucking detailed and I don't want to keep reading it." Erik held the letter out for me, and I took it with a snort of amusement before he turned and headed back outside.

I pressed my lips together as firmly as I could until he was gone, then Montana caught my eye and I lost it. We all burst into laughter once more and I could have sworn I heard Erik chuckling outside too.

ERIK

CHAPTER TWELVE

1000 YEARS AGO

I'd found a small tribe near the north-eastern coast and remained in the mountain range close by. They called me the Night Walker. Their children were told stories about me. They lived in fear of my name; the creature in human form who came at midnight to take blood from their people.

I'd attempted the same tactic we'd employed in our previous village, but these humans weren't so easily tricked. However, the arrangement had worked for me in the end once they'd started leaving out sacrifices for me to feed on. Those who broke the rules in their tribe were tied to a stake and left for me to devour. Though I never killed the victims, my bites were painful enough to strike fear in the hearts of the townsfolk.

I was lonely again. And so bored. The world was a blur, the days merging with the nights while I hid inside a large cave I'd found at the foot of a hollow mountain. I kept the company of bears and wolves. I'd even once tried to sate my hunger on one of their kills. But it was pointless. Only human blood could quench the curse's desire. So I remained there, living for the day that Magnar and his people would succumb to old age and pass out of this world forever.

It had only been a few years and I was already tired of waiting. The rumours of my existence had spread to a few of the closest tribes. It wouldn't be long before I'd have to leave this place behind. It was too risky to stay if word of my hideout reached the ears of the slayers.

I'd probably already lingered too long. Despite the less-than-ideal situation, it was better to have a constant blood supply than to uproot myself again in search of another tribe. I was at my most vulnerable when I was on the move. The slayers could sight me, or I could stumble across one of their camps. I knew they'd moved north in the hopes of finding us in the territories where the nights were longer. I'd heard the townsfolk speak of a fierce group of warriors living close to the sea a few miles south of here. They would head this way eventually. And I would be forced to run.

A storm was rolling in across the sky as I sat at the edge of my cave, waiting for the downpour to arrive. The air crackled with expectant energy, but the rain never came. Instead, a fork of lightning hit the ground in the forest to my right. I watched as it hit the same spot over and over, a frown creasing my forehead.

I'd never seen a storm act so strangely. Apart from...

My gut clenched as I rose to my feet. When the slayers had been blessed by the gods, one of them had wielded the weather with immense strength. But if she was close, surely that meant the others were too?

I growled my frustration. I hadn't had a good feed for over a week. I'd heard whispers of a thief being laid out for me this very night. But if I fled now, I'd miss my chance for blood. The sun was not yet set, though it was close. The storm clouds gave me the reprieve I needed to run in the final hour of daylight. So I flexed my muscles, making my decision.

I'd head into the town and take the blood I needed before I made my escape. It didn't matter if the disturbance caught the ears of the slayers. If they were this close already, they had no doubt heard the warnings of my proximity. Leaving without feeding was too dangerous. I didn't know how far I'd have to go before I discovered another suitable place to take up residence. So I would drink fast then run.

Damn those slayers. We don't even kill anymore, why can't they leave us be?

I started running toward the town, my feet pounding across the rocky ground. As I met the tree line and darted between two thick trunks, the rain was unleashed from the clouds. A torrent drenched me in seconds, but as I moved deeper into the dark wood, I was relieved from it by the thick canopy above.

The scent of a dampened fire hit my nostrils and I urged my legs faster, tearing toward the village.

Get blood. Get out. Run for your life.

I burst out of the trees, arriving at the edge of the village. Men and women were hurrying into their stone houses to escape the downpour. A child stood by the fire as smoke sailed from its doused embers. He was jumping in puddles, laughing as the water splashed up his legs.

I stalked closer, searching for another victim and the boy's eyes found mine, widening in fear.

"Night Walker!" he yelled in his native tongue and I cursed as a panic broke out around him. Those who hadn't made it to their houses turned at the voice, finding me standing at the edge of their home.

My eyes locked on a man as he raised an axe from his belt.

"Get back, monster!" he cried, shoving a woman toward the boy by the fire. She gathered him into his arms, running for shelter.

I let the man come to me, spotting several more gathering behind him with their weapons raised.

"I will not kill you," I told them, like I always did.

"Beast!" the man shouted, charging toward me with a battle cry.

I sighed, wishing I'd been able to sneak someone away rather than cause this much of a stir. But the slayers had forced my hand again. If I didn't get blood now, I was in trouble.

I tensed as the man approached, knocking the axe from his hand with ease before dragging him close to me by the scruff of his neck. His kinsmen backed off as I dug my fangs into his throat, drinking deeply.

Screams cleaved through the air as his friends and family watched me drink from him. A woman slashed at me with a knife, but I knocked her to the ground, lifting the man from his feet as I took the blood I so desperately craved.

When I'd had enough and the man was woozy, I dropped him to the ground, the mud splashing over his clothes. He scrambled back into the arms of his people, clutching the wound on his neck in terror.

Two men stepped forward to intercept me, but I'd gotten what I'd come for. I turned, sprinting back into the trees, leaving their shouts of anger far behind me.

I remained in the forest, heading west under the cover of the canopy. If the slayers were close, they would have been alerted by the noise of the townsfolk. And while they charted a path there, I was going to slip right under their noses into the night.

A grin pulled at my mouth over my victory. I was well-fed and now I could spend my next days heading further inland to hunt down a new tribe. Perhaps this time I could convince them to trust me. To keep my secret from the slayers. So long as I protected their home in return, there was a chance I could find a similar life to the one I'd had before.

The thought alone sent a spurt of energy into my limbs as I quickened my pace, darting through the trees.

Lightning struck the earth ahead of me and I hit the ground before I realised what had happened. I sprang upright, hunting the forest surrounding me, the ground sizzling from the impact of the strike. Perhaps it was a coincidence but I'd seen too much of the gods in my life to believe in that. The slayers were near. I just prayed there weren't too many of them.

When no warriors emerged from the trees, I took a sharp left and headed deeper into the forest. I sensed eyes on me and my skin tingled. I was being followed. But I was faster. I could outpace the slayers. And I damn-well would.

Another spear of lightning brought a tree down before me and I crashed into it, falling over the burning trunk onto the damp ground beyond it.

I bared my fangs, rolling onto my back as I waited for my attacker to appear. "Show yourself!" I roared, rising to my feet once more.

"I only wish to talk!" a female voice came in answer.

I hunted the shadows between the trees, backing up from the blazing fire before me. The rain slowly put it out so darkness reigned again. The woodland was quiet as animals scattered from the scene of devastation, and I listened for the approach of my enemies.

I turned to run but thunder boomed overhead and another fork of lightning ripped the ground in two before me. I backed up, sure I was being penned in, that whatever way I chose right now could equal my end.

Energy surged through me as I prepared for a fight.

She wanted to talk did she? Then why was she trying to burn me alive with the storm's power?

"Stop!" she commanded and I wheeled toward the sound of her voice.

She appeared from the shadows in a blue dress that clung to her lithe figure; it was near-transparent from the rain that soaked it and I quickly dragged my gaze up from the sight. Her face was a picture of beauty, her brown hair spilling down one side of her neck in a braid. In her hand was a golden sword.

I snarled, running to intercept her, but a harsh wind pushed me back, so fierce I had to dig my heels into the soft earth to stop myself from falling.

"Erik Belvedere?" she asked, a smile pulling at her lips.

"Yes, and who are you?" I growled, battling against the wind, desperate to rip her heart out before more of her clan arrived.

"I am Valentina Torbrook. Magnar Elioson's betrothed."

I stilled and the wind eased a fraction as I narrowed my eyes at her. "Why am I not dead yet?"

Her smile fell and she drifted a little closer. "Because I have been scorned by my husband-to-be. I am tired of his games. And I am tired of seeking his comfort and receiving the back of his hand instead."

I frowned at her words. So the great Earl Magnar beat his intended bride, did he? An ounce of pity found me despite the fact that she was a slayer. For all I knew, this could be a trick. But if it was, this woman was playing a long game. She could have attempted to kill me with the aid of her storm powers by now.

"And what does that have to do with me?" I snarled, baring my fangs.

She didn't react to my display of aggression, only seeming keener to close the gap between us. "I have spoken with the gods. They tell me of your family's great calling. That you are to be monarchs one day."

My eyes sharpened to slits. "And what god tells you such a thing? I have been fooled by them too before, but if you hadn't noticed I'm waist-deep in a shitty life here, trying to scrape by. I am hardly a monarch."

"Yes, but I think you might be. One day." Her earthy eyes glimmered and I had the strangest feeling she was admiring me. "I have news," she went on. "A gift of knowledge that could allow you and your kind to defeat the slayers once and for all."

My mouth opened and closed.

"Liar," I hissed eventually. "You must think me a fool if you expect me to trust a *slayer*."

She raised her hands in innocence. "I'm not just a slayer. I am a woman. Human. And I need more in my life than the empty existence my betrothed offers me. My clan disregard me, mock me. And I am tired of living that way. Why should I protect the people who show me no love?" Her voice cracked and a tear slid down her cheek.

If she was lying to me, she was damn good at it. Perhaps she was waiting for her clansmen to arrive and finish me. Perhaps she feared she couldn't do it herself. But I'd seen her wield the heavens; she was a force to be reckoned with.

"What is it you want from me?" I growled.

Slowly, she dropped to her knees, bowing her head. "I'll be your faithful follower. I'll help you ascend to power over the whole land. And I will offer you information that will assist you in ending the slayers. All I want in return is to have a place at your side."

My mind spun at the strange display from her. The wind still kept me from attacking her, but I could feel it easing as if she was about to place her life in my hands.

I bit down on the inside of my cheek, assessing her. "What information?"

A small smile crept back onto her face. "The prophets have foreseen a great war between the slayers and the vampires. They have told us that you and your kin are going into hiding for a hundred years to try and wait out our deaths."

My mouth parted in horror at such news. Could we hide nothing from these bastards? Were the gods so intent on having us fight them?

A feral noise rolled from my throat and Valentina winced, increasing the press of the wind again.

"So? You will all be dead by then," I snarled. "Will you train your children and your children's children just so you can have your fucking war?"

Valentina bowed her head, her dark hair falling around her beautiful face. "I can stop Magnar's descendants from ever being in that war...I will kill him and his brother to rid you of their plight."

My brows pulled together and I released a bitter laugh. "And why would you do that?"

Her eyes twinkled with tears as she looked up at me. "I am hurt and broken by Magnar. I would see him dead as you would."

I observed her closely, unsure if I could really place my faith in her, but I couldn't see the point in her lying either.

She went on, "I wouldn't have come to you if I wasn't desperate. But I have quietly admired your bravery in facing us. I know it was the god Andvari who placed this curse on you. I know you didn't choose it."

My heart softened at her words and I felt the urge to trust her. After so long without company, I couldn't deny it was a relief to speak with someone at last. But Magnar's betrothed? The chances of her truly being on my side seemed ludicrous. Yet I could see candour in her eyes. I could see the hurt he'd caused her. And it stoked a rage in me that begged to be appeased.

Valentina eyed me hopefully, evidently sensing my altered mood. "So perhaps I can stay with you tonight? The clans won't miss me before dawn. They remain south of here for now. And I can guide you away from them to ensure you don't cross paths."

I gritted my teeth, unsure how to respond. Taking the company of a slayer seemed like a fool's idea. But she had offered me a vital piece of information. And if it was true, then she really was betraying them.

"Why come to me?" I asked again. "Why not run from them and start a new life elsewhere? There is no need to take up with your enemies."

"I cannot abandon my vow. But like I said...the gods have spoken of you rising to power. I believe Idun will release me from it eventually. And I am willing to put all of my grievances aside to follow their righteous path."

My brow creased. "I don't do what the gods say."

"We all must, whether we want to or not is irrelevant. Each step we take is designed by them. So if they wish for you to rise to power, you will."

I wrestled with that possibility. I didn't care much for power. But I did care for a peaceful life. One me and my family could exist in without the fear of being hunted.

"Get up," I commanded and Valentina rose from the mud, releasing the pressure of the wind. She lifted her blade and I readied myself for an attack, but it didn't come. She slammed her sword into the muddy ground in a fierce gesture.

"I pledge myself to you," she said, taking hold of the straps of her dress and pulling them down her shoulders.

My face twisted in confusion as she dropped the dress to the ground, stepping out of it as thunder cracked overhead. A lump lodged in my throat as she moved toward me, completely bare, with her hands outstretched. Her naked body was perfectly curvaceous, her breasts full and tempting.

"How long has it been since you had the company of a woman?" she asked, her eyes glittering as lightning arced through the clouds above us.

I backed up, certain she was just trying to get close enough to rip out my heart. That had to be her ploy.

"Don't fear me," she begged, and I couldn't stop my eyes from roaming across her naked flesh, a new kind of hunger growing in me. I had yearned for the touch of a human woman for so many years. But this wasn't just any woman. She was a slayer. And Magnar's betrothed.

Although...the idea of taking something like that from him sparked a heated lust in me.

I cleared my throat, backing away. "I don't know what games you're playing, slayer, but I am not going to fall for them."

"No games." She raised her hand, pressing her finger to a tattoo on the skin above her heart. "Magnar has branded me as his. But he has bedded many woman in all our years of betrothal and humiliated me. Now I am taking my destiny into my own hands. The gods wish me to have a powerful husband, so I am choosing another one for myself."

"Husband?" I murmured, backing up again and my spine collided with a tree.

She sauntered toward me, her hips swaying seductively as she approached. I bared my fangs, stepping forward but she pressed a warm hand to my chest, pushing me back against the trunk. My eyes roamed to her breasts and I cursed myself for my weakness as she moved closer, the scent of her delicious skin rolling beneath my nose.

"I can be everything you've ever dreamed of," she purred, placing a finger under my chin and lifting her mouth towards mine. She was obviously unarmed but I still expected her to turn on me at any second. My muscles coiled as I prepared to intercept the attack she was about to unleash on me.

It never came. Her mouth captured mine in the first kiss I'd had since I'd been turned. She moulded her body against mine, sliding a hand around the back of my neck as she arched into me with desire. Wanting me as I was, as this monster that the world recoiled from.

I was torn between a thousand conflicting emotions as she slid her palm down my chest and took hold of my waistband.

Fear rose in me as I recalled Andvari's words. That we could have children with humans.

"No," I growled, knocking her hand away. "We cannot do this. There's too much at risk." I pushed her back and she stumbled, her eyebrows pinching together.

She ran her hand to a coiling rune above her pubic bone, caressing her skin. "I can't bear children out of wedlock, vampire. If that is what concerns you."

My throat constricted at her words and she closed the distance between us again, her eyes lighting with hunger.

"Have me," she commanded, placing my hands on the silken skin of her waist.

My resolve weakened. I'd been so alone for so long. And despite the terrible repercussions this was probably going to cause, in that moment, I wanted her. I longed to desire someone again. I needed a woman's warm flesh against mine. I wanted to remember what it was like to *feel* again. And I wanted to feel wanted in kind.

Her hand snaked beneath my waistband and I sucked in air as she gripped my cock in her fist. I lost myself, a slave to this single moment in time, forgetting right from wrong and giving myself to my basest urges.

I spun her around, flinging her against the tree with force and giving myself to her tender skin. I hooked her thigh over my hip and drove myself inside her, fucking her with all the pent up fury in my body and taking out my rage with the gods upon her flesh.

She moaned my name and sometimes she moaned Magnar's, which only spurred me on to make her forget all about him.

I knew I was going to regret this. But fuck it. I was going to take Magnar's betrothed and damn the consequences.

MONTANA

CHAPTER THIRTEEN

L aughing with my sister felt like the sun shining on my back. Everything was impossibly alright. We weren't broken. We were entirely whole. And even better than that, we were all actually *happy*. I was standing amongst the slayers with no desire to hurt them. The scent of their blood floated around me, but I didn't care. It was easy enough to ignore it, and I had just *known* that would be the case.

Callie and I were on the couch, going over what had happened at the statue and cursing the gods for all they'd done. When she gently pushed my upper lip up to inspect my fangs, I relaxed at the look of pure curiosity in her eyes instead of fear.

"Erik!" I heard Clarice calling outside and tension built in my chest at her frantic tone.

The slayers stiffened as I headed out of the door into the dreary daylight, spotting Clarice running down the lawn towards Erik.

I joined him and the slayers exited the cottage a moment later with their weapons in hand. They gathered behind me as Clarice arrived, and she darted around the silver Porsche we'd driven down here in and came to an abrupt halt before Erik. Her gaze strayed to the group behind me with a flicker of fear.

"It's fine. They won't attack you," Erik insisted. "What's wrong?"

Clarice dragged her eyes back to her brother. "Wolfe's been sighted right near Realm A. He was with Valentina. I think she's planning an attack on the humans," she said, looking worried. "We have to go. I've called for back-up, but if we hurry, we'll get there first to intercept her and the biters."

Erik clawed a hand into his hair, looking to me. "You can stay here with-"

"No," I said immediately and the word was echoed behind me from the slayers.

I turned to them in surprise and spotted Magnar unsheathing one of his large blades. "We'll go with you. Valentina's death is mine."

"Erik..." Clarice said cautiously. "We can't take them, it's madness."

"No, wait. It's fucking genius," Erik announced. "She won't expect them. And they're a force to be reckoned with."

"You should know," Julius said with a smirk.

Erik ignored him, pointing back up the hill to direct Clarice. "Let's move. They can ride in the back of the van, out of sight."

Clarice stood her ground, shaking her head. "I'm not fighting beside a bunch of slayers."

"I don't exactly want to fight next to you and your parasite friends either, but we want Valentina dead as much as you do," Julius snarled.

"She has betrayed us all," Magnar said, surprising me by being the voice of reason. "Whether you agree or not, we're going."

"Erik," Clarice begged. "I can't bear it."

"Well you can stay here then, GW," Julius said, setting off at a fierce pace up the hill. "That's short for Golden Whore by the way."

Erik shrugged at his sister, jogging past her and I ran to keep pace with him. He threw me a look as if he was fascinated by me and I smiled widely back at him.

"You haven't been trained to fight," he said with an anxious frown.

"I'll have you all there with me and I'm strong enough to do *something*. Besides, I have Nightmare."

He nodded firmly as we crested the hill and started sprinting along the path that led to the house. Clarice tore past us, speeding up the track and racing by Julius. I heard him shouting curses at her and wondered if the slayers and Erik's family were ever truly going to see eye to eye. The hate between them had given way to an alliance for now. But if our common cause ever went away, I wondered how quickly they would descend into battle again.

Callie hurried to my side and fear crashed into me as I realised something.

"Wait." I grabbed Erik's arm to stop him and Callie halted with us.

"Fabian's at the house," I announced, looking at my sister with anxiety bubbling inside me.

Magnar pulled up beside us, gritting his teeth.

"He'll join us against Valentina," Erik said. "We need the numbers. I can't leave him out of this."

Callie glanced at Magnar. "It's okay, I have the ring. He can't affect me."

He brushed a lock of hair from her neck with a gentle caress. "I know, but I'm not sure I can restrain myself around that parasite."

"You have to," Callie urged and I nodded my agreement.

The last thing we needed was another fight breaking out between us. We needed to unite now more than ever.

Erik glanced up the path to where Julius and Clarice were heading out of sight. "We don't have time to discuss it. Fabian's coming. You can ride with me so you don't have to face him."

"So long as he stays away from her too," Magnar demanded and the tension ran out of my shoulders as Erik nodded his agreement.

We started running again and I pushed my muscles to their limits as the air whipped through my hair. Despite being undead, I felt more alive than I ever had. I'd never thought being a vampire could feel so *good*. This curse was so easily disguised as a gift. Without the thirst, perhaps it could have been. But so long as the desire for blood lived in me, I knew I would never stop trying to solve the prophecy. No immortality, no god-given strength and no unceasing energy would ever be enough to change my mind on that.

Erik and I reached the house before Callie and Magnar and we halted beside his van. Julius stood next to it, but Clarice had walked over to a shiny black car on the other side of the driveway. Fabian stared out of the window, looking over our shoulders in the direction my sister was coming from.

"Are you sure it's a good idea to let him near Callie?" I asked Erik.

"We need his help," he said. "We can't risk Valentina getting away again."

"Wolfe's with her," I whispered, hatred boiling in my chest.

Fear ran through my blood at the thought of seeing him again. But I wasn't the weak human he'd known before. I was his equal. More than that. I was Erik's wife. A princess. And I had the strength of my friends behind me too.

Erik nodded, taking hold of my waist. "His death is yours, rebel. I owe you it."

A smile curved my lips as his words started a fire in my soul. "Together?"

"Together," he agreed with a smile, pecking my lips and sending a shiver darting down my spine.

I didn't know if I was ready for this fight, but with Erik by my side I sure as shit felt unstoppable.

CALLiE

CHAPTER FOURTEEN

I rounded the corner of the massive house which had logs stacked up to make the walls, and placed my hand on Fury as adrenaline began to pound through my limbs. This was the nightmare I'd had every night for as far back as I could remember. Vampires breaking into the Realm and hunting humans like we were wild animals. But in my nightmares I'd always been terrified, a victim, unable to defend myself or anyone else. That wasn't the case now.

Magnar walked beside me with Venom and Tempest strapped to his back and I looked up at him, my heart swelling with appreciation for what he'd given me. He'd done so much more than just save me when he'd found me. He'd given me something I never could have dreamed of; the ability to fight back. And even with the cost of the vow and the weight of the gods' eyes resting on me, that was something I couldn't place a price on. Too long had humans lived subject to the vampires' rule, used for their blood and given little attention beyond that. I never would have imagined that I'd be heading to save them with a group of vampires helping me though. Somehow my whole world had been flipped on its axis and I was left hurrying to adapt. But I wouldn't have changed a moment of it.

The van and a black car sat on the drive in front of the house and I stilled as the car door opened and Fabian stepped out.

His eyes were locked on me and Magnar released a feral snarl, pulling Tempest from his back as he shifted into a defensive position.

I drew Fury too and glared at the creature who called me his wife.

"By the gods, Fabian," Erik cursed as he shot into the space between us in a rush of motion. "We have bigger problems than your broken heart at the moment."

"I just need to talk to her," Fabian breathed, his eyes never leaving me.

"Not now," Erik said through gritted teeth, but Fabian wasn't giving up. He took a step towards me and Erik grabbed his shoulder to halt him.

Everyone else just stood watching, wondering what Fabian was going to do as tension coiled through the air.

"Please, Callie," Fabian begged. "I don't understand. I don't know why you won't even talk to me. I know I did a terrible thing but I just, I can't-"

"You can't stop wondering if she's alright?" Julius suggested with a barely concealed snigger.

"Don't," Erik warned as Fabian's eyes narrowed.

"Maybe he needs some water," Julius added, ignoring Erik. "To put out that fire in his burning loins."

Magnar laughed tauntingly as he raised Tempest higher and Fabian lunged at him.

"*Shit.*" Erik wrapped his arms around his brother and Clarice shot forward to help hold him back too. Fabian snarled with a promise of death in his eyes as he tried to fight his way out of their grip.

"We don't have time for this," Montana said angrily. "The people in Realm A need us right *now.*"

"You fucking savages should have died nine hundred years ago with the rest of your people," Fabian spat, glaring at Magnar and Julius as he continued to fight against his siblings' hold on him. "We had you beaten yesterday and you know it!"

"*I'm* one of those savages you hate so much," I growled, stepping between him and Magnar. "So you must hate me too."

His face fell and he stopped fighting as he shook his head. "No. No, I love you. I just need you to hear me out. I need you to see-"

"That she has no flaws? And that she smells like sunflowers and apple sauce?" Julius cut in with another bark of laughter.

"We need to go," Montana insisted and I agreed with her but it was obvious Fabian wasn't going to let this drop any time soon.

"Fine," I snapped. "I'll talk to you if that's what it takes to get you to stop."

"Truly?" Fabian asked, his face written with hope. "Now?"

"You can ride in the car with us," Clarice offered. "No one would question seeing you with your husband."

I bristled at the word but let it go in favour of us getting the hell out of here. "Okay, let's go."

"No," Magnar snarled. "I'm not leaving you alone with him."

I turned to him and raised an eyebrow. "I thought we'd gotten past you telling me what to do?"

"I'm not letting you put yourself at risk," he replied dismissively.

"Well that's where you don't have to worry," I said, rising onto my tiptoes so I could press a kiss to the corner of his mouth. "Because you don't 'let' me do anything. I'm not a possession and I make my own choices."

I took a step back and he caught my wrist to stop me. Fabian hissed angrily, but I ignored him as I held Magnar's eye and waited for him to release me.

"Just... be careful," he said eventually, and I could tell he really hated this idea. "And feel free to stab him if you have to."

His fingers left my skin and I gave him a small smile before moving towards the car. I got into the back and Fabian followed me. I slid across the seats and he pulled the door shut behind him as he stared at me.

Clarice got into the front and started up the engine.

We pulled away and the silence stretched until I was forced to speak first.

"For someone who's so desperate to talk to me, you don't seem to have much to say," I growled.

"I don't know where to begin," he said, leaning towards me across the space which divided us.

I stabbed Fury into the seat between us and left it impaled in the leather. "That's a line. Don't cross it," I warned him.

"Oh for the love of the gods," Clarice swore from the front seat. "Do you know how difficult it will be to get that repaired?"

"Shut up, Clarice," Fabian snapped. "I'll buy you a new fucking car. Just don't interrupt us again."

Clarice scowled at us in the rear view mirror but she didn't say anything further, and I looked back at Fabian.

"So, what did you think of my letter?" he asked me and an amused smile tugged at my lips.

"This is precisely what I keep trying to tell you; you don't know me at all so there's no way you can love me," I replied.

"I don't understand," he said with a frown.

"I can't read. Which, to be honest, you should be well aware of anyway, as apparently you're the one who designed the Realms to be the way they are. So you obviously know we don't have schools. And there are hardly any books either."

Fabian's mouth fell open and he went to reach for me before eyeing Fury between us and dropping his hand. "I'm sorry. That was so thoughtless of me." He smacked his palm into his forehead and I blinked at him in surprise. "So who did you ask to read it for you?"

"Well, I figured you wanted me to know what it said so I asked Erik to read it aloud."

Fabian nodded like he understood but I could see that it made him uncomfortable.

"And...the others were listening too," I added, figuring I might as well be honest. "Sorry." Now that I was looking him in the face I felt a bit bad about us all laughing at it earlier but that poem had been quite something.

Anger flashed in his eyes, quickly followed by humiliation as he scrambled for what to say to me. I suddenly realised this whole thing might go a lot easier if I just used the ring on him.

"I want to show you something," I said hesitantly. "To prove to you

164

that you don't really love me-"

"But I do! You're the only thing I can think about, I can't get you out of my head. I keep trying to sleep hoping that you'll find me in my dreams again and-"

I held up a hand to stop him, embarrassment clawing at my cheeks. "Please stop saying that. It's so unbelievably awkward. You don't know the first thing about me and you're only acting this way because of what Idun did to us. But I can block her sway over you for a little while to prove to you that it's not real. You just have to promise not to attack me if I do."

"Attack you? I'd sooner cut out my own heart, rip off my limbs and-"

"Holy shit, just stop it!" I twisted the ring on my finger and pushed against the bubble of protection it was offering me until it surrounded Fabian too.

He fell unnaturally still. His eyes continued to roam over me but instead of the desperation that had been there a moment ago, I found confusion.

"I... You..." He shook his head like he didn't know where he was.

"It's gone now, right? You don't look at me and feel like you have some weird insta-love connection to me anymore, do you?"

"I still want you," he breathed and I frowned, shaking my head in refusal. How could he still feel it with the ring blocking the bond? "But I don't... I don't..."

I fished his letter from my pocket and held it out to him. "Read that. And tell me if you were sane when you wrote it."

He took it from me hesitantly as if he didn't want to remember the words he'd put down. I watched as his eyes darted over the page, his face scrunching up in disgust before he finally shredded the whole thing into a thousand tiny pieces and let them fall to the floor.

"Dammit Fabian," Clarice growled in response to the mess, but he ignored her.

He stared at his lap for several long seconds then turned his eyes to me again and I almost flinched from the rage I found there.

"Did you say that you let my brother read this *aloud* to those fucking

165

slayers?" he hissed.

I recoiled a little as I nodded and I eyed Fury, wondering if I'd be able to grab it before he could reach me.

"You should be angry at Idun," I whispered. "Not me."

His frown deepened and his gaze trailed over me. I wished I'd worn something which hid my body instead of this stupid thin crop top.

"You're still my wife," he said, his voice low.

I snatched Fury from the seat between us and pointed it at him. "No. I'm not," I replied fiercely. "And you don't love me. So why don't you just forget about me?"

"Just because I was forced to love you, doesn't mean I didn't want it," he replied. "I haven't felt like that in... I don't think I've ever felt like that."

"Love is the most wonderful thing in the world," I said slowly. "But you don't get to take it. You have to earn it."

"But I *can* take it," he replied, his eyes falling to the ring on my hand. "I only have to remove that and you'll feel it again too."

He lunged at me so quickly that I didn't manage to react in time. He caught my wrist, twisting it sharply so I dropped Fury, his other hand grabbing my throat as he shoved me back against the window, my head cracking against the glass painfully.

I cursed, kicking and shoving him as I dragged the ring's power away from him and Clarice shouted at him to stop from the front of the car which swerved across the road as she lost focus.

Fabian blinked heavily as his emotions were thrown into turmoil again and his love for me returned. His face was inches from mine and his hand still clasped my throat but he released me as soon as he comprehended what he was doing.

I stared into his eyes, panting against the adrenaline which had filled me with his attack and only realised he was about to kiss me a second before he tried it. My boot connected with his chest and I managed to kick him off of me before his lips could find mine. Fabian slammed back into the opposite window, shattering it before falling back into his seat with a curse as glass rained down over him.

I snatched Fury from the floor in the moment I gained while he was disoriented and bared my teeth as I tightened my grip on the blade which was chanting encouragement for his death.

"You'd better keep your word and get me a new car after this, you asshole," Clarice snapped as the car sped along the highway behind the van carrying the others.

"I'm so sorry!" Fabian gasped, reaching towards me, but I was done playing nice with him.

I lunged at him with a snarl on my lips, shoving him back against the door as I pressed Fury to the skin above his heart and leaned over him, the threat blazing in my eyes.

"I've tried telling you how I feel. I've tried showing you how *you* feel. But none of it is getting through to you, so I'm going to spell it out. I am not your wife. I am not your girlfriend. Hell, I'm not even your fucking friend. My heart belongs to Magnar. It will never be yours. *I* will never be yours. And if you *ever* lay a hand on me like that again, I'll fucking kill you." I shoved him away from me and climbed into the front of the car, dropping down beside Clarice and looking out of the window while ignoring her shocked expression.

"You know Fabian, I can actually see what you like in her," his sister murmured and I ground my teeth as I refused to acknowledge the comment.

"I don't like her," Fabian replied sadly. "I love her."

I let out a huff of irritation and kept my gaze fixed on the view beyond the window. This whole thing had been a colossal waste of my time.

MONTANA

CHAPTER FIFTEEN

Erik drove down the highway at a fierce speed, overtaking cars with incredible skill. My eyesight picked out every movement of the vehicles around us and I wondered what it would be like to drive something like this. Maybe I'd take his keys sometime and give it a go. It wasn't like I could die now anyway.

The tension in Erik's jaw told me of his anxiety and I reached over to rest a hand on his knee. He threw me a small smile, taking a road off of the highway and speeding along into the city. We took a turn left and the huge river appeared before us, its water dark under the heavy clouds. Lightning speared through the sky on the other side of it, causing my heart to tighten uncomfortably.

"That's the Realm," Erik growled. "She's there. I just hope we're not too late."

I laid a hand on Nightmare at my hip as Erik pulled up to a huge bronze bridge, stopping at a line of guards barring the way forward. One of them hurried to the side of the van, shifting a large gun strapped across his chest. Erik opened the window a crack and I realised the glass was tinted, hiding us from view.

"Prince Erik," the man said in surprise.

"Valentina is attacking Realm A. Send your officers to help," Erik commanded and the man bowed his head, looking alarmed as he ran back to the line of guards and ushered them aside.

We pulled onto the massive bridge, tearing over it at speed. Huge cables reached up to towering stone archways above us and my mind whirled with how such a thing had been constructed.

We met the road with a bump on the other side and I glanced over my shoulder, spotting Clarice's car following us across the bridge. I hoped Callie was alright with Fabian. She could sure as shit hold her own, but he could be a persistent asshole if ever I knew one.

Thunder boomed through the air and hailstones hit the windshield in a torrent.

We took streets left and right and the large wall surrounding Realm A came into view ahead. I toyed with Nightmare in my hand, nerves running through me in a wave as the blade purred excitedly about the deaths it wished to claim.

Erik slowed the van to a halt outside the metal gates. They were closed and there was no sign of any guards manning them. I gazed up at the empty lookout point above and my gut coiled into a tight ball as I spotted a pile of clothes there.

Erik stepped out of the vehicle and I swiftly followed. The hail had turned to a downpour of rain and it slid over my skin, drenching me instantly. Despite the thin dress I wore, I couldn't feel its icy embrace. It ran off of me like I was made of stone, the cold unable to penetrate my skin.

Julius and Magnar exited the back of the van, holding their swords ready.

"Let's break the gate down," Magnar growled.

"Wait," Erik hissed. "We should see what we're dealing with first." He gazed up at the high wall and I moved to his side.

"Can you toss me up there?" I asked and his eyes glittered with the idea.

Clarice's car arrived, skidding to a halt and splattering mud up Julius's legs.

"Argh," he snapped as Callie sprang out of the car and Clarice stepped out of the driver's seat a second later.

"Oops," Clarice said with a wicked grin.

"Oh the Golden Whore is working really hard to get my attention, isn't she?" Julius said, smoothing a hand through his hair.

"You fucking piece of-" Clarice started but I got between them with a firm look.

"Stop, we have to focus."

Fabian exited the back of the car and I noticed an immediate difference in Erik's brother. His jaw was ticking and he moved swiftly away from my sister as if he was actively trying to avoid her. I wondered how their discussion had gone, but I figured now wasn't the right time to ask.

Erik took my hand. "I'll throw you up there. Just have a look and come straight down."

"I'll go too." Callie moved to Magnar's side, seeming anxious to get away from Fabian.

Magnar brushed a thumb over her cheek in greeting, eyeing Fabian with a glare. "Are you alright?"

"I'm fine. He's still not listening to me though," she murmured.

"Up you get then." Magnar linked his hands together and Callie stepped onto them.

Erik moved behind me, guiding me towards the wall, dropping his mouth to my ear. "Be careful."

"I'll be fine," I whispered.

I had to do this for the humans. I was in a position to protect them now and I was more than willing to take on that responsibility.

Thunder cracked overhead and my stomach dropped dramatically. Erik took my waist and with a powerful lift of his arms, he threw me above his head. My heart soared into my throat as I was propelled upwards and I caught the top of the wall with surprising ease. Callie was already there, offering me an encouraging smile as I joined her.

We crouched low, gazing down into the huge town that spread out before us. All was quiet apart from the rain pounding the streets.

"This is how the humans live here?" Callie asked in awe.

I nodded, throwing her a sad look. "Yep, this is Fabian's lie to the other royals."

"Asshole," she snarled, taking Fury from her hip.

"I'm fixing it!" Fabian called, but Callie ignored him.

"Where is everyone?" I breathed, searching the streets for any signs of life.

No blood, no screams, nothing.

My neck prickled uncomfortably. Something wasn't right.

I glanced down at the others below, shaking my head.

"There's no one here," I whispered, knowing they'd hear me.

"Wait, look," Callie hissed, pointing toward a large town hall at the centre of the Realm. A light was on inside, though the rest of the buildings were dark around it. Without another word, she flung herself over the edge, landing in a crouch below.

I followed her and heard Erik swear beyond the wall as I hit the ground, rising to my feet beside Callie. She gazed around, running her thumb over Fury and standing guard while I hurried to the gate.

It was bolted shut with several locks, so I started unlocking them as fast as I could and soon had it open, pushing it wide to let the others in.

Erik jogged to meet me with an anxious expression. "Stay by my side from now on. Don't be a rebel today."

I took his hand, squeezing it as an answer. I didn't even know what this new body of mine was capable of yet, and I had no intention of parting from him or the others.

Clarice hurried toward us, looking down at a phone in her hand. "Back up is twenty minutes away. And I can't get hold of Miles or Warren. Maybe we should wait."

"Fuck waiting." Julius stalked past her, rolling his shoulders. "Let's go gut some biters."

Magnar chuckled, prowling to his side and the two of them set off down the street like wolves on the scent of blood.

"For fuck's sake," Erik muttered before taking chase and Callie hurried to keep pace with them.

Clarice moved beside me, seeming anxious as she tucked her phone away. Fabian pushed his sleeves up, looking ready for a fight.

I took Nightmare from my hip, reaching for its power and it hummed with energy, but that wasn't much use to me, considering it was detecting the royal vampires surrounding me. But as we drew closer to the town hall, its vibrations deepened.

The slayers reached the hall first, ducking down and moving to the side of the building beneath a set of tall windows. I followed suit with Erik, Fabian and Clarice and we shuffled up beside the slayers, leaning back against the wall.

"Better take a look," Julius whispered, slowly standing and peeking through the window. He immediately ducked back down, spewing curses.

"What is it?" Erik demanded in a hushed voice.

"Biters. A fuck-load of them," Julius hissed. "They've got the whole town in there by the looks of it. And they're feeding on them."

Worry clawed at my gut. I'd been like those humans once, too weak to fight back. A fierce anger grew in me. I was going to save them for the sake of all the people I hadn't been able to save in my Realm.

"We should wait for back-up," Clarice reiterated.

"She's right," Fabian agreed. "We can't take them all on alone."

"The humans will be dead by the time your back-up arrives," Magnar snarled, shaking his head. "Me, Julius and Callie will head around back and sneak inside. The rest of you bloodsuckers can cause a distraction."

I ground my teeth, looking to Erik and he nodded stiffly.

"Wait," Clarice grabbed Erik's arm. "We can't."

"We can," Erik insisted. "We'll buy the slayers time to get the humans out."

"How can you trust them?" Clarice growled, raindrops making her golden hair cling to her cheeks.

Magnar answered first. "The whole point of our existence is to protect humans from parasites like you, so I'd worry more about trusting yourselves than us."

Clarice scowled, looking ready to argue but Erik snared her attention. "We have to work with them."

Callie took my hand and I turned to her. "Be safe."

"You too." I nodded.

"Look after yourself," Fabian murmured, his eyes flicking to Callie

173

then back to the dirt at his feet.

She stared at him a moment and I could have sworn a hint of empathy crossed her gaze. She shook her head then hurried away with the slayers, ducking beneath the windows as they moved out of sight.

"Well that's just perfect," Fabian spat, seeming more like himself now that Callie wasn't close. "They can stay out of harm's way while we take on a horde of angry biters."

"Scared Fabian?" Erik goaded and Fabian's eyes narrowed.

"That's not what I meant," he muttered.

"Come on," I pressed, crawling back in the direction we'd come.

We arrived at the front of the building and rose to our feet before the arching wooden doors.

"What's the plan? Knock on the damn door?" Fabian growled.

"I have a better idea," Erik said and he slammed his foot into the doors, sending them flying open and crashing back against the walls inside.

My throat tightened as I spotted Valentina standing on a raised wooden platform at the centre of the massive hall. She wore a crimson dress with a split up one leg and her hair was pulled into a high ponytail. The humans were all on their knees before her, hundreds of them cowering between a large ring of biters. They were penned in by the mass of Valentina's followers like a flock of sheep surrounded by hungry wolves. Several of them were held in the arms of the vampires, their throats torn and their faces pale. My stomach churned violently and I lifted Nightmare, terrified of how outnumbered we were.

"Hello, Erik," Valentina purred. "We've been waiting for you."

"Let the humans go," Erik commanded, baring his fangs. He looked furious, ready to kill every biter in the room.

"Come inside," Valentina encouraged and lightning hit the ground behind us, causing us to leap into the building. The doors caught light and flames licked their way up them toward the ceiling. Fear crawled through my veins, but I willed it away, wanting to face this woman and her vile followers.

Valentina grinned in response and I closed ranks with the others, readying for the fight that was about to unfold.

"Erik...Fabian....Clarithe," the deep, lispy voice drew my attention and hatred burned in my veins as my gaze locked on Wolfe. He stood to my left beside several more biters and I didn't rate my chances at getting close to him. "How nithe to thee you again." He held a young woman in his arms, pressing a blade into her shoulder. As blood dribbled from the cut, he bent down and licked it away, making her scream in horror, and when his lip peeled back, I saw the gaps where his fangs had once been.

"Monster," I snarled at him and his eyes narrowed on me.

"Montana, you're one of uth? So you mutht have tathted the thweetneth of human blood? Do you thmell it? Doethn't it make you hungry?" His absent fangs must have caused the lisp in his speech and it was difficult to understand him.

"I'd never bite a human," I growled, my back tensing as I took a step forward.

Erik caught my arm, holding me in place.

Valentina released a tinkling laugh. "We don't have to fight. Just do as I ask, Erik."

"And what's that?" my husband snarled.

"Come with me," she said simply. "I only want you. Nothing else."

"Why?" I demanded, my free hand curling into a tight fist.

Her eyebrows lifted as she took me in then she turned back to Erik. "So you don't mind having a vampire wife after all?" she asked. "Why is it you denied *me* a place at your side?" she hissed and a flash of hurt entered her dark eyes.

Erik growled at her words. "I'd never have actually married you, Valentina."

"You were just Erik's play-thing. And mine too sometimes," Fabian said with a dry laugh.

Erik's grimace increased and my heart clenched as the tension in the room rose.

Valentina's face contorted in rage. "Liars!"

A gust of wind slammed into us from behind, forcing us toward her.

Valentina shifted irritably on her six inch heels, glaring directly at Erik. "You loved me."

"I have never loved anyone but my wife," Erik snarled at her. "And

I'm not going anywhere with you."

Valentina's mouth curved into a perfect smile. "Wrong." She clicked her fingers and the biters came at us so fast I wasn't ready.

I lifted Nightmare with a scream of defiance tearing from my throat.

"Lead them outside!" Erik commanded as he smashed his fist into a male's face, knocking him to the ground.

I darted toward the fallen biter, ramming Nightmare into his chest and sending him spiralling into death.

Clarice danced between the mass of vampires, bringing several to their deaths with a silver blade, but Fabian was monstrous, tearing out their hearts with his bare hands.

I barely had time to react as a female slammed into my back and I stumbled forward. It took me a second to figure out her strength didn't compare to my own. She was a lesser and I realised with a terrifying clarity, I was an Elite. I tore her from my shoulders, driving Nightmare into her chest as she hit the floor with impossible ease.

I turned to run outside, drawing the biters after me as Erik had commanded. I leapt through the fiery doorway into the rain and two biters took chase, trying to take me down together. The animal part of me took over and Nightmare guided my actions as they raked their nails across my flesh. The shoulder of my dress ripped but the culprit met her end as Nightmare sank deep into her heart.

The male who remained was fast, darting around me like a deadly shadow, evading Nightmare's blows.

The Belvederes led the fight further into the square, ripping off heads and limbs until blood mixed with the rain at our feet. Erik released a grunt as five biters took him to the ground.

I cried out in a panic as I tried to move toward him but my assailant took the advantage, grabbing my wrist and twisting it with all their might.

Pain sped up the bruised bone and I dropped Nightmare, the blade clattering to the ground. Panic swallowed me as the biter leapt at me, and I stumbled back as my ankle hit the kerb of the street, falling to the pavement beneath him. He ripped his nails across my face and I yelled in anger.

My injured wrist started to heal but not quickly enough. I threw a hard punch to his jaw with my other hand and he flew off of me from the power of my strike. I didn't hesitate again, leaping forward to straddle him and grabbing hold of his throat. Nightmare glittered on the ground several feet away. But it was too far. And a feeling of dread pounded through me as I knew what I had to do. I had to let the vampire in me take over.

I wrenched his neck sideways, hearing bones break then punched a hole in his chest. My fingers found his heart and I fought the nausea that gripped me as I squeezed. The vampire exploded to ash beneath me and my knees hit the concrete, my win secured.

I rose on shaky feet, coated in ash and unsettled by what I'd done. I snatched Nightmare from the ground, turning to find Erik amongst the swarm of biters.

He was on his feet again, slashing throats and turning the monsters to dust with a brutal savagery. Relief filled me, but it was swiftly wiped out as a cold voice poured over me from behind.

"Hello Montana," Wolfe growled and I spun to face him, spotting a savage knife in his grip. "Leth thee how thtrong you are againtht a real opponent."

CALLIE

CHAPTER SIXTEEN

We slipped behind the huge building where the wall rose up over us and the only way in was a small window high above our heads.

Magnar cupped his hands and I stepped into them as Julius kept watch behind us.

He launched me skyward and I leapt out of his hold and caught the windowsill, pulling myself high enough to peer inside. I jammed the toes of my boots into the brickwork as I looked down at the humans who were penned inside.

Chaos reigned within the building where biters lined the walls, stopping the panicking townsfolk from escaping and more than one of them was feeding on the humans too, making my lip peel back in anger. A fight was taking place near the open doorways, spilling out beyond the building and making it impossible to see what was happening with my sister and the Belvederes.

I spotted Valentina screaming orders from a stage which was raised towards this end of the building. She was dressed all in red with her dark hair pulled back in a long ponytail and a cluster of her followers swarmed around her, clearly acting as guards.

The humans screamed in panic as they clamoured to escape the fighting and the biters howled with excitement while keeping them penned in. I used the distraction and noise they'd caused to smash the window with Fury's hilt and heaved myself inside.

I dropped to the floor behind the stage and pulled Fury into my hand as I moved towards the left of the room while the biters all swarmed towards my sister and the Belvederes beyond the exit. My heart pounded with fear for Montana but I pushed it aside; she wasn't helpless anymore and I had to trust that she could hold her own against these monsters.

Magnar and Julius scaled the wall outside and followed me through the window, landing beside me in the darkened space.

There was a large pair of double doors set into the wall a little further from us and three biters stood guarding it, stopping the humans from escaping this way.

The chaos at the front of the building was holding their attention and Magnar slid past me, drawing both of his blades.

A bolt of lightning slammed to the ground outside, making me flinch at the raw power of it, but I forced my attention from it as I turned back to the others.

Magnar seized the distraction and raced towards the biters guarding the door, swinging Venom in a wide arc so that it carved through each of their chests, sending them spiralling into dust before they'd even realised he was there.

The humans closest to us screamed in surprise and more than a little fear.

I hurried forward with Julius at my side just as Magnar started slamming into the door with his shoulder.

"Who are you?" an elderly woman breathed as she caught my eye.

I could tell the humans weren't sure whether to be afraid of us or not and I lowered Fury in hopes of convincing them that they could trust us.

"We're getting you out of here," I promised. "Who's in charge among you?"

No one spoke up but many heads turned towards a woman with dark curling hair and she raised her chin in response.

"Looks like I am then," she said as she noticed the attention falling on her.

Julius began to pound the door alongside Magnar as it continued to resist his efforts to break it open and I spied a heavy chain securing it.

"Is there anywhere safe that you can all go while we deal with this?" I asked urgently. "You need to hide until we can clear the biters out of here."

She frowned thoughtfully for a moment before nodding. "The school. It's on the west side of the Realm. It should be big enough for all of us."

The doors finally gave way and Julius grinned at me triumphantly.

"Go," I urged. "We'll make sure everyone follows you."

The woman nodded as the terrified humans started running for the open door and I turned away from her to survey the madness at the far end of the hall. I couldn't see much over the sea of humans so I hoisted myself up on to the stage to get a better look.

The front doors were blazing and the fight outside was little more than a sprawling mess of flailing bodies.

My gaze caught on Valentina's red dress as she swept beneath the burning doorframe and I released a snarl of anger as I tightened my grip on Fury. The blade yearned for her death as fiercely as I did and I ached to race after her and plunge it through her black heart.

I took a step towards her then stopped as I heard a scream. Some of the biters had remained inside and they were tearing a bloody path through the fleeing humans as they drained anyone they could get their fangs into.

I leapt into the crowd without waiting for the other slayers to join me.

The tide of terrified humans surged around me, their shoulders crashing against mine and threatening to knock me from my feet as I carved a path in the opposite direction, following the sounds of the screams.

I shoved a large man aside and spotted two biters ripping into the neck of a woman around my age. Her eyes were filled with pain and terror as she feebly clawed at them, and they fell into a frenzy. They were going to kill her, I could see it coming and pure unadulterated rage swept through my body.

How dare they? What makes them think their lives are worth more than hers?

I'll show them what it feels like to be hunted.

I raced towards the girl, slamming into the first biter with my shoulder and sending him flying to the floor before swinging Fury straight through the heart of the next. The girl tried to run but I caught her arm before she could get away.

"Wash the venom out with water before too much gets into your veins," I instructed, making sure she understood me before pushing her after the rest of the humans.

I turned my attention back to the remaining biter as he rose to his feet, baring his bloodstained teeth at me.

"You wanna take her place?" he cooed, and I rolled my shoulders back as I realised he was an Elite.

"Make me," I dared, drawing on my ancestors' gifts as I prepared to attack.

My kind were made to destroy his and I was looking forward to seeing what I could do when I gave myself to my slayer nature.

The biter leapt at me and I twisted aside, slashing Fury across his back and spraying bright red blood over both of us. He hissed in pain as he shot towards me in a rush of motion, knocking me from my feet and landing on top of me with a feral laugh.

He grabbed my left wrist, dragging it towards his fangs and I gave him a savage smile just as I brought Fury down on his back. The first blow missed his heart and he shrieked as blood poured from his mouth, coating my face. I recoiled in disgust as I stabbed him again, this time finding my mark and destroying him.

I rolled back to my feet, wiping my arm over my face in an attempt to rid it of the Elite's blood but it flaked away into ash as I did so and tumbled from my skin.

I found myself in an open space as the humans continued to flee through the door at the back of the room. Magnar and Julius were cutting through the biters who tried to chase after their prey and I turned to look out of a window at the battle which raged beyond the town hall.

Hairs rose along the back of my neck as I spotted Montana flying across the street outside. She crashed to the floor and rolled out of sight before I could be sure if she was alright. Wolfe stalked after her like a hungry predator and my heart lurched as I turned and raced for the door.

My boots skidded in a puddle of blood and I almost slipped over as I made it beneath the burning entrance.

A huge groaning filled the air and I leapt outside as the massive wooden beam which secured the doorframe fell to the ground, consumed in flames.

I stared back into the town hall as the embers swirled across the blocked doorway and found Magnar looking at me, his swords drawn and ready for battle. The fire blazed hungrily between us, stopping him from following me.

A moment of understanding passed between us. He was alive. I was alive. That was all I had time to convey before I turned and raced after my sister. I was going to end Wolfe's existence once and for all. That monster had taken too much from us when he'd murdered our father. I refused to let him take anything else.

And if I had anything to do with it, then General Wolfe was about to meet his end.

MONTANA

CHAPTER SEVENTEEN

Wolfe came at me like a storm once again and I braced myself, but he was a trained fighter. As strong as me, but with the skills of several centuries worth of training behind him.

Fear made a passage through me as he lunged forward and slammed a bone-crushing punch to my chest.

I flew backwards into an alley, hitting the ground with a wheeze of pain. I righted myself in an instant, but he sped toward me, forcing me further back into the alleyway. He was cutting me off. Driving me away from my friends. And I couldn't do anything but fight for my life.

Though I'd wanted a chance to kill him, I was frighteningly unprepared for doing it alone without any training. But I had to try.

I gritted my teeth, bringing up Nightmare as he grabbed my arm. I tore it across his chest and he snarled his fury, slamming me against the wall so hard my head spun.

"No – get away from me!" I yelled.

He pinned me in place with his fist and prised the blade from my grip with a hiss of pain as it burned his flesh, tossing it to the ground.

"I knew you were a thlayer," he spat and spittle cascaded over me. The scent of rot filled my nose from the gaping wounds in his mouth and my stomach coiled with nausea. "You're the reathon I'm here, outcatht by my own mathter." He squeezed my neck so hard something popped and I screamed in agony. I managed to get my hands between us, forcing him back far enough that I could bring my knees up and ram my feet into his stomach.

He crashed into the opposite wall and I ran to grab Nightmare, desperation tearing through me.

I can't win this fight without it.

Before I reached the blade, Wolfe caught me by the waist, wheeling me into the air. My legs kicked wildly, but I couldn't land a hit before he threw me to the ground again. Pain flared up my back and I was momentarily immobilised beneath him as my body fought to heal from the impact.

He smiled darkly, placing his boot on my chest to hold me down. "I'll take my revenge out on you, and when Erik thees what I've done, he'll come for me. And with the help of my friendth, I'll kill him too." He pounced on top of me, pinning my wrists to the wet ground.

I snarled, bringing my head up and smashing my forehead into his nose.

Blood poured and he yelled in anger, slapping me hard across the face so my head whipped sideways.

"I may not be able to bite you, but I can thtill rip you limb from limb," Wolfe taunted, wrenching one of my arms until I screamed.

Fear built in my gut. I thrashed but couldn't get free from his grip. I wrapped my thighs around him, squeezing with all of my might. But he didn't let go; he was monstrously strong and terrifyingly determined to kill me.

Nightmare caught my eye just a foot away on the ground and I dropped my free arm as he started tugging my other with a strength that made my shoulder joint tear. I screamed through the pain, a seething fury raging in my chest.

I can't die here. I can't let him win.

My fingertips brushed Nightmare's hilt as Wolfe's rancid breath floated over my face.

"Erik will find you in piethes jutht before I tear out your heart." A line of drool hit my cheek and I jerked violently to gain my grip on the blade.

With a swell of triumph, I pulled Nightmare into my grasp, bringing it up and ramming it as hard as I could between Wolfe's shoulder blades.

He roared in agony, rearing off of me and anger flared in my blood, so hot, I lost control. I forced him to the ground with a snarl ripping from my lips, rolling so I was on top and pressing him down onto Nightmare which was still lodged in his spine. He wailed in pain and I revelled in the sound, urged into the hunt.

A hungry beast filled every space inside me and I bared my fangs, succumbing to its desires and losing myself to this animalistic side of the curse. I dug my teeth into his throat, ripping through flesh and sinew, causing as much pain as I could.

He flailed, wailing his pain and throwing punches as he tried to get me off of him, but I was a beast in my own right and my attacks were vicious, filled with the need for revenge. For my dad. For Callie. I was going to make him fucking *suffer*.

I sat up with his blood dripping down my jaw, grimacing at the bitter taste of it. It was nothing like human blood; it was acrid and cold, and I spat it from my mouth, not wanting his taint in my throat.

I had to keep going. I had to end him. Dad was owed his death. I couldn't allow Wolfe to keep living after all of the pain he had caused me and my family.

With a surge of energy, I tore his shirt open, clawing at his chest in a bid to reach his heart.

"No!" Wolfe bellowed in fear, slamming his knuckles into my face.

I was thrown off of him, crashing to the ground and my senses realigned. My nose wrinkled at what I'd done. Attacking him like a true vampire. My fangs hungered for his death with an intensity that frightened me, proving it was more than my revenge fuelling my actions. It was pure bloodlust; exactly what Erik had warned me of. But if I was going to survive this fight, I had to give in to it. I had to let this dark side of me take over. Even if I became a monster in the process.

I sprang upright in a fighting stance, snarling my hatred for him and wiping the blood from my mouth with the back my hand, desperate to get the taste of it from my tongue. Wolfe launched himself to his feet, reaching behind his back, retreating as I advanced.

With a cry of pain, he tore Nightmare free of his spine and flung it at me. I caught it out of the air with ease, rushing forward to end him, refusing to let him escape me.

Someone collided with me from above, forcing me to the ground again and flattening me to the concrete. I shouted out in alarm as several pairs of hands shoved me down and yanked my arms behind my back.

Wolfe's laughter filled the air. "I'm not alone, you thee? I have Falentina'th friendth on my thide."

Terror snaked through my body and devoured my courage as it moved. I was outnumbered by this group of biters and I could sense my death racing closer like a lurking shadow.

I was done for. And Wolfe knew it.

CALLIE

CHAPTER EIGHTEEN

Fury sizzled with excited energy in my palm as I sprinted further into the storm, rain water flooding over me in an icy torrent.

The biters filled the huge square before the town hall but their attention was fixed away from me on the opposite side of the open space where the Belvederes fought wildly. Clarice leapt above the battle for a moment, her snarling face lit by the fire which continued to blaze behind me before she dove back into the mayhem.

They didn't need my help to fight these monsters, but Montana had been alone with Wolfe and I wasn't going to let her face him without me.

I ran to the right of the building, hunting the darkened streets for any sign of them to no avail. Alleyways lined the square but I wasn't sure where to start my search.

Watch out, Sun Child, Fury whispered and I ducked down just as a biter leapt at me from the shadows. He sailed over my head and I swung my boot into his chest the moment he landed, throwing him into the wall of the building behind him.

More of them raced towards me, the whites of their eyes shining with a desperate thirst as I set my feet and let my gifts flood through my limbs.

Three of them reached me at once and I danced between their attacks, slashing Fury across arms, faces, stomachs, burning their skin with my righteous blade as they shrieked in pain. A female clutched at a gaping wound on her arm and I lunged towards her, piercing her heart and using the space her fizzling remains left open to avoid the next attack.

More of them closed in and they surrounded me quickly, using their numbers to overwhelm me. They called out for my blood with desperate cries as I stumbled back, working hard just to keep them away from me.

Grasping hands clutched at my arms, my hair, anything they could reach but I kept fighting, killing and wounding them so they couldn't restrain me.

I roared a battle cry at them, refusing to bow to their bloodlust as I killed again and again, but they were like a never ending tide. Each monster I destroyed was swiftly replaced by another.

One of them caught my left arm in an iron grip, yanking me towards his teeth before I could fight my way loose. I screamed in anger and pain as his fangs sliced into my elbow and I rammed Fury straight through his eye.

I swung away from him as he released me but the biters had me pinned down and more grasping hands caught me, their fingernails digging into my flesh as a second set of fangs found their mark and pain flared in my shoulder.

A bellow of rage filled my ears as someone else joined our battle. I continued to drive them off of me, kicking and punching whilst swinging Fury in a vicious fight for survival.

The biters' attention slipped from me as they were attacked from behind and I managed to twist my arm and drive Fury through the heart of the female who was drinking my blood.

A small measure of space opened up before me as the biters shrieked warnings to each other and the battle turned against them beneath the wrath of their new opponent.

I growled in anger, kicking out at a female who stood before me and taking her head from her shoulders with a deadly swipe of my blade.

A heavy weight slammed into me from behind and I was knocked from my feet, colliding with the concrete. I rolled, bringing Fury up and piercing the heart of the biter before he could follow me to the ground.

I grunted as a boot landed in my side, pain flowing through me as the vampire swung her foot back to kick me again. I caught her boot in my hand on her second strike, gritting my teeth as I twisted her ankle as hard as I could with my gifted muscles until the bone snapped and she fell back.

I started to push myself up but an Elite leapt on me, shoving me down onto the concrete as he drove his fangs towards my throat.

"Callie!" Fabian roared from somewhere close by, but I couldn't respond as I fought for my life beneath the huge vampire who had me pinned.

His hand snared my throat and I scrambled beneath him as his impossible strength trapped me. The Elite grinned at me a moment before his teeth pierced my neck and I spat curses at him as his venom flooded into me.

I stabbed Fury into his side again and again, but he only flinched at the pain as my blood flowed from my body and into his mouth. I couldn't find his heart and his bulk immobilised me as he continued to feed.

His weight disappeared so suddenly that I barely managed to close my eyes as his ashes cascaded over me.

A female Elite with long blonde hair stood over me, offering her hand as I snarled at her.

"I'm here to help," she said quickly, taking a step back as I raised Fury between us.

I scrambled to my feet, glaring at her in confusion as I realised she'd saved my life. But before I could work out how I felt about a vampire helping me, the biters closed in on us again.

The Elite leapt into the fight at my side, swinging a silver sword in a deadly arc which carved straight through two of our enemies at once.

I wasn't sure what to make of fighting shoulder to shoulder with this stranger, but I didn't have much choice as the flood of biters came for my blood once more.

Before they could reach us, Fabian collided with them, tossing them away with his immeasurable strength and tearing into their bodies with his bare hands.

Some of the biters turned and fled from his rage, and he snarled like a feral beast as he placed himself between the rest of them and me.

He fought like a wild animal, biting and breaking limbs, tearing the rebel vampires apart and ripping their hearts from their bodies as he turned them to dust.

The Elite who had helped me rushed into battle at his left, and I moved to intercept the enemies on his right.

I swung Fury over my head, bringing it down with all of my strength as I cleaved a biter in two before hefting it towards the next demon.

Lightning slammed into the ground in front us, striking again and again as Valentina wielded her power and we were forced back as the incredible force of nature divided us from our enemies.

Fabian turned to me, his eyes wild as he took in the bites which marred my skin.

"Are you alright?" he asked desperately, taking a step closer to me.

I stared at him, unsure what to say. He'd been fighting to save me as I was overwhelmed and a surge of gratitude flooded through my chest.

"I'm fine," I replied lamely.

The rain was already washing the venom from my wounds and I had more pressing issues to deal with.

I almost asked if he was alright; he was coated from head to toe in blood and gore and ash, but I could tell that none of it was his.

The biters raced towards us again as Valentina's lightning strikes stopped and panic speared through me.

"I need to find my sister and Wolfe," I said urgently.

"Go," Fabian said. "I'll hold them back."

"I'll help you, sire," the female Elite said fiercely.

He eyed her like he'd only just noticed she was there. "What's your name?" he asked.

"Danielle," she replied. "I was guarding the bridge; I came to help as soon as I was told what was happening here."

"Well, Danielle, let's find out what you've got," Fabian said darkly.

She grinned in reply as she lifted her sword high and waited for the biters to reach them again.

I eyed them with guilt stirring in my chest; they'd both just saved me and I was going to leave them here, but Montana needed my help and Wolfe had to die. I took a hesitant step back and Fabian nodded at me.

"Go," he urged again, rolling his shoulders back as he prepared to dive into battle once more.

"Thank you," I breathed then I turned and fled.

MONTANA

CHAPTER NINETEEN

Four biters held me down and I thrashed wildly, desperate not to give up. My strength surprised me and I managed to loosen an arm, jamming my elbow into one of their faces. A shriek sounded as I broke the female's nose and blood dripped over my shoulder in a steady flow.

Three more were still holding me in place and with their combined strength, I didn't know if I could win. Wolfe watched my struggle with delight, his mouth curved up in a twisted smile. But I was thankful, because if he assisted them, I was dead. But while he continued to hold back and enjoy my plight, I had one single thing left: a chance.

The group rolled me onto my back and I bucked and kicked, jamming a foot into one of their chests. The male hit the wall, his head cracking against it, and he slumped to the ground with a grunt as he waited to heal.

"Kill her, Wolfe," purred the female who held my left arm.

I tried to bring Nightmare up in my other hand, but the male restraining that arm pressed down with all his weight.

"Not yet," Wolfe whispered and fear tossed and turned inside me like a roiling sea. "She hath to thuffer firtht."

Wolfe took a knife from his hip, grinning as he stalked closer then slashed it across my stomach with a vicious swipe.

Pain burrowed through to my core and I bit down on a scream, not wanting to give him the satisfaction of it.

I dug deep for every ounce of strength I had and yanked my arm free from the female. She gasped just as I caught hold of her hair and smashed her face into the ground. The male holding my other arm lunged forward to try and help her. His mistake offered me Nightmare and delight spilled through me as I tore my arm out of his grip. The other males fell onto me at once and I angled my blade toward the closest one with a yell of determination.

Drive me deep, drive me true, Nightmare urged.

The knife guided my movements and sank into his back, somehow skewering his heart as Nightmare burrowed through his ribs. He roared as he died, bursting to dust around me.

Energy coursed through me and I found an ounce of hope to cling onto.

The other males tried to get a grip on me, but I brought up my blade as one of them threw a punch at my jaw. I cried out with effort as I plunged Nightmare into his heart. The final one leapt onto me, gripping me with his thighs and taking hold of my head. I gasped just before he cracked it against the ground. My vision swam, but Nightmare was my eyes, moving my hand and crying out for death. With a growl of effort, I forced the knife into his chest.

The female shrieked, scrambling upright and making a bid for freedom as she saw the tables turning.

"Come back!" Wolfe roared, but she darted out into the battle without looking back.

I was in a cloud of ash but my relief was short lived as Wolfe gazed down at me with absolute hate. I moved to get up, but he slammed his boot onto my knee and a crack ripped the air apart as it broke. I screamed as agony swelled through the bone and he smashed his foot down on my other leg, once, twice, three times, breaking it in several places.

He grinned as I writhed on the ground, needing my body to heal and not knowing how long it would take. The process started, but Wolfe knelt down before me with a wild look in his gaze. I whipped a hand toward his face, but he caught my wrist, snapping that too and making me whimper in agony.

"Perhapth I'll break all of your boneth over and over again."

I slashed Nightmare toward him, needing to see this monster die, but he jerked backwards to try and evade it. He wasn't quite quick enough and the tip caught his right eye, the wound sending blood pouring down his cheek. He threw his fist out, knocking me flat on my back and my head cracked against the stone, causing an injury that left me dazed. I vaguely saw Wolfe slapping a hand over his eye with a groan, slumping back to the ground and cradling his bleeding face. I started crawling backwards, dragging my injured legs along, knowing it was a race for who was going to heal first, trying to reorient myself as blood pooled on the back of my head.

My bones finally started to re-fuse and my thoughts realigned as my head injury followed, but Wolfe was on his feet again and as I tried to get up, he slammed his foot into my side. I hit the opposite wall, my head impacting with the stone and stars burst across my vision before I lost consciousness.

I spiralled into a black pit I feared I'd never wake from, whispering a silent apology to my family.

I've let you down. I'm so sorry.

MAGNAR

CHAPTER TWENTY

I grabbed the last biter by the back of his neck and launched him through the air towards my brother. Julius swung Menace up to meet him and the monster screamed a moment before the heavy blade ripped through his heart and reduced him to dust.

Julius offered me a savage smile and I looked around at the town hall, double checking we'd finished them all as the last of the humans raced out through the back exit.

The far end of the building was engulfed in flames and I had to hope that Callie was still safe out there as I turned in the opposite direction and strode after the humans. My heart beat with worry for her but she was a full slayer now; the strength of her gifts were unparalleled and I had to keep faith that she could hold her own against the creatures who hungered for her blood. I would only feel whole again once we were reunited though and I hurried outside after the humans, hoping to find her quickly.

The rain slammed down endlessly as Valentina wielded a storm above our heads, the gift she had been bestowed to help her fight alongside the slayers now turned against us.

The humans raced away from us, heading for shelter on the far side of the town but the sounds of the battle reached us from beyond the town hall.

I turned towards it just as a terrified scream drew my attention back towards the fleeing humans.

A group of biters raced after them, colliding with those unfortunate enough to have been caught at the rear of the crowd as they tried to outpace them.

I snarled in anger, rotating my blades in my grip as I ran to intercept the vampires instead of heading into the thick of the fight where Callie had to be.

Julius fell into pace beside me, offering me a ferocious smile as we raced into battle side by side once more. This was what we'd been made for; we were born to fight and win. My muscles came alive with the power of my gifts as we dove into the fray and I relished in the power of the Clan of War.

I leapt at the closest biter, striking his head from his body with Tempest before driving Venom through the heart of the next.

I slammed my boot into the chest of the decapitated vampire hard enough to shatter bone and crush his heart beneath my heel, ending his eternal existence.

Julius leapt over the fallen body of a human man, colliding with the vampire who was sucking on his neck and knocking her off as they fell back into the dirt.

I hoisted the human to his feet and he staggered, blinking at me in surprised gratitude.

"Thank you! You saved my life, I-"

I gave him a shove to get him running after his kin, not needing to hear his thanks.

Another biter leapt from the shadows and I threw Venom at him, the heavy blade spinning end over end before slamming through his heart and clattering to the ground as he died.

Julius rammed his blade through the heart of his opponent and rolled to his feet as I ran to retrieve Venom.

The humans raced away but more demons poured from the shadows, chasing after them with a desire for blood lighting their features.

Julius bellowed a challenge at them as he placed himself between the vampires and their quarry, and I moved to his side as they rushed at us.

"Just like old times," Julius said as he raised Menace before him while I held Venom and Tempest aloft too.

"Let's remind them why they feared us a thousand years ago," I growled in agreement.

The biters swarmed around us, using the force of their numbers to their advantage as we fell into a savage battle.

I placed my back to Julius's and we worked together to carve through the monsters like two parts of the same body.

I swung my blades again and again, blood and dust flying in their wake as we carved through the vampires, forcing them back beneath our combined might.

The familiar rhythm of our battle set my blood singing in my veins and I released a laugh as I cut through the parasites who hungered for our deaths. Even fifty lesser vampires such as these could pose no challenge to our combined fury, and Julius laughed with me as the joy of the battle filled us. We were Clan of War; this was what we'd been born for.

I slammed my boot into the chest of a large male and he flew back, knocking his companions over as he crashed into them.

We leapt into the space his fall created, delivering death to all those who floundered to recover and their ranks suddenly broke. The remaining biters turned and fled, and I grinned as I chased after them with Julius at my side.

They led us around the town hall which continued to burn and we emerged in a huge square which was filled with the sounds and smell of battle.

The Belvederes fought fiercely and I noticed other vampires fighting alongside them too; their backup clearly having arrived. I spotted Erik locked in combat with a group of biters and my skin tingled as I tightened my grip on my blades. I still couldn't believe we were fighting alongside him, and I had to turn my face from him before I allowed any memories of our vendetta to cross my mind. Now wasn't the time for second thoughts.

I scanned the square in search of a new prey and energy coursed along my spine as I found Valentina. She had clambered up above the mayhem, standing on the roof of a truck as she raised her hands to cast her power. Her dark ponytail whipped about in a wind I couldn't feel as she wielded her gifts, and I gritted my teeth in anticipation of her gifts.

Lightning scorched the sky above her and the storm flared in response.

I snarled at her, raising Venom in a silent promise as I set my eyes on the former slayer who had betrayed us all.

I dove into battle once more with one goal in mind. Today I'd end my betrothal once and for all.

ERIK

CHAPTER TWENTY ONE

Biters surged around me with obvious intent. Not one of them had attempted to kill me. They were trying to fucking restrain me. And that meant Valentina had another plan for me, but there was no way in hell I was going to be caught by that bitch.

I'd lost sight of Montana and my attacks had grown more feral since. I tried to cut a path to the last place I'd seen her, but the biters kept coming, filling every space I opened up.

As I managed to kill one more of them, an Elite leapt through the swirling ash of his remains, joining me and offering a swift bow of allegiance. He was a slim guy, but he was one of my own. I'd found him mortally wounded forty years ago; the smell of his blood had drawn me to him when his car had crashed. He had been in his early twenties and it hadn't seemed right for his mortal life to be cut short, so I'd turned him instead of allowing him to succumb to his injuries. I wondered if he was still hankering for the promotion I'd denied him in the past.

"Henry," I growled in acknowledgment, trusting in his loyalty as I slammed my fist into a biter's chest, crushing her heart and sending her to her death.

"Master, I will defend you with my life!" Henry cried, swinging his huge sword and ending two biters in one blow.

Dust mixed with the rain, sliding down my skin as I prepared for the next attack.

Two males leapt onto my back and a chain clinked in my ear as they tried to get it around my neck. I launched one of them over my shoulder, knocking three more to the ground as he collided with the crowd. Henry ran to finish them as I tore the vicious female from my back and jammed my foot against her neck.

"No- no!" she begged as I bent down and tore her head from her shoulders.

Henry's blade rammed into her heart, a ringing sound filling my ears as she burst to ash and the sword met the sidewalk.

My heart clenched as the biters closed in again. I started swiping them aside with forceful blows of my arms, desperate to break their ranks and search for Montana. The need sparked a fierce power in me that was unstoppable.

I ripped out hearts as I carved my way forward, determined to find her. I'd sworn to protect her when we'd married and I planned on keeping that promise.

Henry cried out behind me and I was torn as I glanced back at him. Several biters had him on the ground. But my wife wasn't used to fighting like this and I had to make sure she was safe.

He screamed to the heavens and I cursed myself as I sped back to him, kicking a biter off of him and slashing their throat with my fingernails. I snatched up Henry's sword from the ground, wielding it with the memories of my old Viking life. It was at home in my hands and every biter within a foot of me met their death at its sharp tip.

I took Henry's arm, yanking him upright as he clutched a gaping wound on his shoulder.

"Th-thank you, sire," he stuttered.

I nodded and sprinted away from him, leaving him to heal and taking his sword, but I wasn't concerned for him. The biters were after *me*, desperate not to let me escape.

I roared my anger as two of them gripped my right arm, trying to prise the sword from my hand. I slammed my fist into both of their faces in quick succession.

The storm raged around me, coating my skin in rain and washing the blood from my body. I swung the weapon again, taking down a female with bloodstained fangs. As they closed around me once more, panic reared inside me.

They were trying to take me.

A chain was thrown in front of me and several hands yanked on it so I was forced back several steps. As they tried to tie it around me, I jumped away. But there were so many of them, all hounding toward me like a pack of wolves.

Clarice appeared in a fan of blonde hair, screaming her fury as she attacked the biters holding the chains. The second she killed them, I ran to meet her, gripping her arm as the remaining biters backed up in fear. Two Belvederes were more than a match for them.

"Are you alright?" I asked and she nodded with a wicked grin.

"Feels good to fight a real battle after so many years," she snarled, baring her fangs as the endless horde shifted closer, assessing us.

I swung the sword before me, my eyes wheeling across the battle as I hunted for my wife. Henry was fighting valiantly several paces away, using his fists since I'd taken his sword.

"I lost sight of Montana," I told Clarice and her eyes shimmered with concern.

"Then let's hurry up and kill these assholes so we can find her." She lifted her chin, readying her knife as the biters ran at us like an advancing army.

With my sister by my side, I knew we'd finish these fuckers. They were going to rue the day they turned against my family.

CALLiE

CHAPTER TWENTY TWO

I raced away from Fabian and Danielle, searching the streets for Montana.

She'd definitely come this way so I knew she had to be close. I just couldn't figure out where.

Come on, Monty! Where are you?

Fury tingled in my palm, urging me to turn left and I skidded to a halt on the wet concrete. I spun back, flying down the closest alleyway as Wolfe's voice carried to me in the echoing space.

"You're going to beg for deaff before I'm finithed wiff you," he snarled.

Fury burned hot in my grip as I rounded a corner and spotted Montana unmoving on the floor with Wolfe stalking closer. My lungs seized as I looked at her, lying vulnerable on the ground at that monster's mercy.

I won't let you hurt my family again.

I whipped my hand back, launching Fury at him with all of my strength. It spun towards him but he shifted aside at the last moment so it lodged in his shoulder instead of his heart. Wolfe cried out and wrenched the blade from his flesh, throwing it away down the alley.

"Even better," he growled as he turned his icy gaze on me. One of his eyes was destroyed and bright red blood poured down his cheek. "I'll kill both fiffterths."

I released a snarl of pure hatred as I launched myself at him. He shot to meet me in a rush of motion and I took a deep breath, standing my ground, my gifts flooding into me as adrenaline filled my muscles.

I slammed my fist into his face, feeling something crack beneath my knuckles just as he drove his palms against my chest. I was hurled into the air and crashed into the wall of the building beside us.

Pain flared along my spine as I fell to the ground and he was on me again in an instant. He lifted me off of my feet by my throat, raising me above his head as he bared his teeth. I stared at the holes where his fangs had been, the gums bloody and swollen as if his body couldn't recover from such a wound.

He noticed my attention and hissed at me, bloody spittle flying through the gaps in his teeth and coating my face as he lifted me higher and squeezed until I couldn't breathe.

"You're the reathon my fangth were taken. But once the Belfedereth are dead, I'll take them back and drink from the vein for all eternity."

I clawed at his hands then gave up and slammed my knee into his chin instead, forcing him to release me with a curse.

I rolled as I hit the ground, swiftly springing to my feet again before sprinting away from him towards Fury.

Wolfe tackled me before I got ten paces and I smashed into the ground once more. He flipped me over beneath him and wrapped his hands around my throat, crushing me in his grip so I couldn't draw breath.

I punched him in the side again and again, feeling his ribs crack beneath the strength of my blows. But he didn't loosen his hold as he sneered down at me, taking the punishment I was dishing out while knowing I was running out of time. I tried to buck him off of me then swept my hands above my head, searching for something, *anything* to use as a weapon.

"You're going to rue the day you crothed me thlayer." he snarled, his remaining eye alight with glee as he sensed his victory.

My fingers brushed against Montana's cold leg but she was still unmoving as her body fought to repair itself from whatever he'd done to her. I moved my hand back as stars blossomed before my eyes and Wolfe started laughing.

You won't kill me you murdering asshole. I refuse to let you kill me!

Something hot brushed my fingertips and my heart leapt with hope as I stretched my arm as far as I could manage.

Hello, twin of Moon Child, Nightmare purred and I could feel it aching for blood.

I flipped it in my palm and thrust it at Wolfe as hard as I could, catching him in the thigh as my vision continued to darken.

He swore, his grip on me loosening and I stabbed him in the arm.

Wolfe reared off of me and I coughed, sucking in air as I struggled to recover from his attack. I scrambled back on my elbows, bumping into Montana's body as I fought to get away. I glanced at my sister's still form and her eyelids fluttered. She was waking up, I just needed to buy a little more time.

You might be a match for me but the two of us are going to annihilate you.

Yes, let's help Moon Child, Nightmare agreed enthusiastically.

I forced myself upright, backing away from Montana's body and leading Wolfe after me along the alley. His one eye glared at me, his gaze filled with the promise of violence as he closed in on me again.

"Come on then, you fucking psychopath," I growled. "Lethh thee what you can do."

Anger flared in his expression as I mocked him and he screamed with rage as he shot towards me.

He reached for me and I slashed Nightmare at him, cutting the fingers from his left hand and sending them falling to the ground. Wolfe howled in pain and I smirked tauntingly as I backed up again. One of his fingers rolled beneath my boot and I crushed it into the concrete as he shrieked in outrage.

I glanced over his shoulder and noticed Montana stirring.

Wolfe leapt at me again and I batted his left arm aside, but his right fist connected with my jaw. I stumbled back as pain rang through my skull but I danced aside before he could press his advantage.

I threw Nightmare at him as he advanced but he dodged it by inches before crashing into me once more. The collision sent me flying again and I hit the concrete at the far end of the alley, skidding along the ground before landing on my back with something burning hot pressing into my spine.

My face lit with a wicked smile as I grabbed Fury and my blade hummed with excitement as we were reunited.

Feed me, Sun Child. I crave blood!

Montana groaned as she pushed herself to her feet behind Wolfe and he spun towards her, snarling with rage.

I sprinted at him with Fury raised to attack. "Not my sister, you motherfucker!" I screamed as I sprang onto his back, hooking my arm around his neck and stabbing, stabbing, stabbing until the whole world ran red with his blood.

MONTANA

CHAPTER TWENTY THREE

Relief sang in my veins. Callie was here. And together, we'd kill the venomous beast who had taken our father from us.

She was on Wolfe's back, stabbing Fury into his body again and again. Excitement spilled through me but before she reached his heart, he tore her over his shoulder and smashed her head against the brick wall. Fury hit the floor and she groaned from her injuries, stumbling as blood spilled down her face.

"No!" I cried, panic clawing at my insides.

I hunted for my blade, spotting Nightmare on the ground a foot away. Launching myself toward it, I snatched it up and heat sped across my skin.

Drive me into his withered heart, Moon Child.

Callie staggered into Wolfe and he wrenched her head sideways with a murmur of glee, ripping her neck open with his fingernails. He licked a line all the way up to her ear and horror pooled inside me.

I lifted Nightmare, promising his death with all my heart, rage coating my soul at seeing him hurt my twin.

"Get the hell away from her," I snarled.

Wolfe's laughter filled the air as he glanced back at me. "No chanthe."

Callie regained her senses and jammed her elbow into his ribs, thrusting him toward me. I was ready with my blade, stabbing it deep into his side and he screamed to high heaven.

Callie turned around with a fire in her eyes.

"For Dad," she snarled, her gaze locking with mine.

Wolfe slashed out at her, slapping her so hard she hit the ground.

My world spun as I wrenched Nightmare from his side and tried to get close once more. He moved like the wind, diving towards Callie and dragging her up before him. She writhed in his hold, but he gripped her tight, licking the blood from the wound on her head. I could tell it was affecting her; her movements were unsteady and her eyes half shut.

Wolfe groaned, clearly weakened from the cuts of our slayer blades, but he held on tight. He hugged her against his chest and glared at me over her shoulder.

"Get off of her," I growled, readying to tear her from his arms.

He grinned at me. "Get too clothe and I'll break her neck."

Callie looked to me and a small smile twisted her lips. I fought a frown, realising she was faking the extent of her injuries. She looked at Fury on the ground then back at me, and my heart swelled as I interpreted exactly what she meant.

I side-stepped toward it and Wolfe rotated sharply, keeping Callie facing me, his mangled hand on her throat. "I'm going to drain every laft drop of her blood, then I'm going to cruth you like a goothberry."

I inched closer to Fury on the ground, feigning fear, but the glittering malice in Callie's eyes gave me strength. Wolfe lapped at the blood on her cheek once more and Callie lurched violently away from him.

As he moved his full attention to holding her, I bent down, grabbed Fury by the hilt and tossed it to Callie. She snatched it out of the air, turning in his arms and ramming it straight into his cheek. He roared in agony, stumbling back and gripping the hilt to try and tug it out. It burned his hands as he desperately tried to yank it free and the scent of burning flesh seared my nostrils.

I ran closer as Callie kicked him squarely in the chest and he hit the wall, pulling the blade out and dropping it with a gasp.

Blood poured from his mouth, his tongue swollen and half severed. "Ged away you thucking bitheth! Dyou'll pay for diff!"

As Callie approached, he swung a fist at her but she evaded the blow with ease, dropping low to grab Fury and planting it directly between his legs. His screams hit my ears so hard I winced, but satisfaction sprawled through me. We had the upper hand. We were taking down the beast who'd haunted us and making him suffer in the process. Just like Dad had suffered in Wolfe's hands.

My sister twisted the blade in his groin, glaring straight into his eyes. "You're a monster," she snarled, ripping Fury out. His pained yells were the only sound I could hear and they sparked a thirst in me that could be sated by his death alone.

He stumbled past her, suddenly trying to run and I sped after him. He was faster than Callie, but not fast enough to escape me.

I tore Nightmare across the backs of his knees and he fell down in a heap at my feet.

Callie raced to my side, her jaw set.

"You're dirt," I growled, kicking him so he rolled over to look up at us.

"And *you're* dead." Callie smiled darkly.

He clasped the wound between his legs with a pained whimper. "Thuck you and your thilthy, worthleth father!"

With a scream of vengeance that was echoed by my sister, we drove our blades into his heart at once.

Wolfe exploded into ash and the hammering rain swept him away so nothing but his clothes lay on the ground. Callie's eyes glimmered as she looked at me, and a moment of sweet relief filled the air. Then we closed the gap between us, embracing hard, revelling in our victory.

"He's gone," she groaned her happiness, and I squeezed her tighter as bliss flowed through me.

A tear tracked down my cheek as I bathed in the afterglow of what we'd achieved. Justice was dealt and it felt so damn good to have cast our enemy from this world together.

MAGNAR

CHAPTER TWENTY FOUR

I pushed through the crowd of bodies, delivering death to any biter who came at me as I kept my gaze locked on Valentina.

I left Julius behind as the vampires swarmed between us and he was engaged in another fight. It didn't matter though; all I had to do was get to her. My goal was in sight and I wasn't going to leave here without completing it. Valentina had spent too long in her undead form; she needed to die. Permanently.

I was surrounded by lessers and Venom and Tempest bathed in their blood as I carved a path into existence.

She hadn't noticed me yet but I was sure when she did she'd turn her storm against me, so I had to make the most of my advantage. I just needed to get close: I'd spent years encouraging her to hone her battle skills, but she'd always relied too heavily on her gifts. She thought they made her untouchable. I was about to show her how wrong she'd been about that.

Behind you! Venom hissed.

Strike high, Tempest urged in agreement.

I spun around, twisting my blades through the air as an Elite launched herself at me with her own sword drawn.

Venom knocked her blade aside and Tempest cut into her chest before she crashed into me.

I absorbed the blow with a growl of rage as I threw my elbow back into her jaw. She was knocked aside but a lesser catapulted onto my back as I was left exposed.

His teeth grazed my neck and I dropped Tempest before catching him by the hair and dragging him over my shoulder. I slammed him to the ground in front of me and drove Venom between his ribs as he screamed for mercy.

The Elite rushed at me, locking her arms around my waist as she attempted to throw me to the ground. I twisted, stumbling back a step before I managed to right myself and I kicked at her knees, sweeping her legs out from under her. She fell, swearing as she landed on Tempest where it lay on the concrete and the blade began to burn her.

She tried to roll away but I kicked her back, pressing my foot down on her chest so that she was stuck on top of the blade as it burned her flesh from her bones. She shrieked in pain, clawing at my leg as I used Venom to cut through several lessers who attempted to help her.

I looked down at her as she cursed me and I snarled, letting my face be the last thing she saw before I plunged Venom through her heart.

I stooped to retrieve Tempest from the pile of clothes she left behind and the blade greeted me excitedly as I clasped it in my hand once more.

I looked towards Valentina again just as she turned and spotted me. Her mouth fell open in surprise and I could have sworn the twisted bitch looked happy to see me. I bared my teeth at her as I began running to close the distance between us.

The wind caught in her hair and I leapt aside just before her lightning strike hit the ground where I should have been.

"Catch him!" she cried, pointing me out to more of her vile followers.

The biters raced towards me and I noticed some of them holding a length of golden chain as if they thought to snare me with it.

I laughed at the absurdity of it. "You think if you chain me, you might be able to drag me down the aisle?" I mocked as Valentina whipped up the wind around me.

"You will regret scorning me, Magnar Elioson," she swore and lightning hit the ground behind me.

The heat of it flared across my skin but I didn't flinch. If she wanted me alive then I had no need to fear her theatrics.

"I regret many things," I replied loudly. "But never that."

I ran to meet the biters as they raced for me. With a surge of power, I slashed my swords towards them, leaping into the middle of their group as they sought to overwhelm me. But I was a Blessed Crusader, I had no reason to fear a group of lessers such as these, especially if they were foolish enough to try and trap me instead of killing me.

I danced between them, laughing as I evaded every desperately grasping hand and delivering deadly blows with my swords.

The vampires who held the chain approached cautiously, holding it out as if they thought I might actually be contained by such a thing.

I swept the head from the final vampire to have come for me then turned to face them with my arms held wide.

"Come then," I taunted. "If you truly think you can hold me then do your best."

The vampires shot towards me in a rush of motion. The first to arrive snarled, whipping the chain forward so it coiled around my right arm. I laughed as I yanked on it, forcing him towards me and slamming Tempest into his heart.

He disappeared into a cloud of dust, and I shook my arm to knock the golden chain free but it didn't come loose.

The second vampire approached me and I decided to use the chain for my own purposes. I whipped it towards him and the heavy metal slammed into his skull, breaking bone as he was knocked from his feet.

I charged after him and swung Venom down to finish him off.

I searched for Valentina again but she'd abandoned the truck and I'd lost sight of her to the crowd on the far side of it.

I cursed and placed Venom on my back before trying to remove the chain from my other arm.

Pain seared through my wrist as I pulled on it and I scowled as it tightened instead of coming free.

More biters began to hunt me, but they stopped suddenly and just stared instead. I frowned at them in confusion, preparing to cross the gap between us myself.

Idun's tinkling laughter filled the air around me, and I stilled as I looked about for the deity but she didn't appear.

"Now, now Magnar," she sighed, and her voice was full of disappointment as I felt her breath against my ear. *"You didn't think I'd just let you change the rules, did you?"*

"What have you done?" I growled, glaring at the chain as I noticed the power which resided in it was flaring against my skin.

"I've decided to bet on someone else for a change."

ERIK

CHAPTER TWENTY FIVE

I was forced to the ground by a raging storm that seemed hell-bent on keeping me in place. Clarice had intercepted a group several paces ahead of me and I gritted my teeth, pressing my hands to the ground and battling to get to her.

"You can't take me, Valentina," I snarled at the very storm that tried to contain me. "The wind may be your ally, but I have the fiercest warriors at my back. And you. Will. Fail."

A thick fog surrounded me, pressing in on either side and the biters around me withdrew into it. I lost sight of Clarice and anger blazed in my chest as I was cut off from her.

As the pummelling wind eased, I gained my feet and hurried toward the mist. The second I moved, the clouds opened up above me, allowing a single shaft of beating sunlight down on my head. I shouted my rage as its rays fell over me and my body immediately weakened. My shoulders fell lax and my limbs ached as I took another desperate step forward, determined to escape the light. But wherever I moved, the light followed, keeping me trapped within its powerful rays.

The mist shifted and Valentina stepped out of it with a keen smile, her gaze set on me. She was flanked by four biters holding the thick chains they'd been trying to bind me with before.

I snarled at her, raising my sword to defend myself.

"You're under my control now, *Prince* Erik," she said, her eyes darkening. "You've lost. Accept it. You'll find this a lot less uncomfortable if you cooperate."

As I inched forward, the shaft of sunlight shifted with me, never touching her disgusting followers and keeping them strong. They were Elite. And though I may have managed to take them on before, I was weaker than them with ultraviolet light seeping into my veins.

"What do you want from me?" I growled.

I wouldn't give up. There wasn't a chance in hell I'd be going anywhere with this depraved bitch. But my chances of facing her and winning were pretty slim under the influence of the sun.

"I don't want to ruin the surprise," she said with a cruel lilt to her lips, ushering her people forward.

They ran at me with the gold chains in their hands and I snarled to keep them back, swinging my blade in a menacing arc. They evaded my attacks, dancing around me, trying to get close. Two of them grabbed one of my arms, moving faster than I could in my weakened state. I threw the butt of my sword into one of their faces and slashed out at another, but a female caught my free arm, wrenching the blade from my grip with a yell of victory.

The chains were thrown over me and I roared a challenge, wheeling around to try and keep them off. They wrapped them around my throat, my stomach and finally snared my arms. Rage flared in my chest but there was nothing I could do. I was an animal caught in a trap.

Stepping back, the biters yanked the ends of the chains and I toppled over, slamming into the ground. I winced against the sunlight, trying to roll to escape it, but as I moved, the chains tightened around my body as if they had a will of their own.

"You've scorned the gods, Erik," Valentina hissed. "They're helping *me* now. The more you struggle against those chains, the tighter they'll become."

"Fuck you!" I bit at her, rolling my shoulders to try and loosen myself from them.

The chains coiled around me like a python, squeezing my limbs so fiercely I was immobilised.

"Get him in the truck, I'll deal with Magnar," Valentina commanded and the mist moved around her people, keeping them shielded from the sun as they hoisted me into their arms. Valentina headed away at a fierce stride, leaving me alone with her hungry band of monsters.

The fog parted, but the sun remained shining down on my head as they carried me toward a pick-up parked at the edge of the street. The sounds of battle still carried to me and my heart nearly broke at how much I was letting my family down, my *wife*.

The biters dumped me into the open truck bed. I roared between my teeth, managing to move my legs enough to smash them into the side of the vehicle's low walls and dent the metal.

One of the biters produced a gag, hopping into the back of the truck and bending down to put it in my mouth. As he reached for me, I reared up and bit his hand, catching one of his fingers in my mouth. I clamped my teeth down, biting as hard as I could until I broke through bone. He screamed in agony, stumbling backwards as I spat his severed finger at his feet. His blood tasted like piss and I spat out the rest of it beside me.

"You piece of shit." He landed a kick in my ribs and they broke under the viciousness of his attack.

He kept kicking and kicking and the more I fought to get away, the tighter the chains became. All the while, my thoughts were fixed on Montana and how I had brought her to this bloodbath, and now I was abandoning her to whatever fate she faced out there in the fray.

The biter grinned down at me, picking up his finger and pressing it to the bloody stump on his hand so it knitted back together.

"You're no one's ruler now," he sneered.

I ground my teeth against the ache in my body, glaring up at him with acidic hatred, my gaze tracking over his narrow features. "I'll remember your face. Your death is coming for you, asshole."

His grey eyes flickered with fear, but then his mirth masked it. "Yeah? Well my queen will make sure that never happens." He kicked me in the chest and I released a hiss between my teeth, my fury growing out of control.

229

"Your *queen's* dead too, mark my words," I said evenly.

A yell sounded above the battle and I recognised Clarice's voice. "Erik, where are you?!"

I looked to the biter with a deadly smile then shouted, "Here!" just as his foot met my jaw.

I groaned, unable to heal with the sunlight still beating down on me. But I didn't give a damn about the pain as Clarice burst through the mist and her eyes wheeled to me. She sped forward and the biter leapt down to intercept her with a battle cry. Before they met, a lightning strike tore the ground apart and my sister hit the ground.

"No!" I bellowed, terrified for my kin.

I writhed against the chains, managing to sit upright so I could see her again, but every move I made had them snaring me harder and my bones were starting to face the pressure.

Several more biters poured from the mist and fell onto Clarice in a frenzied attack.

Horror pounded through me as I lost sight of my sister beneath the mass of rebel vampires. Panic consumed me as I lost control of the world around me. I couldn't help her. I was useless. Stuck here like a tethered dog.

"Get off of her!" I commanded, but it was pointless. So there was only one thing I could do. "Fabian - Clarice needs you!" I roared, praying my brother was close enough to hear.

A huge figure burst out of the mist and my brows pinched together as Julius appeared, splattered with blood and coated in ash, his sword smeared with it too. He spotted the brawling mass and dove into it without hesitation, stabbing and stabbing his enemies. One of the biters caught him by the neck, biting deep into his throat.

Julius bellowed in anger, shoving her to the ground and finishing her with a fierce strike of his sword.

Clarice battled to get up but too many of them were holding her down, ripping at her flesh, ready to end her.

"Julius!" I shouted in a panic and he dragged two biters off of Clarice by their collars, wheeling them away from her before ramming his blade into one of their chests. The other one dodged his attacks. He was Elite, feral and strong, and I didn't know how well the slayer would fare against him.

Julius rotated his shoulders, grinning as he lunged forward to kill his opponent. The Elite danced aside, sprinting around Julius and slashing his nails down his spine. Julius cried out in pain, turning to try and spear him with his sword. The Elite was too fast, taking him to the ground with a growl of hunger.

"Get up!" I yelled, furious that I couldn't help as both Julius and my sister were incapacitated.

A furious cry filled the air and I spotted Fabian and an Elite, Danielle, tumbling from the mist with several biters in tow. Fabian slammed his fists into their faces, over and over, but their numbers were overwhelming.

Danielle darted toward Julius, kicking the Elite off of him and planting her sword in the biter's chest before he could rise.

Julius sprang upright, nodding to her before running to help Clarice.

He threw a heavy kick into a biter's leg, and he toppled sideways with a yell of panic. Julius thrust his blade into his chest and dust burst around his feet as the bastard died.

He was a monstrous warrior to behold, carving through the vampires with a furious ability which reminded me of precisely why we had feared his family all those years ago. I watched in awe as Julius cleaved his sword through the remaining biters, carving them apart with such brutal efficiency that half of them died without even managing to raise a hand against him, and he dispatched the last of those holding my sister with vicious blows of his blade.

I released a heavy breath as Clarice was revealed at last, shoving the clothes of the biters off of her with a groan.

Julius dragged her upright and she gazed at him in disbelief, her hand staying in his a beat too long before she yanked it away.

"You're welcome," Julius said with a raised eyebrow.

Clarice nodded, looking confused as she turned toward the truck, sprinting to help me. Relief filled me as she approached, but she had to hurry. Fabian and Danielle were barely holding off the horde clamouring to get to us.

"Get me out of these chains," I demanded, not wanting to move again in case they started biting deeper into my flesh.

Clarice jumped into the truck, kneeling down and taking hold of them.

She gasped, withdrawing her hand immediately. "They burn." She turned her palms over in horror, then wheeled around to face Julius. "Come help. Maybe slayers can touch them."

He sprang up too, kneeling before me and laying his hand on the chains. He swore, recoiling just as my sister had.

"Shit," he snarled, curling his hand into a fist before bringing his sword forward.

He pressed it against my leg, easing it under the chain. The blade cut a hole in my pants and it burned like hell as it met my flesh. I snarled between my teeth to weather out the sensation as he gave me a wary glance.

"It's fine, just hurry the fuck up," I commanded.

Julius wrenched the blade sideways to try and break the chains, but as he did, his sword snapped instead, the end clattering onto the truck bed.

"No!" he cried his grief. "My *baby*." He picked up the broken end, horror lacing his features as he clutched the pieces tightly as if they might reform.

"What the fuck are these made of?" Clarice gasped.

"The gods created them; they're helping Valentina," I answered with a scowl.

Julius looked like he was about to break down as he cradled the two pieces of his sword to his chest.

"Get me out of here," I snarled, not having time for his ridiculous display as Fabian released a shout of pain.

"Grab his shoulders, don't touch the chains," Clarice encouraged the slayer, taking hold of my ankles.

Julius sheathed the two pieces of his blade just as the swarm of biters broke past Fabian and Danielle, sprinting toward us.

The storm raged harder and a harsh wind pushed against us. I despised how useless I was as Clarice and Julius were forced to abandon me and leapt from the truck to meet the fight. The rain battered down on everyone but me as I sat in the single shaft of light in the whole town.

As they fought the lessers, the engine rumbled to life beneath me, and my fate closed in.

"Gods be damned," I cursed as a biter drove the truck forward.

I tried to roll in an effort to launch myself from the truck bed, but the chains tightened further, and agony bound me in place.

Clarice glanced back with desperate eyes, but four biters crashed into her to stop her from pursuing. Despite the blinding pain, I tried to roll to the end of the truck bed once again, but between the sun following my every move and the chains biting into my body, I got nowhere close.

Hatred seared my veins at the woman responsible for this.

Fuck Valentina and her damn gifts.

She wasn't just taking me, she was stealing me from my rebel. We'd already been apart too long after our marriage and I cursed Valentina for the injustice of it. If only I'd caught sight of her one last time, to see she still lived. To promise her I'd come back. That the full force of the sun itself couldn't weaken me enough to stop me from returning to her.

I managed to get my chin on the edge of the truck, but the driver veered violently left and right, tossing me back to the middle of the bed. The chains started cutting into my skin and I roared my fury to the sky, swearing on every star in the solar system that Valentina was going to die at my hand. And her death would be a brutal, unforgiving thing.

MAGNAR

CHAPTER TWENTY SIX

A prickle of realisation ran down my spine as the crowd of biters parted and Valentina stepped out from between them, her gaze set on me.

"Oh husband," she purred seductively, though her tone had no effect on me. "When will you realise that I was always going to get what I wanted?"

I glared at her, holding my blades ready as a strong wind picked up. I gritted my teeth and stepped into it as she raised her hands, driving the gale towards me more forcefully until it was all I could do to stand my ground against it. I was trapped in the maelstrom as her cretins flanked me. The chain snaring my right arm blew out behind me, caught in the pressure of her gifts.

My blood flared with my desire to end her but I was immobilised until she released me from the storm.

I spied more chains among the biters as they prepared to come for me again and I glared at them, promising them their deaths if they dared to try and take me.

I couldn't hear Valentina's voice over the wind but I could see her lips moving as she gave her followers instructions.

I tightened my grip on my swords, refusing to allow the storm to take them from me.

The wind dropped suddenly and the biters leapt towards me with their chains, but I was ready. I dove forward, rolling beneath the first chain before gaining my feet beyond it and turning my attention to the vampires who held it.

The closest one lost his head to Tempest, and I kicked his decapitated body so hard that it slammed into three more of them, knocking them from their feet.

I whipped the chain attached to my right arm at the vampires in front of me, cutting them to ribbons with the powerful creation. I was sure such a thing must have been crafted by the gods and I cursed Idun beneath my breath as I fought on, keeping Valentina locked in my sights. This would all end with her death.

The vampire holding the chain to my left slashed it at me and I ducked beneath it, narrowly avoiding its touch. I was sure if it met with my skin then it would coil as tightly as the first, and I refused to let that happen.

I righted myself and sprinted towards the biter as he dragged the chain back into his grasp. Venom cut though his chest before he could try and trap me again, and the chain fell to the ground alongside his ashes.

I turned toward Valentina and she glared at me, lifting her arms to the heavens as she called on the storm for assistance. I sprinted for her, but lightning arced from the sky, slamming into the ground between us repeatedly so I was forced back.

The golden chain rattled behind me as another set of biters took it up.

I turned to face them, daring them to test me.

Ten lessers shot towards me in a rush of motion and I raised my blades to defend myself. Just before they reached me, Valentina drove a gale into my back, forcing me to stumble forward.

The lessers pounced on me as a unit and I only managed to land one fatal blow before they swept my feet out from under me. I snarled in rage, hacking my blades at their legs, and their blood poured, coating me.

I kicked out, launching one of them away and using the space I'd created to roll myself upright.

My right arm jerked backwards as one of the vampires grabbed the other end of the chain and yanked on it. I twisted towards them, bringing Tempest around savagely and cutting into the lessers without taking a moment to aim. The blade sliced through flesh and bone as the vampires screamed, and I closed in on the creature who dared to try and restrain me.

The vampire holding the chain hissed at me as she saw me coming. I snapped my arm back, wrenching the chain closer to me and forcing her forward several steps. Another lesser ran to help her hold it and I bared my teeth in anger.

I raised Tempest high, intending to carve through both of them, but a second chain hooked around my wrist instead.

The Elite who held it shrieked with glee as he pulled the chain tight so it cut into my flesh. More vampires raced to grab both chains as they heaved them away from me, forcing my arms wide and immobilising me.

I bellowed in rage, my muscles trembling as I fought against the strength of so many vampires at once.

Valentina smiled in victory as she approached me and the rain fizzled out of existence.

"What a day this has turned out to be," she said as her eyes travelled over me and she stopped just out of reach.

I strained against the chains once more, aching for her death as my swords burned hot in my palms.

"I had hoped to capture one king and now I've gotten two," she said.

"I'd have thought by now you would have realised that you can't have me," I growled. "Your desperation knows no bounds."

"You should have married me when you had the chance," she hissed. "Now you're going to pay the price for that mistake."

The chains kept tightening around my arms and I sagged my shoulders as I stopped resisting their pull. Valentina smiled victoriously, stepping a little closer.

"I always knew you'd bow to my will one day," she whispered, leaning towards me as if we were sharing some secret.

I smiled at her and her eyes widened in horror as she reached for her gifts, but she wasn't quick enough. I kicked my foot into her chest so hard that she flew all the way into a wooden shed, destroying it as her body collided with it.

I poured every ounce of my will into my gifted muscles and yelled a challenge as I started running after her, dragging the vampires behind me with the chains.

The powerful metal cut into my arms as I fought against its hold and blood poured from the wounds, sending the biters into a frenzy.

Several released their grip on the chains and raced towards me instead, hungering for my blood. I stopped running and kicked out at one of them as she got close enough, sending her flying into the vampires who held the chain on my left.

The two who still clutched it widened their eyes in horror as I yanked them close enough to give me some slack then swung Tempest for their necks. I removed the head from one and the second dropped the chain as he threw himself away from me instead of trying to stand against me.

I roared a challenge at the rest of them as I whipped the chain in front of me before lashing it into the biters who were struggling to restrain my other arm.

The chain slackened and I smiled viciously as I set my eyes on the destroyed shed once more and sprinted for Valentina.

I spied the red of her dress among the broken wood but before I could deliver her death, lightning hit the ground in front of me with such force that I was thrown from my feet. I lost my hold on Venom as I slammed onto the concrete and was momentarily blinded by the blast.

I rolled, trying to right myself but I was knocked off balance as the vampires seized the chains again, yanking them tight. I regained my feet but I was too late; too many of my enemies had grabbed the chains for me to fight them off this time.

I growled in anger as I felt something pop in my shoulder and I was forced to a halt.

My heart pounded a violent rhythm against my ribs. I couldn't move. I thrashed against the chains but more and more of Valentina's foul followers raced to help restrain me and even my enhanced strength wasn't enough to combat their combined might as they pulled me in two directions at once.

A huge Elite approached, forcing me to my knees as the rest of the vampires pulled on the chains so tightly that it felt like my arms could be ripped from their sockets at any moment. The chains themselves continued to cut into my flesh and blood flowed freely over my skin.

Valentina approached me again with a scowl on her face and another chain coiled in her grip. Blood ran from a wound at her temple, but I could see that it was already healing, and she paid it no attention.

"See how the mighty Magnar Elioson bows at my feet," she snarled as she came to a halt before me.

"You can force me to kneel but I'd never bow to you, whore," I spat.

She whipped the chain towards me and it snapped into place around my throat. Valentina tugged on it and it began to tighten, cutting off my airway.

The Elite kicked out at my left hand, knocking Tempest from my grasp and I felt the weight of the blade's presence abandoning me like a blow to the chest.

Valentina smiled wickedly as she took a step closer and pulled on the chain again so I was forced to scramble to my feet or risk the damned thing choking me to death.

"Look at me," she hissed, tugging the chain to make me lower my chin in response to her command.

My eyes met hers and I was filled with the deepest pit of hatred as she surveyed me.

"You're mine," she whispered, stepping closer. "And I can do anything I want with you now."

"And what is it you want?" I growled, the chain around my neck making it hard for me to speak.

"Right now?" she asked and her eyes lit with a feral desire. "I'm hungry."

My muscles tensed a moment before her teeth met with my neck. She held the chain firmly, immobilising me as her venom flooded into my flesh and my blood poured into her mouth. Revulsion spewed through my body as she groaned in pleasure.

Her free hand slid across my chest as if we were locked in an embrace and my skin crawled beneath her touch.

Inside I was trembling, quaking and burning with a rage so intense I wasn't sure anything would survive the depths of it. But I was trapped, unable to fight back as her followers kept my arms pulled wide either side of me and she drank her fill of my life force.

She finally stepped away, smiling up at me with my blood staining her lips.

"Come, dog," she mocked as she pulled on the chain around my neck and I was forced to follow her.

The battle raged on behind me but I couldn't even turn my head towards it as she drew me away. My heart thundered violently as my mind raced with the thousand ways I'd like to kill this creature before me.

Valentina forced me into the back of a pickup and the biters secured my chains until I was unable to move an inch.

"That's it!" she cried as the engine started up beneath me. "We've got what we came for. As soon as I've gotten him away, I'll give the signal to retreat."

The biters cheered in response and she gave me one last, smug look before leaping from the truck and racing away ahead of it.

The vehicle started moving and I craned my neck to look back at the fight, hoping to catch a glimpse of Callie or my brother.

I'd never felt so helpless as this. Never known a fear like it. It wasn't that I was afraid of death. I was afraid of what I was leaving behind. Somewhere out there, Callie fought on and I had the greatest sense of dread that I might never see her again. That thought alone was worse than death. We'd had so little time and I wasn't ready for it to be over yet.

I'd fight a thousand battles just to have one more moment in her arms. And if that was what it was going to take, then let the gods throw that fate at me and see how I fared.

MONTANA

CHAPTER TWENTY SEVEN

The cry of the battle flooded over us and we turned toward the end of the alleyway. "Is everyone okay?"

Callie nodded. "The last time I saw them they were. Let's go finish these bloodsuckers."

My face fixed with determination as we ran together, sprinting out of the dark into the raging fight between the biters and our friends. A thick mist was swirling over one area of the battle, hiding the far side of the town square.

My throat tightened as the scent of blood filled my nose. Callie's own wounds held the same mouth-watering tang, so I was certain it belonged to a slayer.

"This way!" I yelled and Callie ran at my side as we pushed through the mass of bodies.

The biters grew frenzied as my sister neared them, diving forward to try and sink their teeth into her. I slashed out at a female, throwing her away from Callie, and my sister tackled another one to her left.

I locked my hand around the blonde female and she scratched her nails down my arms. I growled my anger, pushing her back and bringing up Nightmare. Her eyes glinted as the blade's golden hue reflected in them. She retreated in fear and I tried to take chase, but she sped away into the surging battle, disappearing into the masses.

I turned to find Callie scrambling upright from a pile of ash and she sprang to her feet, tossing the fallen biter's clothes away from her.

I hunted for the scent of slayer blood again and finally, I found the source. The mist lifted, evaporating and revealing a raging fight beyond it. Julius and Clarice stood back to back, fighting the monsters who came at them. Beside them, Fabian and a beautiful blonde Elite were bringing a muscular male to the ground, working together to end him.

Julius's neck was torn and blood coated his shirt. My heart squeezed as I took off toward him, hearing Callie following as we tried to reach them. The flow of biters was easing, many of them dead, their remains scattered to the wind. I hunted for Erik amongst the last of them but couldn't see him anywhere.

Fear sped through me as I cut down another biter with Nightmare and jumped to Clarice's side.

"Where's Erik?" I demanded, tearing a vampire from her arm. Clarice slammed a deadly punch into his chest and the man dissolved with a wail.

She wiped a smear of dust from her cheek, frowning in fear as she looked at me. "They put him in a truck."

"What truck?" I gasped, my heart tugging sharply.

"It went that way." Clarice pointed, kicking another biter to the ground and diving onto her.

I had no more time to ask questions as Callie stumbled into me and I spotted four biters coming for her.

I screamed my challenge, making a stand at her side as we fought them together. My mind spun with worry for Erik, but I couldn't do anything except try to stop the biters before I searched for him.

Callie slammed Fury into one of them, but the biter caught her by the waist, uprooting her.

I slashed at his side and he dropped her, clasping the wound with a hiss.

Callie hit the ground, rolling and kicking out his legs from under him. With a fierce blow from Fury, she finished him off.

I punched and kicked two males as they tried to get hold of me, but they overwhelmed me in seconds, yanking my arms behind my back. I screamed bloody murder as they pulled one of my arms so hard that my muscles ripped. I knew what was going to happen and I couldn't stop it. I struggled desperately, a panicked cry escaping my throat.

With a horrifying wrench, my arm tore clean off.

I screamed so hard that my throat was rubbed raw. The wound throbbed, the sensation like serrated knives driving into my shoulder. I was immobilised by the shock of it. It was pain in its purest form, my nerve endings alight with hellfire.

I hit the ground, rolling in a filthy puddle as blood spilled out around me.

The two biters laughed and I blinked up at them through blurry eyes, realising they were twins. Males, dark, huge and splattered with my blood. One of them placed their foot on my chest, taking hold of my other arm and pulling with all his might.

I groaned and tears of agony rolled down my cheeks as I tried to get free. The other twin grabbed hold of my left leg and fear swallowed me as I realised they were going to pull my limbs off like wings from a fly.

I released a choked noise, kicking out as I tried to keep them back. But they were Elite. Fierce and well-trained. And I feared I was seconds away from joining the other dead vampires, carried away on the wind as nothing but ash.

"Argh!" Julius crashed into the one holding my arm and I gasped my relief as he was forced to release me.

I curled my hand into a fist as I fought to free myself beneath the pressure of the other biter's boot.

Julius threw punches into the other twin's face, but the biter reacted as if he were made of stone. With a rumbling laugh, he slammed a punch into Julius's gut and he cursed through his teeth.

I kicked out with my free leg, a newfound strength filling me as I fought to keep the other twin from disabling me further. My foot connected with his groin and he stumbled back with a curse, giving me a moment to right myself at last. I spotted Callie in a fierce battle with Fabian at her side, the two of them raining down hell on the biters who surrounded them.

I scooped up Nightmare, dazed from the pain I was in as the huge male stomped toward me. He bared his fangs and I bared mine right back at him.

"Princess" he hissed, cracking his neck. "Shame there's no human blood left in your veins to suck out."

"Get fucked." I slashed at him with Nightmare, but he dodged the attack, darting toward my injured side and slamming his knuckles into the wound.

I bit down on another scream, jerking backwards to evade a second blow. I spotted my severed arm in a puddle of blood and anger cascaded through my chest. I let the animal part of myself take over and lunged forward to meet my opponent with a feral growl. His fist collided with my head, knocking me off balance, but I managed to slice Nightmare across his abdomen. He clutched the wound with a look of dawning comprehension.

I didn't hesitate to finish him, forcing Nightmare into his solid chest with as much strength as I could muster. The tip pierced his heart and he turned to dust which tumbled through the air. The rain swept him away like he'd never even existed and satisfaction dripped through my veins.

I gritted my teeth against the agony in my shoulder, scrambling toward my severed arm and picking it up with a grimace. I'd seen others heal from this before so I knew what to do. I placed the torn edges of flesh against the wound and my skin started to bind together. I sighed in relief as the pain dulled a fraction and a cool sensation ran through my shoulder, moving down the limp arm. My fingers tingled and slowly, my bones and then nervous system reconnected to the limb. I flexed my hand, but my wrist bone was shattered and a new wave of pain found me as it started to heal.

Julius shouted his victory and I looked up just as he plunged Menace into the other twin's chest. As the biter disintegrated into nothing but dust, I noticed the end of Julius's blade was jagged and broken.

I hurried to meet him, squeezing his arm. "What happened to it?"

"The gods," Julius snarled, his eyes glinting with emotion.

"They're here?" I asked in horror.

"They're helping Valentina," he confirmed and my throat thickened at that knowledge.

Anger coursed through my chest. That bitch had Erik somewhere and I was damn-well going to find him. I didn't care if every god in the heavens was helping Valentina, no one, not even the immortal deities could keep me from my husband.

CALLIE

CHAPTER TWENTY EIGHT

The rain withdrew as we fought and the streets ran red with blood and water beneath our feet. I'd lost sight of my sister in the mayhem, but I could only focus on the fight which surrounded me as the biters pressed close. I was like a shining beacon for them to aim for in the dark; my injuries were still bleeding and the scent of my blood drew them after me in a never-ending flood.

I gritted my teeth against the pain in my skull from the wound Wolfe had given me but the constant ache was hard to ignore. It was slowing me down, making sounds harsher and my vision kept speckling with stars. The rain had washed his venom from my neck which was something at least.

Fabian stayed beside me, ripping through the biters like death given flesh. He moved with the speed of the wind and the rage of the deepest pits of hell. It was hard to believe that any of the vampires dared come for me with him by my side, but their thirst for my blood clearly outweighed any fear they held for their own existence.

Danielle was still on his other side, guarding his back while he fought, swinging her sword savagely.

Piles of clothes were building up around them and I moved away as they threatened to trip me.

My breaths were heavy and fatigue started to grow in my limbs but I refused to slow my pace, willing my gifts to fill my muscles with as much strength as I could wield.

Despite Fabian's best efforts to hold them back, many vampires got around him, baring their teeth as their desperation for my blood drove them ever closer.

They were savage, intoxicated by the promise of what lay in my veins and I simmered with unbridled anger as I fought them back.

I swept Fury towards a hulking male as he charged at me, the blade cutting deep into his side a moment before his shoulder collided with my chest.

He fell on top of me, crushing me into the wet concrete as his rancid breath washed over my face. His fangs dipped towards my neck and I slammed my hand into his jaw, grabbing hold of his chin and fighting to force him back.

He pushed down harder and I snarled as I tightened my grip, wrenching his lower jaw sideways until I heard a snap. The vampire reared back in pain, jerking out of my grip and giving me enough space to get my legs up between us. I kicked him off of me, throwing him into more of his bloodsucking friends before I rolled upright again.

Purple lightning arced through the sky overhead and I glanced up at it, wondering what Valentina was up to.

I dropped my gaze to the biters once more, raising Fury defensively.

The male with the broken jaw glared at me for a moment then turned and fled.

I stared in confusion as the rest of them raced away from us too and Fabian grabbed my arm to stop me from taking chase.

"That must have been a signal for them to retreat," he said as he looked down at me. "The day is ours."

"Why would they retreat?" I asked in confusion as the biters sped across the wreckage of Realm A and poured out into the ruins.

"Erik?!" Montana screamed, the anguish in her voice clear.

I turned to look at her as she shot past me, chasing after the retreating biters with a desperate look on her face.

"What's happening?" I demanded as I pulled out of Fabian's grip and ran after her.

The clouds broke ahead of us and the sun blazed down, creating a wide wall of light between us and the biters which the vampires couldn't cross.

Clarice shot past me and tackled Montana before she could make it to the sunlight. "You can't just chase after them," she snarled as Montana tried to fight her off. "Valentina took him for a reason. She obviously wants him alive which gives us time to get him back. If you run after them alone, then they'll just kill you. We have to be smart about this."

"She took Erik?" I asked, wondering how the hell that could be possible.

My heart squeezed with pity for my sister as she continued to fight to get free of Clarice.

"We have to go after Valentina!" Montana shouted, looking to me for help. My grip on Fury tightened as I wondered if I'd have to force Clarice to release her.

I stared about at the bloodstained square and found Julius moving towards me.

"Have you seen Magnar?" he asked urgently and my heart jolted with fear.

"No," I breathed, spinning quickly to try and locate him.

There was nothing around us but the clothes of the destroyed vampires. A glimmer of gold caught my eye close to the burning town hall and I started running towards it, moving past the shattered remains of a wooden structure.

Julius kept pace with me and I skidded to a halt as I found Venom half buried in a pile of clothes. Julius was saying something to me but I couldn't hear what it was as my pulse pounded with panic through my eardrums.

Sun Child, the blade growled in greeting as I pulled it from the ground.

"What happened?" I breathed, unsure if the blade could even tell me.

My vision clouded and I was Magnar for a moment. Biters ran at him from every direction and wrapped chains around his arms which caused pain to flare through his flesh. Lightning hit the ground before him, knocking the blade from his grip and I had no idea what had happened next.

I blinked and the vision was gone. Julius was staring at me expectantly and I shoved Venom into his grasp so he could see for himself before I turned and started hunting for Tempest.

I dug through the heaps of clothes desperately before the blade was revealed. I snatched it up and the heat of its rage washed over me.

"Show me," I demanded.

The vision flooded me. I was Magnar, on my knees as Valentina approached. She was scowling, holding a golden chain between her fingers.

"See how the mighty Magnar Elioson bows at my feet," she said, halting out of reach.

"You can force me to kneel but I'd never bow to you, whore," *Magnar spat.*

Valentina's chain snaked out and snapped into place around his throat, choking him.

Another vampire kicked his hand, knocking Tempest to the floor and the vision was lost.

"What did you see?" Julius demanded, grabbing my arm so tightly that it hurt.

"Valentina has him too," I whispered, unable to believe that such a thing could have happened. "She used chains strengthened by the gods. They were around his throat. He couldn't breathe-"

"Then let's get him back," Julius growled.

I looked up at the determination in his gaze and found my own strength there too. This wasn't the time to fall apart. We had to be strong. And we had to fight for Magnar.

"Okay. Let's go," I snarled.

Julius nodded and we took off across the concrete, heading towards the blazing sunshine which carved a line through the clouds.

Fabian was on the other side of the square, talking to the guards who had helped us against the biters and I noticed Danielle looking our way curiously as we ran past them.

Clarice still restrained Montana and she was sobbing angrily, calling Erik's name.

"Let her go," I demanded as I stopped before them, pointing Tempest at her in a clear threat.

"Just wait," Clarice begged, her arms still locked around my sister.

"That sunlight might weaken *you* but it won't make a bit of difference to us," I growled. "And we aren't hanging around here waiting for nightfall. I'm getting Magnar back now and Montana's coming with us for Erik."

"You can't possibly succeed alone," Clarice protested. "We need to form a plan, go after her united. If you go in there half-cocked you could get both of them killed."

"We might be willing to work with you for the sake of solving the prophecy but this is about family," Julius snarled. "And the day I need to ask for help from a parasite will be a cold day in hell."

"Don't be fools," Clarice hissed. "We have the resources, numbers and weapons needed to execute a successful rescue. You don't."

I glanced at Julius hesitantly. The idea of leaving Magnar in Valentina's hands for even an extra second made my blood boil, but she had a point. Even if Montana braved the sunlight, there were only three of us and I was exhausted and injured from the battle as it was. Valentina still had most of her army and we could do with help even if it was from a bunch of bloodsuckers.

"She has a point," I conceded, and Julius nodded at me.

"If we wait then don't go getting any ideas about us being under your command," Julius spat. "We're using *you*, not the other way around. This is purely about getting Magnar back."

"And Erik," Montana added forcefully.

"Yeah, him too," Julius muttered as an afterthought.

An engine rumbled and I looked up as an armoured truck pulled in through the open gates. Miles leapt from the cab with a rocket launcher over his shoulder, swiftly followed by the dark haired vampire who had been in Erik's dream.

"Oh shit did we miss it?" Miles asked, his face falling as he gazed about.

I scowled at him as he moved closer, my grip tightening on Tempest as I assessed him. He'd been the one to catch me before I'd been forced into marrying Fabian and I didn't trust him one bit. His gaze travelled over me and Julius curiously, but he didn't make any move to attack us so I guessed he was up to date on our current alliance.

"Where the hell were you?" Clarice demanded as she glared at him.

"Well..." Miles glanced at the male vampire beside him and shrugged. "We didn't have our phones with us and I only just got your messages. Sorry. It looks like you didn't need us anyway."

"That bitch has kidnapped our brother," Clarice growled. "Which might not have happened if we'd had your help."

"What do you mean?" Miles asked in fear and Clarice explained what had happened to Erik and Magnar as Montana moved to my side and took my hand.

"We'll get them back," I promised her.

"I'm going to kill Valentina with my bare hands," she snarled, and I nodded in agreement.

"We'll end her just like Wolfe."

Fabian shot towards us and I took a step back uneasily as the three Belvederes stood opposite me. Our alliance was tenuous at best and Erik had been the one to implement it. I still didn't trust the rest of them, and with him gone, I wasn't sure what to expect from them.

"I've organised the guards and they're going to triple the watch here and make sure the human population are cared for. We need to get back to the castle," Fabian said, his eyes falling on me, though he didn't move any closer.

I wasn't sure what to make of him anymore. We'd fought side by side and he'd saved me more than once during the battle, but it was hard to say how much of that had been because of the false love he felt for me or whether any part of it was truly who he was.

"Yes," Clarice agreed, "Let's go." She led the way towards the truck that Miles had arrived in and the others followed.

I caught Julius's wrist as they all piled in, and Montana glanced back at us curiously but I waved her ahead.

The pain in my head was making me dizzy again but I fought it off.

Julius glanced down at me, seeming to realise I wanted to talk to him without the vampires overhearing. He looped his arm around me as if he'd noticed me needing help and we moved away quickly.

"We need to stay close once we head into their castle," he breathed, following my own line of thought. "We're outnumbered and we'll have to keep our wits about us."

"And we need to stick together when it comes to going after Valentina," I replied in a whisper. "The only thing they care about is getting Erik back. Even Montana will focus on him. So we have to make sure Magnar is our priority."

I was so afraid for Magnar that it was making my chest ache. What did Valentina want him for? And why had she taken Erik too? It couldn't be anything good and the longer she held them the worse it could get. She could be torturing them as we spoke.

"Don't worry," Julius replied. "I'm well aware of what it will come down to in the end. We'll look after our own first. Just as I'm sure they will."

I smiled up at him fiercely and he wrapped his arms around me, placing a kiss on my forehead. I leaned against his chest, stealing a moment in his arms to let the panic have me. A tear squeezed from my eye and I took a shuddering breath before banishing the feelings of dread again. It wouldn't help Magnar if I fell apart. I had to be strong. He needed that so much more than he needed my tears.

Julius released me and caught my chin as he inspected the wound on my temple. "How bad is that, honestly?" he asked and I could tell he knew I'd been trying to hide my pain.

"Bad," I replied. "But a bit of rest should be enough to shake it off. I'm just a little dizzy."

"Alright. But tell me if it gets any worse," he said seriously and I nodded my agreement.

We jogged back to the truck and I noticed Montana sitting in the cab with Miles and the other vampire. I smiled at her reassuringly as she looked down at me and I followed Julius around to climb in the back.

He offered me his hand, helping me up so I could cover my injuries more effectively. I released him and lowered myself onto a bench which ran along the side of the covered space. I only noticed I was sitting next to Fabian as I slid along to make room for Julius, and I shifted uncomfortably as he scrutinised me.

Clarice and Danielle were sitting on the bench opposite us alongside some other vampires I didn't recognise. Most of the guards were staying behind to defend the Realm.

"I thought Magnar was the one I had to be jealous of," Fabian muttered irritably, glancing at Julius as the truck started up and Miles drove us towards the castle.

"Oh don't worry," Julius replied for me. "You've got plenty to be jealous of me for. I'm better looking than you, better built, stronger, funnier, more interesting-"

"More full of yourself," Clarice added.

"So you're not disagreeing with anything else I said? Just pointing out that I know it," Julius replied with a smirk. "And I've told you to stop staring at me like that, parasite. My pants won't just disappear because you wish they would."

I sniggered as Clarice glared at him, and a wave of dizziness washed through me.

"I wouldn't fuck you if you were the last man left on Earth," she growled.

"That would sound so much more convincing if you weren't drooling," Julius replied dismissively. "But don't get too excited; I like my women to have a heartbeat."

Clarice seethed and I couldn't help but be impressed with how unaffected Julius was by her anger. If one of the Belvederes had been looking at me like that then I'd have been seriously shaken.

I ran my fingers along Tempest's hilt, stealing some strength from the blade. My thoughts turned to the warrior who owned it again and fear danced along my veins. I'd return the sword to Magnar right after I plunged it through Valentina's heart.

The injury to my temple was sending a slicing pain through my skull and I closed my eyes as the truck bounced along the road. My body was battered and bruised from the battle and unlike my undead companions, I needed time to recover.

"Are you alright?" Fabian murmured, leaning closer to me and I felt his breath on my neck.

I shifted away from him until I bumped into Julius.

"I'm fine," I muttered, refusing to admit just how bad I felt. But the pain in my head was starting to throb and I wasn't sure how much longer I could manage to fight off the effects of my injuries.

Julius glanced at me, seeming to notice my strength waning too. He pulled me under his arm and glared at Fabian, warning him back.

"You just keep your attention fixed on your own kind and I'll look after mine," he demanded.

"Can't she just heal like you do?" Fabian asked him anxiously.

"She's Clan of Dreams, not Clan of War, so it'll take her a little longer, that's all," Julius snapped, closing the subject.

I shut my eyes so that I didn't have to look at them anymore and the pain in my skull lessened as I blocked out the light. I was sure I'd be fine soon enough. I just needed a bit of rest to regain my strength before going after Magnar.

I hoped Valentina knew what was coming for her now. Because I wouldn't stop hunting her until I finished her eternal life for good.

ERIK

CHAPTER TWENTY NINE

I didn't stop trying to escape as the truck tore along a road, bumping wildly over broken stone and crumbled mortar. I'd received more cuts thanks to my attempts and the chains were so tight, blood was pouring from my wounds. The injury Callie had given me mere days ago was split open again and I ground my teeth against the agony it caused.

The sun had been left behind at last as I moved away from the extension of Valentina's powers, but even with my strength intact I couldn't break free of my binds. I focused my attention on the surrounding ruins instead, certain we were heading into the destroyed half of Brooklyn.

I counted every turn, committing it to memory. The second these chains were released, I'd fight tooth and nail to escape. If Valentina wanted me dead, I'd have been reduced to dust by now. But that was a fatal mistake. Because if she thought she could hold me alive, she was going to pay for that stupidity in her own blood.

The brakes whined and the truck finally pulled to a halt. The biter in the cab hopped out and a voice called to him.

"You actually got him?" a male gasped.

"Uhuh. I've got one of our royal rulers right here." Someone banged their knuckles on the truck and I ground my teeth, waiting for them to appear.

Four biters circled the vehicle, gazing into the cab with wide eyes.

"Holy shit," a female said. She had bright red hair cropped short into a bob and an angular face that made her resemble a crow. Her eyes raked over me with vicious delight.

"Hello, Prince Erik." She ran her finger across the edge of the truck.

I snarled but she only grinned in response.

Two of them climbed into the truck bed, lifting me between them. There was no point in fighting them yet; the chains would start breaking bones if I fought them any harder.

They sprang down from the truck while holding me aloft and I eyed the rubble around us between two demolished buildings. They walked with purpose and I spotted a metal sign bent over at an angle as it jutted from the ground.

Rockaway Avenue Station.

I tucked that snippet of information away as they moved past the sign and we descended into a stairway between mountains of debris. Darkness swooped over me but my eyesight quickly adjusted so that I could see the dank, slanted ceiling above me.

They increased their pace, heading ever further into the depths of the old subway station. We arrived beside a large track and they promptly jumped down onto it. Old movie adverts were plastered across the walls and a poster girl watched my plight with her eternal smile. Her blue eyes were cracked down the middle and riddled with mould, the effect strangely haunting as my captors carried me away from her.

The darkness thickened, but I could just make out old cables on the walls, running deep into the tunnel. The biters moved faster and a light suddenly grew around me as we approached another station. Our way was blocked by an old train and one of the biters threw me over their shoulder, springing onto the platform beside it.

The group carried me toward the train and the redhead punched her thumb onto a button on it. The doors opened with a hiss and they walked me inside. The carriage had been gutted and looked recently decorated; the walls and floor were painted red and at the far end was a large throne that looked like it belonged in a museum. It was a huge, golden thing with crimson cushions.

One guess who that belongs to.

The biters wheeled me around to face the opposite direction and a chasm opened up in my chest. Two large cages filled the rest of the space which were big enough for four men to stand in each.

I ground my teeth, unable to fight the urge to writhe in their arms as they carried me toward the cage on the right. One of them swung the door open and they promptly dumped me inside.

I spat air through my teeth as my chin hit the floor. Rolling, I turned my gaze on them as they slammed the door shut and a metallic gong rang out. The redhead slid a padlock into place, eyeing me with glee.

"Prepare to bow to your new queen," she said, her eyes glittering.

"I don't bow to anyone," I growled.

"And yet you were happy to make us all bow to you and deny us our gods-given right," she snarled.

The large man beside her with a bloody cut across his nose nodded his agreement. A sweet satisfaction filled me that a slayer had delivered that blow; it was going to leave one hell of a scar.

"But you're content following Valentina as your queen? You're a bunch of sheep with no brains of your own," I said icily.

"We will feed from the vein under our new ruler," the wounded man said, cracking his knuckles. "She is the true queen of the New Empire."

"So what will you rename it now?" I asked coolly. "The New, *New* Empire? Not quite as catchy, but I wouldn't expect anything more from a bunch of braindead fuckwits."

"It will be the Scarlet Empire," the redhead announced with a wide smile. "The humans will be released from the Realms and we shall hunt them as we please. Our calling will be fulfilled. Our true nature will be honoured and never hidden. We won't be oppressed any longer."

"Well as charming as that sounds, I'm afraid you haven't taken over yet. My family will come for me. And the only blood that will be spilled in my empire will be yours."

The redhead stepped closer to the golden bars, glaring in at me.

"They'll never find you, Erik Belvedere. And even if they get close, Valentina will bake them in the sun's rays until they yield."

"Perhaps...if I don't tear her heart out first," I snarled as anger simmered in my veins.

She threw her head back as she cackled. "You're in a cage made by the gods. They're helping us because they know our cause is just. They gave us this gift of immortality and they want us to spend it well."

"I'd be careful laying my trust in the gods if I were you. They are not on anyone's side," I said.

She turned her back on me and the biters exited the carriage, leaving me alone.

An ethereal laughter reached me from beyond the planes of this world. Idun was close, mocking me. I gritted my teeth, not acknowledging her presence, but as I lay in the silence, the chains around me loosened, uncoiling like living things and slithering toward the bars like wicked serpents. They moved through them, curling into a pile beyond the cage and I released a slow breath.

I rolled my shoulders, wincing from the cuts they'd inflicted on me as I waited for my body to heal. A heavy pressure bore down on me and I gazed up at the red roof of the carriage.

A warm hand brushed my cheek and I grimaced at the invisible touch of the goddess.

"Why?" I bit at her. "What is Valentina offering you for this?"

Her ethereal voice filled the air and her lips brushed my ear. *"Valentina is devout. She honours us."*

"Us?" I spat, realisation hitting me.

"Andvari and I wished for a fight. You and Magnar scorned us, hiding under the gifts of his treasure. Where is it, my love? Which of you wields it?"

I smiled coldly, remaining silent. If they wanted that ring, I sure as shit wasn't going to help them find it.

Sharp nails raked down my chest and I swore between my teeth as my shirt turned to ash around me.

Two dark eyes found me in the reflection of the carriage window as Andvari emerged, gazing at me.

"You have turned on me," he snarled, his face almost pressing against the glass.

"You've never helped me," I snapped. "You expect me to do your will, but I'm done playing your games. You want me dead? Then fucking do it already."

Andvari scowled, baring his sharp teeth. "Death is easy. Valentina will ensure you suffer. And when you are nothing but a bleeding, starving husk, you will beg for mercy from me. Then you will tell me where to find my ring."

As my wounds healed enough for me to move, I rose to my feet and stared at him through the window beyond the bars.

"You're forgetting something," I said, a dark grin twisting my lips. "That ring protects my wife from you. And I would never give it up, not if you tortured me for a thousand years."

"Love is powerful," Idun whispered to us both. *"But it can be wielded. It can be used as a weapon against you."*

"You're clutching at strings, Idun," I said with a hollow laugh.

"Am I?" She stepped from the very fabric of the air before me, her golden skin gleaming as beautiful vines crept around her naked body. She moved toward me with a lustful smile and my love for Montana shifted sharply onto her.

I moaned, stumbling forward, wishing to touch her, needing to with every fibre of my being. She caught my hand as I approached, placing it against her cheek. I stilled before her, enraptured by her. But my mind snagged on a dark-haired girl with skin as pale as the moon and I snatched my hand away.

She tutted, forcing her will into me again as she claimed my heart once more.

"Foolish prince," she purred. "I am the one you adore."

I nodded, reaching out for her again and brushing my fingers through her silken hair. Desire slid into me like a hungry animal and I reared towards her, desperate for her mouth on mine.

She stepped back, surveying me with a smile. "I will make you love whomever I choose."

I nodded firmly, bathing in the sound of her voice, willing to do whatever she bid me to do.

"So where is the ring, which one of your friends wields it?" she asked.

The answer came to my lips, but I bit down on my tongue to stop myself, a renewed flare of loyalty finding me. I blinked, clamping my teeth together as the answer tried to fight its way from my mouth.

The doors sounded again and Idun's presence evaporated. My heart was my own once more and relief spilled through me at escaping her power.

I turned to find Magnar being manhandled into the carriage, yelling his anger as he battled against the gods' chains. One was wrapped around his neck so tightly that his muscles bulged beneath it.

Blood dripped to the floor from his wounds and the biters eyed it greedily as they approached the empty cage beside mine, but they didn't take a taste of it.

Magnar was thrown inside and the door banged shut before the biters locked it too. The chains around him loosened just as mine had, slithering away from him into the pile my own had formed and he spat a wad of blood from his mouth as he raised a hand to his bleeding throat.

Magnar groaned, rolling onto his side as his eyes found mine and I sensed irritation in his gaze. He released a heavy huff. "Great. Of all the fucking bloodsuckers to be stuck here with, it had to be you."

CALLIE

CHAPTER THIRTY

The truck jerked to a halt and I sat up suddenly as I came to my senses again. I wasn't sure if I'd fallen asleep or passed out, but I hadn't wandered into any dreams so I was tempted to believe it was the latter. Julius's arm was tight around my shoulders and I smiled up at him appreciatively as I moved out of his grip.

My head swam with pain and my vision darkened a little as I got to my feet.

Julius leapt out of the truck and I waited for the dizziness to pass as Danielle, Clarice and the other vampires followed him out.

I took a steadying breath as I moved to the exit and Fabian caught my elbow.

"Let me carry you inside," he breathed, his voice laced with concern. "You can hardly stand."

I tugged my elbow out of his grip and shook my head, causing it to spin wildly.

"I thought I warned you not to touch me," I snarled before jumping out of the truck.

The sudden movement stole my energy though and my vision darkened to the point of totality as the ground rushed towards me. I heard Tempest hitting the gravel path as it fell from my grip and the sound resounded painfully through my skull, causing me to wince in preparation of my face following it to the ground next.

Darkness took me before the pain could strike and I lost myself to it for several seconds.

I came around quickly, blinking in confusion as I found myself in Fabian's arms while Julius pointed Venom at him.

"Release her," the slayer growled and I tried to push my way out of Fabian's grip, but he wouldn't let me go.

"She collapsed," Fabian hissed. "I'm just looking after her."

"If you care about her then you'll respect her wishes. She told you not to touch her." Julius stepped closer, violence simmering in the air between them.

"Get off of me," I snapped.

Fabian reluctantly released the arm which he'd banded beneath my legs so that my feet could touch the ground, but he kept his other arm around my waist. I used my gifted muscles to shove him back and I stumbled towards Julius, hoping I could make it that far without blacking out again.

Montana climbed out of the cab as the tension between them grew. "What's going on?" she asked, her eyes darting between the three of us and landing on me with concern.

"Nothing," I replied quickly, not wanting her to worry about my injuries. We had more important things to focus on. "We need to get moving."

Julius stooped to retrieve Tempest from the ground before handing it back to me. The heavy presence of the blade made me feel closer to Magnar as it greeted me, and I held it tightly as I followed Clarice up a wide set of stairs which led into the lavish castle.

Julius stayed close to my side and I offered him a small smile when I was sure the others weren't looking. I didn't want these vampire to realise just how weak I felt. I'd lost a lot of blood as well as having my head smashed into a wall and I was the only one here who couldn't heal quickly.

We moved through expansive corridors and up a spiralling staircase until Clarice led us into an office with a huge glass table dominating the central space.

I dropped into a chair with a sigh of relief and waited while Clarice, Montana, Julius, Miles and the vampire who seemed to be his shadow took seats too. I guessed Danielle and the other Elite weren't going to be privy to this conversation.

The door closed behind us and I frowned as I wondered where Fabian had gone.

"It might be worth cloaking all of us so the gods can't hear this conversation," Julius murmured on my left and I nodded as I pushed the ring's protection over everyone in the room.

The vampire I didn't know had chosen a seat opposite me and he smiled at me as he noticed my attention lingering on him. He was tall with black hair, dark skin and a strong presence. I wondered why he was the only Elite to be given special treatment, my gaze trailing to Miles whose seat had been tugged close to the stranger's.

"I'm Warren." He leaned forward, offering me his hand but I didn't shake it, still too wary of the bloodsuckers to trust an unfamiliar one easily.

"And why are you here, Warren?" I asked.

He glanced at Miles who answered for him.

"He's family." He dropped his voice to a conspiratorial whisper. "Warren is my secret husband."

I didn't smile in response to the wide grin he offered me. "And did you have to kidnap him and force him down the aisle too?" I asked.

"No," Miles chuckled like I'd been joking. "This one is for love."

"How nice for you to be allowed to make that decision," I replied darkly before looking away from both of them.

Being back in this place was putting me on edge. We were surrounded and outnumbered, and I was beginning to wonder why the hell I'd agreed to come here. Fabian still wanted me for his wife with or without the ring's influence. If we couldn't trust these bloodsuckers then there was very little that I'd be able to do to stop him from taking me again even with Julius.

Miles shifted uncomfortably and Montana caught my eye from

Julius's other side, giving me a reassuring smile. She obviously didn't think I had any reason to fear this place and I had to trust in her knowledge of these royals.

"What are we waiting for?" Julius asked as no one seemed inclined to start discussing what we were going to do next.

"Fabian is just sending his Familiars out to scout for Valentina," Clarice explained. "We need to figure out where that bitch is hiding. We can start as soon as he returns."

The pounding in my head was growing sharper again and I touched my fingers to the wound on my forehead, fighting the urge to wince.

Miles watched me with interest and I scowled at him. "Am I making you hungry, bloodsucker?"

"A little, now that you mention it," he replied. "But mostly I'm just fascinated by seeing a wound which doesn't heal instantly."

I placed Tempest on the table in front of me and leaned towards him. "I can give you one to match if you like it so much?" I offered.

"You can try if you want to spar with me." Miles grinned and I got the feeling that was a genuine offer.

"Our kind don't play at fighting with the likes of you," Julius snorted dismissively. "So if you want to fight her then you'd better be prepared to die."

The door opened before Miles could respond and I looked around as Fabian stepped in. He was holding a glass of water and had something else clasped in his other fist. He began to move towards me then halted suddenly as the ring's influence fell over him.

I eyed him warily as his love for me slipped away and I wondered what that would mean. The last time I'd released him from it, he'd tried to steal the ring from me and force the bond back into action. I clenched my fist tightly, ready to remove its power again if I had to.

"Have your Familiars found anything?" Clarice demanded of him.

"Not yet," he replied, though his gaze remained fixed on me. "But they're scouring every inch of the city. It won't be long until they find them."

"I imagine you said much the same thing when they were hunting us," Julius replied scathingly. "But they weren't very effective then."

270

Fabian dropped into the seat on my right and didn't respond, though he was clearly irritated by Julius's remark. He placed the glass of water on the table before him and slowly slid it towards me as if he wasn't sure if he wanted to do it or not.

He hesitated before leaving it in front of me then withdrew his hand. "What's that for?" I asked.

Fabian glanced at the rest of the people in the room before he replied. "It's water. So that you can take these." He held out his fist and I frowned as he opened it to reveal two white pills. "They're painkillers to help you feel better. You're my wife after all and I swore to look after you."

"I've never noticed you paying so much attention to caring for your other wives," Miles commented.

"Well there's not a lot of point in her being here if she can't think straight," Fabian replied dismissively, dumping the pills on the table in front of me before looking away.

"He divorced his other wives anyway. Aren't we supposed to pretend they never existed?" Warren reminded Miles and the two of them laughed as Fabian glowered.

I guessed that he wouldn't have gotten the painkillers for me if he hadn't been under the influence of our bond at the time, and now that it was gone, he seemed embarrassed by the action.

I pursed my lips as I picked up one of the little pills. "What am I supposed to do with these?"

"Swallow them," Fabian growled, obviously wanting to move the conversation along.

My headache was only getting worse so I shrugged as I put the pill into my mouth and washed it down with the water. I repeated the process with the second pill and some of the tension left Fabian's shoulders as the attention shifted off of us.

"We need to quell these biters once and for all," Clarice announced, drawing the subject back around to the reason we were all there. "Once we have their location, we need to go in hard and without mercy. When they were just protesting there wasn't much we could do about them but at this stage I don't think there is any other choice but to execute them all."

"Agreed," Fabian snarled.

"We should try to apprehend Valentina," Miles added. "Then we can broadcast her execution for everyone in the New Empire to see."

"If I get to her before you, I won't be holding back on killing her," Julius replied.

"Me neither," Montana said and I agreed with both of them on that.

"So long as she dies, I don't care much either way," Clarice said. "We can't let this stand. She has flouted our laws, raised a rebel army, abducted a prince and placed a false crown upon her head. It's time she learned the consequences of those actions."

"We should go after her at night so she can't use the sun against you," Julius said.

"What of the other elements she can wield?" Miles asked, pushing a hand through his blonde hair. He and Warren looked oddly clean in comparison to our post-battle filth.

"There's not a lot we can do about the wind." Julius shrugged. "But when I used to spar with her, I would try and contain her within a building or cave to cut off her connection to the rain and lightning. She can't fist fight for shit if you can get that close to her. We always used to tell her to work on it but she refused, preferring to rely on her gifts."

"As far as I'm aware, she hasn't spent any time sparring since she was turned," Fabian added. "So I'm sure if any of us can get close enough she'll be easy to dispatch."

I smiled in response to that.

"Good. Then for now we should rest up in preparation of heading after her once we get a location," Clarice said. "Montana, you can have Erik's room; as he's your husband it's yours now too."

"Oh... sure," Montana said with a faint frown, and it didn't seem like she was entirely comfortable with that decision.

Clarice turned her gaze to me and Julius. "I can have rooms made up for the two of you as well."

"As much as you're obviously looking forward to sneaking into my bedroom tonight, I've told you I'm not interested in you, harlot. So we only need one room," Julius replied firmly.

Clarice opened her mouth to respond, her eyes flashing with rage but Fabian beat her to it.

"If you seriously think I'm going to let you take my wife to your bed in *my* fucking castle then you must be deluded," Fabian snarled. "If she's sharing anyone's bed, it'll be mine."

"Callie belongs with my brother," Julius growled. "And I'll die before I let you lay a hand on her."

"That can be arranged," Fabian hissed.

"I'm right here," I said loudly before they could come to blows. I turned my gaze to Fabian before I continued. "And I'll be sharing a room with Julius and ideally Montana too. We're already outnumbered here and if you think we're going to put ourselves at further risk by separating then you're all fucking insane. This isn't a negotiation and if you try to make any decisions *for* me then I will happily use this blade to cut your head off again. I'd hazard a guess that it might be a little harder to heal from in that scenario?"

Fabian eyed Tempest with distaste and let the subject drop.

"Well if we're done here then maybe you could all go and wash up," Miles suggested. "You reek of death."

"That's rich coming from the likes of you," Julius muttered.

Everyone got to their feet and as I stood, I was pleased to find my head didn't spin. In fact, I could barely feel my headache at all anymore. I realised with a jolt that it must have been because of the pills Fabian had given me and my gut squirmed uncomfortably as the unwelcome feeling of gratitude filled me.

"I'll show you to your room," Clarice said and Julius followed her as she headed away down the corridor.

Montana noticed my hesitation and stopped beside me as Miles and Warren left too. "Are you okay?" she asked.

"Yes. Just tell Julius I'll catch him up."

She glanced back at Fabian in surprise then nodded as she hurried after Clarice and Julius.

"Fabian?" I called, drawing his attention as he stepped out of the door.

He stilled and looked at me like he couldn't quite believe I wanted to talk to him. "Yes?"

"Could I have a moment?"

"Anything for my dear wife," he replied mockingly.

"Would you prefer it if I kept using the ring on you while we're talking?" I asked as I spun the golden piece of jewellery on my finger. I could already feel the others slipping outside of its protection and I just hoped that the gods didn't try anything while they were too far away for me to hide them.

Fabian looked at the ring too, seeming to consider it for a moment. "I think that would be wise if you would rather I restrained myself."

I gave him a faint smile and left the ring's power in place over him so that he wasn't a slave to our bond.

"I just wanted to thank you," I said. "For the pills. And for fighting beside me out there. You might have saved my life once or twice."

Fabian narrowed his eyes at me as if he was waiting for me to add something else, but that was it. I was still pissed at him for what he'd tried to do to Magnar in their fight, but it wasn't as though Magnar would have done any different had the tables been turned. And if they were all able to put their feud aside to try and solve the prophecy then I was willing to do the same. As much as I might have preferred not to, I knew that I did owe him my gratitude.

"Well if you really want to thank me then feel free to use your mouth for something other than words," he replied, shifting a little closer to me.

I rolled my eyes at him. "Do you work hard at being an asshole or does it just come naturally?"

"It's hard to say after all this time." He shrugged playfully and I couldn't help but smile a little.

"Have your Familiars found anything yet?" I asked, trying to keep the desperation from my voice, even though I was fairly sure I failed.

My heart ached for Magnar. I needed to know he was alright. I was desperate for any hint of information and I wasn't sure how long I could bear to wait in this damn castle before we headed after him.

"It's been thirty minutes," Fabian replied scathingly. "Animals can only get so far in such a short period of time."

"Right." I nodded, disappointment pooling in my gut as I began to turn away from him. "Well, that's all I wanted to say so-"

"I could show you something else if you're willing to trust me?" he offered.

"I should probably just go. Julius and Montana will be wondering-"

"Of course, you'd have to get permission. I'd forgotten you slayers are all just slaves to your vow." He turned and headed out of the room, and I scowled as I followed him, knowing full well that he was manipulating me but unable to resist the urge to prove him wrong. I didn't need to ask anyone's permission for anything anymore. I was free and I intended to stay that way for the rest of my days. Besides, if I stayed with him then I'd find out as soon as his Familiars discovered anything.

"This had better be worth my time," I muttered.

Fabian chuckled as he led the way back down the corridor and we descended a flight of stairs. He pointed out things about the paintings on the walls and the architecture of the building as we passed them and I frowned at the opulent surroundings.

"You realise this stuff doesn't impress me, right?" I asked as we headed down another long corridor and Fabian guided me into a darkened room. "Everything you're showing me just highlights how much you kept for yourselves while leaving the humans to suffer in squalor."

"There are those who would argue that humans used to allow their farm animals to suffer in squalor before we took over. As the new apex predators we are simply continuing your traditions."

"Humans used to eat animals?" I asked in disgust. That sounded a hell of a lot like being a vampire to me.

"Of course. But you couldn't really expect us to maintain that level of agriculture just to fatten up our own food supply now, could you? So we got rid of all of that when we seized power."

"Then it sounds like you did at least one good thing."

I looked around at the dark room as he headed on through it and I realised it was a library. The scent of dust filled my nostrils and I glanced back towards the exit, tightening my grip on Tempest as we delved further into the dark. The blade hummed with displeasure and I was sure it was trying to tell me that Magnar wouldn't like me doing this, but it was too late for me to turn back now. And if Fabian did decide to hurt me then all I'd have to do was remove the ring's influence from him again. The version of Fabian who was hopelessly in love with me could at least be relied upon to leave me unharmed.

"Yes, I suppose you *would* be able to identify with the plight of a cow destined to be a hamburger," he murmured.

"A what?"

"Never mind."

"I hope you haven't brought me all the way down here for a reading lesson so that I can decipher your next love letter for myself," I said, eyeing the books. "Because I'm really not sure if writing poetry is your calling."

"Hilarious," Fabian replied coolly. "But you can be assured I won't be writing to you again. Even if you *could* read."

"Well you say that now, while you're not all obsessed with me. But love-struck Fabian deals with things a little differently," I teased.

"What's to say I'm not obsessed with you either way?" he asked as he stopped before a door at the back of the room. "Here we are."

"And where exactly is *here?*" I didn't want to respond to his other comment or think about what it meant so I simply ignored it.

"You'll see." He typed a code into a keypad beside the door then pressed his hand to a scanner.

The sound of a heavy bolt unlocking filled the air and the door slid back into the wall. Then a light flicked on and a stairway was revealed.

"Ladies first," Fabian said, indicating for me to go ahead of him.

A shiver of anticipation ran down my spine and for a moment I could have sworn I heard a thousand voices whispering to me from the space beyond the stairs.

I stepped forward slowly, descending the steps as Tempest and Fury hummed in hungry excitement. No doubt I should have been hesitant to follow Fabian's instructions, but my instincts were urging me on with a sense of excitement which I couldn't quite place.

The hairs on the back of my neck stood on end and goosebumps raised along my flesh the further I went. Something was waiting for me at the foot of those stairs and it was eager for me to arrive. My blood sang for it and my heart pounded frantically like it was responding to the call of a long-lost friend.

When I finally stepped out into the enormous vault, my breath caught in my throat and my lips parted in wonder.

Every inch of space was filled with rack after rack of glimmering golden weapons. There were bows, axes, daggers, hatchets and blades. So many slayer blades that I could have sworn the room was alive with their energy.

I stepped forward, brushing my fingers along their hilts as their names whispered through my mind, one after another. Each of them longing to be held, begging me to lift them into my arms and use them for their sole purpose. To destroy the vampires.

I bit my lip as I turned back to Fabian and I couldn't fight the smile which lit my face.

"Do you think it was wise to bring me here?" I teased. Every weapon in this room hungered for his death with the desperation of a starving man.

"Maybe not," Fabian admitted, his eyes sparkling with a joy of his own. "But the look on your face right now is worth the risk."

MONTANA

CHAPTER THIRTY ONE

I stood in Erik's room with a sinking feeling in my chest, gazing around the space with emotion welling inside me. Black walls stared back at me and his large bed looked like it hadn't been slept in for a while. It was hard to believe how much had changed since the last time I'd been in this room. Erik had captured my heart entirely. We were linked in an irreversible way that had nothing to do with the gods' rune on my palm.

I'm coming for you. I'll save you from that bitch.

What if Valentina was torturing him? The idea set my blood boiling and my throat tightening. I hated her with an intensity that started an anxious fire in my heart.

I moved to the bed, dropping down onto it with an itching at the base of my throat. It grew to a persistent ache and I sucked in a slow breath, trying to will the sensation away. After the battle, I was exhausted. But not in a human way; it was a feeling deep in my chest and I was sure blood was what I needed to feel right again. Perhaps a good night's sleep too. But I didn't think that would come easy knowing Erik was trapped somewhere with Valentina for company.

I ran my tongue across my canines, flopping back onto the mattress and covering my eyes as I tried to will the desire away. Erik's scent floated over me and I rolled, pressing my face to his pillow and devouring the earthy smell. It might have been one-percent creepy but it also gave me an ounce of comfort that helped me fight the thirst. I lay there until I was sure the pain was going to devour me from the inside out. The ache for blood was nothing in comparison to being parted from Erik. Why was everything against us? Why couldn't any of this be simple?

I pressed my fingers into my eyes, not wanting to drown in self-pity. It was a pointless emotion, but one that was gnawing on my insides.

I just want him back. I need him to be okay.

The longer I lay there, the more my sadness evolved into a steely determination. I had my family at my back. Erik's family. Callie. Julius. Today we'd fought those biters and survived. I was certain we could keep doing so. Together, we were a small army. Frighteningly powerful and fearfully protective of our kin. So long as we could keep working together and put our differences aside, nothing could stop us. I knew I was a vital link between the two opposing sides. The bridge between the slayers and the vampires. So I had to be strong and ensure that the fragile ties binding them never wavered.

A knock came at the door and I sat upright, jolting out of my reverie. "Come in."

Clarice stepped through the door looking freshly washed in a silk dressing gown, the scent of coconut soap sailing from her skin. But the smell was nothing in comparison to the contents of the bottle in her hand.

I bared my fangs, unable to help myself as I sprang from the bed and started hounding toward her. I dug my heels in, forcing myself to a halt as my fingers twitched with the need to grab that bottle from her grip.

"It's alright. Here, it's Realm A." She held it out for me and I gritted my teeth, despising this part of the curse more than anything.

I swallowed hard against the sharp lump in my throat, having no choice as I took the blood from her. I was no good to Erik if I couldn't focus. And without blood, the thirst would only increase, snaring me in a net. There was only one way to escape that fate.

Twisting the cap off, I shut my eyes and lost myself to the tantalising scent. I started drinking and the thick liquid rolled over my tongue, so sweet and full of nourishment. I swallowed every drop, releasing a growl as I finished, hungering for more.

"It'll pass," Clarice promised. "That's enough to sate you."

I nodded, digging my fangs into my tongue to try and battle away the clawing urge to find more blood. I blinked hard and slowly the haze lifted from my mind, returning me to myself. In that moment, I was glad I'd chosen to sleep separately to Callie. I never wanted her to see me feed. And I'd known the second we'd arrived at the castle that the curse had gotten its hooks in me again. The less she witnessed that side of me, the better.

"Is it going away?" she asked and I nodded, releasing a breath of relief. She smiled, but there was a sadness in her eyes. "How are you adjusting?"

I chewed my lower lip, shrugging. "It's fine. I mean, it's not as bad as I thought. But the blood thing..." I shuddered. "I feel like a traitor to humans. Like I'm still one of them but at the same time, somehow not."

"Maybe we'll be human again one day," she said, her eyes glowing at the idea. "Erik said you're close to working out the prophecy?"

I nodded, but the possibility didn't offer me any of the relief it had in the past. With Erik and Magnar in trouble, Callie and I couldn't focus on anything but saving them.

"Why do you want to be human?" I asked, the question popping into my mind. "I mean, you have everything here. Is it the thirst?"

She pressed her back to the door and it clicked shut as she toyed with the belt of her dressing gown. "Partly that, yes. It's always been a burden to bear. But I..." She glanced up at me, seeming to consider whether to go on. "I don't want to upset you."

"Why would you upset me?"

"Because when you realise what you've lost, you'll know why it's the most terrible of curses. Especially for a woman."

My mouth parted as I figured out what she meant. "You want children?"

She nodded and her blue eyes sparkled with tears. "I thought if I could have love with a man, that would be enough. But even that's been impossible to find. I don't know if it's the curse or just...me."

My heart twitched at her words. How could someone as beautiful as Clarice not have found love? And regardless of her beauty, I was starting to see such a warmth in her. A kindness. She'd been good to me, even though her intentions hadn't always been for my benefit.

"I love my nieces and nephews," Clarice went on. "Don't get me wrong, I'm so blessed to have the life I do. But it will never be quite enough."

"Where are the children?" I asked.

"Miles and Fabian's wives live in the suburbs with them. They're protected. Human blood still runs in their veins until they come of age. They're vulnerable to our kind before their eighteenth birthday, then they become more like us. Immortal, impervious to the passing of time. Although some of them inherit the gifts of the slayers too. But the curse is still theirs to bear..."

I reached out and rested my hand on her arm. "We'll break it," I swore.

"But what if we don't?" she whispered. "What if there was never an answer? If it's just a riddle to drive us mad?"

Fear spilled into my veins. I hadn't really considered being stuck like this forever. I'd barely had a day to adjust to this new life, but it hit me hard that Clarice could be right. That the prophecy was a lie. And I would be like this for all eternity. Erik and I could never have children. No family of our own.

It wasn't something I'd ever wanted in my life in the Realm. But so much had changed in the past weeks. The possibilities of a free life had been presented to me. One where my children would never have to live in the conditions I'd grown up in. Would I choose to have them one day if it were an option?

My heart splintered as the answer came to me in a resounding, instinctive voice.

Yes.

I looked to Clarice with a sense of pity. She'd been this way for over a thousand years, searching for love, for something to make her immortal life worthwhile.

"That's why you have a harem," I guessed and she nodded in confirmation.

"I give every man in my harem a chance to see if we're a good match in the hopes that they're the one. Don't get me wrong, I care about them all. But never enough. Never more. Maybe I'm incapable of loving someone that way." She shook her head and her damp hair fell forward over her shoulders. A tear escaped her eye and she hastily wiped it away. She always seemed so strong and now she was coming apart right in front of me. We were on equal footing in this castle for once and I suddenly felt the need to comfort her. Although I barely knew her, I was strangely protective of her. As if the vampire part of me recognised her as my family. And I supposed she was now. She was my sister-in-law.

I wrapped my arms around her, pulling her close and she stiffened in my arms as if the action was unknown to her.

Clarice sniffed heavily. "I always wanted a sister." She leaned back, brushing a lock of hair over my shoulder. "Silly, isn't it? I've got everything in the world and yet I still long for more. I should just be happy with what I've got."

She reined in her tears, stepping away from me and tilting her chin up as she regained her composure.

"I don't think we can help what our hearts want," I said with a sad smile. "When I was brought to this castle, the last thing I ever could have imagined was falling for one of your brothers."

"I told you they're not all bad," she said with a grin. "Well, Fabian can be an ass, but he has a good heart. Deep down."

"I like him more when he's in love with my sister," I said, breaking a smile. "He certainly has a way with words."

She snorted. "Did he really write her a poem?"

"Yes and it was atrocious."

She laughed and the sound was light and musical, lifting the heaviness in the air. She glanced down at my filthy attire with a raised eyebrow. "You should get cleaned up." She gestured to the ensuite across the room. "I'll bring you some fresh clothes."

"Thank you," I said earnestly and she turned with a nod, heading out of the room.

I made a beeline for the bathroom, slipping inside and finding a room decorated with navy tiles. A circular mirror encrusted with tiny stars hung on the wall above the sink. I eyed myself in the reflection, wrinkling my nose as I spotted the blood and muck lining my flesh.

I took a long shower, cleaning my skin until its pearly white colour was revealed again. As I dried myself off with a towel, I gazed at the silver cross glimmering on my left palm. I ran my fingers over it, tracing the X, wondering if it would let me know if Erik was hurt, or even dead.

I blinked hard, jamming that thought to the back of my brain. If there was one thing I knew about my husband, it was that he was a force to be reckoned with. And wherever he was, he would be fighting his hardest to escape. Valentina had bitten off more than she could chew if she thought she could break him. And from what I'd seen of Magnar, I suspected the same of him.

I headed back into the bedroom, finding a pile of clothes left on the bed. Some silky pink pyjamas beside jeans and a black shirt for tomorrow.

I tugged on the pyjamas, feeling a little exposed in the tiny vest and shorts, but I wasn't cold, even with my damp hair hanging around me.

I moved toward Erik's closet, opening it and searching through the rack of expensive suits until my hand landed on a casual black sweatshirt. I shrugged it on and it hung down to my thighs. Leaving the zip undone, I rolled up the long sleeves and tugged my hair out from under the collar.

I padded to the door, no longer feeling tired even though I'd probably have been desperate for sleep if I'd still been human. My thoughts turned to Callie and Fabian. I knew she could handle herself with him and the ring's power gave her a weapon over him anyway, but I still didn't like the fact that they'd been left alone together. She was injured and coping with Magnar being taken. The last thing she needed was to deal with Fabian's bullshit too.

I stepped out into the corridor, finding Julius leaving my old room further down the hall at the same moment. He was dressed in navy sweatpants and a white t-shirt. His scent reached me. Blood and shower gel, but as the thirst prickled the base of my throat, I focused on the other scent and the hunger died away a little. I was fed and no longer under the curse's spell. But I wasn't about to tell him about the blood I'd recently consumed.

"Hey," I called and he turned to me with a grin as his gaze flitted over me. "Shit Montana, if you weren't a bloodsucking parasite, I'd almost have thought you look hot right now."

"Thanks," I said tersely, slightly hurt by his reference to me.

"Sorry," he muttered. "You're not a parasite."

I smiled awkwardly, walking toward him, wanting to move on from the massive roadblock between us. We were sworn enemies by the gods' standards. But I didn't give a damn what they thought. And the mere idea made me hook an arm through Julius's in an attempt to prove how much that wasn't true.

"I was going to look for Callie," Julius revealed and I nodded.

"I had the same idea. She's with Fabian."

His expression hardened. "Then let's go save her from him in case he starts spewing poetry again."

I left my arm around his and we headed toward the stairway.

Callie's scent called to me as we descended the red carpeted stairs into the expansive hallway below and I guided Julius along, breathing in deeply as the smell of her untended wounds guided my feet.

"You're sniffing her out," he commented, frowning at me.

"Yes..." I said carefully. "Does it bother you?"

"It bothers me that you have to deal with this curse. But, I guess I'm glad you're like this. Otherwise you'd be dead. And although being a vampire would have seemed like the worst thing on Earth to me a couple of days ago, now I'm having some doubts. And I really don't want to dwell on what that means."

I frowned as we walked, moving down another staircase into a large library. "Because you'd have to accept that the Belvederes might not be all bad?" I guessed.

"I didn't say that. I'm not enjoying keeping the company of the Golden Whore and her siblings."

My frown deepened and my heart tugged painfully. "Don't call her that. She's not a whore. And maybe if you knew her motivations for keeping a harem, you wouldn't think it either."

I released his arm as Callie's scent drew me toward a large metal door which stood open at the back of the room.

"What motivations?" he grunted, but I didn't think it was my place to share Clarice's secrets.

"Maybe you should ask her some time," I said lightly, pushing the door wider and stepping through it. The hairs on the back of my neck prickled to attention and I frowned.

"Yeah, maybe we'll share a picnic on the lawn under the light of the stars. Or maybe I'll gouge my own eyes out with a rusty spoon instead. That would definitely be preferable."

"Don't be a jerk," I said as he followed me into the stairwell and voices reached my ears.

Julius stilled then hurried past me, seeming impassioned by something as he ran down the stairs with a skip in his step.

I followed at speed as a strange humming ran through my veins. It was familiar and yet alien too. I arrived in the room and spotted Callie with a giant golden sword in her hands, standing between racks and racks of slayer weapons.

My mouth fell open as I took in the huge armoury, unable to believe how many of the blades stared back at me.

Fabian was watching Callie with an amused expression, but as we arrived, his eyes darkened.

"This wasn't an open invitation," he growled, his gaze following Julius as the slayer moved between the racks, looking like a kid who'd been handed a bucket of candy.

"Well I'm making it one," Julius said with a grin and Fabian's eyes narrowed dangerously.

"Callie?" I said as I approached her, a smile gripping my face. As I took in her dirty clothes and the scratches and gouges on her body, my smile fell away. "How are you feeling?"

"Fine now I've got this." She beamed as she swung the huge sword through the air. "Maybe I should test it out." She pointed it at Fabian and he gave her a dry look.

I spotted Tempest leaning against the closest rack and sensed the angry vibrations it was giving off.

"Pretend all you like that you want to kill me, but I know I'm under your skin, little slayer," Fabian said coolly and I realised the ring's power was now affecting him. He was back to his cocky I-don't-give-two-shits-about-the-world demeanour.

"Yes!" Julius cried with a wild laugh and I turned towards him as he picked up a beautiful sword with rubies encrusted in the hilt. "Vicious," he announced, turning to us. "This is Valentina's old sword. And now it's *mine*." He continued laughing, swiping it through the air. "She's going to die at the sharp edge of her own beloved blade."

I turned back to Fabian hopefully. "Have your Familiars found anything?"

"Not yet," he said, pressing his lips together. "They're searching the Brooklyn ruins. But that's nearly a hundred square miles to hide Erik in."

"And Magnar," Callie added, arching a brow.

"Who?" Fabian said coolly. "Oh yes, your half-wit slayer boyfriend."

"You're just jealous that Magnar can grow his hair twice as long as yours," Julius called from across the room. "Your little ponytail would be more fitting on a twelve-year-old girl, Fabio."

"It's *Fabian*." He bared his fangs, stalking toward Julius. "And the weapons in this room are Belvedere property. You don't get to take a blade without my say so."

Julius angled Vicious towards him with a casual smirk. "These are all designed to destroy your kind, Fabio. You don't own a single one of them. They were stolen from my people."

"It's not stealing if the owner is dead," Fabian said with a nasty grin.

Julius gritted his teeth and anxiety clutched my heart. Why the hell was Fabian goading a slayer in a place like this?

"Stop it," I said, stepping between them before their bickering escalated. "We're working together now, so can you drop the shit so we can start making a real plan?"

Julius lowered the sword slightly, giving in to my pleading look.

"The plan is this," Fabian said. "We wait for my Familiars to find

287

Valentina and then we go after her covertly."

"Excuse me, sire?" a female voice called from the door and I glanced back, spotting the blonde Elite from the battle stepping into the room. She wore a pair of jeans and a tank top that showed off her ample curves. She was beautiful with full pink lips and lake green eyes, her skin holding a shimmer to it that seemed to light up the room.

Fabian's eyes raked over her. "What is it, Danielle?"

"I had an idea..." She bit her lip and waited for Fabian's encouragement.

"Go on," he growled.

"Well I noticed you only sent birds to scout Brooklyn for Valentina, but you're forgetting about the miles of tunnels beneath the city. Perhaps rats would be more useful for this task?"

Fabian's brows pinched together as if he was going to berate her.

"That's a great idea," I said quickly. "If they're hiding underground, birds won't spot them."

Fabian glared at me then turned his attention back to Danielle. "I'll have it done."

"I have my own vermin Familiars. I could send them? It would save you the bother of making more," Danielle offered.

"Fine, do it," Fabian agreed.

Danielle turned to leave, but Fabian shot to her side in a jolt of motion, catching hold of her arm. "If you need a place to stay tonight, my quarters are available." He threw a surreptitious glance at Callie, but my sister seemed more interested in the sword in her hands. Fabian's eyes darkened as he turned to Danielle again. "If you don't mind bunking with me?"

Danielle raised a brow then laughed. "It's fine, sire, I'm not tired. I'm happy to work through the night and keep an eye on my Familiars."

Fabian shifted uncomfortably, her laughter clearly mortifying him. "Right...sure. But if you need anything-"

"I know where to find you," Danielle said, fighting a smile as she headed out of the room.

"That was embarrassing," Julius remarked. "You're getting shot down left, right and centre, Fabio. It must be really bruising that ego

288

of yours."

Callie snorted a laugh and Fabian snarled, glaring at him. "Shut your mouth."

"Make me," Julius taunted, swinging Valentina's blade through the air.

I sighed, giving up on them ever forming any kind of real bond. So long as they continued working together, that would have to do.

"Callie, are you hungry?" I asked, hoping to escape the tension in the room.

Her eyes widened and she nodded eagerly.

"I'm ravenous," Julius agreed, moving toward me, but Fabian sped into his path, pointing at the rack.

"Put it back," he commanded, but Julius just gave him an amused expression.

"I'm taking this sword. And if you'd rather not end up as a pile of ash in the next few seconds, I suggest you move out of my way, parasite."

Fabian bared his fangs and Callie moved into action, twisting the ring on her finger as she approached them.

"Let him have it, Fabian," she purred.

Fabian blinked hard, turning to her with wide, adoring eyes. "Oh... okay, sure. If it makes you happy, my love."

Julius clapped him hard on the shoulder as he moved past him. "It makes me ecstatic, thanks *bud*." He headed toward the door and Callie threw me a grin.

"I'll fetch a servant to bring anything you want to your room," Fabian said, his cold front lost to the power of their bond.

"Thanks. Maybe some cheese and bread?" Callie asked and Fabian nodded keenly.

"I'll have a feast made," he announced, hurrying from the room and barging past Julius in the doorway. With him gone, Julius moved back toward the weapons, picking up a golden bow and a quiver of arrows before shouldering them.

"I prefer love-sick Fabian," he mused. "I don't even have to try and humiliate him, he manages it all by himself."

Callie released a laugh, placing the sword back on one of the racks and picking up two short daggers instead. "I suppose this bind does have some positives."

"I think you could make him dance for you if you wanted," I said, grinning. "The gods really don't know what love is if they think acting like a doting moron is it."

Callie stilled at my words, her mouth opening. "Shit you're right." She clutched my wrist, her eyes glimmering with hope. "That's their weakness, Monty. It's love. They don't get it. The way Idun made me and Fabian behave over this bond, it's just lust, infatuation."

"So?" I questioned. "What difference does it make?"

"It means they'll underestimate real love," she said with a triumphant look in her eyes. "That's why we were able to stop Magnar and Erik from killing each other before. Because they love us. Truly. So maybe we can overcome anything the gods throw at us with that strength on our side."

"As long as you've got the ring though, we're safe anyway," I said.

"Yes *we* are. But Erik and Magnar aren't." A crease formed on her forehead. "They're on their own. And maybe that's what the gods want. To cut them off from us."

"Why?" I asked, fearful of that possibility.

"I don't know...to punish them? They're helping Valentina. But the gods won't be expecting Magnar and Erik to work together."

"Great," I said, realising what she meant. "So we have to hope they put their differences aside because of their love for us?"

"Yes," Callie said uncertainly. "If we don't find them soon, they'll have to make their own plan."

I sighed heavily, shaking my head. "I hope Fabian finds them in the next hour then."

MAGNAR

CHAPTER THIRTY TWO

I sat at the rear of the cage and waited with my back to the golden bars which held me.

Erik Belvedere was watching me intently but I refused to acknowledge him. Of all the creatures on this planet, I couldn't think of many I'd like to be stuck with less than him. Aside from Valentina of course.

I pulled my knees up to my chest and rested my elbows on them as I pushed my hands into my hair. This was torture of a specific kind. Valentina knew all about my vendetta with this parasite and she'd chosen to cage us alongside each other with the sole purpose of driving us insane with our proximity.

Of course she had no idea about the fragile alliance we'd recently formed. So instead of the seething desire to murder each other which she no doubt planned on, we were caught in the drawn out silence filled with all the things we hated about each other whilst not being able to voice them.

I ran my thumb over the dark tattoo on my left forearm which I'd gotten after my father's death. When he'd been my mentor, my left hand had been marked with a star which joined us and after he'd been taken from me I'd had a replica of that mark etched permanently into my own skin to remind me of my eternal bond to him. Now I sat a few feet from the monster responsible for stealing him from us, who'd changed my mother irrevocably, who'd altered my life and forced me to lead my people before my time should have come. And yet I had sworn not to hurt him.

I thought of Callie, hoping she'd escaped the battle unscathed. For the first time since she'd broken her novice bond to me, I wished it was still intact. Just so I could see that star on my hand and know her heart was still beating somewhere.

"It might help us if we come up with some plan for escaping this place," Erik muttered and I could tell he was growing tired of me ignoring him. But how could I simply start conversing with him like he hadn't done the things he'd done? Callie had assured me that Andvari was the one who was truly responsible for my father's death, but it wasn't so simple for me to relinquish my anger towards the vampire he'd chosen to use as his tool. I'd felt the touch of Idun's power many times and I'd also managed to throw it off on several occasions. Besides, being tricked by a deity was no excuse for what he'd done.

"I plan to kill Valentina as soon as she shows herself. I imagine escaping will become fairly simple after that," I replied in a low voice.

"That isn't a plan; it's an idle threat. You're stuck in a cage just as I am. Unless she decides to unlock the door for you, I highly doubt you'll be able to kill her."

"She'll let me out eventually," I said. "She won't be able to resist."

"To resist what? You can't think that she is so obsessed with you that she'll just open up the door if you flutter your eyelashes at her," Erik said in exasperation.

I shook my head at his ridiculous assumption but didn't bother to respond to it. I hadn't meant she wouldn't be able to resist me in that way, I meant she wouldn't be able to resist the urge to flaunt her power over me. She'd want to bend me to her will in any way possible and to do so she'd have to let me out of this forsaken cage.

I could tell that my silence was really pissing him off and I smiled to myself.

"I mean, she spent the last thousand years crawling in and out of *my* bed so she was hardly that cut up after your supposed death," Erik grumbled.

A surprised laugh fell from my lips at that admission and I looked up at him, finding I couldn't stop.

"What?" he asked angrily, moving to lean against the bars of his own cage.

"You bedded her?" I asked, laughing again. "Was that before or after you made her immortal?"

His eyes narrowed as he answered. "The first time was before. What difference does it make?"

"By any chance, were you motivated by the fact that she was betrothed to me?"

Erik pursed his lips, seeming to consider whether or not to answer. "You cannot understand the hatred I felt for you-"

"I'm sure I can," I growled in response.

I'd never murdered any of *his* family members so any hateful feelings he felt towards me couldn't compare to what I thought of him.

"Well...if you can, then perhaps you would have understood why bedding a woman promised to you might have given me some satisfaction beyond any other motivations."

I looked up at him with a smirk.

"What's so funny?" he demanded. "Shouldn't this just give you another reason to hate me?"

I got to my feet and walked towards the edge of my cage. I leaned against them as I looked at him, draping my arms between the bars. "When I was sixteen, I convinced a member of the Clan of Prophecies to look into my future so that I might take my vow early. He agreed and he foresaw my rise to power and all that I could offer the slayers. I became the youngest sworn clansman in the history of our people. My reward for that pledge was Valentina. Within weeks of me taking my vow, our betrothal was foreseen and I was forced to commit myself to marrying her." I lifted my shirt and pointed out the tattoo which curled around my heart. "Idun was kind enough to stain my skin with that promise. And if I'd ever broken our betrothal then I would have been

295

going against my vow and my life would have been forfeit."

"So you never even wanted her?" Erik asked with a frown. "You were forced to be with her?"

"No. I wasn't forced to be with her. I was forced to honour my promise. So our betrothal stood but it was up to the Earl to set a date for our marriage. My father knew how much I resented being forced into wedlock with her and so he held off on marrying us. After he died, I became Earl and that choice was mine. And I never chose to set a date either. I never wanted her. And despite her best efforts to seduce me, I never even bedded her." I started laughing again as Erik's face fell.

"That's not what she told me," he growled.

"No doubt she made you think I loved her dearly. I'm sure you were mightily impressed with yourself for stealing her from me."

"She told me you were cruel to her, that you beat her-"

"I would never do such a thing," I growled. "Besides I didn't care about her enough to waste time abusing her. I spent most of my time avoiding her."

"So you never raised a hand to her?" he demanded and I could tell he'd really believed I had.

"I never even sparred with her," I replied. "She refused to fight using anything other than the elements and I saw no need to waste my time trying to learn how to battle the wind. Besides it would have meant spending time in her company which I worked hard never to do."

"So she lied to me?" Erik frowned and I could tell the realisation bothered him. "She made me believe you were worse than cruel. A cold hearted murderer with no regard for the lives of others."

"I am all of those things," I replied darkly. "But never to my own kind. Only to yours."

The silence stretched again while Erik fought the temptation to bite back at me for that remark.

"So you decided to take my bride for yourself and I suppose that made you feel as though you'd won some victory over me?" I asked, turning the subject back to our mutual enemy.

"At first, yes. But then she told me she loved me and I found it hard to believe that someone of your blood could ever feel such a thing for one of us. The lust I could understand; the way we look has always drawn mortals to us-"

"No true slayer would covet your unnatural beauty," I growled. "We find it repulsive, not attractive."

"Are you saying I repulse you?" he scoffed like he couldn't imagine anyone not loving his statuesque features.

"More than you can know," I replied evenly.

I didn't care if he believed me or not. Nothing about the way they looked had ever drawn me in. It was just camouflage; a beautiful lie to disguise the ugliness of the rotten souls their bodies housed.

Erik's jaw ticked and I got the feeling he didn't like to be called repulsive. The idea of him being vain amused me though and I was fairly sure he'd regret letting me realise that.

"So you started to wonder about Valentina's intentions?" I prompted, interested in the rest of his story despite myself.

I still didn't understand how my brother and I had come to sleep so much longer than we'd intended and any information about the things that had happened around that time might lead me to fill in the gaps.

"I suspected some trap. I thought perhaps you'd sent her to me, hoping to win my trust so that she might murder me or something of the like. So I asked her to prove herself to me. And do you know what she offered to do?" he asked.

I shrugged, nothing about her would surprise me.

"She offered to kill you and your brother."

I frowned at him. Valentina had never been foolish enough to make any attempt on my life before I'd slept. When my mother had put me into the unageing slumber which had led to me awakening in the present, I'd left Valentina back in our camp without even offering her a farewell. I'd expected to wake a hundred years later knowing she was dead and having the freedom to find love for myself.

"Well obviously she didn't," I said, unsure what else I could offer.

"No. But I believed she had. That was why I rewarded her with immortality. She came to me coated in slayer blood and I recognised the scent of it. I could have sworn it was yours and your brother's. I knew your blood from the times we'd collided and even if I'd doubted it at all, you were never seen again after that day."

"Because we were sleeping, not dead. We should have woken a hundred years later, ready to lead an army to annihilate you. A prophet saw it. But instead I awoke now..." My eyebrows pinched in confusion as something pricked at the edge of my thoughts. Like there was an answer here that I just wasn't seeing.

"Valentina told us about the prophet who had foreseen the reunion of my family. We were ready for your army when it came," Erik replied darkly.

"And my kind were wiped from the Earth because I wasn't there to lead them," I muttered, turning away from him.

The silence grew once more and I folded my arms as I looked up at the red ceiling above us. There was something here. Something important that I just couldn't see. And it came down to Valentina.

"It was war," Erik murmured and I was almost sure I detected a hint of regret in his tone.

There was no point in discussing the eradication of my kind. It was ancient history now, even if it still felt fresh to me. In my mind, only a few months had passed since I'd been among my people. I had just recently been laughing around the fire pit with my warriors. My tent had been pitched beside Aelfric and Elissa's as usual and I'd heard their latest babe wailing in the night. Baltian was still the most fearsome war horse ever to have existed. And I'd just held my mother in my arms, saying farewell for the final time.

I'd known I'd never see any of them again when the sleep had claimed me. I'd given it all up for my cause. But I'd expected to rise a hundred years later, surrounded by the great grandchildren of my friends. The older generations may have remembered some of the people I'd once loved. Life wouldn't have been so very different.

But instead, I'd been trapped in that sleep for so long that the world had changed and changed, being reborn so many times that it was impossible for me to recognise it.

If it hadn't been for Callie, I wasn't sure where I'd be now. I'd been so lost before I'd found her. So confused by everything I came across. And there must have been a reason for my mother's gift to have gone so wrong. She'd never made a mistake like that. Idun had promised to help us so that we wouldn't age or starve, but surely she'd have noticed the time scale being off. So what was I missing?

"Did Valentina ever tell you we were due to rise again? Did she warn you about our slumber?" I asked slowly.

"No. Like I said, I believed she'd killed you," Erik said. "I...well I suppose I was a fool. It seemed like she'd given me everything I'd ever wanted. You were dead. Your people were gone, never to haunt us again. She even kept her powers after I turned her so she could aid us against the sun-"

"And you were fucking her too, just to top it off," I replied. "You must have thought she was a gift from the gods themselves."

"I did," he admitted. "For a while at least. I believed that her coming to us was a sign that Andvari had decided to lessen our curse. To let us live peacefully. Eternally. And that perhaps in time we would be able to solve the prophecy and die a mortal death too."

"So how long did it take for the shine to wear off of her?" I asked.

"It didn't. Not really. Just...she wanted me to love her. But I didn't think I was capable of love while I was in this form. So I kept her at a distance, not wanting to see too much of the hurt in her eyes when she tried to make me fall for her. But I couldn't get rid of her either, we needed her help with the weather so I told her that I would try to love her. And maybe one day it would happen. She seemed content with that, at least until recently."

"Until Montana came along you mean," I said.

"I suppose so. I knew she was jealous, but I've taken other lovers over the years and it never bothered her that much. I didn't expect her to turn against me like this."

"Well it seems as though she's good at turning against men who don't fulfil their promises to her," I replied. "But I still don't understand why she lied to you about our slumber. If she'd told you, you could have been waiting to kill us when we rose again. If she was loyal to you, then why hide it?"

"Because she wanted me to be grateful to her for killing you?" he offered but I shook my head; he'd have been just as grateful of the truth.

While we slept, we were no burden to them and they could have dealt with us easily if they'd been warned that we would rise.

"She must have known that the lie would come out. It's something else. She's hiding something more." I turned back to look at Erik and he tilted his head as he thought about it.

"Whose blood was she covered in?" he asked me slowly. "It must have been someone related to you. I recognised your scent and if she didn't kill *you* then-"

"My mother," I whispered as horror speared through my heart. She was the only family member I'd had left alive. There was no one else. Leaving her behind had been the biggest sacrifice of all. I'd known that once we were gone that she would be broken. Alone. But she'd insisted. She wanted us to exact vengeance for our father's death and in the end I'd agreed because I could see that refusing her was worse than leaving her.

Erik's mouth opened but no words came out. He didn't know what to say to me and I preferred that he didn't utter anything anyway. What consolation could my father's murderer offer me on the death of my mother?

I released a cry of rage and kicked the door to my cage as hard as I could. But the bars Idun had provided to hold me didn't so much as tremble. I glared at them as every inch of my body ached with a thirst for Valentina's blood.

"I'm going to make her suffer more than any living being has suffered before," I growled once I was finally able to speak again. "Valentina made a mistake in turning on me and if she laid so much as a finger on my mother then her pain will be insurmountable. I will rip her limb from limb and tear her black heart from her chest."

"Does this mean you're ready to make a plan then?" Erik asked as my rage simmered into a cold sense of purpose.

I turned back to look at him and prowled across the cage to stand opposite him again.

"If it will help me to kill that bitch any sooner, then fine. What's your plan, monster?" I snarled.

Erik's face lit with a savage grin. "I'm sure we can come up with something, barbarian."

ERIK

CHAPTER THIRTY THREE

Before Magnar and I could develop any semblance of a plan, Valentina stepped into the carriage flanked by two Elite. She waved them back and they turned to stand guard outside as the train doors closed behind them.

She'd changed her clothes into a low-cut white dress that fell to her knees. I wondered where exactly she was keeping all of these fine things in a place like this. Even though she was driven into hiding in my city, she was still walking around like she owned the place.

A bitter taste filled my mouth as she approached us, smiling through the bars. "I had no idea you would show up today too," she said to Magnar. "That trap was for Erik, but I caught you both in the same net." She glanced between us and I stared evenly back at her, hoping she might be tempted to join me in my cage so I could tear her throat out.

"What do you want?" Magnar growled.

Valentina's gaze flicked to him. "I want what I've always wanted. Power. You both had the chance to hand it to me. I would have been an adoring wife. I would have made you both happy beyond your wildest dreams. If either of you had married me like you'd promised then I would have been a queen. But now that chance is gone...and I have taken the power you both denied me. I seized my own crown without either of your help."

I shared a look with Magnar as hatred bubbled in my veins.

"So now, I'm going to do what you both did to me for years. When you toyed with me, dangled my heart's desire before my eyes. I'm going to make you wish you'd married me when you had the opportunity."

"My biggest regret in life is not plunging a sword into your chest," Magnar said dryly. "It will never be not marrying you."

"Agreed," I muttered and Valentina's eyes blazed with lightning.

"You'll change your minds on that," she said after a beat of silence, reining in her temper. "The sooner you come around to the idea, the sooner you can get out of these cages." She smiled cruelly, inching closer to the bars and I wondered if I could reach her through them. "The gods are my allies now." Her smile widened and an energy pulsed through the air which concerned me.

Idun's powers descended on me again and Magnar rolled his shoulders, evidently sensing it too.

"How easy it is for the glorious Idun to control your hearts," Valentina purred. "It's so obvious to me now that the gods were the ones driving your actions when you chose other women. It is why I was denied, but I have prayed to them and they have finally answered."

A shudder ran through me and the feel of warm fingers tightened around my heart. My head swum and I blinked heavily as I succumbed to Idun's power.

My love for Montana was moulded and reshaped inside me, forcing it onto Valentina instead. I growled, trying to fight it but the will of Idun pushed into me and I became a slave to it.

I saw Valentina in a new light, one that intoxicated me body and soul. I wanted her. Needed her.

I moved toward the bars, reaching out for her and I spied Magnar doing the same on my right.

Valentina grinned hungrily at us. "Patience boys...you'll have to fight for a night with me."

"Yes, anything," I croaked, my heart clenching. I had to get nearer. I'd do anything to touch her.

"I'll fight," Magnar promised. "Just come closer."

Valentina shifted toward him, reaching out to caress his cheek through the bars. He shivered at her touch, brushing his fingers along her arm.

"I've wronged you," he sighed. "Let me make it right, my love."

"You can," she whispered. "Soon, but not yet. Let's have some fun first."

Her eyes glimmered with darkness and the power of Idun circled around me. The bars parting me from Magnar bent apart, creating a large gap between them.

"Fight for me," Valentina commanded and a growl ripped from my throat as I lunged toward the opening without hesitation. If she wanted him wounded, I was more than happy to comply. I longed for nothing more than to please her.

Magnar caught me by the neck as I entered his cage, slamming me to the floor and pinning me in place. I clawed at his arms, aiming a rough kick into his stomach. This slayer was standing between me and the woman I hungered for. He would die and then she would be mine.

Jealousy rose inside me like a tide as Valentina gazed at Magnar appreciatively. I forced him off of me, smashing my fist into his jaw and her appraising gaze moved to me instead, filling me with satisfaction.

Magnar came at me with a bellow, driving his knuckles into my gut. I caught his wrist, clamping my fangs down on his arm and drinking deeply.

He cried out as I held on. The slayer jammed his elbow into my back and my fangs came free as he yanked his arm away from me. He caught me in a choke hold, dragging me back against him and I slammed my foot down on his. Bones crunched and he cursed, throwing me forward so I collided with the bars.

Valentina clapped, laughing as she watched.

Magnar caught me by the throat, yanking me upright and trying to tear my head off. I threw my weight back and we toppled to the ground as I crushed him beneath me. Rolling, I snarled down at him and his eyes locked with mine. A memory seeped into my mind of this exact thing, me and him fighting under the dark shadow of a statue. But I'd

305

stopped. Why had I stopped?

The gods.

Montana!

I lurched off of him, shaking my head as I reclaimed my own heart.

Magnar stared at me in confusion as if he was struggling to do the same thing. He panted on the floor, pushing himself upright and backing away from me.

"Alright," Valentina sighed. "Play nice for a while."

Idun's power forced itself into me again and I blinked hard as my love shifted onto Magnar instead of her. A lump lodged in my throat as he gazed back at me and my eyes trailed eagerly down his muscular torso.

Wait...no.

I tried to capture the image of the dark-haired girl who held my heart, but it evaded me. Maybe it was him I loved...

"Why is he looking at me like that?" Magnar growled, turning his attention to Valentina.

He was so fierce...his muscles tensed and firm beneath his shirt. A shirt I had every intention of tearing off as I stepped forward.

"Woah, woah, woah-" Magnar held up a hand, pressing it to my chest and lust impacted with the place he touched.

I smiled, reaching out to skate my fingers over his jaw. Desire coursed through my blood, begging me to kiss him.

"Stop it." He smacked my arm away and a bitter rejection filled me.

"Oh Magnar, don't be shy," Valentina encouraged and Magnar stilled, wincing as Idun's power grew stronger around us.

"No- wait!" he begged then his tensed jaw fell slack and his mouth tilted into a sideways smile.

His golden eyes locked with mine, starting a tremor in my chest.

"Hi," he breathed and a ripple of love fell through me, drawing me to him even more powerfully.

I stepped forward to close the gap between us and Valentina's taunting laughter rang in my ears.

A small scrap of my own self fought its way into my head and I lurched backwards as Magnar tried to plant a kiss on me.

I rubbed a hand over my eyes, trying to rid myself of this strange need growing inside me.

Is Idun fucking insane? Why is she playing Valentina's games?

Magnar caught my arm, dragging my hand from my eyes and moving toward me until my back hit the bars. Idun's claws dug into my heart and I was her slave once more as I reached out to run a thumb across Magnar's cheek.

He smiled dreamily and I smiled right back. Why had we ever been enemies? He was so...alluring.

He fisted his hand in my hair, leaning closer, his breath floating over my face. I caught him by the back of his neck, desire overwhelming me as I dragged him forward. His mouth slammed against mine and my heart sung with joy. I needed to get closer. I needed to get that damn shirt off of him.

I clawed at his shoulders and he shoved me harder against the bars, responding with equal passion as he scraped his nails down my spine.

"Ma'am, we have Familiars in the area." The redhead girl strode into the carriage, looking between us in surprise.

Idun's power evaporated in a heartbeat and my thoughts slammed back into alignment.

"Argh!" I shoved Magnar away and he stumbled, his face contorting as his own heart realigned with the truth.

What. The. Actual. Fuck. Idun?

The goddess's laughter swept over me and I clenched my jaw, practically grinding my teeth to dust. Magnar turned away from me, his eyes clamped shut. If *I* was tormented by this, I imagined he was feeling ten times worse considering he blamed me for his father's death.

Valentina whipped her hand through the air and a sharp wind forced me back into my cage. The bars bent back into place between me and Magnar and she promptly strode from the carriage with the redhead, muttering, "I was just getting to the best bit."

"Sorry, your highness. We need you up top," the redhead replied just before the doors closed and I felt Idun's presence leaving with them.

I looked away from Magnar, dropping down onto the floor, horrified by what the goddess was capable of.

"Don't say a word," Magnar growled.

"Trust me, I wasn't going to," I replied, tucking my knees up to my chest. "That twisted bitch."

"If you ever look at me like that again, I'll rip your eyes out," Magnar snarled.

"I thought we weren't talking about it?" I snapped.

"We're not. I'm just saying."

"Yeah? Well you seemed pretty keen yourself a second ago, Magnar. So if Idun wants my eyes intact, you're fucked."

Magnar pressed his lips together. "We have to beat them somehow," he said eventually.

"The goddess is using us as puppets, what are we supposed to do?"

Magnar shook his head then he turned to me with an idea lighting his eyes. "Idun's only doing this because she's angry with us."

"What's your point?" I asked.

"Maybe we can get her on our side again."

"Well what is it she wants?" I asked.

Magnar fell quiet, brushing some invisible lint from his knees as he avoided my gaze. "I don't know. Maybe she wants me to honour my betrothal to Valentina."

"Great idea, you go through with the wedding while I escape," I taunted.

He glowered at me. "Not happening."

"Then we're back to square one," I muttered.

"Not quite." Magnar rose to his feet, approaching the bars separating us. "The next time she tries that bullshit on us, we'll be ready. You almost fought it off, didn't you? If I focused on Callie, I could nearly manage it too."

I nodded, glancing over at him. "Even if we do fight it off, we're still stuck in these cages."

"Not if she lets us out," Magnar said thoughtfully. "Maybe we can pretend long enough for her to think we're still under Idun's spell."

"There's a lot of ifs involved in that plan," I commented.

"We don't have another option," Magnar bit at me. "It's our only chance."

"Fine," I sighed, falling back onto the floor and cupping my head with my hands. What Idun had done to us replayed in my mind and I grimaced. It was going to take a goddamn century to rid myself of the memory of Magnar's tongue in my mouth.

Valentina was one fucked up woman. But I knew I'd had a hand in causing her anger. I'd fucked her on and off for years, vaguely promising things which I'd never had any intention of fulfilling. I wished I'd never met her. And I wished even more that I'd never laid a hand on her. She'd been trying to earn a place at my side since we'd met and I'd refused it for a thousand years. I had to admit, she had some serious patience. But why she hadn't figured out that I was never going to give her what she wanted was a mystery to me.

Maybe I'd been too convincing in my lies.

Sure we'll marry one day...when the time is right.

I'd told her that once. What had I been thinking? Since I'd met Montana a lot of my former bullshit had ebbed away. I'd changed for the better. No woman had ever sparked that in me. Which was why I knew with all my heart that she was the one. And no scorned biter with a thousand years of pent-up vengeance in her heart was going to change that.

CALLIE

CHAPTER THIRTY FOUR

Once we returned to our room, I made the most of the hot water and washed the gore of yet another battle from my skin. Standing beneath the shower set my skin alight with memories of that morning and I didn't linger as the pain in my chest grew sharper. This waiting around was killing me. I needed to know that Magnar was alright. I needed him back in my arms again. And the longer I had to wait for it, the worse I felt.

It was like a weight pressing down on my soul, crushing me so that I could hardly breathe.

Please be okay.

I shut off the hot water and quickly dried myself before pulling on the nightclothes Clarice had delivered to me. The black camisole and shorts were lacy and pretty revealing but it didn't really matter. I didn't feel the cold like I used to anyway and my body ached for rest. As soon as I'd eaten I fully intended to sleep until Fabian's Familiars located Magnar and Erik. I had to recover so that I'd be ready to help them and if I could get my brain to shut off for long enough for me to sleep, then I needed to do it.

Julius was down the corridor with Montana, giving me space to clean up while he cooed over Valentina's sword. I had no doubt that Montana would be getting fed up of hearing him go on about it by now; I certainly was and I'd managed to escape already.

A knock sounded at the door and I pulled it open expecting to find the slayer and my sister but Fabian stared back at me instead.

I exhaled slowly, wondering if I should just tell him to leave already. It felt like we were building some kind of delicate understanding between us, but all the time the bond was in place it was hard to be sure of his motivations.

"Hello," he breathed, his words faltering as he looked me over.

I cleared my throat and folded my arms across my chest. The pyjamas were suddenly seeming even skimpier than I'd initially thought and though I wasn't particularly precious about my body, the look in his eye made me want to cover up again.

"You know, leaning on my doorframe and staring at me like that is not earning you any favours," I said.

"But you look... If the stars were given souls then they could not compare to you. I have never seen a woman who sets my blood alight as you do. I could spend years staring at the curve of your lips and admiring-"

"Stop it," I snapped and I pushed the ring's influence over him to banish his doe-eyed expression.

Fabian blinked a few times but the desire didn't leave his gaze. It just turned into something more dangerous. He took a purposeful step towards me and I backed up, snatching Tempest from behind the door and holding it between us so that the blade hovered an inch before his stomach.

"I won't warn you again," I growled.

"You know, the longer you keep up this game of teasing me and then pushing me back, the more it makes me want you. And I think you know exactly what you're doing to me," he murmured.

"I am not teasing you, I'm very clearly pushing you back *all* the time," I snarled.

"If you say so." His gaze slid over me again.

"I am. And on that note, your brother reminded me earlier that you've divorced your other wives."

Fabian narrowed his eyes at me and I was sure he understood what I was getting at, but he didn't respond.

"So I want you to divorce me too," I said firmly.

"No," he replied casually.

"No?" I stared at him angrily. "That's it, just no?"

"Well for a start, we can't get divorced if we haven't even consummated the wedding. Which we can do right now if you want to make this conversation relevant? Of course, if we do, I'm sure you'll change your mind about wanting rid of me; you won't be able to get enough."

"That's never going to happen," I growled.

"If it doesn't then what you're really after is an annulment, not a divorce," he said.

"So annul it then. I don't care what you call it, I just don't want to be married to you."

"You haven't really given it much of a chance. You've painted me out like this bad seed and refused to even consider it." He stepped closer to me, shifting around Tempest as I failed to stab him with it. He knew that I couldn't hurt him while this alliance was in place anyway and I needed to stick to my side of our agreement if I wanted their help in getting Magnar back. Fabian dropped his voice as his spoke again. "But I promise if you do, you'll find out that it feels *very* good to be bad."

I glared at him in response and he smiled at me for a moment before turning his attention to something behind him. He snapped his fingers in a command to someone beyond the door and I followed his gaze.

I stepped back as a male vampire pushed a dining cart into the room. He quickly piled the food and drink from it onto a small table beneath the window and left again without a word.

"I thought we might dine together," Fabian said as I eyed the food hungrily. I still held Tempest and the blade was begging me to plunge it through his heart.

Fabian had been true to his word and had delivered a feast. My stomach growled but I resisted the urge to move towards the extravagant meal.

"Seeing as the only thing in this room that you might possibly want to eat is *me*, I think I'll pass on that offer," I replied.

Fabian eyed my neck for a moment then laughed as if I'd been joking. "Luckily for you, I've just had a drink so I have no desire for your blood tonight."

He seemed to have given up on closing the distance between us so I slowly lowered Tempest and moved towards the feast.

"Do I smell dinner?" Julius called excitedly as he bounded into the room. He held Valentina's blade in his fist and he swung it about casually, causing Fabian to step back as it came close to touching him. "Whoops, sorry about that." He chuckled as he grabbed an apple and bit into it.

Fabian folded his arms, failing to conceal his disgust as Julius stuffed his face.

"Were you just leaving?" Julius asked Fabian around a mouthful of food. "Because once we've eaten we really need to sleep."

"You can't seriously think I'm letting you spend the night in a bed with my wife while she's dressed like that," Fabian growled and Julius glanced at my skimpy pyjamas with a frown.

"You don't *let* me do anything." I snapped. "I'm not your fucking property and as far as I'm concerned I'm not your wife either. Besides, Julius is nothing like that to me. He doesn't look at me like that and I certainly don't look at him that way. That bed is huge so I really don't see the problem."

"Harsh," Julius commented. "And true. You belong with my brother so I would never lay a hand on you like that... But if I'm being totally honest, I'd rather not sleep in a bed with you while you're dressed that way. It might be a bit awkward if you roll on top of me in the night, drawn in by my overwhelming masculine appeal, and I don't think Magnar would appreciate me guarding you quite that closely."

"At least the savage can admit that there's a reason for you not to share his bed," Fabian growled.

"It's not like I chose this outfit," I said irritably. "Clarice didn't bring me anything else."

"I'll be fine on the floor," Julius said before the argument could go any further.

"Perfect," I said. "Problem solved, so you can go now." I pointed Fabian towards the door but he didn't move. He was still scowling at Julius and I could tell he wasn't entirely satisfied with his solution to the issue. "Look, if you're that bothered then why don't you just hang out in the corridor all night and listen to the sounds of two people sleeping? Because I'm famished and exhausted and my head is starting to pound again. All I want to do is eat and rest and I can't do either while you're standing here staring at me like a creep."

"Off you go," Julius agreed, waving Fabian towards the door.

The royal vampire bared his fangs in reply before turning and stalking from the room. I followed him and shut the door firmly.

I left Tempest by the door and quickly moved to join Julius at the table.

"You know, I can just kill him if he's bothering you," Julius said as I fell on the food ravenously.

"Tempting," I replied with a smile. "But for now I'll stick to trying to win him around to the idea of divorcing me."

Julius laughed. "Good luck with that. I imagine he's not been very keen on the suggestion so far?"

"I don't really care what he wants. Magnar asked me to be his and I gave myself to him without reservation. It isn't right for me to be married to another man. If I should be married to anyone at all then Magnar-"

A huge crash sounded in the corridor outside our room and I flinched in surprise as Fabian started yelling obscenities. Julius got to his feet and stood before me with his new blade in hand just before the door flew open again.

Fabian stormed in with his fangs bared and I stood too, the hairs rising along the back of my neck as fear filled me at the sight of the monstrous truth of him.

"If you think I'm going to divorce you and allow you to marry that fucking barbarian then you're insane!" Fabian snarled. "You're *mine* and I refuse-"

I withdrew the ring's influence from Fabian and his anger suddenly switched to desperation as he dropped to his knees before me. I caught Julius's arm to hold him back as I could see him warring with indecision.

"Please," Fabian begged. "I love you, I need you. We're married, it *has* to mean something to you too. I know you feel it-"

Miles appeared in a rush of motion, clearly drawn by all of the noise. He caught Fabian's shoulder and forced him to look away from me.

"You're making a fool of yourself, brother," Miles said in a low voice. "Come and have a drink with me, I'm sure we can figure something out." His gaze travelled to me for a moment and I chewed my lip, not knowing what I was supposed to do and not particularly inclined to do anything.

"I won't divorce her," Fabian breathed. "We belong together. I won't watch her marry that heathen."

Miles arched an eyebrow at me and I could tell he didn't think much of the fact that I'd asked his brother to release me from my vow to him. But what was I supposed to do? I didn't want to be Fabian's wife and I never had. After everything they'd done to me, the least I deserved was my freedom.

"Let's go and discuss it in private," Miles urged. "Remember which one of you is royalty here; you're the one who gets to decide if you divorce her, not the other way around."

Fabian nodded eagerly and allowed Miles to pull him to his feet. He gazed back at me before they headed out into the hallway, and I scowled at him until the door closed between us once more. I used my gifted hearing to listen to what they were saying as they moved away.

"If she was immortal she'd change her mind," Fabian murmured. "If I turned her she'd want to be with me forever. She'd see."

I stilled at that suggestion, the threat of it clear even if Fabian didn't appear ready to act on it yet. But if that was where his mind was leading him then I was going to have to be even more cautious around him from now on because I refused to let him turn me into one of them.

"Perhaps, brother," Miles replied vaguely, though I could tell he was just offering platitudes.

"If she was one of us I wouldn't hunger for her blood," Fabian persisted. "She'd have no reason to fear me and she could allow herself to see me for the man I am. She'd see how right we are for each other."

They moved too far away for me to hear Miles reply and a shiver raced down my spine. I glanced at Julius, knowing he'd heard them too.

"I'll never let him do that to you," he swore.

I nodded in agreement, the ferocity in his gaze settling some of the anxiety in me. "We need to get Magnar back as soon as possible," I said. "And then we need to break this curse once and for all."

"Agreed."

We sat back down and continued to eat, but as I grew so full that I couldn't bear to taste another bite, Julius suddenly perked up.

"Before that little show of theatrics from Fabian, did you say that you wanted to marry my brother?" he asked slyly.

"What? No," I replied. "I just said that if I should be married to anyone then-"

"Then you want it to be Magnar?" Julius raised his eyebrows at me provocatively and I narrowed my eyes at him.

"You're making it sound weird."

"I'm just giving your words back to you."

"Yeah, after twisting them up and making them sound all stalkerish," I replied, making him laugh.

"So are you expecting me to get him to propose after we free him or were you hoping to ask him yourself when you rescue him, thinking he will likely swoon at your feet in gratitude for the daring rescue?"

"Oh fuck off," I laughed, shaking my head at him as I pushed to my feet. "For the sake of clarity, I will neither be proposing nor expecting a proposal – but Magnar *will* definitely swoon when I go charging in to rescue his captured ass."

Julius laughed heartily and I smiled to myself as I moved away from him towards the bed. My limbs ached and my head was pounding more violently with each passing moment, the wound there reminding me that it was very much still present. I needed to sleep. I had to recover so I could help Magnar as soon as we figured out where that bitch was holding him.

There were mounds of blankets and pillows on the huge four poster bed and I passed an armful of them to Julius so he could make himself comfortable on the floor. He lay down, blocking the door and a knot of concern eased in my chest. Fabian wouldn't be able to get in without waking him. So I could rest a little easier knowing I wouldn't be woken by the feeling of his fangs in my neck as he tried to turn me into a monster.

I slid Fury beneath my pillow as a backup and curled beneath the blankets before I closed my eyes. I expected sleep to be hard to find as my gut churned with worry over Magnar but as I reached towards the space between dreams, a burning light called me to it and my heart pounded with relief as recognition filled me.

I raced towards Magnar's dream with a desperate urgency and the light consumed me as I fell into it.

A sprawling forest surrounded me and birdsong filled the air. It was hot like the longest days of summer and a bright blue sky peeked between the boughs above my head. I was wearing battle leathers just like the last time I'd entered his dream and I spun about wildly, searching for him among the trees.

"Magnar?" I called as I failed to spot him.

"Callie?" His voice came from somewhere to my right and I ran towards it, desperate to see if he was alright.

I burst through the trees and found a huge pool. The water was shimmering blue and steam rose from it in coiling tendrils.

Magnar was standing in the centre of it, shirtless and utterly devastating as he looked over at me with that wicked smile which set my pulse hammering.

I ran straight into the warm water, wading closer to him as my heart slammed into my ribs painfully with its desire to be reunited with him.

The fighting leathers were heavy and I willed them off of my body, leaving me in the thin shift beneath them so I could move faster, and he waded towards me in turn.

I leapt into his embrace, and he lifted me into his arms as he kissed me with a simmering heat which was tainted with concern.

I wound my arms around his neck, my legs locking around his hips and I felt the firm press of his body against my own, the hard ridge of his bare cock between my thighs.

I was overcome with desire and the dream tried to pull me that way, begging me to merge my body with his and forget why I'd come as I gave in to the aching need of my flesh.

Magnar's hands were already skimming down my spine, tugging at my shift and a fire lit in my veins as I tried to remember why I was here despite the lust which was building to a point of desperation between us.

"Wait," I breathed, grasping for the edges of reality as I almost lost myself to the dream. "We need to... I came here for a reason..."

Magnar moved his mouth to my throat, tugging my shift from my shoulder and sucking my nipple into his mouth. My concentration wavered as my breaths came faster and my fingernails dug into his flesh, pleasure spearing through me, my hips rocking so I ground against his cock between my thighs. I wanted him inside me. I wanted him to destroy me the way he did so easily.

More, I need more of him, I need-

"Stop," I commanded, jerking back, finding some shred of sense before the lust could consume me entirely. "Valentina. Valentina took you."

He released me suddenly, shaking his head as my words broke the spell of his desire and I dropped back into the water, almost falling before his hand snatched mine and he jerked me upright again.

"You're alright?" he asked, his gaze raking over me in the transparent shift as if he could inspect my real body for wounds. "You weren't injured in the battle?"

I swallowed thickly, tugging my shift back up to cover my breasts, though as he could still see my hardened nipples straight through it, it seemed pretty pointless.

I summoned the memories of my fight with Wolfe, showing him the wound to my head and finally revealing how Montana and I had finished him.

"That monster met with the end he deserved," Magnar growled proudly, his grip on me tightening as he looked into my eyes.

I nodded. Wolfe's death had righted a terrible wrong, but it had done nothing to ease the pain left behind in place of my father's presence.

"I'm glad we killed him," I agreed firmly. "But..." I wasn't sure if I should say the rest of my feelings aloud. Magnar had hungered for revenge for his own father's murder for so long that I didn't know if admitting that it brought me no relief from my pain was the right thing to say.

"But it doesn't change what he did," Magnar finished for me softly, running a thumb along my jaw, leaving a line of fire in its wake.

"It doesn't," I agreed. "We got justice but it doesn't bring Dad back. It doesn't change what happened or lessen my grief. It only sated my rage."

Magnar nodded thoughtfully. "Grief fades with time. Eventually your memories of him won't be tainted with the pain of his loss. You'll be able to look back on the things you loved about him fondly. Somehow rage is easier to cling to."

I reached up to touch his face, brushing the frown from his brow with a gentle caress.

"Maybe it's time you focused on love instead," I breathed.

He'd been consumed by what Erik had done to his father for so long that I wasn't sure he'd allowed himself to fully feel anything but that anger ever since. But killing Erik wouldn't fix the wrong that was done to his family. And neither would ending the curse or even destroying the gods. The only one who could set him free of it was him.

Magnar held my eye and I could see the turbulence of his emotions warring inside him.

"Before I slept, the idea of letting go of this anger would have seemed like an impossible idea. But now... Being with you makes me want to surrender all of it. I don't want that darkness to touch us. It has poisoned everything I've ever owned. Each moment, each breath was laced with a piece of the hatred which drove me on. But the more I learn about the things that happened to me, to my family, even to the Belvederes. The more I see the gods' hands in it. And still they seek to use me as their pawn. You are the only thing they didn't intend for me to have. We crossed paths when we both needed each other more desperately than we could have realised and that collision has changed everything for me. I lived my life for the cause. For revenge. But you've given me so much more. And I don't want the worst moment of my life to define me any longer."

"It doesn't have to," I replied softly. "The gods are determined to rip us apart but they can't control our hearts. And no power in the universe is strong enough to stop me from loving you. They can beat us and break us and tear us away from each other but in my heart I'll still be right here with you."

Magnar pressed his lips to mine and in place of the aching lust that had been there before was a pure sweetness which spoke of how desperately he loved me. A tear slipped from my eye as I drew him closer and my soul yearned to be ever nearer to his, but we both knew this wasn't reality.

Magnar pulled back, his fingers tangling in my hair as he looked down at me.

"I dreamed of you every night before I met you," he breathed. "You were the most desperate desire of my heart a thousand years before you were even born."

I bit my lip as I trailed my fingers over his pounding heart and my body was immersed in the warmth of his words. Being with him was like bathing in sunlight. He'd captured every piece of me and made it shine a little brighter as he claimed it for his own.

"Where are you now?" he asked. "Are you safe?"

"We're back at the Belvederes' castle," I explained. "We're searching for you and Erik. Can you show me where you are?"

The scene around us melted away and reformed quickly. I was standing in a golden cage beside Magnar and Erik was held behind bars a few feet away. We were in a train under the ground. Memories of how they'd brought him there flooded me and I drank in every detail.

"You shouldn't risk coming for us," Magnar said darkly. "She wants us alive but she'll kill you if she can."

I shook my head dismissively and wrapped my arms around his neck *once more as I looked up at him.*

"Just let me rescue you for once," I breathed before stealing one final kiss.

I could feel all the protests he wanted to make as I drowned in the feeling of his mouth against mine, but I didn't give him the chance to voice them. If I lingered for another moment then I would give in, I'd stay in this place and worship his body while letting him ravage mine and no matter how much I ached to do just that, we didn't have time to waste.

I drew myself out of his dream and the last thing I saw was a fire burning in his golden eyes.

I hunted around in the glimmering starlight between dreams until I spotted Clarice's consciousness shining brightly ahead of me. I headed towards it with purpose. I was going to show her what Magnar had shown me and then we would get them back.

ERIK

CHAPTER THIRTY FIVE

I turned to face the angry slayer in the cage next to me with a glare. Magnar had fallen asleep and I was kind of pissed off at how easily he'd managed it considering our current situation.

He finally roused, sucking in a slow breath.

"Have a nice rest?" I shot at him.

His eyes narrowed. "I was hoping Callie would come and Dream Walk with me. And she did."

My eyebrows lifted with hope and my anger fizzled out. "And?"

"And now they know where we are. So we have to be prepared. She also showed me how she killed Wolfe with Montana."

A deep kind of satisfaction pounded through me. Montana had gotten her revenge. Wolfe had died at her hands, and I just wished I'd been there to see it.

"They're amazing," I breathed.

Magnar nodded as we agreed on something for once. "They are that. But I still don't know what Callie's sister sees in you."

"Well you saw it earlier when you shoved your tongue down my throat," I pointed out with a snarl.

He scowled darkly. "That was one of the lowest points of my life."

I snorted a laugh. "What's the matter? You're not homophobic are you?"

"Of course not, I'm fucking parasite-o-phobic."

My laughter grew and I was pretty sure it had more to do with Montana's victory than anything else. Magnar cracked a smile - though he fought it damn hard - and for a moment I felt like we'd actually *bonded*.

Doubtful.

I sighed. "Are you ready to take on Valentina?" I asked.

"I've been ready since I arrived in this place," he hissed.

"You didn't look so prepared earlier." I gave him a mocking look and his eyes narrowed sharply.

"Which you insist on bringing up again and again. So I suspect it is *you* who cannot get me out of your head."

"Hilarious," I muttered. "I've actually been thinking about my wife, thanks. She tends to give me a bit more motivation than a seven foot boar."

"I have no doubt my love for Callie will help me escape Idun's hold on my heart, but I can't imagine a parasite loves anything more than blood. Maybe you should daydream about that for a while."

I lunged at the bars, trying to grab him through them but he jerked backwards.

"Don't you *dare* question my love for Montana," I snarled.

His eyes slid over me and his face softened ever-so-slightly. "I know how you look at her. But do you really think you'd pick her over blood if a human throat was cut before you?"

"Fuck you," I spat. "I'd pick her over anything."

His brow furrowed as he eyed me. "Perhaps."

I snarled my fury, backing up from the bars and pacing around the space. It was one thing being locked up with this particular slayer, but another entirely for him to be jabbing at me in the only place I was vulnerable. The idea that anyone could question my love for my wife made me lose my mind with anger. The rune on my right palm itched and I was sure it was pumping rage into my veins. Whatever tenuous connection we'd just been forming was already broken.

"She's back," Magnar muttered and my head snapped up as Valentina appeared beyond the carriage window.

A satisfied smile dragged up her lips as she walked beside her biter lackeys. She stepped into the train carriage and I noticed a line of ash on her shoulders. I suspected Fabian's Familiars hadn't lasted long against her powers. But it didn't matter if the Familiars hadn't spotted her; Callie was already giving my family all the information they required to find us.

"Forgive me for leaving you in suspense," Valentina said as the doors slid closed and we were left alone with her.

"It only gave us time to think of more ways we'd like to murder you," Magnar said coldly.

Valentina laughed as if he was joking then walked away from us toward the red and gold throne at the end of the carriage. She perched on it with a sigh as if her sitting there somehow meant she owned my entire empire. She was going to find out just how wrong she was when my family came for her.

"So we have a little issue," Valentina said with a pout and I didn't think she was talking to us. "They can almost fight off the hold on their hearts. It's not good enough."

Idun's presence washed over me and I shuddered at the caress of her power. She materialised before Valentina, walking toward her on bare feet as shimmering golden smoke coiled up her body, barely concealing her nudity.

The goddess stilled and Valentina bowed her head. "Thank you for coming to me." She clasped her hands together in a prayer and Idun regarded her with delight.

The goddess turned her gaze on us, her upper lip peeling back. "If you were this pious perhaps you would not be in this mess."

Magnar clenched the bars between his fists. "You have played with me too long. You swore I could have love and now you have led me into the arms of my betrothed again. Why?"

"You know why," Idun purred and Valentina lifted her head with a small smile. The goddess ran her fingers through the smoke coiling around her waist. "You betrayed *me* when you used Andvari's ring against us, Magnar Elioson. Remember that." She whipped around to face Valentina again, reaching out to touch her throat. "A gift..." A black lace choker emerged around Valentina's neck with a large tear-drop emerald hanging from it.

Valentina brushed her fingers over it. "Thank you," she gasped.

"It is not just beautiful," Idun whispered. "It is incredibly powerful too, created by the great ruler of the gods. Odin gifted it to me thousands of years ago. It will offer you what you need to control these two adulterers." She gestured at us and ice crept down my spine. Adulterers? Was she fucking serious?

Idun glanced at us, her achingly beautiful face morphing into a smile. "The necklace is unbreakable. Its power unable to be thwarted. It is designed precisely to wield the hearts of men. And this time, it cannot be fought off."

Horror pounded through me and I shared a look with Magnar. If what Idun said was true, the moment Valentina used that necklace against us, we were doomed.

"Go ahead, try it," Idun encouraged with a tinkling laugh.

Valentina rose from her throne, running her fingers over the emerald and sucking in a breath. "Oh... it's wonderful. I can feel its power."

"Use it," Idun urged.

Valentina moved toward us and Magnar tried to bend the bars apart to no avail. I kicked the door to my cage and my boot impacted with a clang. I knew it was pointless, but we had to try.

As Valentina petted the emerald, it glowed a deep green. A green that transfixed me, halting my movements as I was captivated by its glow. I sensed Magnar falling still in his cage too, enraptured by it.

The whole world seemed to fall away and all I could see was that incredible light.

Valentina's words filled my ears, dripping through my body like melted candle wax. "You love me, no one else. And you will do as I bid. You will fight for me with all your heart. You will adore me, covet me. There is no other love in your life but me."

Every word she spoke seemed to brand itself on my skin. I was hot and cold at once. I held onto the image of Montana for as long as

I could, but she slipped away from me, locked somewhere deep inside my heart. Somewhere I wasn't sure I'd ever reach her again.

Valentina filled the place of her in all of my memories, standing at my side as my wife. Kissing me, making love to me. She took my memories of Montana hostage and replaced my love's face with hers. And when the green glow in the room lifted, my rebel was lost to me.

My mouth parted as my gaze fell on Valentina. She was stunning, incredible, and entirely mine. Nothing else existed but her. She was a fierce warrior and the most exquisite woman in the world.

"The twins of dark and light are your mortal enemies. *My* enemies. You will do whatever it takes to kill them," Valentina commanded and I nodded eagerly.

Magnar held the bars, releasing a desperate groan. "Let me near you," he begged.

"You can trust them now," Idun whispered, then disappeared into the ether.

Valentina produced two keys, her eyes flicking between us hesitantly. She released Magnar first and he lunged toward her, gripping her waist and kissing her fiercely. He tried to claw away her clothes and I released a growl of frustration. Jealousy tore through my chest, ripping at my insides.

Valentina pressed him back with a keen smile. "Patience, my love. We must release Erik. You're brothers now. And brothers like to share." She held the other key out to Magnar and he unlocked my cage with envy in his gaze.

I stepped past Magnar and Valentina smiled as I approached. My love. My life. She was everything to me. There was nothing on Earth more important than her.

I reached for her cheek and revelled in the softness of her flesh. She tugged me toward her by my waistband and I released a moan as her mouth met mine. She kissed me deeply, brushing her hands down my bare spine and I shivered under her touch, needing more, desperate to please her.

Valentina pushed me back and I found Magnar beside me, gazing at her with adoration. She skated her fingers down his chest and I eyed her hand with a deep yearning. She placed her other palm on me and I shivered as she petted me.

"We will have time to play together later," she said with a hungry smile. "But we have something to do first."

"Anything," I growled. "Whatever you want, it's done."

"I pledge my life to you," Magnar swore, pressing his hand to his heart.

"Oh Magnar..." She tilted his chin up with a finger. "I'm so glad you're keeping your promises to me at last."

CALLIE

CHAPTER THIRTY SIX

I awoke in a cold sweat and pushed myself upright, frowning around at the dark room. It felt like hours had passed even though the dreams had only seemed to take minutes. I guessed I'd gotten some proper sleep between them too, my body making the decision to rest despite my own urge to get moving as quickly as possible.

"Julius?" I hissed as my heart pounded in excited relief. Magnar was alright. And we knew where Valentina was holding him and Erik.

"I don't wanna eat the little slice, 'snot fair," Julius mumbled sleepily.

I wondered what his dreams would be like to visit and imagined they contained a hell of a lot of food.

Shoving the covers off of me, I ran across the room. I nudged him in the leg with my foot to wake him properly and I could make out his silhouetted form rising onto his elbows.

"Julius, I found Magnar," I said loudly, offering him a hand.

"You did? Where is he?" He took my palm in his and I heaved him upright.

I swept my hand over the wall in search of the light switch but I couldn't find it so I gave up again, cursing the strange room. If they didn't waste so much space then things like that would have been a lot easier to find. My old room in the Realm had been so cramped that the idea of losing something in it was ludicrous.

"Valentina's got them in some underground train station. I showed Clarice in her dream and she knows where it is. She's calling the others and coming here in a minute." I moved away from him in search of some clothes, squinting in the dim light as I navigated the unfamiliar room.

I made it to the heavy wardrobe just before the door to the room flew open and the lights flicked on.

"Oh!" Clarice gasped and I turned around to see what had surprised her. My mouth fell open as I spotted Julius standing in front of her butt-naked. Luckily his back was to me so I could only see his ass but Clarice was staring right at him front-on and she didn't seem too upset about it either.

"Right, I forgot about that - I can't sleep properly with clothes on," Julius said dismissively. "But feel free to take a picture if you want it, whore, because you won't be seeing it again any other way."

He moved to retrieve his jeans from the floor and I looked away before I saw any more of him than I wanted to. I opened the wardrobe and sighed in frustration as I found it empty.

"I don't want to see your cock again," Clarice spat angrily. She was wearing a white nightdress that actually made my own outfit look modest but she didn't seem the slightest bit ashamed about it. "And believe me it's nothing special; I have had countless lovers over the last thousand years and there is nothing particularly impressive about any aspect of you."

"Mmmhmm, maybe you could look me in the eye while saying that if you want me to believe it instead of eye fucking me with your tongue hanging out."

"What the fuck is going on here?" Fabian growled as he elbowed his way into the room and Julius pulled his pants up.

"Oh great, Fabio is here for the cock-watch safari," Julius announced.

"Apparently savages like to sleep naked like wild animals," Clarice said to her brother in disdain.

"Oh yeah I'm a wild animal alright. But that's what you were hoping for wasn't it?" Julius taunted.

"You arrogant-"

"Can we focus on the reason you're here?" I interrupted, not wanting to hear any more of their pointless back and forth. "We know where Magnar and Erik are. We need to make a plan and get moving. And I need clothes."

Fabian crossed the room to stand beside me and I eyed him carefully, wondering if he'd gotten over his anger with me yet. I was using the ring to shield all of us now so he wasn't staring at me like he loved me at least. Thankfully his rage didn't appear to be present anymore either. Hopefully he could forget about it while we had more important things to deal with.

"You found Erik?" Montana asked excitedly as she tore into the room in a rush of motion. It was so strange to see her using her vampire abilities like that. She was somehow this entirely new thing as well as still being the same as always.

She was wearing pink pyjamas which were as revealing as mine but had found a black sweatshirt to help conserve her modesty a little. It didn't look like she'd done much sleeping; her hair was still perfect and she seemed wide awake. Then again, maybe that was a vampire thing.

At least my headache was gone and my strength had been replenished. I was sure I could have rested for longer given the chance, but it would have to be enough.

"I found Magnar in his dreams," I explained. "And he showed me where Valentina took them, then I showed Clarice so-"

"So now we can head there and kill that bitch," Montana growled fiercely and I smiled at her in total agreement.

"We need to be smart about this," Clarice said. "We don't want them to realise we're coming. If we-"

Miles and Warren shot into the room, a breeze rustling the edge of my shorts as they stopped beside me and I flinched away. They both wore sweatpants and t-shirts and their hair was dishevelled, making me think they'd dressed hastily before joining us.

"What have we missed?" Miles asked.

Clarice sighed loudly. "For the final time, I was just explaining that-"

The lights suddenly flickered and died overhead.

I stilled, looking around in confusion as we listened to the pressing silence. A cold hand found mine in the dark and I flinched as Fabian pulled me behind him.

"Stay close to me," he breathed. "I fear that danger has come to our door once again."

MONTANA

CHAPTER THIRTY SEVEN

My eyesight quickly adjusted to the pressing darkness, but it did nothing to ease my anxiety. I searched the faces of my friends as I tried to work out what was happening.

A crash sounded somewhere downstairs and Julius drew his new sword. Callie darted to the bed and took Fury from under her pillow and I bit my lower lip, feeling vulnerable without Nightmare.

"Shit," Clarice swore, curling her hands into fists.

"Could just be a power cut?" Miles offered but Warren shook his head.

"Don't be an idiot," he muttered.

"I'm not. I'm being optimistic," Miles said.

"Shh," Clarice hissed, turning her head.

I strained my hearing and the sound of voices filled my ears. I pushed the door open into the corridor.

"-this way," a deep voice reached me and a tremor crept down my spine.

My eyes darted to Erik's bedroom along the hall and I sped toward it, fear fuelling my movements as I darted silently inside and grabbed Nightmare from my bed.

I ran back to the hallway, finding my friends gathering there.

Clarice pressed a finger to her lips and I swallowed hard as I tip-toed toward them.

A door banged downstairs and I stiffened, sharing an anxious glance with Callie.

"Biters?" Julius mouthed to us, but no one had an answer.

"How could they get in here?" Fabian whispered on a breath.

"The emergency exit tunnel," Clarice hissed. "Valentina knows where it is."

"Fuck." Miles wrung his hands together and Warren placed a palm on his shoulder.

"I'll look upstairs," Erik's voice carried to us and relief slammed into my chest. It wasn't the biters. He'd gotten away.

I gasped, breaking into a run as I headed in the direction his voice had come from. I sprinted downstairs into the dark hallway, sensing the others following me.

"Wait-" Clarice hissed at me, but I couldn't stop.

"They must have escaped," Callie said eagerly as she sped to my side, hunting the dark corridor ahead of us.

A door flew from its hinges as we passed it and my heart lurched into my throat. A swarm of biters fell on Julius and the others in a rush of motion. Chaos descended and fear fell over me in a wave.

Callie turned in alarm, but the cross on my palm was begging me to reunite with Erik. If he was close, I could get to him. And he could help us.

"Go!" Julius yelled and Callie swore as she ran after me.

"Magnar?!" Callie called as we kept running, desperately searching for our men.

I followed the ache in my palm as it guided me into a bedroom. The door slammed behind me and I wheeled around as my sister crashed into it on the other side. Erik stood before it naked from the waist up and I was so relieved to see him that I didn't stop to question why he'd shut the door. I flung myself at him, wrapping my arms around his neck just as a click sounded the door locking. "Are you alr-"

He punched me so hard, my head spun. I crashed into the bed and a gasp escaped me as Nightmare clattered away across the floor.

"It's me!" I cried in alarm as he yanked me down the mattress by my ankles and locked his hands around my throat.

I stared into his eyes, his expression dark and for a moment I could have sworn his irises glimmered with green light. Confusion spilled through me followed by a sharp stab of terror.

I tried to prise his hands off of me, but he swung me upright and threw me across the room. I flew through the air and hit the wall hard, crashing to the floor with a groan. Pain ricocheted through my body and fear consumed me. I righted myself, shaking my head as I tried to work out what was wrong with him. It was like he was possessed.

"Erik, stop," I begged as he came at me like a charging bull. He collided with me, pinning me back against the wall with a feral snarl.

"My wife wants your head," he growled, and anger sped through me.

"*I'm* your wife," I demanded and he slammed my head back against the wall in response. Plaster crumbled and white lights exploded before my eyes.

What's happened to him?

He tossed me onto the floor and I pushed myself to my knees with a groan, trying to regain my senses fast. Erik followed quickly, kicking me back to the floor and dropping down to kneel over me. I grabbed hold of the nightstand, trying to pull myself free but he bashed my head into the floorboards. Pain blossomed through my skull and I tried to align my senses as I fought against his hands.

Callie's screams called to me beyond the door as she threw her weight at it again and again. The wood was splintering but I didn't know if she'd get to me in time before Erik killed me.

I had to fight.

I had to get up.

I pushed my hands against the floor, rearing backwards as I tried to force him off of me. He was so strong but he moved back enough that I managed to roll beneath him. I slapped him hard across the face in an attempt to break the spell that bound him.

"It's me. Rebel!" I cried and he snorted a laugh, his expression cruel and unforgiving.

"You're no one," he snarled, rising to his feet and slamming his boot into my ribs.

I was thrown across the floor, crashing into the legs of the bed. He came at me once more and I moved fast, crawling under the bed and making a bid for the door.

His boots slammed down in front of me as I tried to escape on the other side and I started backing up, releasing a murmur of fright. A glimmer of gold caught my eye and I spotted Nightmare on the floor beside me. I grabbed it, clutching it to my chest, but how could I use it against him? I couldn't hurt him. But if I didn't, he might kill me.

Erik tipped the whole bed up, sending it crashing into the wall across the room. I screamed, leaping to my feet and trying to run past him. He caught me by the hair, yanking me back and my scalp flared with pain. I clawed at his hand and aimed a kick at his knee, determined not to use my blade. He roared in anger, releasing me and I darted for the door once more. My fingertips brushed the handle, but he caught me by the waist, dragging me back against him as he locked an arm around my stomach.

He was so powerful, even with my vampire strength I didn't stand a chance against a royal. I stamped my foot down on his but he didn't react. I lifted Nightmare with a flare of horror ripping at my heart, but my hand trembled and my grip loosened. I couldn't use it. I wouldn't.

I clawed at his arms instead as he brought his hand up to my chest and dug his nails into the skin. He was trying to tear my goddamn heart out.

I kicked and yelled, gripping his wrist to try and stop his fingers from carving their way into my flesh. I threw my head back and caught his chin, making him stumble from the collision. His grip eased and I ducked out of his arms, backing up toward the door.

He grimaced at me, hounding forward like a hungry beast, his head cocked to one side and his eyes wild.

I picked up a chair, smashing it across his head, but it shattered around him and he didn't so much as wince. I caught the door handle behind my back, fumbling with the lock.

Erik sped toward me and a harsh kick splintered the door. I lurched forward into his arms as Callie broke into the room and she looked between us in confusion as Erik held me in his grip.

"Fucking hell, I thought you were in trouble," she said.

"I am," I gasped and Erik launched me into a wall.

My heart soared into my throat as I collided with it. With a surge of fear, I scrambled to my feet just as Erik lunged for Callie.

"No!" I screamed, diving onto his back as he tried to get his hands on her.

She evaded his attack with a curse of alarm, backing away and pointing Fury at him. I eyed the bloody bandage over his shoulder and jammed my fingers against it.

"Argh!" he cried.

"*Run*," I commanded Callie as Erik caught my legs and yanked hard so I fell upside down. He dropped me, stamping on my arm.

Pain flared through the bone as he reached for me and I tried to bat his hands away with my free arm. He grinned cruelly, taking hold of my jaw and squeezing tight. Callie smashed a fist into his face and he stumbled aside allowing her to pull me upright. I could tell she was trying to avoid using Fury and I was overwhelmingly grateful to her for it.

She started dragging me out of the room and I heard Erik take chase as we fled.

"What's wrong with him?" she cried as we sped along the corridor, hunting for the others.

"I don't know," I replied. "We have to get help."

A din of battle reached my ears, but as we rounded into the hallway where it took place, Magnar stepped in front of us with a triumphant smile. I saw the same strange look in his gaze that Erik had and tried to tug Callie back. She shook me off, reaching for him, but he backhanded her so hard that she hit the floor.

"No – stop!" I tried to push him away as he reached for her, but his strength was immeasurable. He shoved me back, sending me stumbling away and panic swept through my veins.

Erik came at us from behind and I turned to intercept him with fear flickering inside me.

"Erik, please listen to me," I said, raising my hands to try and hold him off.

Callie released a pained noise, but I couldn't turn to help her as Erik closed in on me. My death shone in his eyes with a primal intensity.

"Our queen wants you dead," he growled then lunged for me.

I ducked under his outstretched arms, aiming a sharp kick for the back of his leg. He stumbled, but quickly rounded on me once more, cutting me off from my sister.

I caught sight of Magnar forcing her to the ground and terror poured through my veins. We were in an impossible situation. Facing the men we loved. We couldn't hurt them. But they could hurt us.

I wasn't going to die here like this, my own husband turned against me.

I screamed in fury, darting forward to meet Erik's attack. I had to disarm him. But I didn't think I could do it on my own. Maybe if I held him back long enough his siblings would get to us in time to apprehend him.

"Clarice!" I cried above the sound of the battle. "I need you!"

CALLIE

CHAPTER THIRTY EIGHT

Magnar's fingers tightened around my throat as he forced me down onto the floorboards. I struggled beneath him as he cut off my air supply and his eyes blazed with an intense desire for my death. The fire that burned in them was richest green instead of gold. Something had taken his soul captive and he didn't even seem to recognise me anymore.

I threw all of my will into the ring on my finger, trying to block whatever was controlling him and bring him back to me. Power flowed from the golden jewellery but it swept past him like it was a sieve and he was made of sand. Whatever force had taken hold of him was stronger than the ring, or at least not subject to its commands.

My heart raced with fear as he kneeled over me, his weight crushing me to the ground. I threw punches into his kidneys, hoping to force him to release me, but he only gritted his teeth against the attacks, glaring down at me as his hands squeezed my throat even tighter.

I slammed my knee up between his legs and he reared back with a grunt of pain, finally lurching off of me.

I coughed as I scrambled upright, reaching out to him tentatively.

"Magnar? It's me, it's Callie, *please.*"

He stood and turned to me, his face set in a stony mask. "Callie?" he asked.

"Yes," I breathed.

"I'll remember that when my love asks me who I killed for her." He swung his fist at me, and I cried out as I barely managed to avoid the blow.

He didn't know me. He didn't recognise me at all and as I danced between his fists, I quickly realised he had every intention of keeping that promise. He was trying to kill me. The man I loved wanted me dead.

I ducked beneath his fist again and drove my boot into his stomach, knocking the breath from his lungs. While he was doubled over, I punched him in the jaw, my knuckles ringing from the impact.

I turned away from him and tried to run to Montana who was barely managing to keep out of Erik's grip. She kept calling out for the Belvederes, hoping they would come to our aid, but they were locked in a ferocious battle with the biters at the end of the hall.

Magnar charged at me and I couldn't move fast enough to avoid his attack. He caught me around my waist and hurled me backwards over a thick banister, and I flew towards the level below. I screamed as I fell, curling my arms over my head just before I crashed into the floor.

Pain speared through my spine and I winced as I tried to push myself upright again.

Magnar peered over the banister then jumped down after me. The floorboards rattled as he hit the ground a few feet away and I rolled upright, drawing Fury reluctantly.

"Don't make me use it," I breathed, hoping that the smallest sliver of the man I loved could hear me.

Magnar laughed as he advanced on me again.

"I'll use it to carve your pretty head from your shoulders then give it to my love as a gift," he growled and the look in his eye told me he meant it.

A shiver raced down my spine as fear consumed me. I was no match for him and I knew it.

I could still hear Montana struggling with Erik above me and the distant sounds of the others fighting the biters reached me too. But right here, it was just me and him. Except it wasn't him at all. And I wasn't sure if it was worse if I let him kill me or if I ended up killing him.

I shook my head as I backed up, refusing to face the idea that there was no way out of this but death. I just needed to get away from him. If I could lead him towards the warring vampires then maybe I could escape him.

Magnar leapt at me and I ducked beneath his arm, driving Fury's hilt into the side of his head.

He stumbled back a step and I swept my leg beneath his, knocking him to the ground. I slammed my foot into his side to slow him down then ran for it.

I clambered up the spiralling staircase as quickly as I could manage, my heart thundering in time with my footsteps as my bare feet hit the carpet.

Magnar's hand closed around my ankle, and he yanked me backwards with a violent jerk so that I crashed into the stairs with a curse. He flipped me over so he could drive his fist into my face and light exploded before my eyes at the impact.

I kicked out at him, swearing as I tried to fight him off. I flinched away from another punch and the wooden step shattered beside my head.

My heart lurched desperately as I was forced to use Fury against him.

I swept the blade across his arm, making sure I didn't cut too deeply, just enough to force him off of me.

Magnar lunged back to avoid the blade for the second time and I managed to get my foot between us, kicking him squarely in the chest and sending him crashing back down the stairs.

I scrambled to my feet, forcing myself to ignore the horrible sound of his body slamming into the floorboards at the bottom of the staircase as I scrambled to the top of the stairs once more.

I spotted Erik holding Montana against a wall half way along the corridor. He was slamming his fist into her stomach again and again as she cried out for him to stop.

"Get off of her!" I screamed as I sprinted towards him, Fury in hand. I knew I couldn't kill him, but I'd do whatever else it took to incapacitate him.

Erik turned to look at me and his nostrils flared as his eyes lit with hunger. My heart leapt in panic as he lifted Montana into the air and launched her away from us, all the way to the far end of the corridor. She hit the ground hard and Erik sprang towards me.

I stumbled to a halt, glancing over my shoulder to see if I should try and lead him away. Magnar smirked at me as he made it to the top of the staircase, blocking my retreat and fear rolled through me.

I pressed my back to the wall as the two of them closed in on me, holding Fury before me as my arm trembled. I was calling on every memory my ancestors had to offer, every gift that I possessed and yet there wasn't a single thing that I could think of to help me survive a collision with the two of them at once.

I turned to look at Erik and Magnar lunged, catching my wrist with a feral laugh. He slammed my arm back against the wall and pinned it there, keeping Fury out of the way as Erik closed in on us.

"Are you hungry, brother?" Magnar asked him and my lips parted in horror as I realised what he was planning.

"Always," Erik replied darkly.

My heart pounded desperately as I tried to wrestle my way out of Magnar's grip. How could he be doing this to me? He was offering me up like a fucking sacrifice to the creature who'd killed his own father.

Magnar laughed, grabbing my hair and wrenching my head to one side to bare my throat to Erik, using his bulk to immobilise me even though I continued to struggle against his hold.

A whimper of fear escaped me as my gaze met with the feral Belvedere's and I saw my death reflected in his eyes.

The vampire growled at me excitedly as he lunged for my neck and I screamed as his fangs sliced into my skin. The pain of his bite was blinding as his venom flooded into my veins and an agonised cry fell from my lips.

Erik moaned in pleasure as he pressed his cold body against mine, pinning me to the wall while my blood flowed into his mouth at a terrifying speed.

Magnar released me without so much as a final glance in my direction and he turned away to chase after more prey.

My vision darkened for a moment as the pain of Erik's bite claimed my senses again, but I gritted my teeth against it as I pooled all of my energy to fight it off, blinking against the dark and trying to come up with some plan to escape this fate.

Erik Belvedere was *not* going to kill me.

ERiK

CHAPTER THIRTY NINE

I yanked my fangs free from the blonde twin's throat, her face vaguely familiar as she looked up at me in horror.

"Sorry about this, but you need to fuck off." She slashed a blade across my side and fire surged through the wound.

I staggered back, clutching the injury and she rushed past me in a burst of speed. I tried to catch her legs, but she danced away, fleeing toward the dark haired twin who was battling my companions.

Valentina stepped through a door across the hall, her face contorting with rage as she spotted the blood leaking through my fingers.

"Fool," she snapped, and I bowed my head in shame for displeasing her.

Magnar bounded to her side, taking her hand. "Not to worry, my sweet, we're winning." He gestured to the fight behind us and Valentina scoured the scene, not seeming any less angry.

"Then what are you waiting for? Finish them." She shoved Magnar away and he snarled as he ran to join the fight.

Valentina drifted toward me, lifting my hand away from the wound with a frown. I looked into her eyes, hoping to find an ounce of pity there. Or for her full lips to part and tell me how hurt she was to see me like this.

After a beat of silence, she struck me across the face and pushed me toward the fight. "Pull yourself together. End them. Bring me those twins' heads!" She pointed at the brunette and the blonde and their names edged into my mind as if I knew them. Montana...Callie.

I ran forward, filled with the need to please Valentina. I'd do just as she asked. I wouldn't rest until I'd appeased her no matter how much pain I was in.

The twins moved deeper into the fight, glancing over their shoulders at me. I followed them as they fled toward my sister and Clarice's gaze met mine, her brows drawing together. I knew she was my kin, but it didn't matter. If Valentina wanted every member of my family dead, I'd happily offer it to her. No tie was as strong as my love for her.

I shouldered aside some of the biters, forging a path in the direction of the twins. Clarice drove her fist into the heart of one of my allies, moving to meet Montana and Callie as dust cascaded around her.

I bared my fangs, forcing bodies out of my way as I made a direct line for them, spotting more of my family behind her. The sweetness of Callie's blood in my mouth drove me on as I succumbed to the thirst, letting it take over. I wanted more of it, all of it. I'd drain her dry before I was finished with her and present her empty body to my love.

Magnar crashed into Fabian beside me and the two of them wrestled tooth and nail to get the upper hand.

Fabian caught my eye just before I landed a hard blow to his face. He fell beneath us and Magnar and I stood shoulder to shoulder as we prepared to end him.

"Do your worst," Fabian snarled at Magnar. "I'm ready for you, slayer."

Magnar barked a laugh as he leaned down and I bared my fangs, preparing to help him.

"Get back!" Someone swiped a sword above Fabian so we were forced to retreat a step.

Danielle grabbed Fabian's arm and yanked him away from us, wielding her blade to keep us at bay. The biters pressed against our backs as we prepared to take on the group.

Montana met my gaze, her eyes begging. "Erik please."

I didn't know how she knew me and I didn't care. I regarded her as I advanced, tilting my head as I took in her wide eyes. Something blazed in her expression. Something that looked a lot like love. But why would this vampire love me? Rage crept up my spine at the mere idea of it. My heart belonged to Valentina. And this bitch couldn't have it.

I lurched forward to grab her, but Clarice pushed her back, planting a sharp kick into my injured side. Miles braced Clarice, tugging her away from me.

I buckled forward in pain, clasping the wound and sucking air in through my teeth.

Magnar moved to attack them with a feral snarl parting his lips.

Julius swung through the crowd of biters and dust burst around us. "Magnar!"

He shot toward his brother, taking his arm. Magnar planted a hit to his chest that sent him crashing into the wall. Two biters dove on Julius but he battled through them in seconds, casting them to ash. He scrambled to join Clarice and the others, gazing back at Magnar with a heavy sadness in his eyes.

"Run." Clarice commanded, pushing Montana and Callie into a sprint. Julius and Warren ran after them and I snarled through my teeth as I tried to fight away the pain in my side to follow.

Danielle darted forward to intercept a group of biters to my left and as I straightened to attack her, Miles and Fabian closed ranks to hold me off.

"Leave them!" Clarice called. "Come on."

Fabian ignored her, racing to meet Magnar and punching him squarely in the face. Magnar bellowed his fury, snatching Fabian by the neck and tossing him further down the corridor. He skidded across the shiny floor and I slammed my foot into Miles, sending him tumbling after Fabian.

Warren halted behind the rest of the group, turning back for my brother. "Miles – run!" he demanded.

He and Fabian sprang to their feet, glaring at us.

"Erik, listen to me," Miles begged. "You're under Valentina's control."

My upper lip peeled back as I stalked toward him. "I love her. And I'll do anything she asks."

"Oh for fuck's sake," Fabian groaned. "This is the gods' doing."

"It is my heart's doing!" I shouted, rushing forward and snatching Fabian's shirt in my fist.

He started punching my face, enunciating every word he spoke with each blow, "The. Gods. Are. Fucking. With. You."

"NO!" I threw him to the ground, diving onto him as I struggled to keep him in place.

"This is what they've done to me too," he begged, lifting his palm to show me a shining silver cross there. I frowned as he caught my hand, turning it over to reveal a similar mark.

I didn't know what it was and I didn't care. I smashed my forehead into Fabian's and his head hit the floor beneath him. He spat curses and I smiled at my triumph.

Miles was struggling to escape from Magnar's swinging fists, but Warren crashed into the slayer, sending him stumbling sideways and tripping over Fabian's legs.

Miles and Warren came at me together, hauling me off of Fabian and dragging my arms behind my back.

A swarm of biters fell on them at once and they had to release me as too many of my allies surrounded us. They fought ferociously, knocking down my people with heavy blows of their fists and I hurried forward as the biters fell back, determined to finish them.

Warren and Miles shared a look then ran to catch the others with Fabian in tow.

Magnar and I took chase, tearing after them down the dark hallway. My throat tightened and the ache in my side burned. I'd have my revenge for Valentina. I'd do as she willed and seek her forgiveness for my failure so far. I longed for her loving caress, her soothing kisses and the brush of her fangs against my skin.

Magnar threw a glance my way as he ran beside me. "Valentina will reward me greatly when I end her enemies."

"Not if I do it first." I forced my shoulder into his, making him stumble. He darted back to meet me, ramming his elbow into my ribs.

"Bastard," he bit at me. "Valentina loves me the most."

"Liar." I shoved him again. "I'm the one she wants."

Our distraction gave the group time to gain ground on us and I swore between my teeth, quickening my stride and outpacing Magnar.

The lights flickered on overhead and I blinked as my eyesight adjusted to the brightness. The back-up generator had kicked in and that meant we were fucked if our enemies reached the elevator at the end of the corridor.

I quickened my pace but our targets fled into it and the doors started shutting. I shouted out in fury, my gaze locking with Montana's as she stared back at me in horror.

The gap in the doors grew narrower and narrower but I was going to make it through if it killed me.

The doors shut and I collided with them, hitting the ground and spewing curses. Magnar darted past me toward the stairwell with raucous laughter tearing from his throat.

I glowered, righting myself and sprinting after him, determined to beat him. If anyone was going to make Valentina proud today, it would damn-well be me.

MAGNAR

CHAPTER FORTY

I slammed through the door to the stairwell, ripping the door off of its hinges as I went and throwing it down behind me to block the stairs and slow Erik further.

Nothing was going to stop me from killing these enemies first. Each of them stood against me and my love, and I would present their heads to her rather than allow them to live another moment with foul intentions towards her.

"Asshole!" Erik snarled as he clambered over the door behind me and I laughed as I took the stairs two at a time, leaping higher and higher.

Valentina would be so pleased when I did this. I hoped she knew I'd do anything for her. Everything. I just wanted to prove my love. I needed her to understand the depths of my devotion.

I made it to the top of the wooden staircase and slammed into a heavy door which barred my way forward. It shuddered on its hinges but didn't give. I rammed into it again and again, cursing as the delay allowed Erik to catch up to me.

"Let's do it together, brother," he said. "We can't let her down."

"No, we can't," I agreed.

I may have wished to beat him to this, but it was more important that Valentina was satisfied. I couldn't bear the idea of disappointing her. It was unthinkable.

We ran at the door together and it finally gave way as we slammed into it, a cold wind whipping around us as we stumbled out onto the roof of the castle.

A huge metal contraption was rising from the roof, two massive blades rotating above it and lifting it into the sky. It was impossible and yet I was looking straight at it. I simply stared at it for several long seconds, my mind struggling to comprehend such a thing.

"We need to stop that helicopter!" Erik bellowed as he raced forward, forcing my thoughts to focus back on our goal.

Callie stared out at me from within the belly of the metal beast and a snarl left my lips as I started sprinting towards her. My love wanted her head and I would do whatever it took to get it for her.

The strange contraption rose higher, lifting away from the roof at an accelerating speed. Everyone aboard that vessel needed to die. Valentina desired it. And my life held no meaning if I couldn't fulfil her wishes.

Adrenaline pounded through my muscles as I charged towards it, but it rose too high for me to reach. I snarled angrily as it climbed above my head, ascending rapidly and leaving us behind.

"Throw me!" Erik shouted as he shot towards me and I turned to him just as he leapt into the air.

I caught him and used his momentum to wrench him around and fling him up after the helicopter.

The people inside it screamed as he caught one of the metal beams which ran beneath it and the whole thing lurched sideways.

I backed up to get a better view and smiled darkly as I spotted Callie dangling from the open door while Montana fought to drag her back in. With a bit of luck, the two of them would fall back down to the roof and I could finish them for my love.

The helicopter was causing a raging vortex to swirl around me and my hair slashed about violently in the wind. The sound the thing made was a thunderous whooshing unlike anything I'd ever heard before, making it hard for me to pick out the screams of the people aboard it.

Erik was hanging from the metal beam by one hand and yanking on Callie's leg with the other. Once he threw her down to the roof, I'd finish her with my bare hands. A wicked smile lit my face at the thought and my fingers curled in anticipation.

The helicopter spun in a tilting spiral around the rooftop as I stared on, rage simmering in my veins as I ached to join the fight.

Fabian was trying to drag Callie back inside too and my lip pulled back with rage. She needed to die. Valentina needed her to die and he was working against her. I'd have his fucking head for it if they'd only drop lower.

Clarice was screaming at Erik to let them go but he held on, fighting to bring down the girl who had wronged our love.

Julius leaned out of the door with his sword raised and swiped it straight through Erik's arm, severing the hand which held Callie. Fabian and Montana swiftly dragged her back inside and I swore at the missed opportunity.

Erik's severed hand hit the roof beside me and Julius swung the sword straight for his head next. Erik was forced to release the helicopter or face his death and he crashed down on the roof with a sickening crunch.

"Julius!" I roared, running to the edge of the roof as the helicopter swerved away. "I'll fucking kill you for this! We're coming for all of you. You won't get away with wronging Valentina. Your heads will be ours!"

The helicopter sped across the sky, withdrawing too rapidly for us to pursue and I glared at it as Erik groaned beside me. His body was already healing the damage from the fall and I moved towards him, kicking his severed hand closer so he could reattach it eventually.

It took a few moments for him to realign his spine and get back to his feet. As soon as he was upright, I punched him hard enough to break his jaw.

"How could you let them get away?" I roared. "Valentina needs them dead and now they're gone."

"I know," he breathed, cracking his jaw back into place as it healed and I could tell it pained him to admit to our failure as much as it did me. "I don't know how to express how sorry I am."

"We have to tell her," I said as I started heading back towards the stairwell.

I hated to go to her knowing she'd be upset by our failures, but we had no choice. She needed to know and I would take whatever punishment she deemed necessary.

"I've never felt such shame," Erik muttered, hanging his head as he followed me inside.

"Where did you last see her?" I asked as we made our way back down the stairwell.

"She was overseeing the fight but I think she's moved further into the castle now. I can smell her, come on."

"Truly?" I asked, jealousy pulling at me. I wished I could smell her from here, she smelled like honey, lavender, sunshine and miracles. It wasn't fair that he could smell that while I couldn't.

"Yes," he replied. "It's magnificent."

I refused to talk to him the rest of the way. It wasn't right that he should have such a way to feel close to her when she wasn't even present. I ached to see her face whenever I wasn't looking upon it. I yearned to touch her skin and bring a smile to her full lips.

The fight between the biters and the remaining guards had come to an end with our victory and the hallways were lined with piles of clothes and heaps of ash. We moved along them quickly but it wasn't fast enough. I thought of Valentina, her dark hair, full lips, perfect breasts... My pace quickened and Erik's did too. I glanced at him, not wanting him to reach her first. We shared her because that was what she wanted and her happiness was all I cared about, but I ached to be her favourite.

I needed to see her. *Now.*

I started running and Erik growled as he sped along beside me. He was faster but I wasn't going to be left behind easily. We raced down a spiralling staircase and Erik shoved his way through a set of heavy wooden doors and led the way into the throne room.

Some of the biters were carrying three of the thrones away and Valentina sat on the one which remained, right in the centre of a raised stage. The room was opulently decorated with rich golden wallpaper lining the walls and a deep red carpet on the floor. There were intricate works of art hanging from the walls and everything about the place screamed power. But all of it faded to irrelevancy beside the face of my love. My queen.

A glittering golden crown sat upon her head and her dark hair coiled over her shoulders beneath it, drawing my eyes down to drink in her perfect figure. She still wore the white dress and no mark of the battle had stained it. She was beauty personified. The one shining light in the dark abyss of this world. She was all that there was. Nothing else mattered. Everything paled into insignificance beside her.

We hurried closer as she turned her eyes to us, and we both dropped to our knees before her.

"I'm so sorry, my queen," Erik breathed, his voice raw with emotion. "But the royals and the twins you so wished to see dead escaped on a helicopter."

"We have failed you," I murmured, a heaviness building in my chest.

"What?" she hissed, rage simmering in her tone.

"Punish me, my love," I offered. "Take out your anger on my wretched flesh. Physical pain is nothing to me in comparison to the anguish I feel at knowing I failed you."

"No, punish me," Erik begged. "I had Callie in my grasp and I allowed her to escape me. I am the one most deserving of your hate."

"Enough," Valentina snarled and her eyes narrowed with displeasure as she surveyed us. "You will make this right for me."

"Yes, my love," I vowed.

"Anything for you, my world," Erik added.

"You will hunt them down for me," she said. "And you won't stop until you kill them."

"Of course," I agreed and Erik nodded enthusiastically at my side.

"Good. But I will still have to punish you for this failure," she added.

"Please do," I said. "My body is yours."

She beckoned for us to move nearer, and I crawled towards her, looking up at her beautiful face from my position on the floor. It was where I belonged. I'd failed her. I was worse than a worm. She deserved so much better than me. I would be better.

Valentina indicated for me to rise and I stood before her, my body trembling from her proximity. I wanted her so much. Desire coursed through my blood and I couldn't help but stare at the pure beauty of her face as she surveyed me with a scowl.

A wicked smile lit her features and I knew she'd decided how to punish me. I ached for her to do it. I had to unburden my soul of the wrong I'd done her. Failure shouldn't have been possible. It wouldn't be an option in the future.

Valentina reached for my belt and lust filled me as she tugged it free.

"Take off your shirt," she breathed and I instantly did as she asked.

She got to her feet, looking up at me as if she might kiss me and my heart thundered at the prospect. But I wasn't worthy of such attention. I'd failed her. I should be punished. I *needed* to be punished.

I dropped to my knees before her, baring my flesh so that she could sate her rage on me.

"Punish me too," Erik begged behind me and Valentina nodded, allowing him to kneel beside me and accept the consequences for his failures as well.

Valentina raised her fingers and brushed them along my jaw.

"You're my dog, Magnar," she sighed and I nodded with agreement. "And there's only one way to train a dog."

She raised her other arm, holding my belt ready as her eyes glimmered with excitement.

When the blow fell against my chest, I refused to so much as flinch. Pain sliced through my skin as the leather whipped my flesh raw and the buckle drew blood. I grunted but held myself still as she raised her arm again, her face lighting with a savage satisfaction. She needed to do this. I deserved it.

She hit Erik next and he sucked in a breath as the belt licked the flesh from his stomach, but he didn't move an inch either. He knew like I did that this was what she needed from us and that was all that mattered. So long as she was satisfied, our own desires were met too.

Our blood splattered across her white dress, staining it as her eyes burned with a deep sense of satisfaction.

The belt struck me again and again, blood racing down my chest as she took out her fury on my body and I forced myself to remain still and take it.

I focused on the twins I had sworn to destroy for her. Their deaths were etched into my soul. I would come for them like a demon in the night. Their lives would be mine and my blades would run red with their blood. I would see Valentina happy again. Even if it was the last thing I did.

MONTANA

CHAPTER FORTY ONE

The helicopter soared away from the castle, rising higher and higher until we were sailing above the twinkling lights of the city far below.

My relief at escaping was swallowed by a bitter sadness. Valentina had somehow taken Erik and Magnar hostage. She'd turned them against us, and I was sure the gods had to be involved. If Callie's ring couldn't reclaim their hearts, then the power that bound them must have been immense. And I didn't know how we'd ever fix it.

Julius slid the door to the helicopter closed, shutting out the wind. Danielle was piloting the strange vehicle, the back of her head visible through a partition.

I fell into a seat, cupping my face in my hands as Callie dropped down beside me.

"What are we going to do?" my sister asked, resting a hand on my back.

I lifted my head, willing away the tears prickling my eyes. "I don't know." I looked between the Belvedere siblings, searching for an answer on their faces.

Their expressions were grave and offered me no ounce of hope.

"We'll get them back," Julius said as he sat opposite me beside Clarice. "Valentina won't get away with this. I'll cut her heart out."

"And how will you manage that?" Clarice bit at him. "She has taken over our empire. We won't get near her again without an army of biters facing us first."

Julius frowned deeply, shutting his eyes. "By the gods, Valentina is going to do anything she wants with my brother."

"And mine," Clarice muttered.

I recoiled as if the words had struck me a blow. My heart couldn't take it. Callie released a pained noise and I took her hand, turning to meet her eye.

"Maybe they can fight it," I breathed, but I knew how hopeless that possibility was. The two of them had tried to kill us with no regard for our lives at all. They didn't remember loving us. All they could feel was their devotion to that heartless bitch, Valentina.

"If she lays a hand on Magnar, I'll..." Callie shook her head and I squeezed her hand as her hopelessness fell over me too.

"You'll do nothing because there is nothing you *can* do," Fabian growled and I shot him a glare.

"Don't upset her," I snapped at him as Callie toyed with Fury in her hand as if she wished to stab him in response to his words.

"We're royals," Miles said meekly, his hand locked around Warren's. "We can't be dethroned like this. It's not right. Our people will never follow her commands."

"They won't have a choice," Warren sighed, brushing a lock of golden hair from Miles's eyes. "She controls the goddamn sun. What option will our people have but to submit to her? And we underestimated how many wish to drink from the vein; who knows how many more will join her willingly now anyway?"

"The humans," I whispered, my heart clenching. "They'll go after the Realms."

Julius growled his frustration and Clarice rested a hand on his arm for half a heartbeat before quickly retracting it. He eyed her in confusion, shifting an inch away from her.

"Where to?" Danielle called from the pilot's seat.

We were heading away from the city, passing over ruins that extended for miles ahead of us.

No one answered. We were on the run, forced from the city. There was no way we could land near it without a horde of biters coming after us.

"South," Fabian answered at last. "Head toward the farmlands. The helicopter's fuel will get us two hundred miles but no more. There's a military outpost on the edge of Baltimore. We'll have to set down before the sun rises, otherwise Valentina could trap us under its rays. We'll get a car and keep going-"

"We can't just run," Callie snapped. "We have to go back for Erik and Magnar."

"They are untouchable until we can figure out a way to destroy the power holding them," Fabian said calmly. "And at least we know Valentina has no intention of killing them. We have to look out for ourselves now."

I shook my head as a pang of horror gripped my heart. "I can't bear to leave them with her."

"We don't have a choice right now," Fabian growled.

A stony silence descended and I broke apart, knowing Fabian was right. We had to flee. To put as much distance between us and Valentina as possible until we could figure out how to get Erik and Magnar free of her.

"Baltimore it is then," Danielle confirmed and Callie's grip tightened on my hand, her nails digging into my skin.

Thunder rumbled overhead and a tremor rolled down my spine. The helicopter swayed violently under an intense wind and I prayed we'd soon make it further south, away from the limits of Valentina's power.

As the helicopter swung around to face the dark horizon, words burst into my mind that shook the very foundations of my soul.

I swear on everything that I am, I'll save you from her, Erik.

I will not let Valentina have you.

AUTHOR NOTE

Okay, so maybe right now you hate us a bit, and that's okay because Valentina sucks ass and she's totally coming into her stride. Honestly though, I do kind of get her motivations. Those dudes should have just ditched her swiftly from the outset and maybe she wouldn't have spent a thousand years planning her revenge.

Anyhoo, everyone is in peril, our book boyfriends have lost their minds and I'm thinking now might be a good chance to curse our names before plunging on with the series and wondering what it is that makes you return for our particular form of torture.

In the meantime, I'll be wondering what it is that drives us to continue torturing our characters the way we do while simultaneously carrying along the route of destruction at a dancing trot.

We want to thank you for coming on this journey of devious gods and tainted souls with us and remind you that the end is in sight, and we can only strike you with one more cliffhanger before the inevitable end of this story.

So buckle up, grab yourself a flapjack and get ready for more of the gods' interference because we are at the highest peak of the rollercoaster now and it can only be carnage from here.

Love Susanne and Caroline X

WANT MORE?

To find out more, grab yourself some freebies and to join our reader group, scan the QR code below.